The Effect of
Living Backwards

The Effect of
Living Backwards

☙

HEIDI JULAVITS

G. P. PUTNAM'S SONS

NEW YORK

This is a work of fiction. Names, characters, places, and inci-
dents either are the product of the author's imagination or are
used fictitiously, and any resemblance to actual persons, living
or dead, business establishments, events, or locales is entirely
coincidental.

Copyright © 2003 by Heidi Julavits
All rights reserved. This book, or parts thereof, may not
be reproduced in any form without permission.
Published simultaneously in Canada

G. P. Putnam's Sons
Publishers Since 1838
a member of
Penguin Group (USA) Inc.
375 Hudson Street
New York, NY 10014

Library of Congress Cataloging-in-Publication Data

Julavits, Heidi.
The effect of living backwards / Heidi Julavits.
p.   cm.
ISBN 0-399-15049-8
1. Sisters—Fiction.   2. Air travel—Fiction.
3. Women travelers—Fiction.   4. Sibling rivalry—Fiction.
5. Hijacking of aircraft—Fiction.
6. Identity (Psychology)—Fiction.
I. Title.
PS3560.U522 S53   2003   2002036903
813'.6—dc21

Printed in the United States of America
1   3   5   7   9   10   8   6   4   2

This book is printed on acid-free paper. ∞

Book design by Amanda Dewey

BEN

My immense gratitude to the usual embroilees: Henry Dunow, Aimee Taub, Aimee Taub (she deserves twice the thanks), Anna Jardine.

For his research assistance in the elliptical ways of "Intelligence" and negotiation, I am indebted to "Kristin's Uncle."

For their invaluable, pro bono reader services: Dave Eggers, Elissa Schappell, Ayelet Waldman, Ben Marcus, Susan Julavits.

For space and relative privacy: The Writers Room and the Mac-Dowell Colony and 21 South Portland and the Corporation of Leech-field.

The epilogue owes much to track five of *Yankee Hotel Foxtrot*.

My apologies to Thomas Friedman, coiner of the phrase "the Big Terrible," for the unauthorized use of his words.

Reversals and peculiarities fall down upon those too proud of their erotic life.

—ELIZABETH HARDWICK

℮

"The rule is, jam to-morrow and jam yesterday—but never jam to-day."

"It *must* come sometimes to 'jam to-day,'" Alice objected.

"No, it can't," said the Queen. "It's jam every *other* day: to-day isn't any *other* day, you know."

"I don't understand you," Alice said. "It's dreadfully confusing!"

"That's the effect of living backwards," the Queen said kindly: "it always makes one a little giddy at first—"

—LEWIS CARROLL, *Through the Looking Glass (and What Alice Found There)*

Prologue

WHEN I ARRIVED at the Institute, my name was still Alice, I was still the daughter of an entomologist and a population control activist, I was still a dropout student of social work and a former waitress at a western-themed steakhouse, I was still the product of one divorced academic family, various embassy school systems, two state colleges, three-quarters of an overpriced graduate program, and a long, humiliating in-doctrination by the American restaurant service industry.

I was still, in short, myself.

Nor had I been exposed, yet, to the skepticism tactics favored by the professors at the International Institute for Terrorist Studies in Lucerne. It was the sanctioned habit of these professors to scrutinize a file wordlessly while the uneasy applicant faced them across a desk, squirming in a wicker office chair. The professors would peruse transcripts, testimonies, the dull and presumably true details of the appli-

cant's autobiography, before closing the file, administering a patronizing pat to its manila exterior, raising watery eyes and inquiring (not
without a hint of condescension), "But how can you be so certain?"

I was asked this question ("But how can you be so certain?") during
my second admissions interview with Professor Barbara Clifford. The
day was breezy and exquisite, the plane trees outside her shuttered office windows tapping incongruous rain noises against the glass. Clifford
swirled the eraser end of a dull pencil over a transcript describing my
childhood experience at Camp Robansho, where my sister Edith and I
were made to stand naked before the canoe shed so that our spines
could be photographed and our posture analyzed by the camp physician, an agitated cricket of a man who stank of butterscotch drops and
old tennis shoes.

"But how can you be so certain he wasn't a child pornographer instead of a camp physician?" Clifford inquired, her blunted molars
grinding one against another and producing a muted clicking sound.
She wore a brown skirt, brown cardigan, brown heels. The lighting in
her office was massage-parlor dim. Synthesizer East Asian music filtered through a vent behind her dying ficus tree. Clifford drank herbal
tea from a coffee mug emblazoned with the claim "We are multiple beings having a dubious experience."

The synthesizer music tape looped for the fifth time in two hours,
and I asked to be excused to the ladies' room. The fluorescent hallway
grew long and skinny, the walls constricting as I hurried past the locked
office doors, the coffee-vending machine, the utility closet left menac-
ingly ajar, suggesting that you were being watched by someone con-
cealed behind a mop. The ladies' room appeared empty. I put the toilet
lid down and rested there for five minutes or so, staring between my
knees at the beige linoleum. From this height, each scuffed square
looked like a swatch of desert viewed from an airplane, punctuated
with specks of dirt that might be people, goats, a Berber tent. I experienced a twinge of vertigo, and leaned my head against the stall until
the dizziness passed.

Once I'd returned to my chair, I sat silently while Clifford fiddled with an unopened pack of nicotine lozenges.

"Well?" Clifford prodded.

"Well, what?"

She sighed. She despised repetition. "How can you be so certain you weren't victims of a child pornography ring?"

I didn't feel like answering her question, as my vertigo caught a vital second wind, as the synthetic zithers whined out a tune that bore more than a passing auditory resemblance to "Nobody Does It Better." Instead, I said, trying to regain my sense of equilibrium by introducing a light, chatty component to our interactions, "You must be fond of brown."

Clifford dropped the nicotine lozenges onto her desk.

"Pardon me?" she said.

"You must be fond of brown," I repeated, gripping the wicker armrests. The plane trees against the glass no longer sounded like rain, they sounded like a besieging army of carpenter ants, millions of little feet tapping their way down the linoleum hallway.

Clifford fingered her brown sweater. She appeared very offended by my comment, and took a large, white pill. She composed herself and suggested that if I was so upset, I should take a soothing walk through the sculpture park. I gathered my sweater and bookbag, while Clifford poured the contents of her coffee mug into the soil of the ficus tree. Before shutting her office door behind me, she pushed her emaciated face through the crack and said, "I don't know what you're talking about, Alice. I've never worn brown in my life."

After four more bewildering sessions with Clifford, my autobiography lay in penciled tatters on her metal desk. I admitted to the possibility of the pornography ring, yet had trouble conceding that my father, Harold Vickery-Plourde, was not the failed entomologist I'd known my entire life but a highly prized germ warfare scientist; that, instead of a graduate student in social work, I had been an unsuspecting test patient in a mixed gender group behavioral study; that my

mother, the population control activist, actually conducted covert ge-
netic work for a descendant of Dr. Mengele; that the Moroccan Air
plane on which my sister and I were passengers had never been a
proper part of the Moroccan Air fleet. The pilots on Flight 919 were
part of the hijacking, as were the other passengers, as were the police.
It was a far-reaching conspiracy in which everyone was involved, even
Pitcairn.

"What do you think, Alice?" Clifford inquired. "Isn't it possible?"

The trees tap-tap-tapped against the window, the encroaching footsteps urgent and indistinguishable from one another, blending to produce an ominous hum. I was surrounded, lost, friendless; I had been
airdropped deep in enemy territory. More to the point, I was tired of
battling Clifford over the most insignificant details of my life. I toyed,
momentarily, with capitulating to her demands. How easy would it be
to say yes? Yes. Yes. Yes. I practiced it. Hell, I told myself, it might be
liberating to entertain the notion that any experience I'd ever had was
bogus.

Clifford stared me down, sensing in me the heightened receptivity
that accompanies resignation.

"If you blubber at a movie," she persisted, "are you experiencing
actual suffering? No. It's a facsimile of an emotion. We're taught to find
the antecedents to our adult failures in childhood traumas, and so we
spend our lives looking backwards and pointing fingers, rather than
bucking up and forging ahead. But what if your childhood was all a big
misunderstanding? An elaborate ruse? What does that say about failure? Better yet, what does that say about potential?"

I helped myself to one of Clifford's nicotine lozenges. It tasted of
rubbing alcohol and old grass. I caught her subtle, nihilist logic: since I
had never been anybody, I was free to be anyone.

"Alice?" she goaded. "Is it possible?"

I pretended to cough into a tissue, in order to remove the vile
lozenge from my mouth without hurting Clifford's feelings. I swished

some lukewarm vending-machine coffee around my mouth and squinted at her, leaning expectantly over her desk.

"Yes," I said. "It is all possible." In my head I said, *Good-bye,* to no one in particular. But what I really meant was, *Hello.* I felt achy and terminally blue, as a girl will when she pretends she's been forced to do something completely out of character, when in fact she's come face to face with her own essential failure as a person.

Clifford bared her bleached teeth and wrote "Approved" across the top of my folder. Professor Clifford practiced what she preached, suffering from a suspicion so entrenched that she required constant validation from her colleagues over the most indisputable facts of her life. I'd seen her in the cafeteria, frozen before the salad bar with her scarred plastic tray, staring balefully at a chicken cutlet. Her tray began to shake, and on it, the thin silverware, which produced a slightly tense, percussive sound. "Is this really happening to me?" I'd overheard her asking her dining partner, the director of the Institute, Kevin Smythes. He grasped her by the quaking brown elbow and replied with his trademark oily smile, "Let's hope not, Barbara."

THE ROLE PLAY COMPLEX was hidden at an undisclosed location in the French Alps. It had previously been a winter Olympic training facility, back when there was a crystalline form of winter rather than months and months of fog. There were luge runs resembling open sewer pipes, there were ski jumps covered with a vibrant lichen, there were perfectly circular ponds beneath whose glassy surface one could still see the intricate system of cooling pipes, the valves and such, like a series of underwater hearts.

I arrived by bus on a Friday evening with Professor Clifford and ten other approved trainees for a weekend retreat. The bus let us off at a Russian train depot after wending its way past the Turkish souk, the Greek Orthodox church, the Unogen Chemicals industrial office park.

Clifford got on the PA system as we passed a Moroccan Air 747 parked in the gravel lot beyond the ski jumps. The plane was the site, she announced, of one of the most famous role-plays in Institute history. Our bus swung close to the plane en route to the depot, so close that I could see its windows were cataracted with a familiar blue-gray scum.

It's the same plane, I thought, chest thrumming. *Is it possible?* I heard Clifford asking me in my head. No. I shook the panic off. No. No. It is not possible.

We disembarked at the train depot and boarded a shuttle to the dormitory, where we were all assigned to a bunk room with a pile of thin, gray towels, an upended glass, and a bar of shrink-wrapped anti-bacterial soap stacked atop each of the vomity, wood-veneer bureaus. Dinner was served in a solarium that overlooked a partially completed Buddhist temple. I slept poorly that night, shivering beneath an elusive blanket knit of a sponge-furry synthetic material that refused to con-form to my body, levitating one to two inches above my hunched form like a beneficent mold.

The next morning—Saturday—Director Smythes took us on an in-depth tour of the Complex, relating, as he did, scraps of Institute history. The Institute was founded in 1951, he announced. It flourished until the Cold War grew tepid, after which most of the strife occurred within the Institute walls. The two major antiterrorist factions, the In-cursionists and the Brain Worms—"No need to worry about the dis-tinctions, you'll be studying this in depth when you start your course work in Lucerne"—battled for control. In part, this solipsistic faction-alism was allowed to thrive, Smythes believed, because there were no pressing external conflicts to compete for their attentions.

"All of this changed dramatically, however, after the Big Terrible. After the Big Terrible, the Institute received generous amounts of funding, and all international eyes were on us to prevent future terror-ist attacks of such magnitude, calculation, and stealth, like the one that occurred in America. But were we prepared for such an insurgence of money and responsibility?" Smythes asked rhetorically. "No, we were not. The Institute was so stymied by infighting that it couldn't agree upon a training curriculum. As a result, we began terrorizing each other, a fact of which some of you are intimately aware."

Smythes scanned our small crowd. Though he wore reflective sunglasses, I could tell he was looking directly at me.

At the matriculation cocktail party that evening, I drank far too many whiskey sours, became too stupid for conversation and got lost in the Turkish souk trying to find my way back to the dormitory. The next, highly regrettable morning, as I sat alone in the cafeteria and stared into my cereal, Clifford passed my table and dropped my course schedule beside my untouched juice glass. I ignored the envelope, my name written incorrectly on its front ("Alice Vickery Plourde"—she had forgotten, as she would always forget, the hyphen). I tried to eat, but the cereal made me gag. That name, written in Clifford's efficient block letters, seemed to expand each time I looked away and looked back, the black letters bleeding into the cheap bond until they obscured themselves in a spidery blotch of ink. My roiling stomach prompted me to hunt for a soda cracker. In doing so, I caught an unfortunate glimpse of my hungover head in the salad bar's spit-protective plexiglass.

I moved and she moved. I bared my teeth and so did she.

I should have returned to my room to shower before the slide show, but instead I took a walk in the fog. Past the Greek Orthodox church, whose gold dome lay on the ground like an amputated head. Past the Unogen Chemicals industrial office park. Past the Namibian farmhouse, where the llamas gave off a riotous stink.

The fog muffled the Complex. It erased certain things.

I picked my way through the forest of polystyrene packing crates. The Complex's impressively re-created Third World cities, their doors and walls and single-cylinder cars and even their garbage, were imported overseas in large crates, into which, Smythes had told us, a dense packing foam was blown for protective purposes. This foam had the half-life of uranium and was impossible to dispose of, given the new regulations. You could walk through the discarded perfectly split molds, he said, these white shapes of air that had once existed around objects, and try to guess what used to be inside.

The plane, when I was standing beneath it, proved to be in even worse shape than my distant views of it had indicated. The starboard wing was sheared off at the shoulder. Many of the windows were boarded over with plywood. One of the turbine engines lay on the ground; squirrels looped in and out of it.

Behind me, I heard the *stick-squish* of gum-soled shoes. I felt a gun in my side, I smelled Olde Bay Lyme aftershave with a hint of metabolized whiskey and a dash of llama.

I turned. Director Smythes.

"You're curious whether it's the same plane," he said. We stood beneath and peered up at its belly, rusted in a way that appeared painful. Scabs of rust. Crescent-moon scabs, boot scabs, horse-head scabs. Smythes stood laughably straight, as a man who was mocking a sufferer from heartburn might stand. He made strange adjustments to his mouth, turning his skinny lips inside out.

"Maybe I am, Director Smythes," I said.

"Call me Bruno," he instructed.

"Excuse me?"

"Call me Bruno," he repeated, reaching down to turn off the ringer of his red cell-phone.

A prickling sensation climbed up my neck, wedged itself under my hair. I had been warned about this by a janitor. The faculty loved to sneak up on new trainees and engage them in impromptu role-plays. My stomach surged. I ripped open a travel packet of antacids I'd found in my coat pocket, while telling myself to *buck up and forge ahead*.

I tossed the foil packet on the ground and squinted at Smythes. He didn't look a hair like Bruno. He tried to adopt Bruno's habit of puffing out his chest and running his hands up and down the sides of his anorak, but it reeked more of caricature than impersonation to me, and I had to struggle not to laugh. Not that it was terribly funny. I hadn't clapped eyes on Bruno since the hijacking.

"Nice to see you again, Bruno," I said.

I thought to myself: This is ridiculous and cruel.

"What's it been, Alice? Five years?" he said.

"It could never be long enough."

"Haha. Always the joker, aren't you, especially when you're scared shitless. Well?"

"Well, what?"

"Shall we go aboard? I promise to behave myself."

"Your promises aren't worth much, if I recall," I said.

He gestured upward with his gun. I ascended the corroded staircase, Smythes at my heels. We stood on the tiny landing as he loosened a ring of keys from his belt. He reached around my waist in order to spring the padlock, pressing his pelvis into the small of my back.

The door opened. I caught the fleeing odors of old pretzels and mold.

Smythes ushered me into the first-class cabin, pushing aside the nylon curtain.

"Well?" he asked, grinning in Bruno's absent, fake way.

I didn't say, but I was thinking: *It is the same but not the same.* I had imagined the interior of that plane so many times that it had taken on a new, more vibrant existence. These cushions were blue, which seemed incorrect—had they not been a brown-curry-mustard?—the carpet a dull paprika, so distant from the teal I vividly recalled.

Smythes let me into the cockpit. The door had been replaced with a sheet of plywood. I could not check whether it was our door, with its provisional locking system that Bruno—or one of his cohorts—had easily broken through. I touched the pilot's seat, its pleather upholstery peeling away, I draped a pair of overstretched headphones around my ears and fidgeted with the knobs, hoping I might hear Pitcairn's voice. These old knobs, I thought, these dusty, caked switches that searched the air for signs of life—surely they could find the remnants of our chatter, a dismissive snort or even a meaningful, wide silence. I experienced that familiar threading-through sensation in the heart region, but I refused to let it gain momentum, I refused to allow it to weave its way through my organs, to bind my sour insides and make me identifiably sad in a unique, Alice way.

"This is not our plane," I said, "as I'm sure you already know."

Smythes shrugged cryptically. I waited for him at the bottom of the stairs as he closed the door, snapped the padlock. It started to drizzle. We took cover in a foam crate that had once held a giant human head, or that's how it looked to me. We sat on the chin, and Smythes pulled out a half-gone joint.

"I've always wondered what it must have been like for you," he said. "I mean, being as close to Pitcairn as you were."

"I hardly knew him."

"To have been intimate with a man of his stature," he said, ignoring me. "It must have felt very special."

"Don't bullshit me," I said. "He got fired because of you."

Smythes offered me the joint. "It would be more accurate to say that he resigned."

I inhaled an unwise lungful. "Accurate, if entirely untrue," I croaked.

"These things are complicated, Alice." Smythes sighed. "Despite how it must appear to you, that man was my personal hero." He licked his upturned lips and gazed at me as though I were his personal hero, too, just by having known the original.

"Your personal hero was a failure," I said.

"In no small part because of you."

"That's one biased man's opinion." Or was it two men's? I was suddenly very disoriented.

"But regretting what you did, as I imagine you must . . ."

I smoked the joint down to the tiny red tip and dropped the crumbs into a puddle.

"What's your point, 'Bruno'?" I asked.

Smythes reached into his anorak pocket and withdrew his gun. He pushed the barrel under my skirt, his face into my face. Llama Olde Bay Lyme whiskey dope sleep breath. Green irises that expanded beyond the blue of his contact lenses. His eyes were muddy and scarred from too many casual alterations.

"You're a man of mystery, Alice," he said huskily, and tried to kiss me.

So I let him. Why not? It was not the sort of thing that "Alice" would ever do, and therein lay its singular appeal. Besides, there was no use trying to explain what it had been like to be a hostage on that plane, especially to the ersatz terrorist himself. I had tried to put it into words with Clifford, with numerous post-traumatic therapists, but it was easier at the time to be kissed by this stoned, role-playing administrator than to try to say what I really felt. What I really felt, as Smythes tongued the upper reaches of my palate, as his chin scraped against my chin, as he made out, in some distant or projected way, with his own personal hero, was this: Contributing to another person's failure is no small thing. In fact, such contributions can become distressingly addictive, particularly when you're forced into them at gunpoint.

One

But let me describe what Edith was wearing on that day we boarded Flight 919 from Casablanca to Melilla, where, fifty or so hours later, she was supposed to be married: a pale-blue cotton blouse with white threading and sanded wood buttons, an oatmeal wool skirt, a camel's-hair coat folded over her arm, cabled stockings, and a pair of sturdy leather schoolgirl shoes, because my sister believed in the erotic possibilities of cloddish, thick-knit, nubbled apparel.

We arrived with three hours to spare at Gate A-22, groggy and paper-mouthed from the Boston red-eye. We took turns napping; we played rummy; Edith called her fiancé every half-hour. Finally, the stewards and stewardesses arrived with their black overcoats and their wheeled luggage, signaling that it was almost time to board. I washed my face with a towelette and gathered our trash—soda cans, gum wrappers—while Edith stroked the tail of the Seeing Eye dog that was on our flight. She stroked his tail because the rest of the dog was encased in a bulky leather harness, and petting him in the usual way was impossible.

The blind man to whom the dog belonged didn't speak to us, but he did seem annoyed with Edith for petting his dog, probably because such creatures are off-limits to the seeing population, who spoil them back to their canine desires to fetch balls, roll in small animal carcasses, eschew the straightest line between two points. Edith asked the man why Verne (the dog's collar was adorned with a brass name tag) should be forced to wear such an elaborate harness. The blind man cocked his head as the initial boarding for our flight was announced—*"First-class passengers and passengers requiring extra time or assistance."* He rose and, without answering her question, allowed the whining, off-kilter dog (the harness made him wobble) to lead him toward the uniformed ticket woman.

Given that we were burdened with a garment bag containing Edith's fifteen-pound wedding gown and with what she insisted on calling her "trousseau," a single, slate-gray, circa 1979 Samsonite carry-on, Edith believed that we, too, qualified under the special-assistance clause. She dragged us into place behind a line of businessmen and elderly women. We were rebuffed, however, by the ticket taker, who pressed her thin lips together and returned Edith's ticket to her palm while looking beyond her to the next, and presumably more incapacitated, passenger. Edith put the Samsonite on the floor and glared at a robust luggageless couple boarding before us.

"Your prince might have flown us first class," I said.

"So you keep saying." Tap-tap-tap on the Samsonite with her schoolgirl shoes. She whooshed her very long sort-of-blond hair from one shoulder to the other. "But as I keep telling you, he's a former prince."

"He lives in a palace," I said.

"A very old palace with a stone shitter."

"It has a moat."

"Which his parents had to drain, because they couldn't afford the accident insurance." She sniffed and consulted her big rubber watch. "Are we *ever* going to board this plane?"

Edith left me in charge of the luggage while she nipped off to call her fiancé for the seventh time since we'd landed. I had no one to call except my ex-boyfriend, Miles Keebler, and I did consider calling him—Miles and I had been on the same graduate research team, and enjoyed each other's openly hostile company—but wisely thought better of doing so. Miles would complain to me about his new internship at the Revere Social Services Clinic, relocated to a former adult twin cinema. He'd complain that he had to listen to the problems of "blue-collar nutters" (his professional term) while trapped in a creaky old theater seat, its navy upholstery frostbitten with mid-century semen stains. He'd complain about attending a party in Boston thrown by Mindy, our former grad school advisor, in her gulag academic housing complex—one of those tense, beer-from-bottle affairs where somebody, often Miles himself, would tyrannically attempt to introduce dancing, and succeed only in making people feel more conversationally inept, more uneasy in their bodies, more doubtful of their inherent suitability for their chosen careers as social workers.

Instead, I relaxed into a clean orange plastic chair and marveled at the glassy beauty of the Hassan II International Airport and opened a package of licorice whips I'd purchased in Boston the night before. I noticed Edith chatting with animated scorn into the receiver, wedged between her ear and her shoulder so that her free fingers could tweeze apart her split ends. Probably complaining about me to her fiancé. Xavier, or X, as Edith referred to him (he was dyslexic, she said, and needed every available simplification), represented the dreggish finale of a semiaristocratic gene pool that had formerly ruled a Spanish principality in northern Morocco. As far I could tell, X's was the single monarchal family in history without a tragically high percentage of deaths due to syphilis, gout, duels, arsenic poisoning, or incestually produced hemophilia. Working in the Guerrarosas' favor, however, was a family history of dyslexia so severe it bordered on the aphasic, as well as the fact that the royal palace featured a stone "toilet"—a slab of granite with a hole cantilevered over a cliff, where the current below pulled directly toward the palace boathouse, covering the punts, the oars, the windsurfers in a foul fecal slick—on which generations of Guerrarosas had shat, so many generations that a depression had been worn into the stone, a fossilized, bum-shaped memorial more intimate and telling than any kilometer-long portrait hall.

Edith returned, massaging the phone crimp in her neck. She replaced her foot on the Samsonite and folded her arms, scowling at the glowing honeymoon couple, the stout businessmen, the men in djellabahs carrying titanium briefcases, boarding ahead of us.

"How is the formerly provincial Spaniard?" I asked.

Edith pulled a bottle of ginger ale from the side pocket of the Samsonite, tossed the screw cap under a seat, and did not offer me a sip.

"Your passive-aggressive commentary is not desired at this moment," she said.

"What's passive-aggressive about insincere curiosity?"

"If you think I'm ridiculous for phoning so much, just come out and say it."

"No, thanks." I chewed another licorice whip—I would say *innocuously*, Edith would say *judgmentally*.

A chinless man, bobbling papers, a cup of coffee, and a briefcase, dropped a cell phone the size of a small shoe. It smashed, batteries and plastic bits flying. The man kicked the remnants of his phone under the nearest plastic seat, and proceeded toward the militant ticket-taker.

"Is there any more licorice?" Edith asked.

I handed her a whip.

"You really don't think I'm ridiculous?" She bowed her licorice into a horseshoe and bit through the curve. She waved the two shortened whips like a runway controller with her traffic batons.

"I wouldn't say you're ridiculous," I said.

"Why not?" She signaled left, then right.

"Because that would make me cynical."

Rolling eyes. "God forbid."

"You'd accuse me, as you have done in the past, of being jealous, or of being the Woman Who Despised Love."

"You don't despise love," Edith corrected. "You shun it."

"I believe that it has shunned me," I said.

"Whichever does what to whom. So if I'm not ridiculous," Edith said, "what am I?"

I teethed my whip.

"I'd rather not say," I said.

"Say it," she said.

I remained silent.

"Don't make me beg to be insulted, Alice. It's one of the few things beneath me."

"Wouldn't you prefer I save my reservations for the 'shall forever hold their peace' part?"

"We cut that part out for Mom's sake."

"I thought she liked X."

"She *loves* him," Edith clarified. "I just think it prudent, what with her fondness for captive audiences, to eliminate the open-mike portion of the ceremony."

I nodded approvingly. An unfulfilled stage actress, our mother was the impassioned director of theatrics for a spate of population control clinics across Asia. She maintained that theater was a far more effective way to communicate the brutality of overpopulation, more effective, at least, than pamphlets and billboards that nobody could read. Add copious amounts of bad Moroccan champagne to our mother's tendency toward unfocused invectives, and the results would be lethally dull.

"Can I have the ginger ale?" I asked.

Edith handed me the mostly empty bottle. I took the final, flat swig.

"So," I began. "I can't say that I don't think you love him, because you'll just counter with, 'I do love him,' and that will be that."

She nodded in cautious agreement.

"I can't say that I think he's wrong for you, because you'll counter with, 'But you hardly know him,' which is true, I hardly do, and that will be that again. I can only say that your marrying him doesn't seem right to me, which is a little too vague a protest, considering the rather specific circumstances."

"Much too vague," she said.

"I could say more specifically that I think you're scared of being alone, and that as the Spokesperson for People Who are Eternally Alone, I am here to assure you that it's not so bad."

Her eyes narrowed.

"To be alone. Not so bad at all. I am also here to inform you that if you do not marry this man, you will marry a different man. You are a lovely and charming woman who has never been single for longer than the average daily time the American adolescent male dedicates to flossing his teeth. I am here to tell you that it is not yet too late to change your mind."

It was clear from her clenched expression that she was against understanding me.

"This doesn't have anything to do with you, I suppose," she said. Her eyes trolled the shapeless, plaid-dress-encased length of me. I always flew in plaid. Some mixture of habit and superstition. I had never crashed in plaid. In plaid, I had never been airsick, I had never had a high-altitude lasagna dropped facedown in my lap.

"Me?"

"Anyone would understand if you were a little jealous," she said.

"As anyone would understand how you felt pressured to get married to the first dyslexic amateur windsurfer who asked you."

"What pressure? What are you talking about?"

"Nothing," I said. "It's just that . . ."

"What?"

Apologetic shrug. "You haven't been yourself since you've gotten engaged."

Edith pulled a compact from her bag and applied lipstick with three or four hasty slashes. She mashed her lips together and bared her teeth, checking in the mirror for licorice residue. She snapped the compact shut and turned to me, composed.

"I'm sorry, Alice, that I've been responding to certain bridal pressures that *may*, I'm saying *may*, have dampened my usual enthusiasm for bearing witness to your daily toils."

"You know that's not what I'm talking about. You never bear witness to my daily toils. For that matter, I do not toil."

She sighed. Impatient. "Then what are you talking about?"

It was the moment for a trump card, even a trumped-up trump card. I decided, somewhat predictably, to inflame the anxieties experienced by every formerly wild, promiscuous woman on the threshold of marriage. I knew it was a mean and petty sibling maneuver, but couldn't help myself. I was feeling mean. I was feeling loserly and bereft.

I sighed loudly, a sigh that implied, *I'm saying this only because I love you,* and said, "It just seems as if you've lost your spark."

Edith's feet increased their tempo atop the Samsonite. Her fingers wriggled cautiously as though trying to assess, after the abrupt slam of a car hood, if all digits were accounted for. Before she could respond, the flight attendant announced in Arabic, then French, then English, *"Rows twenty and higher, please, twenty and higher."*

We bungled wordlessly down the covered gangway, through the first-class cabin. Despite the fact that our flight to Melilla was short—not even two hours—our plane was gigantic, newly arrived from Cape Town. We were the first of a number of stops; our travel agent had warned us that a flight on Moroccan Air was little more than an airborne African bus ride, usually but not always minus the livestock.

Edith halted at row 28 and attempted to heave her fifteen-pound wedding gown, covered in thick black plastic and zippered like a body bag, into the overhead compartment. The bag teetered on the edge of the compartment before falling on her head with a crackly thump. The man who'd dropped his phone in the lounge was seated in front of us, in row 27. He gave the garment bag a curious look.

"Could you help, Alice, do you think?" she griped at me from beneath the bag. "You're taller."

And uglier, her tone said. And stupider and certain to be alone, always. I smiled at her. She was crabby, poor thing.

"Once," I offered, trying to cheer her, "when I was flying back from Mylandrum, the stewardesses had to tell the mothers not to put their babies in the overhead compartments."

I struggled with the garment bag and the hatboxes, one of which contained the football helmet our father had balanced between his thighs as a permanently benched halfback for the Council Bluffs High Prairie Dogs. The helmet was purple, with a decal of a black silhouetted prairie dog, its face raised and its claws clutched timidly at throat level as though the poor sweet bastard were begging for his life. The animal was a perfect icon for our father. Harold Vickery-Plourde was an entomologist who erred on the khaki side of all things, conferring on his life a neutral invisibility that could pass as functional or meek, depending on your experience of him. He flitted laterally from shoddy academic post to shoddy academic post, relocating his young family to more and more remote corners of the mite-infested subcontinent as his employment options dwindled and his papers remained unpublished by *The Subequatorial Entomologist*.

After the divorce, our father married a Philippine woman and produced two new, bark-brown sons. Edith called them "The Antidotes," because they cured him of any residual guilt or responsibility he might feel toward the two offspring of his first, failed marriage. When he had phoned from Kalimantaan to congratulate Edith on her engagement, she hoped he might offer to pay for her honeymoon; instead he informed her that the older Antidote had demonstrated promising hand-eye coordination with a plastic fork and some fruit bats, and asked her to retrieve for him a sporty relic from the fatherland. I had rescued the helmet (along with the Samsonite carry-on) from a self-storage unit on the outskirts of Des Moines, a ten-by-seventeen-foot windowless locker that functioned as our paternal family's homestead, and to which Edith, our father, and I all kept a key.

"Do you want the window or the aisle?" Edith asked, waiting for me to take the window.

"Window," I said.

Edith settled in with a Spanish beauty magazine—she was trying to learn Spanish—and ordered a Bloody Mary from the male flight attendant once the plane had taken off, steadied out, and begun humming along over northern Africa.

"Should we have gone with the klezmer band? I worry that we should have gone with the klezmer band." Edith turned the pages of her magazine and practiced saying the headlines. I watched her mouth the headline "*¿Quien es más rubia?*" There were small pictures formatted in a way that implied a Golden Gloves match: Grace Kelly versus Mother Teresa; a Spanish pop star in a maroon satin corset versus Patty Duke (in a film still from *The Miracle Worker*). It was, as far as I could tell, an article about blond as a spiritual state of enlightenment rather than as a hair color of many attainable hues.

"Patty Duke *es más rubia*," I said. "'Blond' is one letter away from 'blind.'"

"I worry that we shouldn't have imported carpaccio from Italy. You know how quirky the refrigeration can be on those trans-Mediterranean ferries."

"So we all get botulism," I said. "So it will be a memorable evening that we will resent you for initially, but after a comfortable amount of time we shall retell the story, and to great humorous effect, because wedding fiascos make for the most winsome anecdotes."

Edith shifted her attention to the honeymoon, whose every minute had been described to me in projected, enhanced detail more than twenty-five times in the past six months. Edith and X had tickets to Greenland. They were going to ride sleighs up the sides of mountains while sitting beneath an eighty-pound elk-skin blanket. They were going to eat weird stews in a wood cabin and sleep in a bark-posted bed with a bark headboard.

I might have been jealous if I didn't hate winter so, but I detest winter. I have never been jealous of my sister, even though my hair was never as long as hers, even though my face is broad enough that hats, if I do not wish to be addressed as "sir," are ill advised. I did and do, however, have perfect skin, for which Edith, with her acne scars scattered across her shoulder blades (self-inflicted, naturally; she could never leave well enough alone), has always envied me. Edith also has friction-burn scars along her spine, and for this reason she opposes total nudity during intercourse (thus, I believe, the strategic choice of Greenland as a honeymoon destination). She has never made love in the nude save once, when I was a freshman and she a sophomore at the Maplehook School for Girls in southern New Hampshire. *Never again,* she'd sworn at fifteen and a quarter, recounting the previous evening's clumsy de-bacle, wherein she'd taken off her clothes on the paddle tennis courts just west of the new science building. She pulled up her sweater to ex-hibit the raw patches where her bare back had scraped against the sandpapery tape used to mark the out-of-bounds lines.

Edith poked me in the arm with an elbow.

"Hey," she said. "Recognize that woman?" She thrust her finger across the center cluster of seats, toward a pregnant woman sitting next to a window. The woman appeared to be an American, despite—or maybe because of—the teardrop-shaped diamond glued between her eyebrows, the Indian blouse, the pantaloons, the beatific aura that struck me as chemically induced.

"Uh-uh."

"It's Winnie Sunderland," Edith said.

"Who?"

"Winnie Sunderland!"

"Say her name even *more* impatiently and I'll know exactly who she is." The woman, whoever she was, fumbled with a prescription bottle, popping the lid and spraying pills all over herself and the empty seat next to her.

Edith grabbed her beauty magazine and flipped to the "Vida Nocturna" section. She pointed to a woman sitting in the lotus position in the middle of a ballroom. Guests, or their bottom halves, milled around her in tuxedo pants and slitted gowns. She kind of resembled the pregnant woman in the window seat; the woman in the window seat seemed physically smaller in scope, and less convincingly spectacular.

Edith attempted a translation of the caption: "American heiress makes the flower sitting at the party of her Madrid demi-cousin."

"Never heard of her," I said.

"Don't play highbrow, Alice. It's unbecoming."

"I'm not."

"Winnie Sunderland is the heiress to a western steel fortune. Her mother, Belinda Sunderland, turned her back on her family fortune to become a Buddhist nun in northern Connecticut. She was scandalously discharged from her monastery when her claims of achieving an immaculate conception were disproved by records showing she'd made regular trips to an elite sperm donor clinic in Rhode Island."

"Cool," I said.

"Despite the negative tabloid coverage, Belinda founded a successful perfume company, before she was murdered in a highly publicized case of suburban schoolgirl violence. Winnie, who's her younger daughter, donated a large portion of her inheritance to an ashram in Goa where Winnie lived, and to the guru by whom she was impregnated, free of charge. Winnie's older sister is an organic farmer who stays mindfully out of the papers."

"You've been following her family pretty closely," I said.

"So has everyone who doesn't live under a rock."

"I live in Revere," I said. "We don't have the mental energy for fabulous nobodies."

"You're too busy contending with despondent nobodies," she said.

"Why I live in such a dump, I have no idea."

"Because it depresses the living crap out of you."

A male flight attendant passed by our row with a shallow wicker basket full of headphones under his arm. There were six flight attendants I could see, four women and two men, all of them white and, I assumed, South African.

"What a pity," Edith said, gazing after the flight attendant's small, high, navy-upholstered behind. Inspired by Winnie Sunderland, she had taken an anti-anxiety pill and was becoming more pleasant—sweet, even. She returned to her beauty magazine, and flipped the pages with an aggressive inattention that indicated she was still fretting over my calculated slight in the airport.

The flight attendant pulled up his sagging pants—pants that were clearly not his, pants that sentimentally maintained the baggy outline of someone else's bottom—by the back center belt loop.

"What's a pity?"

"Pity he's wearing a wedding ring, and here he is, poor fellow, a waitress."

I wasn't following her logic. "Just because he's a flight attendant he can't be a good husband?"

"I imagine he's not." Edith leaned into the aisle and watched the man's retreating figure.

His name tag, I recalled, read "Tom."

"His name is Tom."

"I bet I could seduce him," she said, faking exhaustion, as if this were her duty.

Lost my spark my ass, Alice, I could see her thinking. *I'll show you spark, you dim, neutered cipher.* I glanced at her hand to hide my satisfaction, the hand where her wedding ring would soon be. Edith didn't wear her engagement ring, because she hadn't wanted a ring, she didn't want to feel that the world was closed off to her before it truly was. She kept it in her diaphragm case along with her pills.

She skewered her hair on top of her head with her cocktail stirrer without licking off the tomato juice. "What do you want to bet that Tom's a lousy lay?" she asked, then drained her Bloody Mary and pushed the steward call button.

"As opposed to a lousy husband?"

"If he agrees, *obviously* he's a lousy husband. But we need a more ambitious set of objectives."

"Okay. Lousy lay based on what standard of lousiness?"

"Why must you always have standards?"

"Because we're betting," I said. "Because I want to win."

Edith fished a hollow ice cube from her plastic cup and made a loud sucking noise as she attached the ice cube to the end of her tongue.

"He'll come too quickly," she garbled.

"Or take too long."

"Or take too long," she agreed.

"Put a time on it," I insisted.

She considered this. "Under a minute, or over ten."

"Are you proposing to him that this be an impersonal, fast fuck?"

Edith frowned. "He's got the trash collection to think about."

"You're already making excuses for him?"

"I'm just saying," she said tonelessly.

"If he understands this to be a quickie, then ten minutes is too long."

"Fine."

"Anything beyond four minutes, for a cheap, harried sexual encounter, is too long."

"What an expert you are! Fine. Under a minute or over four minutes, you win."

"And what about your pleasure?" I asked.

"Winning the bet will be my pleasure."

"No fair," I disagreed. "You must try to have pleasure. You must at least give him the chance to give you pleasure."

"What do you think I am?"

"A stupid slut," I said.

"Better than a book-smart virgin," she retorted, applying a mock-seductive squeeze to my plaid thigh.

I didn't respond, because there was nothing to say. It was true that I was inexperienced with men, the one exception my brief and scarcely romantic interlude with Miles Keebler. Our sexual interactions were limited to a few groping weekends in the water-stained bedroom of his Brookline apartment that harbored the burn-stink of air-blown popcorn from the previous, anorexic tenant. Miles was fussy about his sleeping, and kept one foot on the floor throughout the night; he wore a long nightshirt, which he insisted I touch him through, when I was allowed to touch him at all. He was not a man of harsh ejaculatory needs; a sweet, rhythmic petting, as you might apply to a crying child, was all that was required to bring him off. My body was not of interest to him. Although I pretended to complain about the arrangement, it was, in fact, a relief.

Edith pressed the steward button again. Tom shot us a hostile look from the flight attendants' station. He huffed back to us.

"Yes?" Tom sounded more German than South African. He was not an attractive man. His skin was alternately good then bad. I could see the powdery flesh-colored attempts to conceal a few problem areas on his forehead, and residual blond highlights clinging to the tips of his hair, which made my eyes water. I cannot but want to hug and protect a man with highlights from the world.

"I was wondering if I might have another Bloody Mary." Edith didn't look up from her magazine.

"We're about to begin the lunch service, madam."

"Actually"—she pretend searched his pectoral region for a name tag—"actually, *Tom,* I'm a tiny bit desperate. Nerves, you see."

I jumped in. "She just lost her lesbian paramour in the . . ."

"Alice! Tom doesn't need to hear about *that.*"

"I thought maybe if he knew the origins of your stress, he'd be more hospitable to your needs as an alcoholic."

Edith clasped my hand and smiled at Tom. "She's always looking out for me. I ask you. Could I want for more in a wet nurse?"

Tom frowned. It didn't take a genius to figure out that he was woefully new to his vocation. Male stewards always seem to be on the verge of lethargy and revolt, their ability to maintain a mask of hospitality challenged by the first request for anything actual—actual lemon, actual milk. Tom did not even possess the flight attendant's terse affability, or the practiced talent of staring at a passenger with a presumed eye-to-eye directness that is a fraction of a millimeter off center, giving the passenger the unnerving sensation that he isn't where he thought he was, spatially speaking, that the world has shifted slightly at this altitude, under this amount of pressure, resisting this amount of gravity, and his body has yet to catch up with the new physics of his airborne circumstances.

"As I said, we're about to begin the lunch service," Tom repeated.

"Of course I'd be *happy* to follow you back to the kitchenette and get the drink myself, if you don't mind giving me a hand."

Tom checked Edith out, but not in a way that indicated he was interested in seeing her naked.

"Of course," he said tersely. "A *hand* I can spare."

Tom minced back toward the galley. He whispered something to the other male attendant, whose red hair was quite long and worthy of a hairnet. He nodded and examined the carpet as Tom spoke to him. After a safe amount of time, he raised his head to look at us.

"So," I said. "Are you going to make Tom tell you a Shame Story?"

Edith regarded me with the exhaustion she reserved for my most pathetic moments.

"You never give up, do you?"

I patted her on the knee. "Come on. For old times' sake." But underneath I was reiterating my earlier jab, *It just seems as if you've lost your spark.* I was issuing a challenge, which Edith did not fail to discern beneath my sham wistfulness.

She handed me her magazine and unbuckled her seat belt. "What the hell, Alice. For old times' sake."

I cleared my throat. "Watch, please."

The man in row 27 regarded us irritably through the seat crack as I played with her rubber watch, beeping it idiotically in my attempt to set the timer to 00:00. Edith braided her hair over her left shoulder, then cinched the split, hoary finale with the elastic she had gripped between her teeth. She tossed the braid over her shoulder and pressed her fingers on the cowlicked heaves by her crown.

I clamped my thumb down on the rubber-nubbed timer.

Go.

Edith sashayed toward the galley in her oatmeal skirt and big shoes, her twisted cable stockings, and disappeared behind the nylon curtain.

In the meantime, I perused her magazine, read the in-flight magazine and did the lame crossword, so lame it had the reverse effect of making me feel dumber than before, even though I filled in all the answers in three minutes. Waiting for my sister to be fondled and loved, even if temporarily, hastily, poorly, was a skill I'd long mastered. She was twelve, just, when she'd lost her virginity. The boy was a hairless Javanese field assistant of our father's who spent the day collecting mutated mites (those with six or fewer legs as opposed to the usual eight) from the rice paddies and putting his captured samples in jars. I watched the field as he unknotted his sarong. I caught the briefest glimpse of his young penis; it craned as high as his belly button and was no more unpleasant to look at than a bare, tanned foot. He and Edith lay down on a mattress of interlocking twigs that he had busily assembled once my sister had made her carnal intentions clear to him. The mattress resembled a beaver dam and thus we called him, for the rest of the time we lived in Java, "The Beaver." We even referred to him as the Beaver in front of our father, who assumed this was a complimentary nickname rightly bestowed on his champion mite-gatherer.

Afterward, Edith and the Beaver emerged and proudly showed me the mud and various other fluids streaked on the inside of her leg and along the hem of her loden-green school jumper. Since then, it has been my role to "watch the field." I have waited near football bleachers and graveyards and newspaper stands. I have waited outside movie theaters, empty classrooms, train station restrooms, parking garage stairwells. I was the seeing, hearing, lucid, stately half of the act of intercourse. It was because of me that Edith could be such a curious slut. I made it possible.

I WOULDN'T TELL CLIFFORD about the Shame Stories until the conclusion of my first semester at the Institute. This is not the sort of confession I would have stooped to had the circumstances not conspired against me; the Shame Stories were not a part of my original file, they were a secret I shared with Edith, and Edith alone. My confession came about, as many confessions do, because of a desperate desire to avoid social discomfort and relieve tedium.

Clifford had invited me to attend a role-playing retreat in Øn, Sweden, along with the five most promising (read: identity-challenged) students from the Institute. Clifford and I were the advance team; we arrived in Øn by boat. (The name of the town led me to make many nervous prepositional puns as we motored through the choppy sea. Continuous tête-à-têting with Clifford made me anxious.) We landed at the rotted dock, unpacked the crates of freeze-dried food into the kitchen cupboards, then lit a fire and tried to generate some painless small talk until the other retreaters arrived.

Unfortunately, Clifford and I awoke to a deluge of sleet and rain, predicted to last through the weekend. All boat and prop plane services were suspended, and Øn was an impractical, three-day road trip from Oslo.

We were stranded, Clifford and I. Alone. In Øn.

Day One we read and played cribbage, but Clifford turned out to be a miserable sport, her expectations far exceeding her faint understanding of the game. Day Two we tried to walk along the bluffs and were nearly blown into the sea, both of us clutching at wet roots, our dry-rotted clogs sucked off our feet by the elongated mud pit that constituted the "path." At Day Two-and-one-third, Clifford suggested we do some role-playing, the both of us, so that the weekend wouldn't be a total bust.

I was just bored enough to agree.

To warm up, she wanted me to tell her something I'd never told anyone about my childhood. The first step to role-playing, she advised, is to revisit your former selves.

So I told her about the Shame Stories. The Shame Stories began when Edith was ten and I was nine. For exactly three weeks, while the Lombok embassy school was being deloused and repainted, Edith and I were transferred to a nearby Catholic missionary girls' academy, where we were taught by Indonesian women in white habits and exposed, for the first time, to the inside of a religion, no matter how awkwardly translated. We memorized the names of saints, and Edith developed a trick knee from praying on the concrete floors without any sort of bolster or blanket. We napped after lunch on the floor of our classroom— thirty girls in six rows of five, thirty girls in plaid uniforms that crept up around their waists, revealing that many of these thirty girls felt little compunction to wear underpants, no matter how much praying they did. Sister Nami awakened us by knocking a metal spoon against the chalkboard, signaling that it was time to inscribe a detailed account of each sin we'd committed since the previous afternoon into individual black ledgers, referred to as our "Shame Books." Though Edith and I were quick studies in most subjects, this particular exercise proved too conceptually foreign to us, two girls who had been raised without a stitch of religion—not because we were innocent of wrongdoing, but because we were innocent of what qualified under the Christian "sin" clause. I left my Shame Book blank the first day, while Edith completed a careful rendering of Sister Nami, right down to her club foot. Sister

Nami beat us on the head with a chalkboard eraser, leaving rectangu-
lar blue-white marks on our temples.

The next day I wrote, *Yesterday I sinned by not writing in my Shame
Book,* and Edith drew an acorn. Both were perceived as further inso-
lence, and we were clobbered with erasers anew. Finally Edith and I decided we must do what all successful people do—mimic. During the
daily lunch of hot rice mush and dried fish, dried papaya, dried milk
invigorated to a gravy texture with the vaguest splash of water, we
sneaked into the classroom where the Shame Books were stacked, spines
vertical if stooped, next to the abbreviated set of *Encyclopaedia Britan-
nica* (culled with such fanatical purpose that not only was the Darwin
volume missing, but so were the Roe-as-in-fish-egg volume, the Beagle-
as-in-dog volume). Edith and I stole three notebooks each and retreated
to the coatroom.

There, beneath the moldering ponchos and damp wool jerseys, we
lost ourselves in these schoolgirl testaments to "sin"—in most cases,
reenactments of supposed wrongdoing featuring, at their cores, a reve-
lation of personal humiliation. The beautiful Pavrita Baksh, for example, confessed to stealing a lipstick from her grandmother; her real
regret, though, was being caught by her brother as she kissed her own
reflection in a hand mirror. Clever, scheming Devta Sinha begged for-
giveness for wanting her own sister to be disfigured in a bicycling accident, yet her real concern seemed to be that her sister had given their
ugly, wealthy cousin Devta's diary, in which she'd expressed a hope to be
this cousin's wife someday, because "money turns a blind eye to otherwise repulsive men." Edith and I devoured book after book after book
that afternoon, keeping a quick ear against the coatroom door for the
sound of Sister Nami's lumpen footfalls. While we failed to glean much
specific information about Christian notions of sin, we did become familiar with our own inky attraction to other people's secret disgraces.

"Intriguing," Clifford said, scribbling in her notebook. "Tell me
more."

Because we were our father's daughters, I continued, which was to say because we were attracted to the justified manipulation of the scientific method, we decided to initiate our own secular Shame Book project, starting with him. Our first official entry in this Shame Book was the carbon of the proposed eulogy our father had typed on his curmudgeonly black Royal (the keys forever clumping), to deliver at his mother's funeral in Council Bluffs, even though the woman was not yet dead, and would not die for another decade.

Our mother supplied the second entry. She wasn't much of one for letters or writing, but she did represent a wealth of a certain kind of massively revised oral history, particularly when she'd had a few scotches. Her favorite story recounted the time she first met our father, at Machu Picchu. She'd sit on the edge of my bed, doused in lily-of-the-valley perfume (she had an overly sensitive nose; she wore a lot of perfume to mask the olfactory world), and tell me about her spinster aunt, the Peruvian waiter, the amazing clouds, eventually falling asleep on the floor beside my bed.

Edith and I soon branched out into the population at large, and began compiling our subsequent Shame Books using the petty manipulations available to us at the time, trading a melted lipstick or a primitive menstrual belt for a tale of personal degradation. But our means were limited, until our parents divorced and Edith and I were shipped to America, to attend the Maplehook School for Girls. In the idyll of the White Mountains, along a New Hampshire stretch of I–89 teeming with fourth-rate prep schools, we discovered that time-tested female economic boon. Edith would appear amenable to sleeping with a student from the neighboring boys' academy, licking his waxy ear and unbuttoning a single shirt button, rewarding him with a peephole's worth of skin. At the moment her subject became aroused and unthinking, she would pull back and demand a different variety of nakedness from him. One boy told her how he'd masturbated with his mother's oven mitt. Another admitted that he used to tuck his penis between his legs and take Polaroids of his new body, and that his mother had found the pictures and grounded him for playing doctor with an unidentified neighbor girl. At last count, we possessed fifty-five notebooks, of all sizes and colors, with browning pages and bent spines, sticky furred soda spills, tea stains, the occasional spot of nail polish or blood.

Clifford liked the Shame Stories, a lot.

"You'll be a role-playing natural, Alice," she said.

The perverse glint to her kelp-green eyes made me a tiny bit queasy.

"And when did Edith lose interest in the Shame Stories?" she inquired, pencil poised above her notebook.

Edith lost interest in the Shame Stories, I told her, at about the same time she lost interest in me. After we got to college and she wanted to be close to a man in the traditional sense.

"The traditional sense," Clifford clarified. "You mean, instead of humiliating a man as a way of becoming intimate with him, she wanted to fall in love."

"I guess," I replied. The Shame Stories were no longer cruelly entertaining to her: they'd become a contagious source of disgrace, until it was no longer clear where the teller's humiliation stopped and the listener's began. She was still a slut of impressive proportions, but her objectives had changed. She didn't want to exhume through sexual manipulation the apex of a man's shame, she wanted to pretend that the men she slept with (there were a great many of them) were perfect individuals, without unattractive desires that coded them as weak. She wanted to become infatuated with a man who hadn't revealed his secret uglinesses to her. She succeeded in falling in love, again and again and again, with the most inexplicable string of losers. This was her new experiment, from which I was patently excluded: to see how many dismal, petty men she could adore.

Clifford and I broke for a snack. When we returned to the living room, she announced that we were going to role-play all of the Shame Stories that I could recall from my childhood. To begin, she wanted to play me while I played my mother. The results were not successful. As my mother, I could not hold my pretend liquor, I became uncharacteristically (for my mother, at least) silly. Clifford counseled me against ironic impersonation, but I was too "drunk" to listen. Finally I settled down and did an admirable approximation of my mother telling me the story of how she had met my father, while Clifford pretended to be me listening.

I had just fallen asleep beside the "bed" (a couch), when Clifford blew the silver whistle around her neck, ending the session. We shared a pot of tea; then she changed the scenario.

"Alice," she said, "I believe you're ready for some freestyling."

"Great," I said. I didn't mean it. Clifford and her role-playing enthusiasm exhausted the hell out of me.

"We're going to transpose the Shame Story template onto your hijacking experience."

"Huh," I said.

"I want you to role-play the passengers on Flight Nine-nineteen," Clifford said.

"They didn't tell me Shame Stories, per se," I corrected her. "We were scared witless and bored. People tell you personal stuff when they're scared witless and bored. I'm a good listener, or possibly I'm just bland and forgettable. The passengers confessed things to me, without my resorting to any forms of extortion."

"This isn't about them."

"But if I retell their stories, I'll get them wrong," I lied. "I'm actually not a good listener, as it turns out. I just look like one."

"The stories they told you were already 'wrong,'" Clifford said. "Reliving an experience alters it, until there's no way of knowing the truth from the story. And this isn't about them. This is about you."

"Right."

"Think of it like this," she said. "If you were this *person*, how would you behave disgracefully? You can learn a lot of things about yourself by acting badly as other people. I promise."

"You've lost me," I told her.

"It's about living in the hypothetical," Clifford said. "In order to divorce oneself from the actual, one must re-create the hypothetical as oneself. Think of it as your own personalized fairy tale."

I was too bewildered to argue. I spent the remainder of that sleet-shot afternoon role-playing the passengers on Flight 919, while Clifford pretended to be me, the fake-able listener. (My Winnie Sunderland portrayal proved the creative highlight of the day, because I chose to do Winnie under the influence of the impressively strong painkillers to which she was addicted during our hostage tenure.) The role-plays were easy, since I was "freestyling," as Clifford put it; they were also bizarrely fun. I noticed, however, that with each person I blithely became, I experienced more and more unsettling cringes of self-discovery. I was digging up parts of myself that hadn't been exhumed for years, and they were creepily unfamiliar, they mutated and morphed into ugly, unrecognizable aspects of myself that felt nonetheless *true*.

We took a break for lunch. We didn't speak as I set the table, as Clifford laid out the smoked herring and condiments. I picked the seeds out of the rustic bread, too unsettled to eat.

"So," Clifford said, layering herself a hefty sandwich. "Did you learn anything of value this morning?"

I shook my head.

"What did you learn, Alice?"

I gave her a look that said, *Alice who?* But it was all an act. I knew too well who Alice was.

"Alice," she repeated. She trilled a birdcall on her whistle. "What did you learn?"

"Hell is other people," I said.

"And?"

I crushed a flaxseed with my thumbnail. I didn't respond.

"You are other people," she said, answering for me. "Thus?"

I stared into her kelp eyes.

"Thus?" she repeated.

"What do you take me for?" I asked. "A stupid donkey? Do you think you can whip me into action? Do you think I can be led by the nose to damning conclusions about myself?"

"Answer the question, Alice," she said.

"No," I retorted. "You answer *my* question. What do you take me for?"

Clifford dropped her hands, clutched around her herring sandwich, to rest on the embroidered tablecloth.

"I take you for a girl who's eager to grow unstable at the first indication that things can come back to haunt a person, even after she has given them up for dead."

"Fuck you, Clifford," I said.

Clifford tucked her whistle inside her sweater and hefted her sandwich to mouth level. She refused to speak to me for the rest of the meal.

EDITH REAPPEARED at exactly 06:45 on her watch timer. An announcement over the PA alerted us to the meal choices: minute steak kabobs or curried turkey Tetrazzini. Edith and I glanced at each other and nodded. We would both choose the minute steak, for it brought back childhood memories of a busy mother, too preoccupied with her theater productions at population control clinics to be bothered with foodstuffs that required peeling, heating, waiting to become a meal. Often we were left to rustle up our own dinners, which led to a disgusting and vengeful culinary experiment. Edith trapped a mongoose in a bat net, drowned it in the toilet, then skinned it with a camping knife and made it into a curry. She served it over rice to our mother, who was too tired to notice the reptilian springiness of the meat. Once our mother's plate was clean, Edith informed her of the prank. Our mother, to her steel-stomached credit, seemed to care only about which one of us had killed the mongoose. Edith blamed it on me, and I was sent to my room after a brief whacking with a soup ladle. My mother loved the mongooses, because they kept the house free of snakes.

"I'm *loath* to bring this up," Edith remarked. She was growing woozy from the anxiety pill and the alcohol. "But there's a distinct and horrifying chance that they will run out of the minute steak before they get to us."

I stood to count the number of passengers seated in front of us, each person represented by a tuft of hair rising above the brown tweed seat backs. I could see only the tops of heads—bald heads, Rorschached heads, turbaned heads. Middle parts and side parts, greasy hair and scorched hair, implanted hair featuring precision-tooled scalp spurts, hair dandruffed with what looked to be insidious crumbs of packing peanuts. They broke my heart, these innocently groomed people who were entirely unaware of their aerial disappointments.

But we had been warned. While supplies last.

"I'm older," Edith said. "And prettier."

"You should be more mature about this," I responded. "You should watch your weight."

"We never did say what we were betting," she said.

"Winning will be my pleasure," I taunted.

She scowled and flipped furiously through her magazine.

"So," she said. "He wouldn't."

"He wouldn't what?"

"He *wouldn't*," she repeated frostily.

Tom, she reported, had been calm when she'd unbuttoned her blouse. Moderately aroused, he'd pushed her into the nearest lavatory, lifted her onto the metal sink, and hiked up her skirt. He'd felt around the waistband of her underwear, he'd removed her bra and massaged the cups between his fingers. His erection disappeared after he'd determined the sharp object beneath the nylon to be nothing more

lethal than the underwire. He'd dismantled the smoke detector and enjoyed a cigarette while she checked for tears in her skirt lining.

"So," I said, "it appears to be a forfeit."

"It appears that I won, you mean."

"You didn't win," I argued. "You've provided no evidence one way
or the other."

"I most certainly do have evidence. Not being able to perform, in
my book, is uncontestable proof of a bad lover."

"That's ungenerous," I said. "He's preoccupied. He's got the up-
coming lunch service to think about."

"Now who's making excuses?"

"I'm just saying that he might be a perfectly fine lover but that, as
a *lover*, you have no experience of him."

"Not true," she said. "He touched me with the sensuality of a
prison guard conducting a body-cavity search."

"Maybe he's on probation for conducting airplane affairs with passengers. Maybe he thought this was a human-resources sting operation.
Your approach was a bit abrupt, after all."

She glowered. "At any rate, I didn't get a Shame Story out of him."

"Of course you didn't. He didn't even *want* to screw you. Plus,
you're woefully out of practice."

Edith pulled her hair over her shoulder and began the steady
process of unbraiding. "Now I know why you've decided to become a
social worker. People will tell you their most humiliating secrets *and*
you get to keep your clothes on."

"Brilliant, isn't it?"

"I thought so."

"Pity you dropped out of school."

I bristled. "I'm on a student sabbatical."

"Hah!" She finished unplaiting her hair and whipped it over her
shoulder. "Conducting cutting-edge social research at the Tip Top
Steak House. How hip! How inventive!"

"You have to take an innovative approach to education if you want to distinguish yourself from the masses of plodding, do-good job applicants."

Edith caught a fingernail—pearl-polished, manicured for once—on the woolly upholstery. She swore and, after dislodging the Samsonite from beneath the seat in front with her foot, bent into the aisle to rummage in the side pocket for an emery board.

Because she was preoccupied by her search, she failed to register Verne's indignant squawk as his tail was trod upon by his clumsy, sightless owner, ten rows behind us. I turned to see the blind man bump against the overhead bin, then make his methodical way toward the front of the plane, counting seat backs as an antique, abacus-like way of self-location. He had a shiny forehead and the merest spoutings of hair on the top of his skull, so timid and fledgling that they looked to be the promising beginnings of something rather than the slow, sad end. He wore glasses with opaque black lenses, behind which, I imagined, he was hiding a hideous injury. His hands seemed to lack muscle tone, and were suspiciously clean for a man who had to touch every surface, wall, doorknob, molding, who had to put his fingers in gum or spit or seagull droppings in his daily attempts to get from place to place. Over his shoulder he had slung his carry-on bag, one of those cheap canvas satchels you receive upon giving money to a fading bit of culture, such as the wind symphony or the bookmobile.

The bag said "Institut Sprecht von Lichtenfreug, Bern."

Edith, still bent over her carry-on in search of an emery board, did not see the blind man approaching. Because I was feeling cross, I said nothing. What I mean is that I *did* nothing to prevent the blind man from kicking her, however gingerly, in the head.

Edith shot upward as the blind man reared back. I could see him wondering, not without a certain amount of defensive indignation, *Which Moroccan idiot did not store his muskmelon properly beneath the seat in front of him?*

He recomposed himself. "I'm so *awfully* sorry," he said. He laid a hand over his heart. "Was that your . . ."

"Head. Yes."

"I'm *awfully* sorry," the blind man repeated. "It was the last thing I expected to find with my foot."

He had a strange accent that I could not place.

"As a blind man, you should learn to expect the unexpected," Edith advised.

"Yes, well."

"Your seat is behind us," Edith said. "This is row twenty-eight."

The blind man pedaled his lips. No doubt he was unaccustomed to hostility from complete strangers, even strangers whose heads he had punted in an airplane aisle.

"Perhaps I've misunderstood," Edith persisted, rubbing the back of her skull. "Are you not lost?"

The blind man presented us with a row of jaundiced European teeth. He stared at Edith, as much as a blind man can stare, fixing her with his black goggles. He took off his glasses and began to scratch his eyes, or rather, the wizened concavities where his eyes used to be. His bag swung and struck Edith's shoulder.

He returned his glasses to their proper place.

"Maybe you could help me," the blind man requested. He looked not above us, beyond us, beside us, as so many blind men are prone to do, but directly at us.

"Require a little assistance in the lavatory?" Edith grabbed my crossword pen and wrote across the bared stomach of the blonde on her magazine's cover, *There once was a blind man from Switzerland.*

"I can manage myself in the lavatory, if you could assist in getting me there without my kicking any more unsuspecting passengers in the head. May I know your name?"

I took the pen from her and added, *Who was as bald as that French guy named Mitterrand.*

Edith raised an eyebrow, as if to ask, *Was Mitterrand bald?*

I shrugged. Anything for a rhyme.

Edith told him her name and held out a hand. He grasped it immediately, and made me question, as I did so many times over those next few days, his rightful claim to sightlessness.

"My name is Bruno."

"You look like a Bruno," Edith said.

"Shouldn't your dog be able to find the lavatory?" I asked. Something about the guy bothered me. He seemed too confident of his puzzle place in the greater interlocking world; he was too spatially comfortable for a man who lived his life floating, untethered, in an infinite, black void.

Bruno ignored my question. "And what's your name?" he asked.

"Alice," I answered. "But shouldn't your dog . . ."

"Are you girls on holiday?"

"Not exactly," I said. When we had gone through immigration at Hassan II, the customs agent had flipped open Edith's passport and asked her whether she was visiting Morocco for business or pleasure. Edith had replied, "I'm getting married." The agent, initially uncertain how to classify this, proclaimed her to be traveling on matters of business.

"I'm getting married in Melilla," Edith informed Bruno.

"How nice for you."

"How did you lose your eyesight?" I asked.

Bruno tried to mask his testiness with bemusement. "Is this a quiz?"

"No."

"It sounds like a quiz."

"I'm curious."

"She's a social worker," Edith explained.

"I was riding a train along Lake Leman. A girl threw a rock and shattered the window as I was gazing out at a field of . . ." Bruno trailed off.

"Of what?" I asked.

"Of lupine."

"How awful!" Edith exclaimed.

"She's the last thing I will ever see. An ugly girl with a poor throw in a field of lupine. Of course, I have made love to her since. She came to find me when she turned twenty, and I made love to her."

"Yikes!" said the social worker.

"She felt sorry for you," said Edith.

"I felt sorry for her. Even with two eyes she is the less perceptive. She still has a terrible throw, her aim is abominable."

"Every tossed rock lands somewhere," said the social worker.

"We practiced in the backyard of my house, and she couldn't hit my face again with a rock from my garden. She tried and tried, before collapsing on the flagstones. I'm the one who took pity."

The chinless man in front of us raised his head above his seat back.

"Would you mind conducting your conversation more quietly?" he asked. He had a British accent.

I could see only the top part of his freckled face. I guessed that he had once suffered from a shopworn English pastiness, but after years of short-brimmed hats and lazily applied sun cream, his skin was a permanently chafed purple-red. It appeared unsuitable for the air, as hairless mice can appear unsuitable.

"Does this talk of lovemaking as an expression of pity disturb you?" asked Bruno.

"I have work to do," the man said, waggling a ballpoint.

"And you, sir," Bruno said, "have you never made love to your wife because you found her pitiable?"

Edith giggled.

The man slid back down into his seat. "If I had, I would scarcely confess it to a stranger."

"But better a stranger than, say, your wife, if you feel the need to confess."

The man cleared his throat. "I feel no such need."

"It's commendable that you know yourself so well," Bruno replied.

The man returned to his legal pad, choosing to ignore us.

"So you will help me?" Bruno asked Edith again.

The plane encountered a patch of turbulence, which tossed the presumed Winnie Sunderland, en route to the lavatory for the fifth time since takeoff, crashing into the other male attendant, the twitchy redhead with "Stephen" on his name tag. Bruno rode the interruption easily. He shifted his balance to his wide-spread legs and bent his knees, absorbing the plane's jerks with his sizable thighs. The seat-belt lights blinked, and we heard a beverage cart clang against the galley wall. The stewardesses—interchangeably patinated ladies who kept to themselves in the galley—each braced themselves against the cork walls with a single long fingernail.

Edith sighed. She unbuckled her seat belt.

"Order me the steak kabobs." She dropped the completed limerick in my lap.

He might be a fool
Or a perverted ghoul,
But a blow job might make a less bitter man.

She walked ahead of Bruno toward the lavatory. At one point she extended her hand behind her, which he somehow sensed and took in his own. It was not an act of kindness, or even brusque parental impatience, on Edith's part. It was an act that came from the same unconscious place that makes a couple, even if they go to bed in a fight, wrap themselves around each other lovingly in their sleep.

Mother's
Shame

WHEN I WAS an unworldly girl of eighteen, I traveled to Peru with my spinster aunt to see the Inca ruins and climb the peaks of Machu Picchu. Aunt Bea was a dynamic loner, and the sort of peevish yet pretty woman who derived her sole erotic pleasures from mocking any man who was kind to her in even the most indifferent fashion. I watched how she spurned taxi drivers and hotel concierges and lonely married businessmen.

We arrived by train at the base of the mountains and stayed in a log lodge with pyramid-shaped stone fireplaces and Incan-patterned silverware, napkins, towels, carpets, stationery, toilet paper. The first man Aunt Bea spurned at the lodge was the concierge, a balding Englishman who tried to bury his native Cockney cadences beneath an optimistically delivered Scottish Highland lilt. He called her "Mademoiselle," and accused me of being her sister.

You're not her niece, he said, grinning like a rabbit, long upper teeth and stumpy, over-alert nose, his desk clean of everything but a burly telephone that appeared too cumbersome to ring. You two girls could be sisters. Twins, I'd say.

He scoffed goodheartedly at our attempt at deception. My aunt took her key and turned away without a word to him. To me she said, quite audibly, You'd think they could find some miners' bastards locally, without having to import them from overseas.

I turned back to watch the man's expression deflate. His windlessness stayed with me, so that I could not enjoy our game of cribbage, our cocktails on the log deck, where we stared upward at the swelling flank of an Ande. We ate in a dining hall lined with photographs of Hiram Bingham and his archaeological team in the prolonged act of discovering Machu Picchu, digging it out with pickaxes and spades, looking as triumphant and first-time as men on the moon. Aunt Bea gestured toward them with a gravy-smeared knife. She said they exemplified the deluded ways of scientists who in their excitement forgot that Machu Picchu was not formed by the excavating motion of their pickaxes, who forgot that they were digging out the homes and graves of people who preceded their elevated discovery with the daily discoveries of copulating, eating, dying close to the top of the sky.

Scientists, she said. Aunt Bea was almost married, once. He might have been a scientist. She never spoke about him.

After dinner, I found the balding concierge drinking alone at the bar and gave him a fragment of bone I'd found while walking in the woods behind the lodge. It was a truly unremarkable fragment, gray and blunt and from a bird, but he accepted it with a resigned pleasure, as he accepted me, the niece of a mean woman on vacation in the Andes. He took me to a room in the staff building, a hangar-type structure hidden behind a wall of conifers. I slept with him because of his meager living conditions, because he was balding, because I believed it was my duty to correct the misbehavior of other people, especially those to whom I was related. Afterward, the Englishman was full of a scary number of apologies. I didn't dare to tell him I was, or had been, a virgin.

The next morning at breakfast, I sat across from my aunt, who turned her pickled face toward the Peruvian waiter, so dapper and sweet in his pressed white uniform, and said, A shame they weren't all killed by Spanish pestilence. What has survival ensured them but a life of servitude?

She asked for more coffee, and the waiter poured her a cup, spilling not a single drop onto the Incan-patterned saucer or her tweeded lap. Before the waiter's luncheon shift, I brought the brown underfeather of a sparrow to him, in the back room where he was polishing water glasses. His body was tougher than the Englishman's, his manner similarly apologetic and rueful. I did not tell him I was but one man from a virgin. I did not tell the other men that I was two men, three men away.

I thus passed my vacation, dodging contrition from men during the day, feeling a heartbeat in my sore, newly excavated places at night. It was little wonder, then, that I mistook my future husband's lack of interest for actual love. It was little wonder that I became besotted by this man who treated me with total indifference.

I mistook the day we met, even, mistook it for foggy when, in fact, we were inside a cloud. We boarded a tram, my aunt and I, guided by a small man who might have been a sherpa, one of those dense, low-center-of-gravity men, as wide as they are tall, who form geologically beneath the crushing air of mountainous climates. Water condensed on the windows as we were pulled upward.

At the top, the visibility was less than six feet. It was a terrible day to visit Machu Picchu. We might have been anywhere. My aunt accused the sherpa, who extended his hand to help her, We might be anywhere.

The sherpa did not understand English. He did not notice when she snatched her hand out of his. She disappeared angrily into the cloud, her failure to strike at the heart of a person causing her to reflect on her fading nasty allure, something that is always advisable to do in private.

I stayed with the tour, which was given by a young Peruvian woman who was beautiful from the front but who suffered an unattractive recession of her features when viewed in profile. We visited primitive kitchens, high-up holes in a rock face with blackened walls where fires once burned. We visited deep basins chipped into the stone by the singular dripping of an icicle over millions of winters. We visited a somber chamber with a stained floor, where sacrifices were thought to have taken place. At the Hitching Post of the Sun, a giant rock where astronomical observations about winter were made, I pocketed a tiny stone.

The Peruvian woman led us to a row of granite-slab picnic tables and passed out sandwiches and thermoses of tea. My aunt had been missing for more than an hour. I assumed she was off conducting her own examination of the kitchens and the sacrificial chambers, until I saw a bony figure being led through the cloud by a man with what sounded like bells around his waist.

My aunt collapsed next to me on the picnic table. Her clothes were filthy with a brick-colored mud. The man was thin, with the put-upon redness of skin that has been forced to act as a hide or a pelt rather than just an underthing to clothes. He had deep crevices around his eyes that marked his smile, though he was not smiling. He wore a tool belt that jangled, not with bells, but with tweezers and magnifying glasses.

My aunt did not speak. She pushed her muddy hair from her face and asked for a cup of tea. The man sat at our table. He lit a cigarette and pointed at my aunt with the breathing end.

Found your auntie here neck-deep in a mud pit, he said.

My aunt smiled. She had mud on her teeth.

Lucky for her, the man continued, I was looking for fossils. He exhaled and looked out into the cloud. Amazing acidity levels in the bog here, he said. Best-preserved insect fossils in the Pacific basin. Better even than Borneo.

You're a bug man? I inquired.

In training, he said. But bound to be a bug man.

Brilliant, I said.

We were silent.

But it must be a bore, I said, this bug business.

The man played with his match. He flicked it over his shoulder.

Beats baking bread, he said. Beats building bobsleds.

My aunt leaned forward and grinned with her muddy teeth. This man saved my life, my aunt said. She delivered the news as an accusation.

"Man," I thought, was a bit ambitious for the bug man. He was more of a boy. A bug boy.

What's your name? my aunt asked, sneering.

I could see the bug boy form a "buh" with his lips, but his mouth relaxed.

Harold, he said.

Well, Harold, my aunt said. You should know better than to waste your time rescuing old ladies from the bogs of this world.

He nodded. I've learned my lesson. You're the penultimate. He winked at me and wandered off into the cloud, tweezers clinking.

That night I found Harold the Bug Boy in the hotel bar. I drank five scotches and gave him the rock I'd stolen at the Hitching Post of the Sun. He identified it as a piece of concrete some archaeologists had used to buttress a failing wall, and threw it at the bartender, who laughed. Later that evening, he was unchanged after our encounter in his small hotel room, unchanged and unapologetic. He disappeared into the cloud the next morning without saying good-bye, even though he knew that my aunt and I were leaving on the evening train. When he tracked me down in the States ten months later on his way from one bog to another, I agreed to marry him without his even needing to buy a ring. I agreed because I was his ultimate bog woman, and I wanted to be rescued from the bog of my life. I didn't realize that his idea of rescue would be just another sticky form of entrapment. I didn't realize he was a man who preferred fossils, who could properly love only those people who were a hollow outline of their former selves.

Of course, I have a wedding ring, now. I tell everyone that Harold gave it to me, but the truth is, I bought the ring myself after I realized how much I'd come to adore the plastic emerald ring my younger daughter, Alice, received at the dentist's. I stole it from her bureau and wore it on my pinkie finger. When she asked me where it was, I hid my hand in my skirt and said the maid had thrown it out. Alice cried and cried. Even after I bought myself a real ring, I didn't give the ring back to her. If anyone had asked me why I did this, I'd have said it was because Alice was such a sensitive girl, so eager to grow unstable at the first indication that things can come back to haunt a person, even after she has given them up for dead.

Two

After Edith led Bruno into the first-class cabin, I took a casual stroll to the threshold between first and coach. I could see neither my sister nor Bruno—she was in the galley, I presumed, waiting for him to finish up his blind man's business in the lavatory—but I did notice a pair of Japanese businessmen seated in first class, along with an attractive Indian man wearing "work-casual" Western attire: linen suit pants, a button-down shirt, substantial leather sandals that might have been carved out of mahogany blocks. As I returned to my seat I clocked a boy of five or six dressed in suede lederhosen. He was traveling with his mother, I assumed, a plump woman in an ivory suit with big gold buttons.

Behind the boy in lederhosen was a university-aged fellow whom I recorded with a sentimental fondness, because he was the exact blueprint of a boy Edith had dated when we were in college, a peach-fuzzy physics major named Hal Pipkin. This boy exuded the same air of belligerent laziness that had made Hal such a coed catch. He breathed with his lips flared, revealing gums that were bad for a boy his age, livid and receding. He was cute, however, and would be for approximately three more years, if Hal Pipkin's fate could be seen to represent any common path of devolution, at which point the source of his appeal— a lingering boyishness—would be smothered by heavy jowls and distorted by a widening jaw. His eyes, already on the small side, would be squeezed by the thickening pith of his man's flesh, and the smirking green would dull to the color of dried lentils.

The center seats of the plane were occupied by a boisterous group of twenty male archaeologists en route to a reunion at Volubilis, the ancient Roman outpost in northern Morocco. I heard them complaining about their roundabout itinerary (our plane overshot Fes, flying to Melilla first, then retracing its path east and south), questioning the decision to hold the opening reception at the former site of the House of the Ephebus, and speculating jokily whether or not their hotel, the Gordian Palace, had finally purchased a fax machine. They all wore the same corroded wire rims, and all seemed equally relieved that their wives, already checked in at the Gordian Palace, had spent a ladies' weekend at a spa in Fes, and would thus be more agreeable than wives usually are who are dragged to remote locales to look at the resting places of Roman tablet fragments.

I returned to my seat and checked Edith's watch, still set for Boston time. By now Edith had been gone nearly eight minutes.

If Stephen and Tom had disappeared for a suspicious length of time, I did not notice it. If an unnatural hush emanated from first class, I did not notice it, because I was not, as yet, a notably observant person. Becoming such a person took years, and plenty of humiliation, the sort that the Institute was skilled in doling out. The most famous example of this, the Banal Reassembly Test, was administered stealthily to unwitting new trainees. On a particularly sweltering October afternoon, I sat with twenty-seven other trainees in the Curtis Fishbeiner

Lecture Hall, waiting to be given an exam in a survey titled "Mobile Civilian Container Victim Reaction Trends, 1970 to the Present." This required course offered a historical study of the ways in which passengers on airplanes, buses, and trains responded to hijacking situations, and how these responses had altered after the Big Terrible.

In preparation for the exam, I'd been up all night in my dorm room reading and rereading case studies of various post–Big Terrible hijackings. None of these case studies followed a pattern, and thus trends were difficult to spot, and possible countermeasures by passengers difficult to contemplate. Two particular hijackings stuck in my mind as representative of the new brand of unpredictable disorder.

The first was the case of Malaysian Air Flight 879, which departed Bangkok at 10:15 a.m. on November 23, 2003, en route to Kuala Lumpur. It carried, among other passengers, a British rugby team, a famous Malaysian industrialist, and ten infants who were being escorted by five adoption authorities to a Malaysian orphanage. Less than an hour after takeoff, the flight was hijacked by the adoption authorities—in reality members of a Burmese liberation front known as the Red Veil—who had smuggled knives aboard in their charges' diapers.

It was an unusual case, made even more unusual by the black-box transcripts, which created a highly atypical terrorist portrait. The lead operative, a man who called himself King Tabinshweiti, stated repeatedly to the passengers that he did not intend to crash the plane into any building in Kuala Lumpur, the destination city; he intended only a "regular old hijacking," in which, at worst, a few people on board might die if his demands were not met. It would not be hyperbolic to describe Tabinshweiti's speech to the passengers as a strange and supplicant form of salesmanship; his pitch was devoid of the usual terrorist threats, it was reasoned and beseeching in tone, indicating that he was acutely aware of his need to "sell" his hostages on the terms of their captivity, for fear of being terrorized himself.

Despite Tabinshweiti's artful talking, nobody believed him. The hijackers were overpowered by the members of the British rugby team, the plane went into a tailspin and crashed into a harbor off Koh Pipi, and all sixty-nine people aboard were killed. Interviews with Tabinshweiti's family suggested that he had been telling the truth, and the members of the British rugby team, worldwide heroes for twenty days, were rebranded as overzealous hotheads. After the incident with Malaysian Air Flight 879, passengers were counseled not to act too hastily in the case of a hijacking; an international coalition of mental health professionals met with the World Airspace Coalition to generate an "Is Your Hijacker Suicidal?" checklist, to be laminated and placed in airplane seat pockets along with emergency procedure brochures.

Less than nine months after the Malaysian Air debacle, four Basque separatists, who had fuel supplies hidden at more than six hundred airfields around the world, overpowered the crew of Aire España Flight 2019. The impeccably behaved fifty-three passengers and six crew members did nothing to challenge the hijackers, and were held hostage for a record-breaking 543 days. Once they were rescued at an airfield outside Buenos Aires, the hostages exhibited some of the most severe cases of Lansberger's syndrome ever documented. None of them wanted to get off the plane, even after their captors had disappeared into the pampas. They took up the arms left by their captors and fought off the rescue workers for an impressive forty-seven hours. The photos in my textbook showed the passengers and crew being dragged down the metal stairs in handcuffs; one woman clutched the railing, another flailed her fists against a uniformed man while unleashing a perfect arc of saliva into his face, her spit photo-frozen like a beautiful icicle. A passenger coalition formed a few months later and won a legal suit against Aire España that claimed the hostages deserved frequent flyer credit for all 1,234,890 miles flown by Flight 2019. Subsequently it was almost impossible to fly Aire España without encountering at least one of the former hostages. My mother sat next to Merced Rillarado, of the beautiful spit, on a flight from Madrid to

London. This woman, she said, peered around nervously throughout the flight, fixating with desparate expectancy on a turbaned man three rows back. When the plane landed safely in London, Merced Rillarado burst into a bout of tears as reflexive as a coughing fit. She cleaned up her face with the towelette from her utensil packet, and hurried off to make her connection.

On the day of the "Trends" exam, we waited and waited in the Curtis Fishbeiner Lecture Hall. After twenty-five minutes, three-quarters of us resorted to a nap, cheeks pancaked atop the ink-stained writing platforms, legs thrust into aisles, pencils falling onto their pin-sharpened points. We were, all of us, sleep-deprived because of the midnight interrogations that found us deep in abandoned train tunnels, wearing pajamas and hastily donned bluchers, answering, to the torturous drip of underground condensation, barked questions about an assumed identity we had each been forced to memorize in three minutes.

After forty-five minutes, Director Smythes entered the lecture hall in his scabrous wide-wale corduroys, his filthy-edged files protruding from his Guatemalan tote. He informed us that our instructor, Professor Hinckels, had moved the test to Room 33, because the lecture hall was scheduled to be painted, a brighter shade of ecru. That's what he said: *a brighter shade of ecru.* He apologized for the confusion. We shuffled, half asleep, drool and ink stains patterning our cheeks, down the corridor to Room 33. We retook our seats, resharpened our pencils, restowed our book bags. The windows were closed, had been closed, it felt, for the duration of the summer and fall, and the stale, chalk-stinking humidity was unbearable. What little resolve we'd had against sleep melted away; we pressed index fingers against liquefied eyelids to prop ourselves awake. Smythes apologized again, for the heat, for the confusion. He extracted our exams from his Guatemalan tote, gave a handful to the first person in each row, and left the room.

The test was multiple choice, a hundred questions, easy. It concluded with an innocently posed extra-credit question:

What color were the original walls in the Curtis Fishbeiner Lecture Hall?

(a) shell pink
(b) British khaki
(c) petit beurre
(d) ecru

Ninety-three percent of us bubbled in confident number-two unison, *(d) ecru*. We were somnolent and heat-dumb, but we had listened, we had been paying attention to the man in the mustard-colored suit. After two months at the IITSL, our brains were tautening into ropy, muscled switchblades of gray matter, processing, storing, digesting information through miles of looped track as intricate and mechanistic as intestines.

We left our exams in the wire basket by the door, then bumbled back to our dorm rooms to prepare for our Role Play Complex pre-orientation workshop.

"Civil unrest is spawned by lassitude," Professor Hinckels intoned the following afternoon as she replaced the chalk in the chalk well. She dragged her powdery fingers across opposing suede-patched elbows before handing back our "tests." The exam, it turned out, had been a cover, and was thus unscored. The walls of the Curtis Fishbeiner Lecture Hall, she informed us, had been a vitamin-pill shade of pink, notably caustic, hard to mistake. It was not, she insisted, "even a neutral shade." She chastised us for our "willingness to accept as fact the claims of an authoritative man in a corduroy suit" and gave everyone a failing grade, even those two students who had answered *(c) petit beurre*.

From that moment forward, we were never allowed to be bored again. The lesson of the Banal Reassembly Test rendered the notion of simple existence forever obsolete; even now, all these years later, I find myself unable to cease counting the number of outlets in hotel lobbies, the number of light switches, or memorizing the number and placement of every egress, bellhop, davenport, faux fireplace, equestrian oil painting. During the flight from Casablanca to Melilla, however, I still harbored the softest and slowest of minds, I stored pulp between my ears that did not whiz and click at the sight of strangers and neutral shades of classroom paint.

I heard a creak and a rustle in front of me as the Englishman peered at me between the seats.

"Where's your sis sprung off to?" he asked.

"She's helping that blind man," I said.

"Brave of her, escorting that creepy chap to the loo."

"Maybe you have issues with afflicted people," I observed, feigning engrossment in Edith's beauty magazine.

The man coughed into the folds of a financial paper. "I beg your pardon. The wife, who is overloved, is a diabetic. Tends to afflict the *healthier* ladies." He moved left, then right, so that different longitudinal segments of me were visible through the crack.

"Why do Brits always use the indefinite article instead of the first-person singular possessive?" I asked.

"Keeps us from having to claim responsibility for anything," he replied. "Always some other poor bloke out there to take the heat for the old betty, the old pension, the old overwrought ticker."

"That's a fine answer," I said. "People don't tend to supply such fine answers to rude, rhetorical questions."

The man thrust three fingers through the crack. "Cyrus Bing."

I shook his fingers, but did not offer my name.

A voice came over the loudspeaker announcing that lunch had been canceled because of an oven mishap. He added that he was sorry to announce this flight as our captain's, Aboul Somebody's, last before retirement. He followed this announcement in French and Arabic, and three different groups of the passengers clapped at three different times.

"It's the opposite of a maiden voyage," I said through the seat crack.

"We're his last gasp. His widower's walk. Your sis seems a bit riled up. Wedding jitters, I suppose."

"Or wedding rage."

"And not a day married? Isn't she precocious."

"I told her I thought it was a mistake to marry the man she's marrying."

Cyrus made disapproving ticking noises. "You might have told her sooner, before she bought the dress. Once the dress is bought, the ability to make clever choices departs a girl's head entirely."

"You can return a dress."

"But now she's seen herself in it, and damned if a girl isn't going to wear the dress she's bought herself, even if the occasion is hell-bent and shoddy. After the first wife bought her dress, she didn't have the courage not to go through with the ceremony."

"How can you be so sure she didn't want to marry you?"

"A man knows these things," he said. "And the woman was right, after all."

One of the stewardesses came around with the beverage cart and handed out "snacks"—packages containing two pulverized tea biscuits. Cyrus ordered a beer.

"Stork beer," he said, showing me the label. "As in, 'Drink too much of this at your peril, for you may drunkenly shag a pub sweetie and receive an undesired visit from our bird friend.' You'd think there were Catholics running this country instead of Muslims."

"Perhaps the stork symbolizes something else in Morocco," I said. "Loyalty. Nobility. An icon against pestilence."

"Don't be so certain," Cyrus said, jiggling the can back and forth. "I think it might be an insidious fertility potion."

"You're belying your own guilty Catholicism."

Cyrus chuckled. "Or my weakness for pub sweeties." Though he was an older man, in his early sixties perhaps, he contained an inner youthfulness that made his crimped, skinny body seem an error. "You can see straight through me," he said. "What's your name?"

"Alice."

"You can see straight through me, Alice. What do you do with yourself when you're not chatting up the oldsters?"

"Chatting up the youngsters," I said. "Or the medium young."

"You're a pederast?"

"I'm getting a master's in social work."

"Ah. Can't say I've ever met a master of social work before. You people don't fly much, do you?"

"We fly enough," I said.

Cyrus took a long sip of his beer. "The wife wants me to see a therapist," he said. "Says I need to detoxify myself. Says you can see it on my skin that I'm a liar."

"On your skin?"

"She's a gels-and-potions lady. Sells products for the face and neck area, but branching soon into joints."

"But not for lying skin," I said.

"No, not the lying skin, for that you need to see the doctor. Says so right on her labels. 'If lying persists.' So what do you say?" he asked, turning his face from side to side. His moles were sprawling, mottled cityscapes, each outlying town expanding, one ragged-edged suburb bleeding into the next. "Is there hope?"

"I don't know," I said. "Maybe you could start by telling me if you've ever made love to your wife because you pitied her."

Cyrus blanched as much as was physiologically possible for such a crisped English specimen. "Oh, you're a cheeky one, Alice. Your bedside manner's a bit lacking, though."

He regarded me balefully. And then, as is always the case with people who have been ravaged, browbeaten, eternally disappointed, abandoned, he delivered an honest and heartfelt response to my insolent question, telling me in candid detail the manner in which he had met his second wife. What is it about the cruel that renders them trustworthy? Because cruelty has become synonymous with honesty, compassion with chicanery?

I have tried the compassionate approach—in graduate school, at the Revere Social Services Clinic—but this made me a target for some stranger's mischanneled wrath. The moment I turned mean was the moment the humble honesty came trickling out of my counselees— usually hostile, cigarette-smelling accounts-payable executives from Quincy or Danvers who had taken an unthinking swipe at a wife or a pet. The moment these people became victims of a similar abuse was the moment they became tolerably docile.

This had certainly proven true with Miles Keebler. Our brief rela- tionship, during which I was rejected again and again while remaining endlessly understanding, reversed itself alarmingly once I decided, out of boredom plus the tiniest dash of self-respect, to reject him, to refuse to rub his groin down beneath his nightshirt, to refuse to find adorably eccentric his sleeping habits or noble his vegetarianism, which was so extreme it made savage kissing ethically complicated. I dropped out of school. I got a job at a steak restaurant. Instantly, Miles grew love- sodden and desperate to communicate with me. He would show up at the Tip Top near the end of my shift, and order a pair of baked pota- toes and read the cast-off sports pages while I refilled saltshakers and pried the gummy black residue from the screw-top grooves of ketchup bottles. He would drink black tea, which never got much blacker than light brown, even if he steeped three bags of the Tip Top's cheap-ass pekoe simultaneously, lightened further with dribbles of soy milk from a plastic container he always kept on his person, and wait until the manager had gone to his office to run off the night's receipts. Casting worried glances toward the kitchen (where my elderly co-waitress was stealing rolls), he would corner me at the coffee station, push me up against the stainless-steel bread warmer, fondle beneath my white frilled apron, and mutter excuses about himself as he drove his pelvis into my abdomen.

It was always touching, at least for a while. Miles whispering into my hair, coiled from the kitchen steam tables. Miles kissing my cheek, soured with the oily evaporated sheen of condiments. Miles feeling me

up with a hand coated in bread crumbs. I would struggle free and toss
my apron in the hamper, I would grab my ski parka and my canvas bag
full of books and lip balm, I would allow Miles, his mouth quivering
with some unspoken sense of deep injustice, to drive me back to Revere. Silently disapproving of the world music station to which his radio was eternally tuned, I would listen, bland-faced and sleepy, as he
told me about his Baltimore mother's fear of communicable skin diseases, and the way she used to wrap his private parts in medicated
gauze whenever he went to a public pool, the way she would clean beneath his foreskin with a stinging alcoholed Q-tip, the way she would
rock him to sleep so violently that he developed a severe sense of nauseating disequilibrium whenever he lay down on a bed.

But one must take these disclosures in stride, and see these "hon-
esties" as the extreme fabrications they frequently are. I didn't need
three-and-change semesters of grad school to learn that people rarely
tell the truth about themselves. I have been lied to enough times to
realize that a lie, when delivered in a confessional context, is really a
fussied-up truth; that people do not tell accurate stories about themselves when they are given the chance. They tell, as Miles Keebler
called them, "representative anecdotes." People concoct stories that
capture the essence of an emotional experience, sacrificing factual precision in hopes that an emotional truth can be conveyed to a listener.
People turn their lives into fairy tales, into myths, not as a way to self-
aggrandize, but as a way to convey their human distress. As Clifford
concurred, many years later, "the seeds of neuroses are literally seeds."
Seeds, requiring cultivation through enhancement—or in Clifford's
world, role-playing enrichment—until they blossom into the menacing, carnivorous plant life that can believably be blamed for the failure
that is *this person.*

IT IS WORTHWHILE to note the following detail, which I do recall
with utter clarity: Save for a few gasps, the sort that a low moon or an

unexpected view of the sea might elicit, nobody in coach screamed, not a single passenger, when Tom, the steward, emerged from the first-class cabin with a gun.

A gun. It seems impossible in this paranoid age in which the elderly are deprived of their canes by airport security officials, women of their fingernail and hair extensions, but a respectful delicacy still exists between humans (this is heartwarming to me) in our knee-jerk, petrified world, and as such the blind, and more specifically their dogs, are seen as having suffered enough invasive insults that their heavy harnesses are not removed and checked for weapons. An off-kilter canine wobble is viewed not with due suspicion, but with the same relieved pity that arises upon witnessing the Alzheimer's counselor nodding off on the train—pity for his futile trials, combined with a tangible relief that there exist people in this world who derive pleasure from the daily task of helping those whose situations will never, never improve. And so Tom held a gun, a small gun, granted, small enough to be hidden inside Verne's harness, but still, a gun. There was no mistaking its realness. It was matte and cast of a brown metal, sufficiently ugly to imply that its concerns were merely functional.

Tom spoke in a normal voice that might have been asking us to do something as banal as return our seat backs to their upright position for landing. He still wore his steward outfit, his steward apron, which contributed to our fear disconnect.

He asked us to "kindly shut the fuck up," even though no one had said anything. He promised that no one would die—not in our plane, not on the ground—as long as we behaved ourselves.

"Tick me off," he said, "and we'll crash this plane right into Volubilis."

The archaeologists paled. Their leader, the man with the largest and most corroded pair of wire rims angled over his much-broken nose, glanced around nervously, indicating he might tackle anyone who tried to overwhelm Tom or "tick him off" in any way. I couldn't help wondering what he was more concerned about losing to the obliterating heat of a jet-fuel inferno—the former site of the House of the Ephebus or his wife.

The little boy in lederhosen let loose a Doppler-effect wail—intensifying, arcing, receding—which inspired the ten or so Moroccan women aboard to moan and rock in their seats, touching their foreheads to their folded tray tables. A woman in a ponyskin vest and turquoise bead earrings started to hiccup.

Tom pointed the gun into her face. "Button it," he threatened, and knocked her, hard, under the chin. Tom's highlights flashed; even with the gun, he was hard to take seriously.

I was not, as yet, taking him seriously.

Like Ponyskin Vest, I was overcome with a need to hiccup, as urgent as the need to vomit. I pushed my fist into my mouth, but the sound came out anyway. I rattled open the airsickness bag and put my face in it. I filled it with nervous breathing.

Stephen, wielding a short-barreled pistol, ushered the first-class passengers back to coach. The Japanese businessmen shuttled, eyes low, briefcases and papers held tight against their chests; Work Casual Indian Man hurled an indecipherable expletive at Tom when he tried to force him into a spare seat.

The airsickness bag still pressed over my lower face, I peered forward to locate Edith. I caught a glimpse of brightness, which might have been the reflection of the overhead light on her whipping hair as she was shoved into a seat or pushed onto the floor. I did see one female flight attendant, her hands tied behind her back with the clear tubing from an oxygen mask.

During these initial moments of the hijacking, I did not for one instant consider that we might die. This response seems unimaginable, I know, particularly given the then recent innovations in airplane terrorism. Our hijacking took place after the Big Terrible, but before the Malaysian Air debacle. Passengers still felt compelled to get involved.

Cyrus—foreman of the Elk and Crown Cricket Club, editor of the

Plastics Tomorrow newsletter, booster club president for the Manchester Girls Football League—exhibited a more immediately civic approach.

"We have to do something, Alice," he whispered through the seats.

I swallowed. "We do?"

"We have to charge him. You and I. He'll never know what hit him."

A clumsy, unathletic woman and a rather old man. That's what would hit him, and to what effect? I looked around at the other passengers. They seemed to be on my wavelength: *Let's trust the man with the gun.*

"But what about Volubilis?"

Cyrus regarded me blankly.

Volubilis. I had written a paper on Volubilis when I was in school at Maplehook, I informed him. The land surrounding Volubilis was some of the most fertile in northern Africa. Nine thousand lions had been sailed over the Mediterranean to their deaths at the grand opening of the Roman forum by the residents of Volubilis. My history teacher's miniature schnauzer was named Volubilis. Volubilis was hit by a car, but lived. My history teacher had to carry him on walks, lowering Volubilis's bandaged body to bushes so that he could pee.

Cyrus sputtered, impatient. "You don't *believe* this man, do you?"

I chewed my lower lip.

"He's just preempting any trouble. What would you say, Alice, if you wanted to hijack a plane in this day and age without being tackled?"

"But if he's telling the truth, we'll be responsible for the deaths of innocent people." I told him about the archaeologists' wives at the Gordian Palace. They had just been to a spa. Surely they didn't deserve to be incinerated.

Cyrus frowned. "'Responsible for the deaths of innocent people.' Listen to yourself."

"I'm not saying I'm against it," I said. "I'm just saying we should wait."

He grew flustered. "For what?"

"We can't rule out the possibility that this is a good old-fashioned hijacking, Cyrus. We really cannot underestimate the retro-movements of the terrorist world."

Cyrus glowered. "And you can live—so to speak—with the blood of innocent people on your hands."

I paused. I could have said, *I'm too scared, at the moment, to parse moralities with you, Cyrus,* but instead I said, "I have learned, in my brief time as a social worker, that it is wisest not to indulge haste in a time of crisis."

This response mollified him.

"You're the social worker," he conceded. "I will adhere, for the time being, to your good judgment."

I craned into the aisle again to secure a glimpse of Edith. There was a commotion beyond the curtain—bodies moving, the pop of overhead compartments being sprung open—but it was impossible to make any sense of it, so I leaned back in my seat and pushed the recline button as I waited for the real extent of the danger to make itself clear.

This arguably timid response was predicated on a childhood of theoretical decision-making, foisted on me by my own father. Never one for the usual bedtime stories, he preferred to lull Edith and me to sleep with anecdotes involving people at an ethical crossroads. For example: Two people are trapped in a jeep hanging over a cliff, and the jeep will soon topple over, killing them both, unless one of them agrees to jump to his death. Or: Two people are stranded on a sinking ship, and there is but a single life preserver that can keep but a single body afloat. Or: Two people are starving to death in a cave that is being guarded by a bear, and one of them must volunteer to be eaten, so that the other can escape to safety. Of course, he would always distinguish between the two potential survivors in the jeep, on the ship, in the cave, so that it was not a mere question of drawing straws. One of the people was always a doctor on the verge of discovering a cure for cancer, or the mother of three children, or more pleasing to the eye, while the other was a lonely, unaccomplished body that required nourishment and took up space. The true test was this: Was the person in possession of the less valuable life willing to sacrifice it so that others could benefit from the survival of the worthy party? Because if that person was willing, where there had previously been inequality there now was parity. The sacrificed life was of equal value to the life saved.

To him, these riddles were beautiful spirals, double helixes of human behavior that could be tested and proven. Ultimately, my father's behavior raised the unambiguous possibility that "worth" was a shifting quality. Despite his ethical (and scientific) sense that worth was a black-and-white issue, where his personal life was involved, worth was both relative and changeable. His first marriage turned out not to be "worth" much to him in any ultimate way, nor were his first two children. He had chosen to align himself with a new family, thus conveying that he found neither Edith nor me terribly worthy, no matter how we behaved in a jeep, in a cave, on a sinking ship.

I couldn't help being reminded of these ethical dilemmas as Tom walked down the aisle, pointing his gun into people's faces. I felt the plane tightening with our collective terror like an artery fossilizing from overstrain. The only sound was that of breathing, fast and deep, staving off panic.

Tom patrolled the aisle, making his way toward me, his head scissoring back and forth, looking for a quiet insurgence in somebody's lap. As he walked past me, he paused.

I kept my head down. It was calming to have him next to me. I knew where danger was. I held my breath as I saw his arms rise. Tom brought the butt-end of the gun handle down on my head and continued down the aisle.

Nausea. Nausea behind my ribs and forging its dizzy way upward. I coughed repeatedly and opened a second airsickness bag. A hand snaked back from between the seats in front of me. The fingers wiggled, playful.

"Come on now," Cyrus whispered. "We must keep our wits about us, Alice. We must remember that we are the ones with the final say, not them."

I smiled at him inside my airsickness bag. It was admirable of him to be so optimistic, but my hand was clammy and I felt more self-conscious than empowered as I took hold of the proffered fingers. I counted the minutes before I could retract my hand from his without seeming rude.

Aboul, the pilot, came over the loudspeaker. He assured us that he was still the captain of the plane, despite the change of command in the cabin, and that there was no need for anyone to do anything foolish. He apologized for unlocking the cockpit door—but could we blame him? How was he to know that a steward was a hijacker? What had happened to trust in this world? Why wasn't anyone who he was supposed to be anymore? He admitted that he was quite ready for retirement, because he no longer understood how things worked. Trust, he said again, what had become of it?

From time to time a passenger would hyperventilate—a pair of elderly Moroccan women clasped at their chests, turned a terrible sweaty gray color, rubbed each other's temples—but for the most part we were obediently silent, many of us staring out the windows to watch for a sign that we had been lied to, and that our plane was intended as a bomb. The plane felt reassuringly aimless as it banked to the south so that the sun streamed in the windows, then north, then south again.

Ten minutes after the pilot's announcement, Bruno appeared at the front of the coach cabin. I heard Cyrus whisper, "Good Lord, Alice, did I warn you about that man, I did, I warned you about him."

Bruno stood in front of the movie screen, which showed a crude graphic of Africa, our intended flight path represented by a blinking line, merrily unaware of the altered plans. If Bruno *was* a terrorist, he was underdressed for the role. He still wore his pastel polo shirt, khaki trousers, gum-soled shoes with the obvious stitching that sought to correct some deep orthopedic wrong. His hands were the lone indication of his potential for ruthlessness; though unmuscled, the backs were lined with prominent veins, tense and forceful irrigation tubes that continued up his wrists and forearms, disappearing under his shirtsleeves and forging onward, invisibly, to his heart.

He wasn't holding a gun. His head swiveled from side to side, as though he were taking careful note of us from behind his opaque glasses. The fact of his blindness seemed to relax most of the passengers. The blind, we presume, are not prone to the violence or covetousness that seeing engenders; they cannot defend themselves, and thus they do nothing that might precipitate an attack. They are peaceful by design. And so despite the fact that there were seeing men with guns, the ruling presence of this blind man reassured us.

Midway through this sightless surveillance, Winnie Sunderland began sobbing dramatically. She chugged along, her heavy arms and breasts jiggling inside her cotton tunic. The diamond glued between her eyebrows commenced a southwest slide.

People looked into their laps. No one moved to help her.

"*My u-u-u-uterus,*" she blubbered wetly. "*Pressing on my b-bladder.*"

Tom pushed his gun into her stomach and told her to "shut the fuck up." Winnie balled up a fist and delivered a useless, downward girl punch, hitting Tom's forearm.

I heard a noise from first class as Edith appeared from behind the curtain. "Don't fucking touch me," she said, Stephen's hand pushing at the small of her back. Her hands were bound, and a button was missing from her blouse. Her eyes were puffy and pinched, her skin mottled, her mouth swollen and vaguely blue. She was unable, because of her bound hands, to push the hair out of her eyes. She swung her torso and neck around, trying to dislodge her mane from one shoulder to the other.

Edith refused to look at me. She cast her placid eyes over Tom's gun, still thrust at Winnie's stomach.

Winnie continued to weep in a grandiose fashion, making us all feel helpless and cowardly and—it must be admitted—vaguely resentful.

Cyrus Bing folded his paper, muttering, "This is too much, this really is." He stood up and, to everyone's surprise and embarrassment, struck out toward Winnie, cutting through a row of seats to the opposite aisle. Bruno tracked his approach, listening to Cyrus's leather loafers on the carpet.

"There, there," Cyrus said, offering Winnie a handkerchief. She blew her nose, producing an impressive racket that, however poorly, seemed designed in its rebuking affront to induce sympathy and shame in all who heard it. Cyrus, even as her designated soother, could not prevent a flicker of disgust from tightening his features.

"You should be ashamed of yourself," he addressed Tom. "Endangering the lives of the living is one thing, but endangering the lives of the unborn is unconscionable."

Tom raised his gun and pointed it at Cyrus's temple, but Bruno, ears alert and interpreting the sounds, advised Tom to back off.

"So you are a Catholic," Bruno stated.

"I am English," said Cyrus.

"You are a Catholic sympathizer."

"I sympathize with this poor woman. Beyond that, I would say that my sympathies are unknown to you."

Bruno nodded. "That is a problem, is it not?"

"For you, perhaps. I, personally, am untroubled by it."

"And how about my sympathies?" Bruno inquired. "Are you not curious about my sympathies?"

"Not particularly," Cyrus replied. "Any sympathies you profess to harbor are no doubt small concerns to you, and are showcased under the rubric of 'cause' so that you can justify your misguided actions on this plane."

Bruno ran his hands up and down his polo shirt.

"In other words, you find the criminal mind lacks sincerity."

We struck a patch of turbulence and the cabin lights flickered. A darkened Bruno was silhouetted against the crude-hewn African continent.

The lights returned.

Cyrus struggled to help the awkward, overstuffed Winnie out of her seat and to the restroom.

"My bladder," she explained to him, reversing her malady, "is pressing on my uterus."

Cyrus experienced considerable difficulty with the folding door and Winnie's stomach, but soon she was wedged inside. Minutes later she emerged, face flushed, gaze hostile. The diamond had continued its migration across her forehead, affixing itself to the outer fringe of her left eyebrow.

Once Cyrus had returned Winnie to her seat, Tom dragged him before the screen. He whispered in Bruno's ear. Bruno turned to Cyrus.

"You pride yourself on being a good citizen, Mr. . . ."

"Cyrus Bing."

"Mr. Bing. There may even be further chances for you to test your fervor for good citizenship, given your renewed set of circumstances."

"You have the gall to test me?" Cyrus's complexion had deepened far past its usual chafe, his breathing was harried. I recalled what he had told me about "the old overwrought ticker," and wondered whether there was any truth to it.

"I prefer not to think of it as a test," Bruno corrected, "but as a game."

"I will not indulge you in any moronic game-playing," Cyrus retorted. "And you cannot threaten me with my life—it has already been long and decent. The girls are grown. The wife will be well taken care of. There's a retirement home in Wales all paid for."

"But what of the lives of the unborn?" Bruno asked. "Surely to endanger them would be unconscionable."

Winnie—I could see directly across the aisle—appeared oblivious to this conversation. She was busy digging into the upholstery creases of the seat beside her. She retrieved a pill with an index finger, and jammed the pill furtively into her mouth.

Cyrus worried his bottom lip with his left canine.

"It's simple, really, what I want you to do," Bruno said.

"It's of little consequence to me what you want," Cyrus answered. But his body said otherwise. His shoulders pointed toward his ankles, and his head drooped atop his pipe-cleaner neck.

Bruno drew some hasty signage in the air. Tom walked to Winnie's row and took her by the arm, then dragged her into the aisle. She fell, emitting sloppy foaming noises—eventually identifiable as laughter— as Tom pulled her up before the screen and pressed the gun into her ear.

Winnie sniggered, even as her expression remained antagonistic. The diamond now slipped down her cheek like a shiny fake tear.

Cyrus combed his fingers through his feeble hair, leaning against the movie screen. He looked truly unwell, his face white under the pink and his narrow chest heaving, trying too hard to accomplish the simplest respiratory action. He wiped his mouth repeatedly with his cuff.

"Mr. Bing," Bruno said. "Are you familiar with the Ottawa Summit?" Cyrus shook his head.

"Nor should you be. The Ottawa Summit is a yearly *trade show,* to put it in business-class parlance, for terrorist negotiators. A trade show held, because TNs consider themselves a clever bunch, on the out-skirts of Spokane."

"Fascinating," Cyrus remarked weakly.

"It is, in fact. It's fascinating to watch men—it is still mostly men, I'm afraid—create rules for anarchy. It's fascinating to watch futility at work."

Cyrus swaggered into one fleshless hip. He wasn't defeated yet, the dear fellow. He still had a bit of the old kick in him. "I suppose I'm de-veloping a taste for it firsthand," he said.

"But there is something pleasant about rules, even if they fail to re-sult in order," Bruno continued. "Rules are also about maintaining integrity in a losing situation. They are about instilling a project with a sense of moral highness, not control. Thus"—he smiled—"thus we have imported a few of the Ottawa Summit proposals for our own purposes."

He nodded at Tom, who I half expected would roll out a chalk-board from behind the first-class curtain and give us a lesson. Instead, Tom maneuvered Edith by the arm-crook until she was side by side with the sweating, giggling Winnie. He positioned Cyrus in front of the two women. Edith remained expressionless, her bound hands fiddling by her pelvis. The blouse, missing its one button, revealed flashes of her brassiere.

"This is theatrical and perverse," Cyrus protested.

Bruno shrugged. "Checks and balances, sir. Even terrorists must avoid the temptations of tyranny and give the choice *back to the people*. Of course, too many choices tend to fuddle up the mind. Before our dry runs with a test audience, we might have given you the gun and made you cast your vote with a bullet. But seventy-five percent of the people in your situation indicated that they would take the bullet themselves rather than kill an innocent person, which was *not* one of their choices. These, Mr. Bing, are your choices."

Tom pointed to Winnie again with his gun. Her mouth hollowed into a perfect circle, so round and wide it reminded you that the mouth was in fact *an orifice*, it is an entry point, it is *the way in*. I thought, *She swallowed a baby*. Winnie giggled hysterically and the plane shook—from turbulence, true enough, although it seemed that she had become the receptacle for our pent-up terror; she had opened her mouth and allowed all our terror inside, where it mutated into grotesque laughter.

Tom gestured to Edith, who, despite her unhealthy pallor, did not flinch. And yet the numbers were stacked against her. It was one and three-quarters to one, if you counted Winnie's baby. Cyrus's choice, if Bruno forced him to make one, was a no-brainer.

"I simply, simply refuse," Cyrus said.

Bruno clucked. "It's both of them or one. You've seen the movies. There's no way to extort the extortionist, I'm afraid."

Cyrus picked at his shirt placket with extreme agitation. He was not convinced, as none of us was, that this was happening. He would choose *Edith* or *Winnie,* and Tom would lower his weapon to the unlucky temple and pull the trigger, and a "POW!!!" flag would eject and flutter at the end of his trick pistol. Stephen would come around with champagne and we would all toast and laugh and say, *I knew it was all a big send-up, really, I mean the* Ottawa Summit? *What a bamboozle, really—wait'll the old wife hears this one!*

"I'll count to ten," Bruno said.

Cyrus inhaled loudly; his breathing was clogged with something cumbersome and wet.

Edith remained erect and confident, although I detected a spasm in her left eye.

The rest of coach class was motionless.

Bruno swayed on his orthopedic shoes. He was sweating under his glasses, the drops riveting down his cheeks.

One.

Cyrus glanced at me, but I was no help. My vision was obscured by my father's pensive face, his eyes pinched and yellow from years of seeking out the tiny camouflaged bodies of mites on the forking roots of rice plants. He was saying, *The sacrificed life was of equal value to the life saved.*

Two.

Three.

Cyrus raised his arm, elbow bent, palm down. His limb was being levitated by another's telekinetic brain, or so it appeared. He disowned that limb as it wobbled with a divining rod's indecision, Winnie–Edith–Winnie–Edith, as Bruno counted, *Four. Five. Six. Seven.*

All the passengers, except me, cowered in their seats, unable to watch. The mother of the little boy in lederhosen had covered his head with a felt blanket and was singing to him.

Eight.

The disembodied arm had stalled between Edith and Winnie, favoring Edith. Had a stop-time photograph been taken of the moment, my sister would have lost by a minimal distance, equal to the height of two or three stacked plastic knifeblades.

This was the instant that I jumped from my seat to take my sister's place on this unnerving airborne game show, forgetting that I had yet to unbuckle my seat belt. The belt was loose, and I was able to lift more than a few inches into the air before the strap cut into my pelvis, knocking the lower wind out of me. I ricocheted onto the concave foam cushion with an unattractive *ufff.*

I yanked at my belt buckle. *Idiot! Idiot!* The buckle was stuck. At last I freed myself, just in time to watch Cyrus, that subversive devil, that extorter of the extortionist, grab at his heart and emit a strangled groan. He stared at Edith as his body slid out of sight behind the seats. This was not, I thought, to indicate that Edith had been his sacrificial choice, one he wished to make known to all his fellow passengers in his final moments so that they would not think him indecisive; it was so that Edith would be his final vision, so that Edith would be the reason for his death, so that she would live and thrive on the condition that he perish. It was Edith he saved. It was Edith who stared at him as his eyes wilted and his soul departed through some spiritual portal, culvert, or vent.

I stood, dumbfounded, two hands atop Cyrus's former seat back. My sister's eyes met mine for the first time since she'd escorted Bruno to the lavatory. Winnie hung on her arm in hysterics. Her high-pitched, glassy laughter cut into my brain, and made me see iridescent lights, dissection colors. The phrase—irreverent, true, monstrous even, but I cannot excuse the way the brain seeks to calm itself in inappropriate ways after a near-trauma—entered my head and would not leave it for hours afterward. I repeated it even when I thought my mind was resting, over and over I said it and it calmed me, it did, because it might have been the first sentence to a very fine memoir or the epitaph on a tombstone:

We were spared by the old overwrought ticker.

Cyrus's
Shame

I met my wife when I was a spry and only marginally bald young fellow, just sprung from a fifth-rate university and inexperienced with women. My mother, who suffered from a watery lung, was desperate for me to marry a girl, any girl, even a girl who resembled, on her softer days, a sleepy old man. The sleepy old man in question was the daughter of her friend from the gardening club; my mother arranged a meeting between us one autumn weekend, when the gardens would be at their peak of romantic shabbiness.

That Friday of the autumn weekend I was in a bad head. My superior at the insurance house where I was employed had berated me—in front of the house's only attractive secretary, a Belgian girl whom I'd been supplying with Japanese cucumbers and avocados I'd pick up at the market on my lunch hour—for my sloppy figures, my insolent phone manner, my yolk-stained cuffs. I was also dreading the meeting with the daughter of the friend from the gardening club, for I knew her mother, and found her horsey yet grotesquely female, as if she were constantly trying, through some distorted masquerade of femininity that included noxious toilet waters and protracted giggles, to persuade others to overlook the equestrian tendencies of her face. I called her the Equifemme, which made my mother, that churlish lady, chortle with the unchecked glee of the dying. It sounded of rocks and consommé, that chortle, so revolting that it made me wish I could restrain myself from being funny for my mean old dying mum.

I mention my bratty humor in order to explain why I was not acting as a recent graduate from a fifth-rate university should act. In North Station, I cut off a young woman with a baby in a pram, shaving the baby across the pink knees with the corner of my briefcase, causing said baby to hurl her spit-shiny rattle and commence a yowling that bounced off the Ionic columns and the marble busts of Generals Mackelthwaite, Fibbetts-Roy, and Thom. I glared at the woman, I glared at her baby, and I continued, without apologizing, toward the ticket counter. The queue was endless. While trying to discern the time beneath my fissured and befogged watch crystal—a graduation present from my mother which I had, in a beery graduation stupor, cracked beneath my dress oxfords—I noticed a woman in front of me with one untied shoe. I stared at the shoe for some time—an attractive shoe, despite the fact that its dour antecedents lay in the sort of footwear favored by nurses, with soundless bread soles and off-center eyelets—and found myself experiencing an intense dislike for the woman. I hated the way her plaid skirt made her hips look wide and padded, I hated the way her ankles were thick and suggested an unchecked appetite for puddings, I hated the way she'd allowed her shoe to remain untied. She was chatting up an old woman in front of her, and I hated the way she complimented the woman's fuzzy hat, which no sentient being could have admired. Though I knew that I should alert her to the untied shoe, part of me believed that she deserved to trip for being so insincere with her compliments to old women in ticket queues. I made a bet with myself: If she trips on her shoelace, I will not have to marry the sleepy old man. If she falls on her face, the Belgian girl and I will feed each other persimmons in the stockroom, and she will let me lift her blouse and touch her belly with the stainless-steel ruler she holds against her cheek to keep her cool on hot days.

The woman with the untied shoe bought a ticket to Manchester and waddled off, shoelace slapping, toward the café adjacent to the quays. After purchasing my own ticket, I followed her to the café, ordered a whiskey, ate nuts and watched as she drank a coffee. She befouled the white mug with her lipstick, each time taking a drink from a different place, until the rim was bordered with a stripe of cheap carnation red. She struck up a conversation with another lonely-looking woman. I overheard her asking prurient questions about the woman's dead husband and the woman's dead son. The lonely-looking woman started to cry, and the woman with the untied shoe dug a stained hankie from her purse and patted the lonely-looking woman on the back of the hand with it.

I finished my whiskey and checked my watch. Our train was scheduled to depart in ten minutes. The woman with the untied shoe, however, was involved in comforting the crying woman and seemed unaware of the time. She set her overstuffed leatherette purse on the floor, where any thief could have snatched it. It tumbled over, and her train ticket and a set of keys spilled out on the tiles. A lipstick rolled out and was trod upon by a businessman, who tripped, making a desperate grab at the nearest thing, the delicate sleeve of a young lady's dress. The sleeve tore at the shoulder, the young lady screamed, and a police officer tried to arrest the businessman. The businessman gave the police officer some money and offered to buy the young lady a drink. He escorted her to the table next to the woman with the untied shoe and ordered champagne. I saw their wedding announcement in the society pages not six months later, but it might have been two other strangers, because strangers in love do tend to share the same gummy faces.

A giant clock hanging by the thinnest wire ticked off the minutes audibly. I contemplated alerting the woman to the impending departure of our train, but concluded she should learn to be more careful with herself and that other people's tragedies are not the automatic province of any nosy, cipherous creature. I was disappointed that she had yet to trip on her shoelace, fall on her face, and guarantee me a carefree bachelor's erotic office life, but I had already decided such bets were foolish superstition, indicative of nothing certain. I heard her urging the lonely-looking woman to inscribe her phone number on a café napkin and promising to invite her to tea.

Once in my seat I tried to nap, tried to interest myself in the ingredients of my nougat bar, but instead felt myself growing mindlessly irritated with the woman the longer she failed to show up. What a muttonhead, I thought to myself, so prying, so irresponsible, so "caring," and yet incapable of being assiduous with herself. No wonder she wasn't married (I'd noticed her bare left hand). No man could put up with this sort of recklessness. Imagine what a terrible mother she'd be, foisting her baby at the first shifty stranger to hold while she dashed in to have her bangs trimmed; what a terrible cook, singeing teakettles and scorching chops; what an enthusiastic, unchecked lover, giving the neighbors adequate reason to chuckle in private and examine the tilework when she crossed paths with them in the mail hall.

When the train's pistons began their slow pumping, I left my compartment to stand at the end of the car. I saw nothing at the far end of the quay but smoke. As the train began to move I spotted a figure, running frantically in the white gloom. It was the woman, her bosom and shoelace flying. Her leatherette purse, clutched in her left hand, was unlatched, and her handkerchief blew out, along with a number of coins. She saw me and yelled, *Hold the train! Hold the train!* I descended to the bottom step and bent low. She tossed me her purse, which I juggled and nearly dropped before managing to sling its frayed strap around my shoulder. I reached out to grab her hand. Our fingers touched, just the tips.

Come on, I said.

She pedaled her legs faster, her skirt riding midway up her thighs. Our fingers touched again, parted, and touched again, until I was able to grab her around the wrist.

It was at that second, unfortunately, that she tripped on her shoelace. Her hand wrenched from mine. My body flung outward, my face crashing against a compartment window, followed by the grommet clatter of the woman's whipping purse. With one squashed, aquariumed eye I saw the shocked *Oooh* of a woman knitting a blue scarf. I swung back onto the stairs and, in doing so, dislocated my shoulder. I banged it against the side of the train to relocate it, and because of the departing whistle, no one heard my howling.

The woman, meanwhile, had disappeared under the train. I presumed she was dead, crushed beneath the cog wheels, until the train cleared the quay and I saw her, sprawled on the concrete, her face bleeding and her leg crooked at a very wrong angle. She stared at me and I at her until we rounded a curve and she was blocked by the toggling serpentine passage of the cars.

I went to the lavatory to wash my hands and make a sling with my tie, and returned to my compartment with her purse. I opened her wallet and learned her name. I pulled out four lipsticks, an old airplane biscuit, a mother-of-pearl-handled pocketknife, a small glass flask filled with crystallized honey, a pot of lotion with the label "Lying Bros. Face Cream." I found a toffee tin filled with six aspirin, which I swallowed without water. I used her money to buy nuts and a gin drink in the dining car. I arrived in Manchester that evening and enjoyed a serviceable date in a shabby garden with the horsey woman's daughter, who was color-blind and wore unmatched wool socks, one red, one green, with her leather sandals. She was touched by my makeshift sling and my bruised cheek, which I told her I'd acquired while preventing an old woman's knitting basket from tumbling off the train. I smothered my face in Lying Cream, which made it easier to ask the horsey woman's daughter to be my wife. The wedding announcement I submitted to the society pages, "Graduate of Fifth-Rate University Marries Sleepy Old Man," never appeared. It wasn't until my old man and I were on honeymoon in Majorca that I recalled my bet with myself, which I had presumably won, to no visible effect. I laughed to myself with affectionate bitterness, which made my wife, Lydia, a fidgety, insecure girl, remark worriedly, *Are you really so tired of the beach, Cyrus?*

A few months after my wedding, I was scrounging in my closet for a pair of golf trousers and found the leatherette purse, stashed behind a framed map of Africa (a place I used to think I'd live). I had forgotten about it as soon as my shoulder stopped aching. I popped open the glass flask and tasted the old honey. I spread the Lying Cream on my dry hands. I pulled out the woman's driver's license and made note of her name and address again. There was no phone directory listing under her name, but in the purse was a napkin from the train station café with a number on it. I called it and the lonely-looking woman answered. I introduced myself as a friend of the woman with the untied shoe, and did she have her phone number handy, for I had misplaced it. The lonely woman complied and then inquired, confused, But how did you get my number?

I paused.

I was a distant business acquaintance of your former husband's, I said. Lovely chap, a real go-getter, it's a shame he's dead, and so forth. The woman said, But, and I cut in, Thanks really, appreciate your help, and hung up before she started crying.

I called the woman with the untied shoe, but there was no answer, not for weeks. I called her basement flat four, five, ten times a day. I walked past her house, I peered into her low windows, which were covered with pretty iron bars on the outside, water-stained flowered curtains on the inside. When I one day rang her bell and found her at home, I told her I'd found her purse in an alley, just the past week. I had grown a mustache, walked with a slight stoop, and was in many other ways unrecognizable after my marriage.

She was accepting of the fact that I was a strange man doing a good deed. She invited me in. We sat at her kitchen table, covered with a sticky, unwashed oilcloth, and she told me about her accident in the train station. She started to cry when she got to the part involving myself. She couldn't understand how a man could steal her purse after she'd been hurt. She couldn't understand how a person could behave so hatefully toward a woman he didn't even know. I realized the only way to make her quiet was to take her clothes off. I made love to her with a strange sort of precision, a quilted sofa cushion protecting her hip. I told her that I loved her, as a way to apologize for what I'd done. I said, I love you, and she didn't understand what I was saying to her, she didn't say, You're forgiven, or even, Thank you. Instead, she fell asleep. I dressed in the dark, forgetting my cracked watch on her bedside table. Her house smelled of vitamins and curry, and I couldn't leave swiftly enough.

For the next few weeks, I walked around with a foggy head. I was let go from the insurance house, and the Belgian girl did not say good-bye to me. Lydia returned to Manchester in search of an annulment. Eventually I was hired as a sales associate for a plastics manufacturer with offices outside Tunis. I removed the framed map of Africa from my closet and hung it on a pink wall that Lydia had painted, in her opinion, ecru. I would walk past the house of the woman with the un-tied shoe from time to time, but never dared to ring her bell. I always caught a strong, acrid whiff of vitamin-curry on the sidewalk, my stomach would roil, and I would run to the nearest pub for a soda and bitters. I had given the woman a false name—Ralph Sneed—and a stranger's phone number. I dialed the number once and said, This is Ralph Sneed, by any chance has a lady phoned me at this exchange? but the person who answered thought I was a salesman and hung up.

Early that spring, my mother died. I was traveling to her funeral, on a mostly empty train, when a woman entered my compartment. She unwrapped a white cheese sandwich, but when she tried to eat it she began to weep. She attempted to hide this from me, staring out the window and pretending to find entrancing the charred villages.

It seemed somehow appropriate, because the train was so empty, to put a hand on her knee. She covered my hand with hers and kept it there as we ticked past some of the ugliest places in the world. I asked her what was wrong, and she told me that she was running away from her husband because she was in love with a man who had died.

In love with a man who died, I said.

Indeed, she said. In all the time she was married she couldn't work up the courage to leave her husband for the man she had thought about every waking minute for five whole years. They had met at a business convention and had slept together once. When he died in a plane crash the month before, she confessed everything to her husband, who loved her even more for the sacrifice she'd made in staying with him all those years. But once she'd confessed, she couldn't think of any reason not to leave her husband. And now she had no one, and nowhere to go, even though her husband loved her more than ever.

Her story made sense to me, and so I didn't ask, as the woman with the untied shoe might have asked, Why hadn't she left earlier? Why hadn't she left her husband to be with the man she loved? Instead, I told her that my mother had died, and that I was queasily infatuated with a woman who was once late for the Manchester train, whose purse I'd stolen, whom I'd made love to once and lied to repeatedly.

The woman's eyes lit up. Oh, but you must marry this woman, she said. She knew the forever binds of misrepresentation.

I pulled my hand off her knee; my shoulder was starting to ache. My head cleared and became verdant, tropical, even as my vision was cluttered with familiar moldy townscapes and train-chasing ruffians in red knit hats, cycling their sickly legs after us. I could move to Africa, I thought, I could marry the woman who was late for the Manchester train, because I was nobody's son now, I was nobody's husband.

You're right, I said. You're utterly right.

We rode together all the way to Manchester. I invited the woman who had nowhere to go to my mother's funeral. She stayed in my mother's bedroom, she wore my mother's chenille robe, she smoked her leftover carton of cigarettes. We made love together, on the cramped guest-room cot, because she seemed so lonely and yet so unconcerned with being alone. When we returned to the city, she stayed at my flat for a few days, a week, four months, a year. It was the unspoken quality of our communication that made her such an unparalleled flatmate. I knew, without her needing to tell me, that she wanted there to be things I hid from her. Thus I never told her that I loved her, I merely said, I'm sorry, I'm so so sorry. After we were married, I never again spoke of the woman who was late for the Manchester train, so as to restore our marriage to its proper height with secrets and duplicity.

Three

When Moroccan Air Flight 919 finally landed—after flying for hours on a modified course, hugging the contours of a coastline with smooth, modest cliffs and meager strips of dark beach, before cutting inland over clusters of derelict shacks and torn-up earth, flying so close that our shadow could be spied slippering across the brown, the brown, the more brown—I hadn't the faintest idea that we were the designated prey of a Brain Worm.

The rivalry between the Brain Worms and the Incursionists, although it had certainly dimmed, still fractured the Institute in a ghostly way when I matriculated. As we learned in the seminar "Anti-Terrorist Theory: 1950–2001," the rivalry was all the more potent and malicious because it involved two Institute men—Guiomar Atxaga and Seymour Packs—and a potent, "kill the father" variety of betrayal. Guiomar Atxaga was the father figure, and his Incursionists dominated the Institute through the late fifties; his aggressive Ottawa School method advocated immediate force, and held that the number of quick civilian casualties usually equaled the number of casualties after weeks of exhausting, dead-end negotiations. Atxaga was an able icon for his cause, black as a beetle, an obsessive single-sculler, who, legend had it, would, in the dead of night, scoot along a shallow tributary that wound through the Institute's property, his motion no more discernible to the eye than wind.

Atxaga was in his early sixties and searching for a suitable protégé when he first encountered Seymour Packs, a shy and scarcely educated man from Santa Barbara who hosted a radio confession show called *Forgive Me, F***head*. Although drab and largely forgettable in person, Packs could evoke an enigmatic and soothing persona from the shallows of his gaunt, drawstring-panted frame when faced with a microphone and an hour's worth of empty airwaves. Atxaga stumbled across the radio show while on vacation in California, and mesmerized by Packs's perfected "white-voice" interrogation method, he pulled his rental car into the nearest taco stand parking lot and called from the pay phone to confess (to what, it is unclear: the tape has disappeared). Atxaga then drove to the radio station, broke into the studio, pulled a gun on the sleepy-faced host, and flew him to Lucerne. Atxaga and Packs worked together with peaceable efficiency for ten years, strengthening the Incursionist curriculum and limiting their competition, the Parasites, to a few under-enrolled talk-therapy courses.

Everything remained harmonious until Atxaga began to explore ever more macabre forms of negotiation. His favorite involved removing the lower cranial plate of a terrorist's mother (or, if the mother was deceased, then wife, daughter, sister, in that order), snipping out her medulla oblongata, and delivering this portion of the brain to the terrorist, usually in a long flip-top metal safety-deposit box. Packs stood firmly against this negotiation tactic; the two had a very visible argument in the Institute cafeteria, after which Packs fainted and had to be administered intravenous fluids. Packs started to whisper about

Atxaga's forced retirement, while Atxaga changed the key codes, thereby excluding Packs from the Incursionist labs. Packs officially severed himself from his former mentor by announcing the resurrection of the weakened Parasite faction as the newly Packified Brain Worms. The two men never exchanged another word, and Atxaga perished from brain cancer a decade or so later, a viciously bitter and violent man.

Atxaga was long dead by the time I arrived at the Institute, but I met Seymour Packs once, when he was in his late eighties. Dressed in his usual white robes and pantaloons, Packs visited the Role Play Complex during my second tour there, to read from a paper entitled "Inertia as Motion, Motion as Regret, Regret as Rumination, Rumination as Death." He shook my hand at the luncheon that followed and pressed a small, sharp tack into my palm while feigning a mild swoon. He had heard about my brutal tactical decisions during my Beirut role-play, and intuited that I would never become a member of his camp.

Nonetheless, I had never heard of the Brain Worms or the Incursionists, or of Seymour Packs or Guiomar Atxaga, when our plane struck the sand—a soft bump—and lurched to the left before initiating a slow sideways skid toward a collection of parked vehicles. Men in uniform hopped out of their vans and scurried out of the way, guns jumping on their backs. At the last millisecond, the plane recorrected, the tip of the right wing lightly brushing the side of a media van. Sparks jumped and died on the sand as we came to a sludging, eighty-degree halt.

There was weeping, of course. There was praying, as well as a general sense of relief that we had made the right choice in trusting the man with the gun, that we had behaved not cowardly but with commendable foresight and prudence.

I pressed my face against the window, hoping that my framed countenance would be captured by one of the cameras so that our parents could rejoice that one of us, at least, was alive.

A sharp object poked between my shoulder blades. A muscle spasm, I thought. My back was killing me.

"Get up."

I turned, driving the point of a gun deeper beneath my left blade. It was Tom.

"Let's go, princess." Jab jab.

I stood.

"Walk." He punctuated the word with another sharp dig between my shoulder blades.

Tom pushed me into the now squalorous first-class cabin. Soda cans and foil wrappers littered the aisles and the empty seats. Stephen struggled with an unwieldy map. Edith dozed on the floor, propped against an emergency exit, her wrists and ankles bound with rubber tubing. The four coach stewardesses, now joined by their first-class colleagues, were seated with wrists and ankles similarly bound, their mouths covered with duct tape. (Post Big Terrible, all flight attendants had been trained to give coded oral instructions to one another.) The body of Cyrus Bing was belted into one galley jumpseat, a pilot's blazer over his head, a toppled soda can leaking brown onto his trousers. Bruno was nowhere to be seen.

"I've got the sister," Tom announced.

Edith stirred. She squinted her puffy eyes at me. I thought she'd be relieved to see me, but instead she seemed surprised, almost mad.

Stephen didn't look up from the map—of the air or the desert, of a space where the only markers were currents, downdrafts, invisible tangents and through-lines created by gravity and mathematics— spread over his jittering knees. It made a low rattling sound.

Tom shoved me toward the closed door of the cockpit.

"Knock," he said.

I knocked.

Some muffled yelling ensued, to which Tom answered, "Got her." The door opened, and Tom pushed me inside. The primitive locking system (a metal bar; some brackets) lay bent and useless on the floor.

My palms were sweaty. I imagined I might vomit. The more I

imagined vomiting, the more it seemed possible, until I imagined I was fine, and that seemed possible, too.

Bruno sat in a cramped, cross-legged position, smoking a cigarette and tapping the ashes into a plastic cocktail glass. He was too lanky and composed, too easy in the world, too liberated from the straight-spined posture of overpreparedness that most blind people adopt. Edith had been on to something when she'd observed, *As a blind man, you should learn to expect the unexpected.* Bruno's posture seemed to state that *he* was the unexpected, that we were the ones who ought to watch out for him, not vice versa.

The pilot and co-pilot seats were occupied by two men with hair-less pates and very evident skulls beneath their brown hides. Verne had wedged himself between them, his tail curling up into the wires and fuses that sagged beneath the instrument panel. He stared at me anx-iously through his blond eyelashes, perhaps thinking, as I was, *So this is what it comes to, our vast flying machine with its news loops and beverage carts: this pair of old men.*

"Hello again, Alice." Bruno exhaled a long, steady vector of smoke in my precise direction.

"Hello again," I said.

"Aboul," Bruno said. "Meet Alice."

The pilot appeared belligerently confused.

"This is Mjidd," Bruno indicated in the general direction of the co-pilot, a middle-aged man tilting fast toward aged, with a beaker-wide face and tar-colored divots beneath his eyes.

"Alice is here," Bruno continued, "because it has been said of her that she speaks Sasak."

Sasak, I thought. How odd. How . . . odd. Sasak was the Lombok language I had learned quite effortlessly in Mylandrum, because I was talented in that way in which timid girls with uninhibited sisters strive to be talented.

"We've run into a bit of a negotiation obstacle," Bruno said. "The negotiator they've assigned now pretends to speak only Sasak. This is his way of discovering what sort of *passenger depth* we have."

My role was explained: The Sasak-speaking negotiator needed to be informed that Bruno would execute one hostage just before night-fall unless he received fuel and food and water. I was not to mention, under any circumstances, Cyrus Bing's heart attack. I was to insist that no further negotiations would be possible until a man named Pitcairn was procured from the International Institute for Terrorist Studies in Lucerne.

"Pitcairn," I said.

"It's a family name," Bruno said. "And I can understand Sasak well enough to know if you're saying anything unnecessary. I advise that you keep to the essentials, unless you want me to disfigure your sister."

I wanted to say to him, *But how can you be so certain that is not my fondest wish?* It was not, of course, but you never can be certain with female siblings, especially those close in age.

Aboul handed me a pair of headphones and flipped the switch that broadcast the radio noise through the cockpit. The volume was loud; the static made everyone recoil except Aboul, whose reflexes were so calcified that he scarcely flinched.

"Turn it down!" Bruno hollered.

Aboul reduced the volume. He rolled his eyes over me.

"In the Koran," he said, "evil arrives in the form of beauty, re-demption in the form of ugliness." The right side of his mouth was full of gold teeth.

"Oh," I said.

I wiggled the headphones over my ears. The staticky emptiness stretched as far as the outer limits of the desert.

"What do I say?" I asked.

"How should I know? I don't speak Sussex," Aboul said. His eyes probed the softest parts of my neck and face. Mjidd scoffed, or maybe he swallowed some lint. He hacked into his long hand. Neither of the pilots appeared especially unnerved by the hijacker in their cockpit, a fact I found consoling on one level, disquieting on another.

Aboul donned a second pair of headphones and announced our airline, flight number, original departure city and destination, and the news that we were under the control of a terrorist group. He pointed a finger at me.

I said, "Hello." Nobody responded. The radio made the zithering sound of loose electrical wires in a hurricane.

I said, "Hello," again.

More zithers.

"*Snamo?*" a voice said. "*Gno mnabo nay?*"

"*Snamo,*" I responded.

"*Gno mnabo nay?*" the man repeated. His voice was toneless and hurried.

"I am Alice," I replied. My Sasak, never exemplary, was pretty rusty. "We have been hijacked."

There was a pause.

"Your Sasak is barely adequate. Not quite as fluent as your file claimed."

I paused, thinking, *My file?*

"My apologies," I said, disconcerted, "it's been a few years." (Literally I said, "Look away from this sorry girl, many years until Sasak talking.") "Barely adequate" was a more than polite assessment. My Sasak sucked.

I told the man that people would be killed if we did not receive food and water, fuel, a man named Pitcairn. I had to say the name a few times, because the man said, "What? What? Speak more adequately, Alice."

"Ah, *Pitcairn,*" he said at last. "And everyone on the plane is healthy?"

"Yes," I lied. It wasn't exactly a lie. Cyrus Bing wasn't unhealthy, per se.

"And yourself, Alice, you are well?"

"I am a wallet head of exuberance," I told him in Sasak.

The man seemed pleased, or at least his momentary silence indicated pleasure to me.

He started to say something, but the radio emitted a sudden and deafening twang.

"You are not in our heads after the hurting noise," I said.

The radio continued to emit excruciating whines.

"More voice," I urged, "you are still not in our heads."

The static, when it stopped, stopped instantly, replaced by the rustle of papers. The voice was the same. The voice said, in Sasak still, "I see your Thai is more adequate."

"Much," I said. I had learned small amounts of Thai in college. It was either that or Mandarin, to fulfill my tonal language requirement.

Switching to Thai, the man informed me that he would be happy to give us food, water, and fuel, as long as the majority of the passengers were released. In keeping with the rules of hostage negotiation, he claimed he would not try to befriend me or create any sort of emotional bond, because I was "the conduit." He told me that many a negotiator had lost valuable ground by becoming "too attached to the conduit," and thus he hoped I would not be put off by his apparent lack of personal investment.

I assured him I would not be.

"You seem a nice girl," the man said. "You're not scared, are you?"

"No," I said. "Yes."

"There's absolutely no reason to be scared. This man would no sooner hurt you than kill his own brother."

This, I thought, was an odd analogy.

Out of the corner of my eye, I saw Bruno stiffen. He'd caught on to the fact that we had switched languages.

"Who is that? Who is that man?"

"It's the same man," I said.

"He's not speaking Sasak."

"He's speaking Thai."

"It's the same man? You're sure of it?"

I nodded, before recalling the pointlessness of the nod. I said, "I'm sure."

"And you speak Thai?"

"I speak it poorly."

Bruno smiled in such a chilly way that it made the skin behind my shoulders constrict. "And how did he know this?"

I glanced at Aboul. He had unearthed a pack of cigarettes from his shirt pocket. He watched me watching him extract a cigarette, but did not offer me a smoke.

"Excuse me?"

Bruno's mouth was steely. "And how did he know this?"

In my ear I heard, "Tell him I've done my research."

"He says he's done his research."

Bruno's mouth trembled. He yelled at Aboul to fix the radio so that the Thai-and-Sasak-speaking man could not hear the cockpit noises. Aboul complied while Mjidd lit two cigarettes in his mouth at once.

Bruno ordered me to give him the headphones. He struggled to fit them over his gourd-shaped head, stretching them to their limit.

"Hello, Pitcairn," he said, his voice guttural.

The man responded in English.

"I will only speak to Alice," he said.

"So did you enjoy your flight?" Bruno asked. "Catch a good animal detective flick?"

No response.

"Pitcairn? I warned you this would happen. I warned you, didn't I? But you didn't listen to me."

Nothing.

"And what if we kill this Alice?" Bruno asked.

Silence.

"Pitcairn?"

More silence.

Then: A quick-fire of Sasak.

"Speak English, damn you!" Bruno yelled into the microphone.

More Sasak, mixed with Thai. Pitcairn was quite the fellow with languages.

Bruno turned to me, exasperated. "What's he saying?"

I couldn't speak. I sensed that this was my opportunity to negotiate, to wager my new crucial position against some demand I might have, but I couldn't think clearly or speedily enough.

"What's he saying!" Bruno lunged at me with his feet, and succeeded in nicking me in the ribs with one rubbery orthopedic heel. He might have kicked me harder. He might have snapped a rib if he'd cared to. I understood: I was a thing of value.

I swallowed. "He's saying . . ."

Bruno's mouth quavered.

"He's saying, Do you want to play or not?"

Bruno's face contorted. A laugh popped out of him, or some creepy combination of a laugh and a cough, a burp, a yelp of pain. He kicked the wall of the cockpit with his foot, and Stephen appeared. Bruno removed the headphones and handed them to me.

"Tell him we'd be delighted to play," he said.

I WAS NOT ALLOWED to go back to my original assigned seat.

"We'll need her again," Bruno said.

Stephen pushed me into a seat littered with wrappers and crumbs. Edith watched from the floor, eyes upturned, chewing her fingers. Her tubing squeaked and rubbed as she tried to get a better purchase on a thumbnail with her left canine.

"Give me your wrists," Stephen said. He ripped an air mask out of the ceiling and bound my hands with the tubing. "Now behave your-self," he said, punching me in the diaphragm.

My stomach spasmed. The stewardesses, hearing my desperate wheezing, attempted to see what had happened. Their mascara had run, their nostrils were snotty. I watched, swooning, as Edith struggled to a standing position. She used her bound hands as a crutch to pull herself up the curved side of the plane. She shuffle-hopped down the aisle, her skirt hiked around the tops of her thighs, her skin imprinted with the bumpy molar texture of the carpet.

Stephen regarded her noncommittally. He reminded me of Miles when he was stoned. He possessed Miles's stoner elliptical interest in women, an inkling of sex that is acknowledged and even momentarily pursued before the equivocal attention span refocuses on the previ-ously abandoned cheese taco or the well-thumbed office supply cata-logue. Stephen slid his map aside and stood, placing a hand on Edith's shoulder. He shoved her, hard. Edith fell on her hip and shoulder, un-able to brace herself with her bound hands. She writhed in a graceless heap as Stephen returned to his map, unmoved. After a minute or two, she righted herself. She collapsed next to me and pressed her face into my lap. I scratched her scalp, not minding the chalky residue of hair conditioner and old sweat, a halvah-like substance that wedged under my nails. She groaned.

"It'll all be okay," I said, lamely.

She shook her head, grinding her forehead against me. I thought I heard her say something about the wedding into my thigh.

"You can get married next weekend," I offered. "Or the weekend after. The carpaccio will spoil, but maybe carpaccio wasn't such a swell idea, anyway."

I could feel her breathing through my skirt, long exhales that snagged wetly at the trough. "And if the string trio's not available, you can go with the klezmer band, or we can buy kazoos for the Antidotes, or Mom can put on an antifertility musical. We've got a fair bit of tal-ent in the family that you can always rely on in a pinch."

Edith continued to press her skull into my thigh, although it was unclear whether she was agreeing or disagreeing with me; she rotated her head in an ambiguous oval pattern, as she frequently did when she suffered from a headache rather than definitive opinions on a given topic.

"And I'm really sorry what I said about Xavier, Edith. He's a really great guy, for a formerly provincial Spaniard."

And I *was* sorry. I felt pretty fucking crappy about my behavior in Hassan II Airport, massively chagrined that I should have stooped to manipulate my poor sister on the eve of a happy occasion.

Edith raised herself from my lap and grabbed me in a clumsy hug. It hurt, her hugging. Her mouth fell open by my ear and I could feel her breath, the coarseness of her hair, the chapped skin of her lips scratching against my lobe.

Edith was crying.

I let my own stoicism give way. I paused to catch my breath so that I could hear Edith's sobbing, so that her despair could push me to access deeper and deeper wells of anguish. This was a familiar rhythm, carried over from childhood: she would cry, and I would cry, and she would cry louder, and I would cry louder. Such overwrought gamboling was never terribly effective in our getting our way, whatever way it was we wanted, but it did achieve a certain *startlingness*. The upshot of this little trick, however questionable its effectiveness, was that I became reliant on Edith to assist me in the most basic expressions of sadness, and found it difficult, still do, to cry without her help.

And so I paused in my seat as my own engine of sadness stalled and sputtered; I listened for the sound of Edith's grieving to give me the necessary fuel. I held my breath at the top of an inhale—but heard nothing. I held my breath longer, waiting for the telltale catch in Edith's chest, the chug, the windy, weighty exhale. When it came, it was ephemeral, flighty. I could feel her hot teeth pressing against my cheek as her lips curled back, I could feel the tickle of her hair against my temple.

Edith was not crying. Edith was laughing.

❧

SIX P.M. EVENING. Still in the desert.

In addition to being bored (which replaced scared), we were highly uncomfortable. The windows of the airplane were nearly liquid in the heat, every bit of landscape viewed through them melted and undulating. Most distressing was the fact that the "police" had rejected us once they discovered we were neither disembarking nor releasing passengers. They had filed back into their canvas-topped trucks and sped back, I presumed, to the nearest town, though none was visible through our windows. Even the media vans had departed, now that the light was fading.

I found this not just disheartening; I found it strange.

The only people visible from my window were goatherders in black burnooses, leading their indolent charges. The herders hardly cast a glance at the shiny jagged thing that had landed in the middle of their sand and scrub. At most the plane was an annoyance to them, as their goats dawdled over and dropped to their bellies in our cylindrical shadow. The herders hurled rocks at the goats to wake them, rocks that jangled off the side of the plane and gave me a headache.

After her laughing fit, Edith had fallen asleep in my lap; I, too, eventually slept. We were both awakened by angry yelling from the cockpit.

"What's going on?" Edith grumbled. She tried to swallow, failed, then fired a meager condensed spitball onto the carpet.

My mouth was paste.

I shrugged. I could make out incensed tones, if not exact words.

Bruno emerged from the cockpit, his hair, the thinning part, wild and forward-leaning like those trees you see on coastal hills, their trunks and limbs blown by the wind to appear in a perpetual state of almost-falling. He opened a can of soda and drank gravely. I heard him say to Stephen, "I want the fuel and food *first*. No passengers until we get fuel and food."

Stephen coughed into his hand. "I don't know if it works that way."

Bruno's thinning hair trembled. "*Make it* work that way!" He counted seat backs until he was at the last row of first class. He slid into an empty seat, tore his glasses off, pressed his thumbs into his empty eye sockets.

Stephen folded his map and placed it in a duffel bag. He ran his hands over his face.

"So," Edith asked me, "what did the man on the radio say?"

"Nothing, really. He wanted to know if we were healthy."

Her mouth tightened. "Odd that he would speak Sasak, of all things."

I shrugged.

"If I'd known it was going to get me anywhere, I might have tried to learn a word or two of that stupid language." She pushed up her skirt to examine her thighs, which were covered in a heat rash.

"You never know what's going to get you somewhere in this world," I replied.

"You mostly know, Alice. Don't get all gloaty because you spent four years learning a language that you've now used once, for thirty seconds."

"There's something very, very strange about all this," I said. "Something's not right about this hijacking."

"And you would know, being such the veteran."

I frowned. "So where are the police, Edith?"

"Napping," she said. "Selling arms to children. God knows. This is Africa, Alice. The police might be worse than the terrorists."

"Where are the reporters?"

"Filing their stories, I guess. Where do you get these expectations? The movies?"

I stared at her as if to reply, *Where else does one get one's ideas about anything?*

"It should come as no surprise to you," Edith went on, "that movies fail to convey what it's really like to be a prisoner. Why? Because the prevailing torture inflicted by hijackers on their captives is not fear, but tedium."

Edith pried the Samsonite (at Edith's request, Tom had brought it from coach) from beneath the seat in front of her and unlatched it with her clumsy proliferation of fingers. She pulled a makeup bag from the interior and dropped it on her lap.

"Help me." She clutched the bag at both ends with her bound hands so that I could help unzip it, and retrieved a compact mirror, a cotton ball, a tiny bottle of rubbing alcohol, and a vial of tea rose perfume. "Hold this," she insisted, opening the compact.

I held the mirror with my bound hands as she swabbed her face. She tucked the soiled cotton balls into the seat-back pouch and put a few dabs of tea rose under her jaw.

Stephen, meanwhile, had busied himself over Cyrus's corpse. He examined him with medical thoroughness, checking his wrists, unbuttoning his shirt, feeling his chest.

"So," Edith said, "I don't suppose you told Sasak Man to give word to our loved ones that we were alive."

"I didn't really get the chance."

"I don't suppose it occurred to you that I have a *fiancé* who is probably worried sick, and might be interested to know that I was distraught, but bearing up under the strain."

I glanced at my plaid thigh, on which there was, inexplicably, a hard splotch of wax.

"I suppose it would only be gracious for me to accept the blame for your shortcomings," Edith continued. "Who else might have taught you that you never give unless you get back? 'Cooperation' is just another word for self-advancement."

"I guess I do not learn well from example. I guess I am irretrievably dumb."

She sighed a conflicted sigh, not wanting to agree with my assessment of myself, yet finding no alternative but to do so.

"I guess I am also dumb in the way that I don't understand your lack of fear or even vague concern, given our current situation," I said.

Her eyes glinted in the middle of her alcohol-smelling face. "That is because you have no interest in being a participant in history. You are, as you have always been, too scared to be notable."

I lost my temper, but only inside my head. Inside my head I raged, *Give a shit about something important, please! Care, for one second, that a man is dead!*

Outside my head I heard myself saying, "Oh."

"Human nature is well disposed toward those who are in interesting situations," Edith said in a high voice, her chin tilted upward, indicating that she was quoting someone, our mother perhaps.

"Meaning what?"

"Meaning that, for a girl who is losing her spark, I am going out with a blinding flash."

I stared at her, awestruck. Edith transmogrified optimism into the basest form of opportunism; it made my eyes burn.

I cleared my throat. "A man has died, Edith."

"By accident!"

"Not by accident!" I fumed.

"If a man has a heart attack while making love to his wife, has she killed him?"

"That's different."

"Is it, Alice?"

"It is."

She sniffed. "Then I suppose that means you *believe* all this gun-waving nonsense."

I stared at her. At the flight attendants, coughing and slurping behind their duct tape gags. At Stephen, trying to lift the stiff eyelids of Cyrus Bing with the laminated corner of an emergency procedures brochure.

I lowered my voice. "What am I missing here?"

She leaned toward me, her hair falling over her face.

"They're not using bullets," she said.

"What do you mean, they're not using bullets?"

"They're not using bullets."

"How do you know?"

She smiled, triumphant. "Because I saw them!"

"You saw the bullets?"

"I saw them spinning the . . . the . . . whatever those spinning things are in guns, to make sure there were no bullets."

"I don't understand. Why wouldn't they have bullets?"

"All I'm saying is that we're not in any true danger, unless they try to get up in the air again and crash the plane, which I can't imagine them doing, because Bruno keeps saying to Stephen, 'When we return to Lucerne,' and talking about 'the Failure Project.'"

"What's the Failure Project?" I asked.

She looked around at the duct-taped flight attendants, at the carpet covered with biscuit crumbs, at Cyrus's soda-stained trousers, at me.

"We are," she said.

I watched as Stephen walked back to confer with Bruno. The two of them whispered and nodded. Stephen then hurried to coach class, and reappeared five minutes later with the Hal Pipkin doppelgänger. I was still trying to process the possibility that our hijackers weren't using bullets. What the hell were we doing here, in that case? Why didn't all of us passengers just mutiny and leave? Surely Edith was missing something crucial. Maybe they didn't have bullets, but they had something else. A briefcase bomb. A penknife. We were captives for a reason. Weren't we?

Stephen pushed Hal Pipkin into a seat three rows ahead of us.

Bruno replaced his glasses and stood, then counted his way forward. Upon reaching Hal Pipkin, he thrust out a hand.

"Bruno," he said, lowering his behind onto an armrest.

"Justin," Hal Pipkin replied, shaking the proffered hand.

"Drink?" Bruno inquired.

Justin blinked. "Beer, if you got it."

Stephen fetched a can of Stork from the galley. He popped the top and handed it to Justin.

"It's warm," Justin said. Despite his rueful college-boy façade, his body vibrated visibly. He took a small sip, then a larger one. He finished the can in three gulps.

"Another?" Stephen asked.

Justin nodded. He nursed this one, taking sips and burping loudly in between.

Bruno rested his elbows on his knees in a pose of mock enthrallment. "Tell me about your travel plans," he said.

Justin peered at the doodled-on leg of his jeans. "I'd have to say they're a bit uncertain at this point."

"But initially."

"I was studying in Casablanca," Justin said. "Archaeology."

"Archaeology." Bruno nodded approvingly. "Have you had a chance to chat with Team Volubilis?"

Stephen snickered.

"But I'm on my way home now. I had a connection in Melilla, then an overnight in London, during which I had to switch from Gatwick to Heathrow, then I had to change planes again in Reykjavik, then fly to Chicago, then on to Atlanta."

Bruno tapped the end of his bulbous nose. "How thorough," he said.

"It was one of those discount tickets they sell outside of the student union. They're not refundable, under any circumstances. My father says the price of escape is always hidden."

"Aptly put," Bruno said. "But surely a hijacking would qualify as an extenuating circumstance."

"Doubtful."

"And where are you from, Justin?"

"Outside Atlanta."

"Do you have a girlfriend?"

"Sure."

"I bet you want to see her."

"I don't care one way or the other."

"And . . ." Bruno said.

"And?"

"You haven't completed your thought."

Justin concentrated on his beer, bewildered.

"Don't you mean, 'And she's not going anywhere'? Or possibly, 'Like a lot of women, she's not going anywhere'?"

"I'm not following you."

"I'm just hoping you feel comfortable being honest with me," Bruno said. "Honesty will prove indispensable, if this is all going to turn out pleasantly."

Justin's hand tightened around his beer can, producing a cricking noise.

"The real question," Bruno continued, "is *why* she's not going anywhere. Because you're the heir to a tobacco fortune? Because she's a good Catholic southern girl? Because she visited you in Casablanca, where prophylactics are in scarce supply? Because she's been weeping for weeks in Atlanta, which is not, from what I understand, the easiest place to procure an abortion, at least without being stoned by right-wing Christians?"

Justin purpled.

"Let me guess. She refuses to get an abortion. She's Catholic, sure, but those girls are only ever Catholic after the fact. It never stops them from taking their panties off in rubberless African countries, does it?"

Justin scowled, but did not reply.

"Do you have something to say, Justin?"

Justin remained silent.

"Justin?"

"Christ!" Justin snapped. "You get off on this or something?"

"What do you mean?"

"I mean interrogating people about their sex lives."

"Is that how it looks to you?"

Justin's jaw wriggled in its socket.

"I can't get laid, isn't that what you're thinking? You're thinking, Who'd want to have sex with a blind man? Is that it, Justin?"

Justin drank his beer. He swallowed a burp. "Took the words out of my mouth."

Bruno nodded toward Stephen, who wound up and delivered a whipping, backhanded slap.

Justin's skull struck the headrest with such force that his seat jerked on its floor bindings. He flounced forward, his head between his knees, hands protectively over his hurt face.

"Man!" Justin howled. "Why do you even give a fuck?"

"Who says I give a fuck, Justin?" Bruno asked, standing over him. "Maybe I'm just very, very bored. Maybe I'm just playing you and you're too stupid not to be played by me."

Bruno shoved his hands in his pockets and rocked on his orthopedic shoes, waiting for Justin to surface.

After a minute or so, Justin emerged from between his knees. "Why can't you just act normally?" he said through his teeth. "Why can't you just shoot people or fly us into a building?"

Bruno considered this question. "Because, Justin," he said after a time, "that would make me a common terrorist."

Bruno turned to face my direction. He gestured in the air, his usual semaphoric tangle of fists, thumbs thrust sideways, elbows pumping. Stephen strode back toward Edith and me. He pointed. I followed him.

"I prefer"—Bruno fingered his patchy, whiskered chin—"to mix in a little education with my hijacking. Because I, for one, cannot stand to waste an occasion to learn something new about humanity."

Justin paled.

"Let me tell you what I'm interested in at the moment, Justin."

"Like I care," Justin said.

Bruno ignored him. "Did I mention that I was an anthropologist? Sorry. *Am* an anthropologist?"

No one responded.

Bruno nodded at Stephen, who positioned me in front of Justin. Justin's eyes cased the length of me.

"Well, I am. I'm not terribly interested in rain dancing or menstruation huts, but I am very interested in essential human morality, particularly as it is influenced by guilt."

Edith and I exchanged a fast look. A man after our own hearts.

"Guilt," said Justin.

"Guilt," repeated Bruno. "Are you familiar with Fechner's Paradox?"

Justin shook his head.

"Well, then. Your study abroad continues. The tribe I was working with—their name does not matter, their continent does not matter, people are people whether they wear bone skirts or girdles—submitted to a few tests that I devised. I wanted to chart the lengths to which people will go to minimize tragedy while avoiding culpability. I drew up a scenario in the mud. You are here, I said. You are riding a water yak that refuses to heed your commands. You gallop over a hill, and there, in front of you, is an old woman. To the left of the old woman is a group of children, to the right of the woman is a group of children. If the yak runs straight, it will kill the old woman. If it veers to either side, it will kill a group of children. Which would be preferable, if your yak is out of control—to kill the old woman, or to kill the group of children? Everyone decided that killing the old woman would be better than killing the group of children. It was a matter of numbers; there is no ageism in this society, quite the opposite—these plagues of nameless children are far less rare than an old person who has survived God knows how many diseases. But when I changed the scenario, when I told them that they were able to control the out-of-control yak, that the yak was headed straight for a group of children rather than the old woman—who, I added, was sick and would be dead within the month—every single person refused to intercede. *Every single person,* Justin, refused to force the yak to hit the old woman, even though it was in their power to be the agent of a less terrible act. They'd prefer to kill ten children than command the yak to kill a single dying lady."

He paused. "So how about it?"

"How about what?" said Justin.

"Fechner's Paradox. What do you think?"

Justin raised his chin. "I think you're a fucking freak who gets his pathetic kicks fucking with strangers."

"That might be an insightful comment, Justin, if I hadn't already told you that about myself. What I didn't tell you is that I've done similar things to people I know very well. To my ex-wife, for instance. It was a new marital counseling technique that was popular in the eighties. Deceive and conquer. But maybe if I told you something more about *myself*, you might feel able to respond more honestly to the situation you're about to find yourself in."

Justin scowled. "Who says I want to know anything about you?"

"If I told you how I lost my eyesight, you wouldn't be interested? It's a deeply embarrassing story, I promise you. Not remotely self-serving."

Justin was confused beyond reason, and starting to hate it. He stared at me, but not at me, exactly. I just happened to be in front of him.

I smiled at him.

Bruno slid his glasses off his face, exposing his eyes, or the not-eyes, the holes that once were eyes, or not-holes, for they weren't even holes, or even dimples, but little sewed-up mouths, two sour expressions of disapproval crimping the skin.

Bruno told Justin (and me, and Stephen, and Edith, and the stewardesses) the story of How He Lost His Eyesight. When he finished his story, which made no mention of a train ride, of a girl with a poor throw, of lupine fields, of Lake Leman, Justin responded by saying, "Can I go now?"

I cringed. I thought Bruno would be offended. He was not.

"That's what I meant by 'honest,'" he said. "Nothing would make me happier than to let you go. However, it might be wise for you to keep in mind that *the cost of escape is always hidden.* It's a very small price in this case, really minuscule. But you see, Justin, we need a dead body, so that the negotiator, with whom Alice here has had some regular contact, will not mistake us for insincere. I think he finds us a bit insincere at the moment, and I wish to disabuse him of this idea. We have one dead body, which, I would argue, is the most symbolic measure of one's sincerity in any endeavor"—Bruno indicated in Cyrus's direction— "but he is not appropriately deceased, Justin. And it is this problem with which you might be able to assist us, in exchange for the freedom you desire."

Justin nodded, utterly lost.

"What I'm saying," Bruno clarified, "is that I want you to 'kill' Mr. Bing."

Justin stared at the blind man, as I stared at him, as did Edith, as did the stewardesses.

"Now that's gruesome," Edith called out from her seat.

I felt sick.

"But not the most gruesome," Bruno countered. "The most gruesome would be if I commanded Stephen to shoot Alice, if Justin refuses to 'kill' Cyrus. We must have a convincingly dead body—I care little how we attain one."

"But I speak Sasak," I protested. I looked back helplessly at Edith, who mouthed at me, *Remember what I told you.*

Remember. Try to remember. Ah, yes. The bullets, or lack thereof. Thus the fact that this was merely a game, where to lose was not to die but to be humiliated before a planeful of strangers. This hijacking was unlike any I'd ever heard of, and so the stakes, and the punishments, were impossible to predict.

Stephen pulled his gun from his waistband. He made a big show of spinning the barrel, flipping it back, announcing that there was one and only one bullet available for Justin to do his work, and that this one bullet would, depending on his choice, soon be lodged in either Cyrus's body or mine.

Justin stood slowly, wincing as the blood banged into the recently beaten areas of his skull. Stephen knocked at Cyrus's chest with his covered fist, his knuckles encouraging an incongruous hollow thunk from the rib cage.

"Right here," Stephen instructed. "Aim for the yolk stain on his tie, poor bastard."

He stood behind Justin and placed the gun in his hands. He held Justin's arms below the shoulders, to ensure that he shot the right person. The stubby barrel slumped down toward the floor.

"I'll count," Bruno offered, "if it will make you feel less responsible."

Justin nodded. He attempted to wipe his mouth with his arm, sending the gun pointing toward the ceiling, and causing Stephen to yell, "Whoa, whoa there, little cowboy," and jerk Justin's arms forcefully downward.

"Ten," Bruno began. "Seven, five, four."

"Hey," Justin said, his voice trembling. "That's not fair."

"Two." Bruno paused.

"Two," he repeated. Justin's hand shook, even as Stephen sought to steady it.

"*Two*," he said a third time.

Justin complied by turning his head to the side and coughing a watery mouthful of bile onto Stephen's shirtsleeve.

"Goddamnit!" Stephen whipped Justin against the wall. The gun skittered between Cyrus's skinny legs and thumped against the wall beneath his jumpseat. Stephen yanked off his shirt and stormed into the lavatory.

"Stephen!" Bruno yelled. "Stephen, what happened?"

Stephen emerged from the lavatory, shirtless. "Kid puked on my arm," he said, rubbing at his skin with a paper towel.

"Where's the gun, who has the gun?"

Stephen dropped on all fours and felt around beneath the jump-seat. "I've got it," he said. He stuck the gun between Justin's eyes. "You shithead. You chickenshit shit-brained shithead. Now we have to kill Alice. Is that what you wanted? Huh?"

Justin didn't respond. His face was green.

"This is very disappointing," Bruno muttered. "Very disappointing."

Stephen sidestepped toward me and grabbed me by the hair.

"Please," I said, but he wasn't listening. He shoved me, face first, toward Justin.

"So this is what you wanted?" Stephen said. I wasn't crying, necessarily; I was leaking profusely from the eyes, true, but it was more a physiological response to having my hair yanked.

I was inches from Justin's face when it crumpled, in service, I feared, of another bilious emission. I turned my head away as far as I could, despite Stephen's grip on my hair. I braced myself for the worst and thus was deeply thankful when I opened my eyes to see that Justin was bawling.

"Christ," Stephen said.

"What?" Bruno asked. "What's happening now?"

"Kid's lost his stuff entirely."

"That's too bad," Bruno said. "He knew the consequences, however. Didn't you Justin? You knew the consequences."

Stephen released the safety and pressed the gun into my head.

"You're going to have her brains all over you, Justin, buddy," Stephen said. Justin bawled harder. "Just as a little thank you and fuck you."

"Go ahead," said Bruno. "Shoot her."

Poor guy, I thought, what was Justin going to do when he found out the whole business was a big, rollicking fake? He'd be wrecked for life. "Shooting blanks" would come to take on a whole new erotically problematic meaning for him, it would no doubt translate into a literal form of lifelong impotence; he'd be paralyzed before any ejaculatory trigger, he'd be doomed to wither at the crucial moment of climax, to yield nothing more fertile than snot and tears, which some girls might accept as the Broken Man's Ecstasy, and consider him "gotten off" in his own pitiable way.

Poor, poor Justin/Hal.

I wanted to witness the moment he realized he'd been duped, so I kept my eyes open, wide open, and waited for the echoing metallic *click* as Stephen pulled the meaningless trigger.

But instead of the echoing metallic *click*, I heard my sister's voice, floating forward from a few rows back.

"Wait."

Stephen turned. Justin turned. Bruno turned.

Edith strode up the aisle, not like a ray of light, not like an avenging angel cast down from the heavens to do the humble work of a just God who favors the meek. She looked like hell, to be frank, her hair knotted and frizzed out around her shoulders, her skirt creased, her blouse unevenly buttoned.

"I'll do it," she said.

Bruno listened to her approach. "You'll do what?"

"I'll shoot Cyrus," she said.

Stephen removed the gun from my head. Snot gleamed on Justin's upper lip.

"That's very generous of you," Bruno said, "but this is between Justin and Alice." Yet he seemed relieved.

Edith frowned. "But don't you want to learn new things about humanity? You could learn something about sibling sacrifice. You could learn something about familial love and commitment."

I scoffed under my breath: "You could learn something about strivery one-upmanship."

Edith beamed at me, and I beamed back, dutifully playing my part as the grateful sacrifice with a new lease on life.

Bruno's nostrils shivered, picking up, no doubt, the fading smell of alcohol from Edith's face, the scent of her tea rose perfume.

"Stop." Bruno held up a hand. "Stephen," he barked. "I need to talk to you."

Stephen and Bruno huddled in the galley and whispered while Edith picked at her split ends, pulling them apart at the tip and making two new hairs.

Of course we loved each other, in a complicated manner, Edith and I, our love expressed more often than not through our attempts to confound each other, attempts that were nonetheless infused with the knowledge that we depended on each other's hostile presence to feel defined and alive.

Our father owns—catalogued and chronologized in the Des Moines storage unit—the movies to prove that Edith, before I was born, which is to say before I came along to inspire her to spiteful action, was a lethargic infant, free of passion. (Our father related to us best through his camera lens. I spoke to my mother once about the childhood experience of being filmed—we were both drunk and post-sauna stupid on the patio of an Arizona spa—and compared it to being a deer tracked by a hunter through his rifle sight, to which she said, "Darling, how *literal*.") Our mother feared that Edith was autistic, or at least this is what she exclaims to the camera in "Edie Meets Gammy Vicks," as she squats in a plastic lawn pool with an infant Edith dangling motionless between her thighs. In the movie "One Lost Mitten," shot at the bottom of a toboggan run in Iowa for an uninterrupted twenty-seven minutes, Edith sits in the snow, somberly chewing a ski glove. In "Daddy's Failed Vasectomy," Edith sits on a Persian carpet wearing a red-and-white-striped frock, her body a pale, hunchbacked lump, a pendant of drool dawdling on her lower lip. A hand—from the hair on the thumbs, our father's—tweedles a paper clip in front of her spiritless six-month-old gaze. She fails to put the compelling metal object in her ear, eye, mouth, throat, and instead allows it to tumble onto the carpet to become lost in the Persian's frenetic cartouches.

It was not until "Alice's First Picnic," in which I make my debut in the Vickery-Plourde family drama, that Edith shunts aside all traces of toddler autism. She is sitting upright in an embroidered smock of stiff Egyptian canvas, her hair a white dandelion fuzz around her face, making her resemble some old woman. I am larval on my back before a plate of rice. Edith is staring off at an object in the distance, a sheep, perhaps, or a tank, or a maid piled high with laundry. My hand reaches out and grabs Edith by the ankle. This was an accident, no doubt. My eyes were still that gummy shade of newborn blue, undiscerning and dim. If I may speak for my preverbal self, I suspect I flung out a hand and caught the first thing I encountered with my fingers. This happened to be my sister's ankle.

Edith stares at my hand. And stares at it.

The camera swings between my hand around Edith's ankle, and Edith's face. She grabs me by the arms and hauls me into her lap, where I loll and gurgle and spasm my legs. She clenches me around the wrist until my hand is purple. The camera catches—again, by accident—the exact moment when Edith's face cracks open with its first human expression, her eyes flooding with an appetite for affection and damage.

Bruno and Stephen returned from their galley huddle.

"All right," Bruno announced to Edith. "We've decided to take you up on your offer."

Stephen escorted Edith toward Cyrus. Standing behind her, he yanked her tubing, untied it, placed the butt of his gun into her palm, then closed her fingers around it.

Edith bounced the gun, weighing it.

"Ever shoot one of these?" Stephen asked.

Edith looked to me. "Have I, Alice?"

I stared at the becrumbed carpet.

"I suppose I haven't, no," she answered.

This was a lie. Attractive girls did not graduate from the Maplehook School without first acquiring impressive rifle skills. The neighboring boys' school was chock-full of third-generation trust-fund kids, sons of gentlemen New England watercolorists, who took their Maplehook girlfriends to their parents' sprawling farmhouses on long weekends, and shot at dead trees and live squirrels as a form of heightened teenage foreplay.

Had Stephen known this, he might have remained standing behind Edith, he might never have taken his hands off hers. Stupidly he stepped away from her, just enough to allow her to spin around and point the gun at him.

Edith expertly released the safety.

"Hey now," Stephen said, dumb-faced.

"Stephen?" Bruno asked.

"Now, now," Stephen said, palms tamping calm into the air.

Edith flung her hair over her shoulder and the gun swerved. Stephen ducked. When the gun stabilized, it was pointed at Bruno's big head.

"Stephen?" Bruno asked again.

"Why don't you tell me how to shoot this thing," Edith said sweetly.

"Stephen, what's going on?"

Stephen was sweating in earnest. "Let's not be creative here, shall we?"

"Why not?" Edith asked. "You're not scared of a little gun, are you?"

"A gun is not a toy," Stephen said.

Edith looked directly down the barrel. One-eyed squint. "I don't know, Stephen. This gun looks like a toy to me."

She reversed the gun and aimed again at Bruno's forehead, his stomach, his knees, then returned to his head.

"You know what they say," Stephen said. "Looks are deceptive." He was trying to keep the panic out of his voice, and no wonder, considering what Bruno might do to him if he discovered this amateur fuck-up.

"Stephen!" Bruno barked. He was panicking, just a little.

Edith's finger tensed around the trigger as she aimed at Bruno's chest. I cringed, even though I knew there weren't any bullets. I put my hands over my ears anyway. But I never heard the click.

"*Pow,*" Edith said. She jerked the gun, faking a kickback, then giggled and blew a strand of hair out of her eyes.

She pointed the gun at Stephen's face.

"*Pow,*" she said again, before rotating on her thick schoolgirl heel and pointing the gun at me.

"What do you say, Alice?" she asked. "Don't you want to beg or something?"

I held up my bound hands and, after some effortful twisting, thrust the middle finger of each of my hands into the air.

Edith laughed. It was a touch disparaging, that laugh, a tiny bit exhausted with me.

"Always the joker, aren't you, especially when you're scared shitless." She shook her head. Then she shifted her attention to the body in the chair and, with a teenage-foreplay sort of quickness and accuracy, took a cool marksman's aim at Cyrus's tie.

"*Pow,*" she said, and pulled the trigger for real.

There was a single, jarring explosion, and then, except for the screams from coach class, it was intolerably quiet.

I lifted my head to see the body of Cyrus, tossed partway out of his jumpseat, the jacket turban holding tight to his head even as smoke rose from his chest and his left hand grazed the teal carpet.

Tom sprinted from the back of the plane. He immobilized Edith in a wrestling lock and struggled the gun away. My sister's face maintained the ghost of a confident smile, as she stared at the wrapped head of Cyrus Bing. I wondered, as I often did, what Edith thought to herself at moments such as this. Perhaps she was blaming me for putting her in the position in the first place, thinking, *Goddamned Alice;* perhaps she was thinking, *Whoopsy!* saying it in her head as she says it to me when we're playing rainy-day croquet in a hotel lobby in "Monsoon School Break" and she wants her malicious send to appear an accident.

Or perhaps she heard a more deadly honest refrain in her head, as I often hoped she must, a refrain that she heard in her head at all times, like a white-noise machine, its hiss condensing occasionally into a clumpy fog that turned into letters and then words, linking themselves to form a mean, unceasing accusation in the depths of her ear canal: *Stupid slut, you're a stupid, stupid slut.*

Bruno's Shame

I MET MY WIFE at a campground in the mountains above Vienna while I was a student of anthropology, studying the nomadic theater troupes that traveled through the Transdanubia mountains. My wife was a member of the Szemlő-hegyi troupe; one steamy July evening, I watched her deliver a performance as a wood sprite who grants the power of sight to a blind couple poking their way through the woods with sticks.

Her gift, as intended, proves a curse. The husband and the wife become obsessed with the idea of beauty, even though neither of them knows what beauty is. They've been blind, poor people, and can't put a finger on prettiness. Nevertheless, they point to each other, to kitchen stools, to saltcellars and forks, and say, *Has this beauty, darling? Has this?* They each have love affairs with seeing people who laugh at them and fail to find charming or innocent their inability to know a chipmunk from a woodpile, a sock from a bedroll. After much disappointment and rejection, the husband and the wife decide to put out each other's eyes, so that they can return to their life of uncomplicated darkness. The final, stormy scene featured my wife, the wood sprite, chuckling on a branch above the blind couple. All at once she is struck by lightning, and as the curtain drops, is heard screaming, *I cannot see! For the love of beauty! I cannot see!*

It was a terrible play, featuring absurd thespian desecrations, a play that encouraged the many audience members to get raucously drunk afterward and burn a dining tent to the ground by accident. I found my wife dancing around the inadvertent fire, and it was not until after I had made love to her in my pup tent that she confessed she was not a member of Szemlő-hegyi, but a nun.

A nun, I said.

A nun, she grinned. And not a terribly good nun, as you must suspect.

I said she was worse than a bad nun, she was a blasphemous disgrace. We took an apartment together in Vienna and were married after I received my degree. We moved to Bern for a job at the university, and she accompanied me on my summer research trips to Borneo to study the theatrical habits of the Penang tribe.

We had been married for a little more than three years when my wife began to behave in an unusual manner. She refused to go outdoors, and hired a neighbor girl to do our shopping and our errands. She began wearing a crucifix over her boiled-wool sweaters, even though she'd long before renounced her religious affiliations, she'd drunk cow's blood from a coconut shell with a lofty member of the Penang governing society, she'd watched a gibbon eat his sickly young, she'd danced around a fire wearing nothing but a towel and hiking boots.

Trying to be gentle—trying, that is, to avoid skepticism or judgment, two quick, bad things I default to when disoriented—I asked her one evening why she was wearing her crucifix again.

Because I have committed acts of wickedness, she replied, stabbing her finger into a glass of wine and licking it.

I asked her to describe the acts to me. Did she love another man? She denied this. Was she falling back under the sway of God?

No.

I should mention that a few months earlier, a man had moved into the apartment above ours. He was an accountant, who had the annoying habit of pacing around his apartment late at night wearing one wooden shoe. Every night I would awaken to find my wife crying next to me in bed, rolling the crucifix between thumb and forefinger, and every night I would take the broom and bang on the ceiling with the handle. I would bang, and the upstairs neighbor would bang back, and I would bang again, and he would bang back. He seemed a musical fellow, with a strange series of banging rhythms, quick-quick-quick-slow-quick. After a week of these staccato interchanges, I mounted the stairs in my slippers to compliment him on his percussive acumen, and to request that he wear slippers at night.

I knocked on the door. The man opened it, holding a bottle of kirsch in his right hand. He wore pajamas. He had one bare foot and one wooden leg.

At last, he said to me. I have been inviting you up here for a drink for weeks. I was beginning to think that you didn't know Morse code after all.

I accepted a kirsch, and we stayed up until dawn. He was a jolly, nervous man, who made so many jokes about his wooden appendage that you felt he was relieved to have lost his leg in a horse-riding accident, because it gave him something interesting to talk about with strangers. He said he had belonged to the priesthood as a young man, but had left the Church after his accident.

Because you could not serve a God who was prone to acts of random cruelty? I asked.

No, he replied. Because I was no longer made in his image.

But how do you know? I countered. Perhaps the old fellow has three wooden legs and a big, rheumy eye. He is getting on.

The man shook his head. I read it as a message that I should become a junior partner at my father's accounting firm, Holzbein and Kurz, he explained.

Holzbein and Kurz, I'd heard, was a very good firm. I asked him if he would solve an estate dispute I'd been having for years with my brother. He agreed.

When I returned home, my wife was asleep. Over breakfast, I told her about the man upstairs with the wooden leg.

I invited him for dinner this evening, I told her. You two have a lot in common.

I doubt that, she said.

How do you know? I asked. You've never met him.

He has a wooden leg. Her mouth twitched. He's known obstacles that I have never known.

There are more mean bastards with wooden legs than you can count, I said.

That's because they were shot in wars. That's because they were crushed in earthquakes or malnourished as children.

Perhaps you're overromanticizing the handicapped.

She didn't reply.

Besides, I said. He used to be a priest. But he left after his accident.

Good for him, she said, and shut herself in the bedroom.

Our neighbor arrived at six, bearing a strudel. Over dinner my wife was appallingly rude. She would not look the man in the face. She did not ask him questions about himself. She served him the smallest piece of pot roast and gave him the burnt potatoes scraped from the corners of the gratin pan. She disappeared into the kitchen, and never returned. I apologized to our guest, but he was far more sympathetic than hurt. He invited me upstairs for a nightcap, which I accepted. We stayed up until dawn.

When I returned to our apartment, my wife was sobbing in our bed. What's wrong with you? I inquired.

She wept and apologized. She said that the man upstairs made her think wicked thoughts.

I was stunned. She loves him, I thought.

I accused her of this. You love him, I said.

I've tried to love him, believe me I've tried.

How nice of you to try so hard, I said.

You misunderstand! she wailed. I am an animal! I am hardly more advanced than a gibbon!

She told me that she'd seen the man on the front stoop without his leg, sunning himself. She'd watched him detach his leg and pull up his trousers so that the patchwork stump was revealed. The sight of his pruned limb made her sick, and the noise of his wooden leg on the floorboards was a constant reminder of her personal failures. She confessed to me the reason she'd left the Church. She had always found people without limbs, noses, crucial body parts to be loathsome. They made her sick, no matter how many times she went to confession. The night she'd met me in the Transdanubia mountains, she'd seen a man without arms dancing around the embers of the dining tent. She knew then that she could never return to the convent.

So it was not out of affection that you made love to me that night, but out of disgust for a dancing man without arms?

She cried harder.

I told her that I didn't believe her, that I knew she could love a person without arms or legs, that she would love me if I were to lose a limb. She denied it, and I insisted, because I loved her so, and trusted her to be a better soul than she believed.

It's not true, she said. If anything terrible happened to you, I'd leave.

I pulled her bothered head into my lap. As she slept, I unlatched the crucifix from around her neck and put it in my shirt pocket. When she awoke in the morning, she seemed relieved to find her crucifix missing. This did not mean that she stopped scrabbling at her throat with her right hand; this did not mean that she did not finger that ghost trinket as she walked to the market, keeping her eyes on the cobblestones and praying that she would not see the neighborhood child in the red go-cart who was born without hands.

In a weak moment, I confessed everything to my upstairs neighbor. His face gloomied in a way I'd never seen in him, but he didn't seem insulted.

She's a tragic woman, your wife.

Not so tragic, I replied, just badly bred.

He limped into his kitchenette and put on some water for tea. He wore a thick sock over his wooden prosthetic, and took care, I saw, to favor his good and quiet leg. He was an exemplary neighbor.

He put a mug of tea in front of me, and doused the top with cognac.

Because it is a matter of breeding, I continued, I imagine that I can unbreed her.

My neighbor shook his head. You could more easily remove her skin. This, I need not tell you, is impossible.

I glared at my neighbor. He was usually such an optimist; even with his wooden leg and all, his cheeriness was unfaltering.

I didn't come to you for talk about impossibility, I said. I came to you for help.

The man sighed. Then you should pray you never become disfigured.

I shook my head. I respectfully disagree, I said.

My neighbor shrugged. We finished our tea in silence.

For the next few weeks, I spent every afternoon in the library studying cultures where fear presided. I learned, for example, about young married girls in the Congo who were scared of intercourse and refused to give themselves to their husbands. These girls were stripped naked and barricaded in what was typically used as a menstruation hut, filled with sides of raw pork. The girls were not given food, only little jars of water. They were imprisoned in the pork hut for five days while the pork spoiled and the maggots ate themselves into flies. At the end of the fifth day, the girls were released and given, unwashed and partially mad, to their husbands. The husbands wrapped them in blankets and brought them to the marital bed, where they were quietly relieved of their virginity.

The scared girls gave me an idea. I called Hans Nagy, who had been the makeup artist for Szemlő-hegyi. Hans and I met at a dark pub with a woodsy interior, where tiny women served us beer in long, thin steins. I told him I wanted him to make me blind.

Excuse me? Hans said. He eyed an impish waitress with a trayful of drinks, her breasts multiplied and stretched long and rangy by the steins.

I told him about my wife's troubles, of which I was seeking to cure her. I wanted Hans to make it appear that I'd lost my eyes.

Right this second? Hans asked.

I stared at him. Indeed, why not right now?

I drove Hans back to his house. He sat me in front of a mirror, in a barber chair he'd found on the street. He blackened the skin around my left eye; he glued the black sprouts of stitches to the lid. Then he mixed up a compound of petroleum jelly and glue, and applied it to my shut eye. It shrank as it dried. It squeezed my eyeball and caused me considerable discomfort.

Voilà, said Hans, spinning the barber chair.

I looked in the mirror with my good eye. The paste had dried clear. The tightness produced a lovely concave effect, which made it look as though my eye had been removed.

I gave Hans my phone number and told him to call my wife to inform her that I'd been in an accident on the way home from the pub, that I was in the hospital and refused to see her.

She'll understand, I said.

Hans dialed my number. I could tell my wife did not cry upon hearing the news.

She was very upset, Hans lied, hanging up the phone.

I stayed in his house through the weekend. When he was out, I sat in his barber chair and tried to give myself convincing bruises with his pastes and purple blushes, but instead I made myself look all-over burnt.

After three days, I asked Hans to call my wife and tell her that he'd be bringing me home that evening. He asked her if she would be there, and she paused a while before saying yes.

This time, Hans did both my eyes, first the left and then the right. I grew anxious when he closed my right eye. I felt trapped; I had trouble breathing.

Pretend you're asleep, he advised.

I pretended until I fell asleep. When I awoke, I was confused.

Hans? I asked.

Just a minute, he said. He was far away. He was talking to me through water, or through a long, long pipe.

Hans, I can't say I'm enjoying this very much. I was beginning to sweat. I touched my eyes. They were sharp. I cut my finger on a stitch.

What's to enjoy? Hans said. Let's get going. I have a date.

He put me in a coat and pulled me down the stairs.

You're not a terribly patient caretaker, I complained as he shoved me into the passenger seat of his car.

It felt to me that Hans was driving very fast. It felt like daylight outside, even though I knew that it was dark, and that the trees were naked, and that there were black patches of ice on the road. But it smelled of fall, not winter; I could see the red flashes of the leaves I knew weren't there as we drove beneath them.

Here we are, Hans said.

He helped me out of the car. The sidewalk did not feel familiar; the steps to my building did not feel familiar; the halls did not echo in a familiar way.

Doesn't seem that anyone's home, Hans said, knocking. The knock sounded strange. It was a cinematic knock, very pure and laid over the regular, unremarkable sound of knocking. It was a knock with color, with meaning, with import. It stayed in my head and I could see it there; it had the quality of a stain.

I heard the hinges grind as the door opened. Remember to oil the hinges when this is resolved! I said to myself.

Come in, my wife said.

I smiled toward the voice.

Where are you? Hans asked.

Hiding behind the door, she said.

Hans shoved me forward. How about some lights? he asked. The door shut behind him.

Silence.

Well, I've got a date, Hans said. I heard him fumbling for the knob. He let himself out gently. The door's latching was no more than the sound of a cracker breaking in two.

How are you? I asked the dark. It was dark and then dark, I surmised.

Fine, she answered. How are you?

Well enough, I said.

So, she began. She was on the verge of weeping. What happened to you?

I paused. I hadn't thought about what had happened to me.

I was at the pub, I began. There was a fight.

You were in a fight?

I considered this. No. Two men were in a fight. One of them squeezed the bosom of a very small waitress.

How rude, my wife said, shakily.

I tried to break it up.

Oh, she said.

And then, I continued, the man who fondled the waitress put his hand into his pocket.

He had a knife, she guessed. She started to cry.

He may have, I said. But he didn't pull it out of his pocket.

Oh, she said, snuffling.

He did have little vial.

Of acid, she offered. My wife had a gift for worst-case scenarios.

Could have been, I said. But before he could unstopper it, the other man threw me out of the way.

What a selfless fellow, she said.

Except that he tossed me through the plate-glass window, I said.

My wife didn't say anything.

Though he tossed me through the plate-glass window, I am amazingly unscarred.

I swear I heard her spirits lift. I could hear that sort of thing all of a sudden. It made me think in terrible clichés along the lines of, *Blindness is a new way to see.* I was not even embarrassed to think this.

Really? she asked.

Except for two perfectly aimed shards of glass, I am unscarred, I said.

Two shards, she said.

Think of the worst sort of luck or the best sort of aim, and you are looking at it.

She started to weep. I am not looking at you, she told me. Every few seconds I saw a sweep of red behind my lids. She had a flashlight. Or cars, I thought. Their headlights.

I will wear dark glasses, I offered. We can live with the lights off.

That won't matter, she said.

She wept until she was beyond weeping. I began to feel a little bad about the joke I was playing on her. I was also growing scared.

But I am your husband, I told her. I was your husband, I remain your husband.

She didn't reply.

In sickness and in health, I reminded her.

We removed that, she said.

Excuse me?

We removed that, she repeated.

I guess I've forgotten, I said. I felt my way toward an armchair, crashing my shin against a side table and sending a lamp clanging to the floor.

We removed that, she said a third time, somewhat stridently.

I believe you, I said. But this is not a matter of legal semantics. To reduce it to that is to exonerate yourself too easily.

I never promised you I could behave differently, she said. Thus there is no need for exoneration.

But that's monstrous, I pointed out.

Exactly, she replied, not without a self-pitying hint of regret. I could tell she was proud of this regret, the way a racist is proud of experiencing a hint of humanity toward a Pygmy. It made me want to hit her.

I heard her moving about. I heard her hands sliding over the furniture, I heard them opening drawers, I heard the silk as she slid her hands into the sleeves of her lined coat.

I'll be back, she said.

Where are you going?

I need time to think. I'll be back.

The door shut.

I kicked at the broken pieces of lamp on the floor. I heard my wife's boots going up the stairs, then a knock, the muffled thump of a wooden leg, the low sound of conversation.

Soon there was a knock on my door.

Come in, I said.

The sock foot thumped over the runner.

You told me so, I said.

I heard the sounds of lights being flicked on. My eyes swarmed red.

That's a foul business there on your face, my neighbor said.

I heard him running water in the kitchen. He returned and started scrubbing at my eyelids.

After my first eye was freed, it wouldn't stop crying. The water ran down my face, not in drips but in a torrent. I tasted it on my tongue and it was barely salty.

That's just the effect of the makeup, I explained.

My neighbor worked on my second eye.

She'll be back, I said. She simply needs time to adjust.

He made me tea. He told me that he'd settled my estate dispute, and that my brother had agreed to pay me the money he owed.

It took me days to get the glue off, even with repeated scrubbings with a loofah mitt; people stared at me on the street, perhaps believing I suffered from a disease that made my face turn translucent and slough off in dried bits.

This was, in part, why I failed to go to the hospital until I was so ill that daylight hurt me. My eyeballs burned and chafed beneath their dry lids. It's just a reaction to the glue, I told myself, to the stress of my wife's leaving me. It wasn't until too late that I discovered I'd contracted a virus, something I'd picked up in Borneo, at least that's what the doctor deduced, having never seen this particular sleeper mutation on the European continent. According to the doctor, the virus had lived in my system for years and was a cousin to leprosy. Blindness occurred in only the rarest of cases. He asked if I would be willing to visit with medical students; my disease, he claimed, was truly exceptional, and he gave me the incredible statistics, as if he expected me to share his wonder. He wrote me a prescription for a topical ointment, and said, I think you'll find that blindness will produce its own form of seeing. If I'd had eyes, this is what I would have done with them: I would have given him the foulest look imaginable, and then I would have cried them out.

My wife never came back.

Four

With Cyrus dead a second time, Bruno ordered Stephen to release some passengers.

Coincidentally, the police had regained interest in us; they'd
brought spotlights that cast the dimpled sand into a regular pattern of
shadow and light, like a snakeskin. The uniformed men stood in an
olive-green semicircle to the east of the plane, and although they were
not so close that I could see their eyes, I could make out mustaches
here and there in the lights, I could make out red cell-phones attached
to their belts, and guns strapped around their shoulders and torsos.

Stephen didn't say anything as he chose the passengers for release,
preferring, in his detached way, to punch the back of the headrest
of each lucky person. At the time his choices seemed random, not
conforming to any selection system I could divine. I was given cause
during my third semester at the Institute, however, to entertain the

possibility that Stephen's choices were far from haphazard. I had enrolled in a class taught by Director Smythes called "Trumps, Shills, and Antes." On the first day, Smythes walked into the Curtis Fishbeiner Lecture Hall, corduroy jacket held over his shoulder with one hooked, nicotined index finger, and broke his stride just long enough to dash the following command across the chalkboard:

RESPOND IN A REAL (READ: SELF-INTERESTED) WAY

"You are on a bus," Smythes said, assuming a back-and-forth strut before the pitted chalkboard, his corduroy pants producing a nappy inner wind as his thighs brushed against each other. "You are tired. You've just worked a twenty-hour shift at a salmon-canning factory." This drew appreciative laughs from my overachieving classmates. As if any of us would work at a canning factory, their laughs said. Within a week, we were all participants in a salmon-canning role-play in Juneau. "You drop, exhausted, into the one remaining seat, reserved for the elderly," said Smythes, "because it is midnight, and the elderly are asleep. The bus stops. An old, old woman clambers aboard. She is attractive, for an octogenarian, silvery hair in a bun, wearing a royal-blue cardigan that brings out the color of her eyes. She thanks the bus driver for being patient. She looks for a seat and, seeing none, grabs the nearest metal pole."

Smythes stopped, fingering his nascent goatee. "Thinking as a self-interested individual, do you surrender your precious seat to the sweet old lady? Raise your hands, please, if you want to surrender your seat."

A self-interested no-brainer, since we all recognized the inherent benefit in martyring ourselves for classy old ladies before a busful of strangers. All of us raised our hands, indicating a yes vote, except for one petite, self-lacerating girl from Osaka, who stared at her open notebook and turned a vicious shade of pink.

Smythes nodded in approval, then altered the scenario. "You're on a bus, et cetera, et cetera, stinking tired from canning salmon, et cetera, et cetera. This time, though, the old woman is hideously deformed by age, but well dressed, with a big diamond ring and a designer purse. Do you surrender your seat?"

The yes votes dropped by a tenth or so. The ugliest people in the class refused to offer their seats, while the attractive ones, the guilt-ridden pretty ones, raised their arms ramrod straight, without a moment's hesitation.

Smythes continued to tinker with the scene. "Now the old woman isn't only deformed by age, she's dressed in rags and smells bad." Only a third of us voted yes. "Now she behaves rudely toward the bus driver when she boards, she curses at you for sitting in the 'Reserved for Elderly' seat, she tries to spit at you but the saliva lands on her chin and stays there, gleaming under the fluorescent lights. The driver orders her off the bus, but she is stubborn and remains. The other riders look at the old woman with disdain. She is not of our kind, the looks say. She is barely a human being, and thus fails to qualify under the elderly-seating clause. She is a crone, a harpy, a dumb, drooling witch."

One person raised a hand—the girl from Osaka.

Smythes turned to the chalkboard and wrote the results. "Now," he said, massaging chalk absentmindedly into his goatee, "consider this: The spitting, smelly, badly dressed, hostile old woman is blind. She hobbles past the conductor and feels around for an empty seat. Finding it occupied, she strikes you with her cane. The bus hits a pothole and she topples over. Her skirt flies up and you catch a hideous glimpse of her old-lady legs sausaged into support hose, her twisted garters, her lumpy underpants."

"*She's hit you with her cane,*" Smythes reiterated. "She smells bad, she is a nasty shrew who hates everybody. Do you help her to her feet? Do you give her your seat?"

We stared at our desks. We spun our pencils around on their erasers. One by one we raised our hands. With reluctance, of course. We resented the old blind bitch, but we were going to give her our seat, even though we were deaf from twenty hours inside the incessant hum of an industrial canning plant and our legs were so tired the muscles had liquefied and our skin stank of antique salmon.

All of us raised our hands.

Smythes wrote on the board. INADVERTENT MANIPULATION: The ability to make people do the last thing they want by shaming their sense of humanity. Beneath this, he wrote, IDEAL HOSTAGE CLUSTER.

The ideal hostage cluster, Smythes informed us, should be assembled with an intense amount of care given to the potential for inadvertent manipulation. Old people were essential for this, as were children, the handicapped, the mentally retarded, pregnant women, family members. These "trumps" must be surrounded, however, by "shills," individuals susceptible to the manipulations afforded by public shame. Think of it as a dinner party, Smythes suggested, and of terrorists as a form of socialite. If the terrorist assembles his guests with sagacity, the party will run itself. He can sit back and let "humanity" dictate the behavior of his hostages; he need barely possess a gun.

So it was, in retrospect, unsurprising to recall the passengers who remained after Tom waved the chosen people through the doorway of the plane with his gun and ushered them down a rickety emergency gangway that folded out from beneath the threshold. The pregnant, vaguely malicious heiress Winnie Sunderland. Edith and I, sisters with a provably complicated relationship. Sadath Namboodiri, the arrogant and self-centered work-casual Indian man. Brita O'Kerrigan, a woman known to us at this point only as Ponyskin Vest, a needy, desperate woman who seemed capable of taking humane acts to a self-destructive level. For ballast's sake, Bruno also kept five Moroccan men, three Moroccan women, a pair of Germans, and an American ophthalmologist.

The released passengers (Team Volubilis, Justin, the stewardesses, the lederhosen boy and his mother among them) staggered down the gangway while Stephen arranged Cyrus's stiff body on a plastic orange first-aid stretcher. This proved rather difficult, as Cyrus had rigor mortised in a seated position and would not be flattened; his hands and feet beetled upward, his head and face still burlapped like the roots of a nursery tree. Stephen fastened the safety straps around Cyrus's middle and cinched the lower ones tight around his elevated ankles, so that he wouldn't roll from side to side. Stephen pushed the stretcher to Tom, who knelt at the door, trying to ease the stretcher down the gangway. He lost his grip just as the stretcher passed through parallel.

"Shit," Tom said.

The stretcher bumped down the gangway and hit the ground, its momentum carrying it ten feet or so over the sand dunes before it frictioned to a stop. The released passengers stared at the sled. Justin grabbed the reins, put them over his right shoulder, and started toward the sickle-shaped arrangement of green men, dragging Cyrus behind him. The passengers fell in line, following the depression the sled drudged through the sand. Once they were a safe distance from the plane, the police surrounded them and escorted them into vans.

A fuel truck appeared, as well as a jeep piled high with plastic tubs. Food, I prayed. Water. Thirty minutes later, our plane jerked to life, the engines revving to hysterical registers, the hydraulics groaning ominously as the wheels spun in the sand. We taxied for what felt to be five miles before the wheels extracted themselves from the shifting earth.

It was nine-fifteen p.m., Moroccan time.

Edith and I continued to be held hostage in first class; the other passengers spread themselves out along the empty rows of coach, unpacked their clothing and erected tents by slamming airplane blankets, jackets, djellabahs into the overhead compartments. Their intentional spacing was a secret code, like the human brain turned inside out, flattened and gridded. I was reminded of a paper our father had written about the flight distances of mites. Edith and I had misunderstood the term as *fright distance*. Fright distance, like flight distance, was a way to measure fear, even if the units changed. We measured the fright distance of Sister Nami when we hid behind a stone wall and tossed coins at her (five car lengths); of the mongoose, who hunted rats under our porch (two rice paddies); of our mother after a frosty row with our father (five scotches).

After we'd reached our cruising altitude, Tom distributed couscous, cold and clumped together, and round wheat bread the consistency of old moccasins. We each received one can of warm orange soda and one package of antiseptic towelettes. Stephen followed Tom and unbound Edith's wrists and mine so we could eat. He never bothered to bind them up again.

We tried to sleep, and succeeded. Although it seems counterintuitive and naive, I confess I was greatly relieved to be airborne again; it was nice to feel, albeit falsely, that we were going somewhere, and that there existed the potential for improvement. Stasis intensified my pangs of claustrophobia, and the monotony on the ground afforded little room for optimism.

Midway through the night, Tom poked me awake. Edith stirred beside me. Her eyes were crusted shut. She'd been crying steadily since she'd shot Cyrus, retreating into a self-pitying and semi-catatonic state.

She opened her eyes and watched with undisguised resentment as Tom hauled me toward the front of the plane.

"Pitcairn on the radio," he said, pushing me into the cockpit. Mjidd watched the controls while Aboul dozed.

Stephen squatted to one side, holding a can of orange soda. He nodded toward the headphones. "Make him give us a destination."

I slid the headphones around my neck. "Shouldn't *we* be deciding that?"

Stephen tapped the top of his soda can testily with his forefinger. "Leave the hijacking to us, okay?"

The lights in the cockpit were dim. We were high in the sky but the stars looked farther away than usual, feebler.

"Hello, Alice," Pitcairn said. English this time.

"Hello," I said. I was still asleep. I heard scratching through the headphones, different from static. A pencil, maybe.

"Hello?"

The pencil noises ceased. "I'm here. Sorry. Listen."

I didn't say anything.

"Alice? Are you there?"

"Yes, I'm just a little groggy."

"Let's try to wake up, shall we? We've got some important matters to discuss. I've estimated the damage projection, based on your hijackers' known criminal profile. As long as your sister keeps to her assigned seat, you shouldn't have anything to worry about."

"The known what?"

"I apologize. I'm in a different time zone."

"Really, I . . ."

"No, no, you're sleepy still, I can hear it in your voice."

This struck me as a very personal comment, perhaps because I had woken up next to a man so few times in my life. No man had called my voice sleepy, certainly not Miles, who slept until noon. We had never exchanged that groggy, half-dreaming morning babble. We had never shared that unprotected moment when you are allowed to say sweet, babyish things that are otherwise largely out of character.

"Why don't we talk about something less heady while you wake up?" Pitcairn suggested. "Why don't you tell me something about yourself?"

Stephen wasn't watching, but he was listening, while pulling out arm hairs with a certain detached interest. He would not tolerate this sort of chattiness, I feared. Or maybe he would. There was little predicting what would be tolerated in this hijacking.

"I am but the conduit," I reminded him.

"Yes, but . . ." Pitcairn said. "That does not preclude civilities. If we're going to work together, we should make at least a superficial attempt to get to know one another."

"Okay," I said.

A long pause.

"So?" he asked.

"So what do you want to know?"

"What do you want me to know, Alice?"

I rubbed my eyes. The stars. Inside, outside. Everywhere. Dizzying. "I'm too tired for this," I admitted.

Stephen stopped pruning himself long enough to pinch my thigh. "Make him give us a destination," he whispered.

"You could ask *me* a question, if you prefer," Pitcairn said.

"Fine." Eyeing Stephen.

"It can be personal, if you prefer. I'm not opposed to personal questions."

"That's good," I said.

"Because it's all about trust, Alice, you know what I mean?"

"Of course."

"It may seem obvious to you, but I find a lot of people in my line of work forget how important a role human trust plays in a situation like this. This is not a mere chess game, after all, no matter how much it resembles one. You are not a pawn."

"Right," I said.

"So," Pitcairn said. "Shoot."

I looked at Stephen. He had dug his gun from his waistband and was pointing it at my head. He yawned.

"Okay," I said, and paused. "Where should we land next?"

Stephen lowered his gun. He nodded approvingly.

Pitcairn didn't respond immediately. "That wasn't exactly what I had in mind."

"Huh?"

"I said, That wasn't exactly what I had in mind. I thought you might appreciate a little superficial get-to-know-you conversation, but apparently you're all business this evening."

"I . . ."

"Let's just cut to the chase here." Pitcairn's voice came and went. He was a smoker, maybe. I had a strange thought. It glimmered weakly in my head like one of those stars: *I'd make him quit.*

"What was that?" he asked.

"Huh?"

"Did you say something?"

"I . . . no."

Pitcairn exhaled. "So. Cutting right to the chase, now, Alice: Whose side are you on?"

"What?" What kind of negotiating was this? I was thoroughly bewildered, both by Pitcairn's chatty negotiation methods and by Stephen's apparent tolerance. It was just another example of the many ways in which the hijacking failed to live up to what I expected, even if my expectations were based primarily on fictions.

"You see, I *believed,* perhaps erroneously, that I could trust you. But perhaps I'm a bad judge of character. Perhaps, as they've been saying, I'm losing my touch." Pitcairn's voice was high now, fracturing.

Stephen glared at me. I made motions with my hands (patting motions, then circular ones), trying to indicate that I was getting to it and this was all part of my process.

"They say that, you know," Pitcairn continued. "I hear them whispering at the salad bar in the cafeteria. They say, *Time for the glue factory.* They say, *Every old dog has his old, old day.*"

Confusion on my end. What the hell was he talking about?

"But most importantly, Alice, we—you and I, that is—can't be working at cross-purposes."

"Of course not."

"If you're planning on pulling some idiotic attention-getting stunt like your sister, I need you to inform me of your poor intentions so that nobody else winds up dead on my goddamned dime."

I lost my patience. Why? I was tired of being goaded and kicked and manipulated by pretty much everybody, that's why. Terrorists. Negotiators. My own sister.

"Alice?"

"Don't be stupid," I said.

Long pause. "What did you say?"

"I said: *Don't be stupid.*"

Another long pause. That was it. I'd blown it. I'd pissed off the negotiator. He'd order Bruno to have me killed, or maybe Bruno would just decide to kill me, for the hell of it. Fuck. Fuck. Oh well. I was too tired, too hungry, too inexplicably giddy, to try to influence anyone in my favor.

I'd worked myself into a state of deep and insincere apathy when the texture of the silence changed. I can't explain this, but silence can have a texture.

"Our Alice doesn't tolerate fools," Pitcairn said. I could almost hear him grinning through the static.

My body deflated.

"She prefers not to," I said. "But she'll put up with anything in a pinch."

"That's exactly what Miles Keebler said."

"Pardon?"

"So what are you, Alice. A graduate student? A waitress?"

"As you apparently know, I dabble in both."

"I ate at the Tip Top, once. Early eighties, must have been. Back when I had my hair, or enough hair, at least, to drag through the German potatoes. I was doing a lecture at . . ."

"In the early eighties, I was still a kid."

He paused. "What does that have to do with anything?"

"You tell me."

"Nothing, as far as I can see."

I was still worried about Miles Fucking Keebler. "What did Miles tell you?"

"Miles is not the most reliable character. I wouldn't let anything he said bother you."

"He's reliably very weird," I said.

"Miles said you were the sort of girl his mother would have liked, if she hadn't died of lung cancer. Of course, he hated his mother. How were you in math?"

"Math?"

"Yes," he said.

"I enjoyed the parts of math that didn't have any numbers."

"I'm brilliantly good at math," Pitcairn said. "When I was in the navy, I worked air tower control on a carrier. There was no war. We were bored. My colleagues and I used to have contests to see who could fly the planes around the longest and land them with the least amount of fuel in the tanks."

"Did the pilots know?" I asked.

"I had them running on fumes as they coasted onto the carrier deck. Won every damned time, but never fully enjoyed my victories. I have trouble living in the moment."

"That's so . . . alarming," I said.

"It's science. It's numbers and gravity and air and aluminum. Nothing could be less alarming. And no, the pilots didn't know. I'll tell you what's alarming. Human beings are alarming. Speaking of which, why don't you tell me about your sister."

"She's getting married. Was getting married. I mean, I don't imagine we'll be done with this in time for her to be married when she's supposed to be."

Pitcairn clucked. "You have so little confidence in me." Then: "You're probably right."

"Her husband-to-be is a dyslexic formerly provincial Spaniard."

"Tell me something useful about her," Pitcairn said.

I considered this. But I was fake-considering. Whenever people want Edith explained to them, there is no more useful anecdote than the movie our father shot of us when we were living on the outskirts of Cairo, the summer before we moved to Mylandrum. He agreed to take us to a Bedouin encampment where a man dragged tourists around atop his camel and snapped Polaroids with a broken camera. The gray photos promised to turn into something recognizable, but never did.

The opening shot of "Camel Ride" featured white mountains,

onion-drab sky. My father panned down to the sand and up, past hooves and ankles and a pudendal bobble of brown flesh, a belly, then past two dusty left feet with Magic Markered blue toenails, two red leather sandals.

Close-up: Camel chewing cud, or whatever it is that camels chew.

Our father walks backward, revealing Edith and me seated on a pile of sheepskins and wool blankets, balanced on the camel's extreme hump.

I usually supply some context at this point in my telling. Something along the lines of: *Until the age of six, Edith exhibited a meekness that made her the least likely child any strange swathed Egyptian woman on a bus might pull onto her knee and sing to in Arabic. She carried a book with her, always, as protection against the neglect of others. She was sullen and smart and didn't cater to the frilly, prancing needs of adults as I did.*

Cut to: Camel walking. Its knees are all old rubber and arthritis. Crunch crunch crunch go the joints.

Boring now. Edith starts to read her book.

Two unexpected extras wander into the leftmost part of the frame. Egyptian women, carrying baskets of spun-wool yarn. I wave to the pair of them. They smile and chortle at me. They reach up and hand me a figure eight of yarn, thick and gray, which I wave at the camera with a victorious grin.

Edith watches the women walk away without so much as patting her on the knee. Our father manages a close-up. There is a new set to Edith's pretty mouth, a new resolve in the wrinkling and unwrinkling of her nose.

Boring now. Five minutes of boring camel ride. Ride ride ride. Boring boring boring.

Now, entering the leftmost part of the frame again, a second pair of Egyptian women. They carry baskets of grain that flies into their faces, forcing them to close their eyes as they trudge into the wind.

Close-up of Edith, beginning to wave. Close-up of her book,

hurtling toward the sand. Close-up of her torso, her unnatural smile. Her arm is long and unwieldy. She waves hello, aggressively, without the cloying sweetness that most girls her age have learned to adopt for even the least unreasonable request.

Close-up: The women, who do not see or hear her. Their eyes are closed tight, except when they occasionally look down to ensure they are not, by accident, stepping off the edge of a sandy dune.

Close-up: Me. Oblivious. Playing with my yarn. Tasting it. Ick. I sputter my lips, hang out my tongue.

Close-up: Edith. Edith stands up, teetering twelve feet above the sand on the hump of the camel. Her red sandals slip in the sheepskin. She almost loses her balance (close-up of her contorted, terrified face), but then digs in her heels, finds purchase in the dingy pile. Her body is stiff, it jerks in time to the camel's plodding steps. Just before she's tossed off, Edith lifts her hands above her head and dives, headfirst, into the desert.

Here I usually introduce a dramatic pregnancy by describing the following events that transpire off camera and into the future. As Edith is gliding through the air, as she strikes the ground headfirst, her body collapsing into a somersaulted heap of blond pigtails and clothing, the camel continues to amble at its knobby-kneed pace, its lips rubbering imaginary grass. The camel man snaps a photo of Edith's swan dive, yanks out the photo, peels off the paper, and waves it around, thrilled. It is this failed picture that causes the man, finally, to throw his stupid camera into the sand and stamp on it with his knock-off American jogging sneakers. It is this picture that causes him to shift careers, to become the very stonemason who, less than one year later, will steal our father's movie camera while remortaring our toilet.

But back to the film. Our father, the cameraman/scientist/hunter, finds himself faced with a difficult choice: to record the response of the child on the camel, or the response of the child on the ground. The viewer becomes acutely aware of his indecision as the camera makes queasy swings between me, sobbing into the sheepskin, and Edith, splayed out in the sand, her dress flown up to reveal her matching underwear.

Eventually, our father settles on the girl on the ground as his primary subject.

Close-up: Edith, who in and of herself is not a very interesting subject; but the response of the Egyptian women, it seems, wins our father over. They drop their baskets. One of them rearranges Edith's dress while the other smooths back her hair. The two women wail over my sister and talk to the sky.

The scientist focuses on his daughter's face while her consciousness slips around inside her. The hands of the Egyptian women are black against her cheek. They poke at her jaw, feeling for a rotted tooth or some soft way into her head so that she can be pulled back into the daylight. Finally, her eyelids flutter and part. The Egyptian women hoot; they pinch her cheeks and holler.

From the bottom right corner, a small hand, smudged with blue marker, invades the frame. (Off camera, I had been helped down from the camel by a strange man, a tourist with a tourist's new straw hat and bag, who quickly disappeared.)

The blue hand touches Edith with the confidence of the only one who ever touches her. Eyes wide open and the sun on her face, she pushes the hand away. The blue hand trembles, uncertain how to take this. The blue hand moves toward Edith. The blue hand stops. Withdraws.

The scientist stumbles backward in the sand for the wide shot. He trips, and for a second there is nothing but sky, a lung-shaped cloud, a fiery white shot of sun. But he steadies himself. And this is the frame composition, the final frame, before the film goes black: I am curled on my side next to my sister, clutching my yarn. She is stretched across the sand, her head in the lap of one of the Egyptian women. She stares into the sky, at the lung-shaped cloud, perhaps, unblinking, as if at last she has gained possession of the one thing she's been trying to steal from me all along.

I stopped talking. Pitcairn didn't say anything. I suspected he was gone.

"Hello?" I said.

"Hello."

"Well, so." I felt sweaty. I felt dirty.

"That's very enlightening, Alice," Pitcairn said. "You've told this story before, I take it. I'm ready to give you your destination now. Do you have a pencil?"

I tapped Stephen's foot. I made writing motions.

"This is very important, Alice," Pitcairn said. "You mustn't get this wrong."

"I won't get it wrong," I told him.

Pitcairn rattled off numbers, degrees. Landing coordinates. I wrote them down. He made me read them back to him three times.

I heard the click. I said, "Hello."

No answer.

My silence alerted Stephen that our conversation had concluded.

"So?" he asked.

I passed along the piece of paper. He struggled to focus his eyes on the coordinates.

I loitered in the galley before returning to my seat. The lights were low; everybody was sleeping, except for Stephen and Bruno. I searched through the metal drawers for a forgotten packet of pretzels. I found a towelette and scrubbed down my palms, my neck, my armpits. Pitcairn was right in observing that I'd recounted the plot of "Camel Ride" many times, so many times, in fact, that the original movie's importance had been superseded by that of my narrative. Edith and I fought over this, as each of us had a competing version. In hers, Edith fell off the camel, with no ulterior motive but to get away from me (I was pinching her, she claims).

What I typically didn't tell people about were the movies that followed "Camel Ride." These movies—what few our father shot that summer, before the camera was stolen by the camel man turned stonemason—document a rapid shift in power. In "Outdoor Bath," Edith is shown, glorious and water-dappled, as she forces my face under a corroded copper faucet that protrudes from a stone wall and spews a brown sewage; in "Birthday Dinner," I am requested to eat a roach which she has brought me as a present; in "Aunt Bea Visits from St. Paul," I am lured by Edith into a defunct quarry and, in order to be lifted free, forced to promise that I will tell Aunt Bea that she "stinks of old goat." There is no footage of this telling; the camera was nicked that afternoon. Briefly, the evening went as follows: I told Aunt Bea that she stunk of old goat, and she smacked me with the backside of a bejeweled hand, slicing open my cheek and requiring me to get three stitches at the local hospital, where Edith and I saw our first leper.

EDITH AND I were shaken awake just after dawn by the quick lurch and drop of the airplane.

"Holy," Edith said, peering out the window. It was the first word she'd uttered since she shot Cyrus.

We stabilized. I presumed it was just the usual turbulence, until it happened again—there was a measured, mechanical quality to the jerking, which did not feel like the irregular contours of weather.

Tom and Stephen ran forward to the cockpit. I pressed my face against the window. Colorless mountains stretched as far as every visible horizon. There was no landing area that I could see.

Aboul came over the loudspeaker and instructed all of us to take our seats and fasten our seat belts. Bruno, Tom, and Stephen strapped themselves into the first two rows.

I could see rocky peaks now, clearly enough to make out the blur of scrub bushes. I could see individual branches on individual bushes, skeletal traces of lichen on the rocks. We were so close that I could see the ants fleeing to hide in shelters provided by the corrugated rock.

We were going down.

I grabbed Edith's hand and we both watched, petrified, as the plane came within two feet (it seemed) of the peak. She screamed. I screamed. Seconds before the plane's underside scraped the rock, the ground dropped away with the nauseating surge of an ocean swell.

"Holy Christ," I said. Edith grabbed for an airsickness bag. In the center of the flat valley below I spied a tarmac—a little worse for wear, with deep fissures and drifts of white dust—but a tarmac nonetheless. An old air terminal deteriorated at one end, its windows mostly glassless, its tower initiating a slow, Pisa-like lean.

We struck the ground with the left wheel first, bounced skyward, then struck with the right wheel, bounced again, and settled into a wobbly coast along the uneven landing strip. The cabin lights flickered and the overhead compartments shimmied with an incongruous, fluid motion. We were still coasting when I heard the engines quietly expire, the fading whine as the turbines spun themselves still.

We were out of fuel.

I laughed. Pitcairn, the bastard. I didn't even mind that he'd almost killed us. I was too busy being impressed, and even a little starstruck.

Aboul turned off the seat-belt sign with a self-congratulatory *ding!* I could see the dusty approximation of a runway under all that colorless dirt. There was nothing green for miles.

It became clear, as the yellow-white day droned onward, that Pitcairn's strategy was to condemn us again to monotony, stasis, inertia. This was not difficult to accomplish at an abandoned airfield in the dry northwestern region of Kashmir, just across the Pakistani border. We waited and waited for the promised trucks to emerge with our supplies, but none did.

Just after dusk Stephen yelled, "He's coming." We looked out the left-hand windows to see long snowy tubes of headlights paralleling around the tarmac. The truck was small. Indeed, there was no fuel. A stunted man who spoke no discernible language unloaded some hasty packages at the bottom of the gangway and sped off into the dark. The packages contained warm boxes of sweet red punch and black licorice whips. Edith and I were asked to pass these frugal repasts to the people in coach. "But no fraternizing," Tom warned.

Edith worked the port aisle, I the starboard. People accepted the food from us greedily—because they were ravenous, I supposed, until I saw the look of mistrust on their bleary faces, noticed the subtle attempts they made not to touch our hands. No one looked me in the eye except for Work-Casual Indian Man, who winked at me when I handed him his licorice whip. Verne, who had preferred to hang out in the cockpit, now tagged along, whining at my heels. I felt his breath on my calves and, every once in a while, a hot slide of saliva.

I stopped by Winnie Sunderland's seat. She'd been asleep during my first pass. She was still asleep. I nudged her arm.

"Dinner," I announced, unlocking her tray table.

Winnie stared at the licorice, the box of punch, then offered her name and a flaccid hand.

"Sit down a minute," she demanded.

"I shouldn't," I said. I checked to see if Tom or Stephen was watching me. They were not.

"Aw, don't be such a goody-goody. One minute," she insisted. "Hello, doggy. Hello, sweet doggy." Winnie jaggled her manicured nails toward Verne, seated in the aisle, waiting for handouts. He sniffed her foodless fingers with appropriate caution. He lifted his nose and exhaled snobbily.

I sat. Up close, Winnie was an attractive enough girl, despite the swimmy, unpredictable, and slightly dumb quality to her gaze and the strategic splashes of herb tonic that made Verne sneeze. Her eyes, though, were too close to her temples; coupled with her domed stomach, from which her thin neck and head emerged, she resembled a mildly irked snapping turtle.

She struggled with her punch box.

"Here," I said. I freed the straw from its clear condom and jammed it through the foil hole.

Winnie sucked on the straw. Edith caught my eye from the opposing aisle and shook her head disapprovingly.

"So," I said. "When's your due date?"

Winnie lit up. "Are you a doctor?"

"A social worker."

"Do you carry a lot of prescription painkillers?"

"I . . . no."

"Too bad." Winnie's eyes half lidded. She was high as a kite. Probably had been the entire hijacking. Still, I could smell a manipulative opportunist a mile away. She might have given my sister a proper run for her money, had she not been so high.

"When's your due date?"

"Three weeks," she said.

"I didn't think women in your condition were supposed to fly. Anything special planned?" Her glossy hippie stylistics and bottomless cash flow suggested that she would subscribe to all measure of innovative gymnastic childbirth schemes. She would be hung from a bouncy harness with a hole at the bottom or splayed out on a beach at the exact latitude of the Tropic of Cancer or made to swim with bottlenose dolphins at the peak of her labor.

"Just a natural childbirth," she said.

"You'll make it home," I assured her, even though she seemed patently unconcerned with making it anywhere. "Next time I talk to the negotiator, I'll tell him you're not feeling so well."

"Some acts are beyond the intentions of good men." She massaged my wrist with her reptilian fingers. "As a social worker, I guess you don't take much stock in astrology."

"As a social worker, I don't take much stock in social work."

"I met an astrologer in Goa," she said. "She told me, 'You will die many miles from earth.' I puzzled for months over what she meant. How could one die many miles from earth? Unless one is an astronaut, of course."

"You could be on a boat in the middle of the ocean," I offered.

"But *earth*," Winnie said, irritated. "She said *earth*, very specifically, not *land. Earth*."

"Earth, I see." I thought: Isn't there a horoscopic watch group that regulates the imparting of that kind of morbidity?

"This same woman told my friend that she would *die behind the wheel*. Of course she gave up driving, never again drove a car. You know what happened?"

I shook my head.

"She was bending over to tie her shoe near a temple and a tourist bus backed up over her."

"Huh," I said. "Still, I don't think you can take these pronouncements too seriously."

Winnie nodded, but I could tell she disagreed with me.

"Can I ask you something?" she said.

"Of course." I prepared myself for the *Do you believe you might be reborn as a jaguar or a plastic spoon?* sort of question.

She paused, her pupils constricting.

"What?" I asked.

"I forgot," she said.

"I have to go, Winnie."

She gripped my hand again, firmer this time.

"Let me tell you about my mother. She was a real bitch."

"I don't doubt it."

"But nobody knows the real story," Winnie whined. "Everyone thinks they know about my life because they've read it in the papers, but it was so much worse than that."

I allowed her to hold me captive with her cold hand, her pleading eyes, her shifting skunky scent, as she told me about her neglectful upbringing. I took the opportunity to dig around in the seat pocket, in her batik satchel, searching for her pill stash. I found an empty canister of opiate painkillers from a pharmacy in Greenwich, Connecticut. I dug around in the cushion crease as Winnie talked. I came up with lots of crumbs, a hair elastic, four old euros, *et voilà*, two pills.

"Alice," she said, "are you listening to me?"

"I'm listening."

"Then you'll do it!"

"Do what?"

"If anything happens to me, Alice. Promise?"

"I'll promise nothing."

"But it's already in my will. You'll both be provided for."

"What will?"

"The astrologer told me I'd meet a savior far from earth. That wasn't how she phrased it exactly, she didn't use the word 'savior,' she used a less, well . . ." Winnie dissolved into a clatter of mean giggles. She was laughing at me, I thought.

"You're high, Winnie."

She sobered up enough to frown at me. "So?"

"So don't give anything away you might later regret."

She grinned. "Like a baby?"

I could see the silhouette of Tom and his gun. I tried to shake Winnie's hand from around my wrist. Her arm was rubbery and whipped about, but her grasp held firm, suctioned there.

"Give it back," I said. "I have to go."

"Will you? Alice? If I die many miles from earth?"

"I might be a pedophile, Winnie."

She blinked at me. She was having a rough time staying awake.

"I might have Munchausen by proxy."

"You remind me of my cousin Pammy," she said. "Pammy was a real joker. She died of a heroin overdose in Goa."

"Are you following in her footsteps?"

"I was," Winnie said. "But then I got pregnant. You can't very well overdose when you're pregnant."

"You very well can. It was nice that you didn't want to."

"I suppose."

"Who's the father?"

She wedged a pillow against the window. "Oh, Alice. Who cares?"

I patted her on the hand. "Not me," I said.

Winnie had already nodded off.

I returned to my seat, swiping a newspaper from Cyrus's former seat pocket en route. Edith was stretched out beneath a blanket, pretending to read the emergency procedures brochure.

"Aren't you popular," she said. "What did Winnie Sunderland want?"

I opened my palm. "The more appropriate question is, What did I get?"

Edith peered at the pills. "She's a junkie?"

"She's a spoiled fruitcake who's in a lot of 'pain.'"

Edith tried her best to act dismissive. She accepted her Winnie pill from my palm and put it into her diaphragm case and settled down again to sleep.

"You're sleeping too much," I warned her.

"And how do you suggest I better spend my time?"

"You could learn something about humanity."

Edith turned away from me.

I settled in with Cyrus's financial paper. Verne pushed his head into my lap and drooled over a pie chart showing the fourth-quarter earnings of a South African tech company. I tried to sleep, but was unable. It was the first night I'd slept in a grounded airplane. I hadn't realized how much, in such a short period, my sleep depended on being airborne, on that subconscious sense of flight. Earthbound I was sleepless, dreamless.

THE NEXT MORNING was excruciating, as anyone who has ever had candy and punch for dinner can attest. We suffered extreme intestinal discomfort, which made the lavatories more unspeakably filth-ridden, and tempers, whose foulness is always proportional to the decrepitude of a WC, began to fester. We curled up in our seats and waited for the true, dull beginnings of starvation to relieve us. Winnie was in the most amplified distress, and claimed to be unable to reach the lavatory without the assistance of Work-Casual Indian Man and Ponyskin Vest. She called out for me, but I pretended not to hear.

I was watching the sun rise between two mean peaks when Aboul poked his head through the cockpit doorway.

"Hello, Sussex lady," he said. "Pitcairn calling for you."

I hurried forward, but encountered Bruno blocking the entrance.

"Alice," he said. He stood closer to me than was comfortable. His head smelled bad, like an old sponge. "You're not proving very adept at your job."

I didn't answer.

"Are you? Maybe we chose badly when we chose you. Maybe we should get your sister on the radio."

I squinted at him. He was screwing with me, the jerk.

"Okay," I said.

"Okay?"

"Okay."

He sneered. "That's not very honest of you, Alice."

"Well."

"Well, what?"

"It's not very honest of you to try to manipulate me, is it?"

"That's *my* job," he said, "which I am doing very competently."

"But we're still stuck here, aren't we? I don't know if I'd start patting myself on the back just yet. I mean, *honestly.*"

He grabbed me by the blouse, misjudging the distance and jabbing me in the chest. He caught hold of the fabric and yanked me downward. I knocked my bottom lip on his knee as I fell. Blood pattered onto the carpet.

"Don't get cocky," Bruno warned. "It feels forced."

"About as forced as your interest in learning about humanity," I countered. "You're just a bully, and bullies don't tend to be interested in much more than humiliating people."

"Spare me the analysis. Just go in there and communicate to that man that I will kill someone—*I will kill someone, Alice*—if we don't have fuel before nightfall."

It took great restraint not to spit in his face, *Bullshit*. What Pitcairn had said was dead right. This guy stank of harmlessness.

He unfingered my blouse and felt his way to the lavatory. I ignored Aboul's inquisitive look as I stretched the headphones over my ears. Stephen was nowhere. Nobody watched me as I spoke to Pitcairn; nobody managed our interactions. I found this strange, but I was careful not to take liberties with my unusual freedoms—everything, if I was reading this situation correctly, was a potential trap that Bruno set, then waited for his victims to walk blithely into.

"Hey," I said.

"Hey," Pitcairn said. "How're things?"

"As bad as you hope they are."

He tsk-tsked. "You misunderstand me, Alice."

"Do I?"

"I'm doing my absolute best. This is a rather, well, unusual case. I probably don't have to tell you that."

"I'm finding it highly unusual."

"But even so," he said. Then he lowered his voice. "My job is on the line here."

"And?"

"I mean more than usual. My professional *reputation* is on the line here."

"Really."

"What if I told you that . . ."

"What? Told me what?"

"Nothing. I shouldn't have mentioned it."

"Told me what?"

Pitcairn sighed, as if to imply that I'd forced this out of him. "Things aren't as they appear, Alice."

"They rarely are."

"But I mean in this case. Nothing you've taken at face value has, well, much value."

"Meaning what?"

No response.

"Give me a break, Pitcairn."

"I'm asking you to be patient."

"I don't see that I have much of a choice," I said. "So what's the next move in this chess game? Your pawn wants to know."

Paper rustling.

"I want you to . . ." More rustling. ". . . I want you to tell him that I refuse to give him fuel unless he releases Winnie Sunderland."

"He won't do it," I said.

"I'm aware of that. We're going to throw him off, using what's called *false gambiting*."

"I don't care what it's called. You tell me too much, for a conduit. He said he's going to kill somebody."

"He won't," Pitcairn replied.

He stayed on the radio while I presented the offer to Bruno.

"He says fuck off," I reported back. "That's a quote."

"Excellent," Pitcairn said. "So next, I want you to tell him that I'll give him fuel if he . . . Hold on a second, Alice."

I heard Pitcairn saying, "Great, no, tell Patrice I'll meet her at nine, and get that file back from Phil, thanks, righto then."

"Hi there. Sorry."

"Business or pleasure?" I asked, thinking, *Patrice?* A Frenchwoman? He prefers French girls. With little brown bobs, brown sweaters, brown lipstick, chewed-up fingernails. I saw Patrice holding a cigarette between her snaggled digits, charming and girlish and prematurely world-weary, in the manner of all good Frenchwomen, God damn her.

"I wish. So here's the plan. Ready?"

I didn't answer.

"Tell him," Pitcairn began, "tell him he'll get his fuel if I'm allowed to meet with one of his associates."

"Fine. Which one?"

Silence.

"Pitcairn?"

Throat-clearing.

"Actually, you."

My heart galumphed. "I'm not one of his associates."

"Don't ask him now. We need to kill a little time."

"Okay," I said. Positively glowed the word.

"Why don't you tell me about— Oops. Sorry again."

This time Pitcairn covered the microphone on his end. I heard curt, muffled noises, but could make out no words.

"I'm back. So what haven't we gone over, Alice? I've got your file in front of me here. . . ."

"So you keep reminding me."

"Why did you become a social worker?"

I cleared my throat. "It's somewhat debatable that I *am* a social worker."

"Let me rephrase: Why did you choose to pursue social work? Following in your mother's footsteps?"

"My mother?"

"It's in the file, Alice."

"What *file?*"

"You have a file. Everyone has a file. It's nothing to get paranoid about."

"Maybe not, but I don't see why I should assist in its compilation."

"You'd prefer I get my information from unreliable sources like Miles?"

"Then at least you'd get to wonder about me."

"Oh, Alice. If only you knew how much I wondered."

And so, of course, I told him everything he wanted to know about me. What was the harm in it? The sun was rising, the white dust was diamondy, the empty airstrip and the colorless mountains filled with the certain hopeful warmth and familiarity that a blooming infatuation can inject into even the most homely, rutted landscape.

Our mother, I informed him, wasn't a social worker, per se. She was an activist against world overpopulation. Pitcairn inquired why this, why world overpopulation, and I could state only that I couldn't say without making crude guesses about her own ambivalent relationship to motherhood.

Edith and I were ten and nine, respectively, when our mother started to volunteer at the Mylandrum Birth Control Clinic. Run by a general practitioner named Dr. Miswo, the clinic was a cinder-block box, its exterior painted the same candy pink as the hollow plaster uterus Dr. Miswo used to teach the local girls about the urn-shaped organ that was the source of all their troubles. He let them hold the uterus in their hands, hoping to inspire their disgust, but most of them cradled it like a newborn as he piled his handwritten pamphlets in front of them. The plaster uterus was part of a larger model of the female reproductive system, many of whose removable pieces had been lost or co-opted for other purposes, such as the ovaries, which had been painted white to serve as sheep outside a mini-manger erected every Christmas at the Catholic missionary academy.

Our mother rode her bike to the clinic because we had only one car, a fusty '57 Peugeot that a French entomologist had donated to the university after he caught his wife cheating on him in it. Our mother helped Dr. Miswo leaflet the outlying villages, but soon learned that his pamphlets were incomprehensible to the majority of women; they were wetted down and employed as nappies, they were used to wrap gristled leftovers, but they were scarcely ever read. She spoke passionately to Dr. Miswo—a stringy, fatigued bachelor who possessed an impotence of will she found both ironic and enraging—about the need to reach the illiterate masses. He would say, "I agree with you, of course,

Agnes," removing his glasses to blur her chattering form while gently gnawing the writing bump on his right middle finger.

With Dr. Miswo's express disapproval, our mother appointed herself the clinic's first director of theatrics, and set about raising funds for a summer series of outdoor plays to be performed in the clinic's backyard, the site of the doctor's failed medicinal herb garden, now nothing but a weed patch littered with forgotten gardening tools and soda cans tossed from over the fence. Our mother called it the Theater of Discouragement, and hired a man with a rickshaw to drive her around to publicize that evening's performance with a megaphone during the hottest hours of the day, when she knew people were napping and fornicating.

Her early productions were one-woman shows; she played three or four characters, grabbing a hat, a pitchfork, a rattle, some prop to signify each lightning-quick thespian shift. But the people didn't understand her plays, which were in English, and which frequently involved long, ranting soliloquies from a character called the Unborn. She complained of her failed efforts one evening over a dinner of canned beef curry and instant potatoes. The audiences had been waning, and Dr. Miswo was growing unpleasantly smug.

"It's simple, Agnes," our father said, chewing, as he always did, with his mouth wide open; we could see food flinging between his molars.

"Close your mouth, Harold," she told him.

"You have to tell them a story they already know," he said, ignoring her. "Nothing has any weight unless it's happened before. Why do you think people wait in line to see the Mona Lisa? Because it's a great painting? Because they've seen it *before*. Why do people keep rewriting the Greek myths? Because people don't like new things. People don't want to be surprised. They want to hear the same story. Tell them the same story and they'll listen."

"What the hell do you know about theater, Harold. You barely finished college," accused our mother, who had entirely failed to finish college.

Less than a week later, she had Edith and me wrapped in sheets, acting in her reworked version of *Medea* in the clinic backyard.

"Who's Medea?" Edith asked.

"You know who Medea is," I whispered. Our combined grade had just read Euripides in summary form at school.

Edith elbowed me and whispered back, "I want to hear what she says."

"A temperamental Greek lady who chopped up her children because she didn't get what she wanted in the divorce settlement," our mother explained.

Dr. Miswo kept a suspicious eye on us from his office window.

Our mother tore large strands of leaky blue crepe paper, meant to be water, and taped them to the stage floor. She'd taken her bedroom fan and placed it on a stool in the wings; she hoped it would blow the blue strands sideways to approximate a storm.

"If these people can't read or understand English, Mom, its doubtful they'll be familiar with *Medea*," I pointed out. I wanted to go home. I was sweating. Edith was sweating. The sheets were wrapped around our loden-green school uniforms, which were made, inexplicably, of a lightweight wool. Wool breathes, we were told by the school principal, even though half the girls in our school passed out in the lunchroom from heatstroke every spring. The green helped us blend in with the landscape. We were all but invisible when we crossed the rice paddies.

Our mother brushed her hair away from her perspiring face, leaving two blue streaks across her cheek. She turned on the fan to examine the effect. The crepe paper wriggled like Medusa hair; one by one the strands ripped free of the floor, floating into the empty audience pit. The fan fell off the stool, and the vibration caused the boat she had erected out of Dr. Miswo's medical journals to topple over.

She sighed and put her blue hands on her hips. "Alice, sweetie, every culture can appreciate a good infanticide yarn."

As the crowds later indicated, she was right. The play's summarizing title, which Dr. Miswo translated into Sasak, was *We Were Poor, He*

Left Me, and He Made Me Kill Our Baby. Dr. Miswo's herb garden had
never seen such fertile activity. Our mother played Medea, Edith the
scurrilous Jason, and I their child of indiscriminate sex, "Our Baby."
After detailing their considerable financial woes, as well as his love of a
young woman whose "quiet womb was not a wild rumpus," the script
called for Jason to "hit" Medea, an act of convincing injury accomplished by his taking a far-off swing while Our Baby, backstage, slogged
an upturned cast-iron pan with Dr. Miswo's broken stethoscope. After
leaving Jason, Medea "slaughtered" Our Baby with a knife—in fact, a
stretch of bendy medical pipe—while Jason, backstage, hacked away at
a gourd. As she sailed away in her sturdy medical-journal boat, Medea
held up Dr. Miswo's plaster uterus and delivered this bulkily metaphored
soliloquy:

> *O womb, ye foulest funereal urn,*
> *may you teem with corpse dust instead of baby's breath.*
> *You are no better than a cricket cage*
> *where I trap the hoary-winged locusts,*
> *a plague of fertility*
> *inseminated by this penniless marriage.*
> *But nothing can grow in you now,*
> *ye blighted vessel,*
> *I rip you from my body*
> *with my own murdering fingers.*
> *This is not another death I perform,*
> *but a wise pruning*
> *of these dead-headed roses*
> *that threaten to topple me*
> *in the slightest wind.*

Despite the fact that no one understood what our mother was saying, you could hear the whoops as far as our house in the rice paddies,
our father later told us. While Edith and my mother took numerous

bows, I walked among the crowd with the hollow plaster uterus, collecting coins. As was our postproduction habit, we would take the womb to a nearby pub so our mother could have a celebratory whiskey. She would buy drinks for everyone, she would give money to women she suspected were prostitutes and beg them to have their tubes tied. She was a good mother when she was drunk, if only because she liked to hug us then. Normally we smelled too terribly of sour socks and little-girl sweat, but on these nights she didn't seem to mind. She'd nuzzle our heads into her lily-of-the-valley neck; the white-flower stink so saturated her skin that it gave me a raging headache, which I nonetheless enjoyed. By the time our father came to fetch us in the Peugeot, the womb was always empty.

WHEN I RETURNED to my seat, Edith was crying. She rubbed her eyes with a blanket.

"Don't," I said. "You're going to make it worse." She had yet to say one word about Cyrus, and I certainly didn't plan on bringing him up.

"Are we ever leaving this hellhole?" she asked.

I shrugged. I decided against telling her that I was scheduled to meet Pitcairn. She seemed too upset already by my semi-favored status among the hijackers.

"I've really fucked up, Alice, haven't I?"

It wasn't clear what she was referring to. The Cyrus incident? "Camel Ride"? Her sluttish comportment as a so-called adult?

"Try not to think about it," I said, patting her knee. "Confrontation is overrated. I support denial in certain extenuating circumstances, for which this certainly qualifies."

"But he looked a little bit like Dad, didn't you think?" she sniveled.

"Who?"

"Cyrus." She put her head in her hands.

"He didn't look anything like Dad. Maybe you wished he looked like Dad."

She lifted her head, scowled. "Don't analyze me, Alice. It's patronizing."

"But he didn't look anything like Dad."

"That's your *opinion.*"

I opened the in-flight magazine, which I'd already read two hundred times. "I think we both need to lie low and wait for this thing to resolve itself." I started the crossword again. *Pretend you don't know German Death Attraction, Minor Avon Scribe, Yogurt Sauce to Gandhi.*

Edith sniffled. "But . . ."

"But what?"

"But I was supposed to be married today," she wailed.

She didn't have a tissue. I let her blow her nose on the corner of my blouse.

I didn't say, peering at my watch, that we were only hours from the scheduled reception; soon the belly dancers Edith had hired would be blubbering their bared stomachs around the stone fountain, soon the table beneath the red silk wedding tent would be full of dates and olives and bottles of undrinkable Moroccan champagne, soon Edith would be, for the first time in her life, wearing a thong. I imagined her clinging to X's arm, smiling that crazy bride's smile that is always a thin mask against some kind of mixed-up sobbing. I imagined our mother trying for the fortieth time to aggressively befriend our father's second wife; the larger Antidote beating the smaller one over the head with a letter opener the size of a fire axe; my father in his cheap professor's suit standing in the middle of a dry field with a martini, listening for maimed crickets. I imagined myself—as I had imagined myself since Edith announced she was engaged—looking around at the foreign people, the people who smelled bad or just wrong and unlived-in. I imagined the brilliant cloudlessness of the day turning oppressive and bleak, as it does when isolation descends with the weight of happiness upon the forehead. Now this image felt outdated and self-pitying. Now I saw myself feeling happy for my sister, or at least indifferent to her so-called success. I didn't feel abandoned, because I had brought a date to her wedding. Pitcairn. He was off in that dry field, talking with my father, both of them with their hands in their pockets, staring at their shoes.

I searched around for something comforting to offer. "Look on the bright side," I said, gesturing toward her eyes. "It's sort of fortunate you're not getting married today."

This made her cry harder. "Maybe I don't ever want to get married," she gurgled. "How long have I known him? Nine months? Ten? What can you know of a person in nine months?"

"Sometimes more than you can know in ten years, depending on the person."

"I was despondent when I said yes," she said. "I'd just read an article about decreasing fertility in American women. I'd just spent another Sunday alone, watching couples walking home from brunch with the paper."

"Sometimes we're most honest in those moments."

"Sometimes we're just more desperate."

"But you love him," I said.

She shrugged. "I love him *fine*."

"That would be enough for some people."

"But is it enough for me?"

"It might be," I said. "If so, that's nothing to be ashamed of. Look at the women in Japan."

Edith leaned back against her headrest. "I don't know the first thing about women in Japan, as you're well aware."

"The women in Japan," I told her, "marry as a business arrangement. They never vacation with their husbands. They don't look to them for love or even companionship. Thus they are hardly ever disappointed. At least that's what I've read."

"I couldn't care less about disappointment. Disappointment is a Western cultural necessity. What I'm talking about is erotics."

"Oh," I said.

"Why do you think they chose you to speak to Pitcairn?"

"Because I speak Sasak."

"You hardly do. You really hardly speak Sasak."

This was true.

"It's because I'm betrothed. Hence: I'm no longer of erotic import. Marriage neuters a woman. I might as well have my tits lopped off."

I frowned. "That doesn't really stand to figure."

"Of course it does. How do you figure that you've been chosen, for once, that you're the chosen one?"

Chosen for what? I wanted to ask. Chosen to be kicked in the ribs, to be potentially shot in the head because of a cowardly boy who was the spitting image of Hal Pipkin?

"This might be one of those 'careful what you wish for' moments," I responded.

Edith snuffled into her sleeve. She found her diaphragm case and popped it open, tilted it back and forth to sort through the pills, the earrings. She set the case in her lap, extracted a big blue allergy pill, and swallowed it dry. Then she withdrew her engagement ring. The one she'd never worn. She rubbed the diamonds on her skirt and fitted the ring over her thumbnail.

"It's sort of pretty, don't you think?" she asked noncommittally.

I nodded. It was absolutely pretty.

"I think it makes my hand look kind of sexy."

She pressed her hand against the folded-up tray table. She had beautiful hands, muscular and lithe.

"So what's he like?" she asked.

"Who?"

"Pitcairn."

I thought about this. "He's a bit like Dad."

"You *wish* he was like Dad."

I ignored her. "In the way he asks questions. Like he's just collecting data."

Edith nodded. "And when are we getting out of here?"

"Soon," I said. "He keeps telling me not to be scared."

"That's just protocol," Edith replied.

"He's a little insecure," I said.

"He's arrogant, you mean."

"I think he honestly impresses himself, but fails to impress anyone else. This confuses him."

"He sounds like an idiot. Which means we're not getting off this plane anytime soon."

As she said this, I realized, *Yes,* or rather, *No, we're not getting off this plane anytime soon.* Or perhaps I should say, I hoped, *Please, no, don't let us off this plane.* There was a warming area in my chest the size of a plum pit when I talked about Pitcairn. Maybe it was just because he made me feel important. Or maybe it was something else altogether.

Edith put her diaphragm case away. But not the ring. The ring she moved from her thumb to her forefinger. She wriggled it around beneath the overhead light, shooting sparks around the cabin.

"I miss him," she said unconvincingly. She tried it again. "I *really* miss him."

"At least there's one good thing that's come of this," I answered, settling down for a nap.

She blinked at me, miserable yet expectant.

I touched her ring. "There's nothing like a hijacking to make you put a finger on the things that really matter."

Edith fell back to whimpering. I let her.

Winnie's
Shame

I GREW UP outside Greenwich, Connecticut, on an old onion farm, with a mother who was always sick. When she was a girl, a doctor diagnosed her with a rare form of epilepsy, triggered by smells; he gave her pills that made her fat and sad. In the midst of a depression she decided to join a Buddhist monastery, where she learned to shut off the world without the help of medications or nose plugs. After my sister and I were born, however, her sickness returned, and we were never allowed to cuddle with her because we smelled too strong.

In hopes of fixing the problem, my mother consulted a Tibetan seer, who told her in his oblique seer way that *meat makes you odorless to the enemy.* My sister and I were put on a strict, meat-only diet. My sister, who had a tendency to take things too far, claimed that meat made her want to kill things. Instead of playing house, dolls, hopscotch, she practiced trapping small animals in our backyard. I followed her as she slip-noosed rats, squirrels, chipmunks, then skinned them and fed them to the neighbor's beagle. During her teenage years, while her hormones were surging, she moved on to bigger prey. Stray cats. Beavers. The day she decided to kill the neighbor's beagle, I ran behind her, arm levered against my joggling breasts (the seer claimed that brassieres caused cancer), begging her not to kill the beagle. She killed it anyway, crushing its skull with a spade. She dared me to say something to our mother. I never did.

If my sister and I didn't get along, it was probably because we had different fathers. I had never met my father, but I had seen his certified file from the sperm bank. He was a white male of mixed Irish and German parentage, aged twenty-two at the time of his donation. He was pursuing a mail-order proficiency degree in boat building from a distantly located technical college; according to his application, he resided in rural Nebraska. He had written about himself, in the four-line space denoted for a personal statement, "I am rarely sick and when I am an aspirin suffices. My palate can withstand very spicy foods. I have survived a January night in the Nebraska wilderness without a sleeping bag or frankly hope." I asked my mother why his application had seemed promising to her, and she said that she was touched by his pursuit of boats in a landscape without water, and his willingness to admit that he was occasionally without hope.

We left home, my sister and I, to attend a small rural college in Maine. During my second year, I left the dorm and moved into a vegetarian cooperative. I consumed lettuce, carrots, pears, onions. I voided great tracts of my childhood through my stimulated intestines; it was popular, at the cooperative, to receive ocean colonics at a nearby health spa, and I allowed a thin German woman to pump me full of the Atlantic while I lay on my stomach under a recycled-paper blanket. My life changed. Our mother could smell my obvious self across three states. She sent me a typed note on her business stationery that said: *An odorless girl is a winning girl.* When a shipment of shiny brassieres I ordered was mailed to her address, she sent me a postcard along with the forwarded package. The card said: *Think to succeed.* Beneath her handwriting were little pencil drawings: a girl in a nightgown choking a burglar with her brassiere; a girl shooting an arrow with a bow made from her brassiere; a girl employing her brassiere—one arm loop knotted to an apple tree branch—to swing over a crevasse. She also sent me a box of beef jerky. She taped letters from her great-grandmother's scrimshaw Scrabble set on top of the box—*Eat and be quiet.*

At or around this time, my mother used her considerable inheritance to start her own perfume company. Her perfumes smelled like a glass of very cold water, and they became the brilliant centerpiece for a certain minimalist fashion movement that had recently caught on in Europe. Soon she was also writing diet books that taught people how to inhibit their own natural smells, and at the urging of her seer (now PR consultant), she founded a survival skills camp for girls from the suburbs. She turned our backyard into a campground, and was photographed in a red suit for a business weekly, standing at dusk before the lit-up tents.

She ceased writing to me at all.

After college, my sister purchased an organic farm in Iowa and I moved to Rhode Island. I joined an all-girls urban housing cooperative on the eighth floor of a corporate low-rise with a plastic banner across its lobby that said "Retail Space Available." My co-op mates and I cooked vegetables together on a chain of hot plates, spread out along a lengthy conference table. We slept in office cubicles, our futons tucked beneath the desks. We each had our own telephone with six different lines, and upholstered bulletin-board walls.

I got a job at an advertising firm. My supervisor was a man whose specialized niche was the mass deodorizing of American women. My mother was his personal hero. For practice, he gave me photographs of women in stressful situations: a woman jiggling a crying baby on her hip while giving a talk before an auditorium full of frowning doctors; a woman construction worker who has just discovered that her co-worker has mangled his own foot with a jackhammer; a solo woman pilot whose plane, its tail section ablaze, is about to crash into the sea. I stared at these photos for weeks and could not think of a single slogan. I realized that I was not a creative woman, merely a strangely raised woman, and that exposing one's children to exceptional situations will not protect them from mediocrity.

I asked to be excused for a creative replenishment day. When I returned to the office, I brought my slogan for submission: *An odorless girl is a winning girl.*

I was promoted to write copy for a campaign advertising a new brassiere that inflated to four different cup sizes. I was given the same three photographs—the medical lecturer, the construction worker, the pilot—because our firm believed in the subconscious power of repetition. I wrote *Think to succeed,* and on my computer manipulated the photos so that the lecturer held a baby with a brassiere gag, the construction worker was applying a brassiere tourniquet to her injured co-worker's leg, the pilot had inflated her brassiere to the supersized option to use as a balloon to keep her plummeting plane aloft.

I was promoted again, and given the firm's prestigious Mank Award, bestowed biannually on the associate who best exemplified the forthright, pragmatic ideals set forth by the firm's founder, Alford T. Mank. I was given a year off to travel and, as my supervisor suggested, "find new markets." But I continually postponed my flight to Cairo. I stayed in my cubicle in the co-op and fingered the scrimshaw letters spelling *Eat and be quiet,* rearranging them to yield *A quaint bee Ted.* I started eating meat again. I ate cold kielbasas under my cubicle desk, because cooked meat was forbidden in the co-op. I gnashed through dozens of kielbasas at a time and stashed the wet plastic packets down the mail slot between the elevators.

I decided it was time to find my father.

This was a mistake, perhaps. But I was starting to suspect I was bound to be a failure, and that it must be his fault. I wanted to face my future squarely, because after you think you don't need them anymore, your parents still serve the useful purpose of mapping the future trajectory of your decline.

My father, Theodore Hummelman, was easy to locate through the matriculation records at the boat-building school. He owed the school money, the snippy bursar informed me, which I paid with a credit card in exchange for his address. He lived in Nebraska and was, I learned, a poet. I called and pretended I was a journalist doing an article on emerging poets of the Nebraskas. We arranged a meeting date.

He answered his door in a flannel bathrobe, holding an unopened can of diet cola.

Ted, he said, hand outstretched, cola can clenched in his armpit.

A quaint bee, Ted, I thought.

He apologized and quoted himself as he ushered me into a sitting room with flowered wingbacks and crocheted mantel hangings:

> *a man is only as naked as his next meal*
> *and yet the spring peas are too innocent to flavor*
> *the broth of his regret*

I'm working on a series of poems based on the Fannie Farmer cookbook, he said, offering me a cigarette. I declined. A cat crawled into his lap and whet its claws on the stringy arms of a wingback.

How interesting, I said. I pulled out a notebook and feigned an experimental shorthand.

Tell me more about yourself. Do you have a wife?

I don't care for women, he said. Although I have written a series of poems about my mother called *Hanging by Apron Strings*. It's also a passing critique of capital punishment.

You are politically active, I observed.

Hardly, he said. I haven't voted in thirty years. I haven't paid taxes since before the second-to-last war.

I was told you once had an interest in building boats, I said.

He coughed and said, That was my brother you must be thinking of.
You have a brother? I closed my notebook.

He looked afraid. No, he said. No, that was me who wanted to
build boats. Because I cannot swim.

Ah, I said, reopening the notebook.

You're not a bill collector, are you? he asked.

I shook my head.

Because if you are, there is a disability act which excuses my inability to pay for a water-related degree. You'll find it under the flota-
tion failure clause.

I said I'm not a bill collector.

He settled back into his chair. Good, he said. And then:

is it you
noose lover of the underdone?
everything must retain its crunch
even the boy's neck
especially the boy's neck

How evocative, I said.

You didn't know my mother. She was not an evocative woman. I
have made her evocative. I have made her unimaginative neglect into
something spectacularly evocative. That is the role of the artist.

But how do you feel about hope? I asked.

Hope?

Hope.

He scratched his head and said, Good question. You hungry? He
pushed the cat off his lap. A microwave bleeped and hummed in the
kitchen. The smell of cheese filled the house.

He returned carrying a plate on which was balanced a plastic pan
of lasagna. He rearranged himself in his chair.

Hope, he said, blowing on an oozing forkful of white. I know as a
poet I'm supposed to disagree with it.

So you're not a hopeful man.

Is this for the article? he asked.

I scribbled on my paper. I'd forgotten to scribble. Yes, I said.

What kind of distribution? he asked.

Mainly rural, I said. Rural with some lakeside distribution.

Okay then. I am an immensely hopeful poet.

Really? I was disappointed.

I am an immensely hopeful poet. I am hopeful for the future.

But in the past?

In the past, I was hopeful for the future, which is now, in which I am also hopeful. Hope gets you up in the morning. Hope gets the job done.

Right, I said, thinking how upset my mother would be. If she hadn't already forgotten me, she would do so after hearing that the man who produced the sperm that subsequently produced her daughter was not a survivor. He would wander into tall reeds and be eaten by a horned, tufted boar. I would be condemned to pass along this hopeful foolishness in my genes, creating weaker and weaker versions of my already weak self.

Thank you for your time, I said to the man. He smelled terrible, of fake food. I did not want to shake his hand.

I drove through the bland heart of Nebraska and stopped, when the sun set, at a steak restaurant. I passed up the stuffed potato and the free salad bar. I ate three T-bones wrapped in bacon. I checked into a hotel room and washed myself with water, only water. I threw my brassiere in the trash. I turned on the TV and saw my own advertisement, *Think to succeed,* with the image of the construction worker applying the tourniquet to the leg of her injured colleague, and I rescued the bra from the trashcan. I tied it around my neck and hung the arm loops from the shower nozzle. This was not a serious attempt to take my life. You should not confuse this with a serious desire to stop existing. This is what I told my therapist at the hospital in Connecticut.

This was just an experiment. This was just a way to cut my losses and approximate a fresh start.

After my release from the hospital, I returned to my mother's house in Connecticut to convalesce. I steered clear of the girls in the backyard, because they were never the same girls week to week. My mother was very affectionate with these strangers, rumpling their permed hair and visiting their tents at night. She had conquered her sensitivity problem with everyone except me; when I was around, she kept her distance, she pressed her nose against her wrist to smell the reassuring nothing of her odorless perfume.

One morning I found my mother unconscious on the back lawn, one side of her face sliding over her cheekbones. A stroke. She wouldn't let me call an ambulance because she didn't believe in Western medicine. She wouldn't let me feed the girls in the tents, because she was scared I would upset them. She was behaving in a highly irrational manner, so I e-mailed my sister on her organic farm and said: *You must come home.* Downstairs, I caught one of the girls trying to order a pizza on the den phone, and chased her back into the yard. She sobbed that she was hungry. I reminded her that this was survival skills camp, and that there were no goddamned pizzas in the wilderness. My mother had spoiled these girls, with all her hugging and visiting them at night. They were more helpless than when they'd arrived.

My sister appeared the next day and filled the house with the stink of seedlings and manure. She took one look at our mother—laid out on her antique bed—and said, She's history. Our mother glowered at her with her one good eye and said through her crooked sliding mouth, I always knew you'd be the failure. I got you from my third-choice donor.

My sister didn't reply. She strode into the backyard and marched between the tents, screaming, *Come out, you mewling pussies.* The girls crawled out of their tents, where they'd been hiding. Nobody had fed them in almost two days.

My mother heard the commotion downstairs. You must make your sister leave, she whimpered. She's ruining everything. I ran outside to hush up my sister. The girls cowered inside their tents, refusing to come out. My sister scoffed and walked deeper into the backyard to check her old traps. She returned holding two handfuls of squirrels by their tails.

The girls in the tents watched my sister as she killed and skinned the squirrels and started a fire in the outdoor cooking pit. Timidly, they emerged. They circled the blaze.

Mom wants you to leave, I said.

My sister said, You're a moron, Winnie, you've always been a moron.

The girls let loose a few nervous titters.

I'm not a moron, I said.

She laughed and turned her stick, on which an animal was impaled, anus to eyebrow; its little forearms clenched as she thrust the stick over the fire.

You'd be less than a moron if it wasn't for me, she said.

That's true, I said. That's true for a lot of people.

They'd be morons if it wasn't for me?

A lot of people would be morons if it wasn't for other people. The world is a web of interconnected dependencies, I said.

My sister grinned. I swear you're some form of retarded.

The girls reddened and stared at their moccasins. I heard their stomachs growling.

One of the girls, a girl with pretty hair and skinny arms, whined, We're hungry.

My sister grinned at her. I wonder how hungry you are, she said. Will you cut off your own hair for food? Will you allow me to hang you from a tree branch by your nipples? Will you jump off a bridge? Will you kill your own mother?

The girls trembled and looked at me. I shook my head to imply, She's joking, ladies. But in truth I couldn't be sure. My sister was full of a record-breaking kind of hatred.

The girls watched as she spitted and seared every squirrel she'd caught. The scent of cooked meat made a few of the girls weep. My sister laid the food on the ground in a neat pile before her feet. I stepped outside the circle but nobody noticed; the girls were prone before my sister, gnawing on bones.

I drove to the police station and, employing a purposeful obliqueness, told the officers there that we'd been taken over. I followed the squad car back. The police, their nightsticks resting on their forearms, wandered through the clusters of girls weeping on the lawn. They found my mother, dead. There was a pillow over her head. She'd been suffocated. My sister told the police that the hungry girls had done it. They were arraigned and brought to a detention center. My sister flew back to her farm in her private plane, and I haven't seen her since.

The funeral was attended by nearly five hundred people, plus a documentary film crew and a handful of Buddhist monks. The mayor of Greenwich's wife sang a very beautiful hymn, and the monks chanted. At the film crew's request, I lingered by my mother's casket after the nearly five hundred people and the monks had departed for the reception. The cameraman said, Let's see some grief here, lady. In the producer's opinion, there was not enough grief in his movie. He turned on his lights and the camera made a thunking, whirring noise. He suggested I lift my mother's stiff hand and hold it to my nose. Her wrist smelled vaguely of embalming fluid, if she smelled of anything. I tried and tried to weep for her beneath the bright camera lights, but her odorless body recalled nothing gone to me.

Five

BRUNO, contrary to my expectations, kept his promise and allowed me to leave the plane in order to meet Pitcairn.

It was late morning. Verne and I stood at the top of the metal gangway, listening to the wind frittering the sand over the tarmac. Overhead, the sky was tan-colored, the sun straining from behind a thin layer of clouds. There were no birds here. There were no flies. I thought I saw a scorpion, but it turned out to be a flattened piece of copper wire, curled up at the end.

"*Hello!*" I called out. "*Yayayayayayayay.*" No echo. None at all. I called out, "*Yeep yeep yeep!*" and heard nothing in return. Even the wind had halted.

This land was dead.

I hardly cared, it felt so good to be outside, even an outside as bleak and unpromising as this. Verne and I walked, as we had been instructed by Pitcairn, toward the defunct air terminal. He had said "main entrance," so I tried the most main-looking option. The door handle was covered in scaly bits of rust and paint.

The door was unlocked.

Verne whined.

"Verne," I said. "Where is he?"

Verne lifted a single, fluffy ear, conveying his partial enthusiasm.

"Go find him, Verne," I urged. "Go find him."

Verne slumped over the dark threshold, head between his front paws, gaze abject. He required a few encouraging kicks before groaning to a standing position, shaking the dust from his fur with a half-hearted butt-wriggle, and trotting into the gloom.

He led me past office doors with smoked glass. We climbed a staircase and Verne quickened his pace, his tongue slapping the underside of his chin as he took the stairs two at a time. The second floor offered a hall identical to the one below it, except that all the rooms were filled with wooden crates, which blocked the windows. It was hard to keep track of the white blur ahead of me. He scurried up a far staircase that led to a tower. In no time, I'd lost him.

"Verne!" I called his name up the stairwell. Nothing. Nothing but my own voice jittering off the petrified linoleum. The staircase listed alarmingly to the left. I climbed with one hand flat on the interior wall for balance. Greedy, sniffling dog noises came from above.

"Verne!" Stupid dog, gnawing a pigeon carcass at best, a rat or the corpse of a Kashmiri air traffic controller at worst. At the top of the stairs, the door was ajar; a bright light shone from beyond it. I found Verne with his head deep in a bowl of something.

"Idiot dog." I pulled on his collar. "Get out of there."

Verne growled. He braced his forelegs. He strained toward the bowl.

"Go ahead and poison yourself, then." I released his collar and he fell forward, his nose jamming into the bottom of the bowl. He squeaked, composed himself, resumed eating. I tried to get a look at what was in the bowl. A muddy substance, liver-colored and wet, maintained the concentric circle pattern and the cylindrical shape of the bottom of a tin can. It appeared to be, and in fact was (as a brief whiff informed), dog food.

Huh.

We were in the old control room, from the looks of things. I walked over to the communications console and sat in a metal chair, waiting for Verne to finish. Most of the knobs and dials were gone. The panels had been removed, the wiring stripped. Huge, many-paned windows looked out onto the tarmac and our airplane. From this height, there appeared to be a purposeful design to the fissures in the antiqued asphalt, a message, maybe, that if the dirt were swept away would be apparent to anyone flying overhead. It would say: *Keep away*. It would say: *Yayayayayayayay*. It would say: *This land is dead*. People fought over this land, and why? It was dusty and cold and had a black heart. It was beyond new hopes of ruin. This was just the sort of place I should meet the man of my dreams, a girl like me. On a crapped-out tarmac. Beneath the busted glass of a looming metal control tower. This was romance, when you've never had it.

The sun disappeared behind a beige cloud and the wind picked up, shrieking through the teethy remains of the windows. The sound was discordant, menacing, and recalled to me a sound I'd heard at the Hindu funeral I'd attended for a colleague of my father's, a man named Mr. Veerappan, who had died of a water-borne virus. Mr. V. was a visiting irrigation theorist at the university; his wife was a colonial feminist scholar. The Veerappans were friends of my parents', their relationship based on a handful of informal cocktail gatherings spent complaining about university politics. They had one daughter, Harja, who did not return from her boarding school in Düsseldorf for her father's funeral, an event that was sparsely attended, by a smattering of students and colleagues, by our family, by the few lonely local stragglers who attended free public events.

My mother, father, Edith, and I were late to the ceremony. We'd hurried through the rice paddies from our bungalow, encased in the somber silence that had been generating between our parents for months; it spread outward, surrounding Edith and me as well, making us unwilling colluders in their furious quiet. I was surprised to note, once we'd reached the clearing in the center of town designated for funeral pyres and a weekly fruit market, that Mrs. V. had forgone her hemp-and-amulet academic uniform, opting instead for a traditional sari, a garment that looked incongruous with her asymmetrical bob, her mismatched earrings, her round pewter-rimmed eyeglasses. A robed religious man handed Mrs. V. a torch. He indicated with an impatient gesture (he knew her feminist scholar's opinion of Hinduism) that she was to apply her torch to the pyre, a crisscross of wood and irrigation textbooks, atop which her husband's body lay on a platform, beneath a gold cloth. Mrs. V. shot an inscrutable look at our father, who cleared his throat and stared at the dirt. She specifically did not look at our mother standing beside him in slingback sandals and a pink cotton dress, her eyes disguised behind sunglasses purchased on a sidewalk in Bangkok and her mouth pursed unreadably.

Our mother seesawed a lit cigarette between her thumb and forefinger. She flashed a menacing smile at no one in particular. She'd soaked her dress in her lily-of-the-valley perfume, to ward off the smell of the fire. She was surrounded in a pungent haze; it almost had a texture.

Edith and I wore our usual green school uniforms. We were so worn down by the heat that we hardly cared about the dead body, either the fact that it was dead or the fact that we had known it once. We wiped our sweating faces on our wool jumper straps.

The religious man checked his watch (the fruit market was scheduled for the afternoon) and grabbed Mrs. V. by the shoulder, urging her toward the pyre. She managed not even three doddering baby steps before collapsing onto her knees, her torch tumbling to the dirt beside her.

The religious man paused, flummoxed, as Mrs. V. commenced a

tasteful and composed hyperventilation, her bob knifing back and forth above her shoulders with the steadiness of a metronome. After a few moments, she turned her teary face toward our father, and extended a pleaful hand. Our mother seesawed her cigarette faster and faster, until it almost blurred to nothing. I expected her to levitate at any moment in her pink funeral outfit, her cheap sunglasses, a sub-equatorial Mary Poppins drifting through the sky on the aerodynamic strength of her cigarette alone.

"Go on, Harold," she said, tonelessly, giving him a light push with her elbow. "Make yourself useful for a change."

"Agnes," our father said. He looked chagrined. He tried to kiss her, but she shied away from his mouth. He said, "I love you, you know," and we could hear the contrition in his voice, we could hear the apology that constituted the true essence of this outwardly amorous claim. Our mother laughed and said, "Fuck you, Harold."

He shot her a poisoned eyeful, as if to say, *You chose this*, before striding, mechanically, toward Mrs. V. His back to us, he knelt beside her and delivered three strangulated pats to her bowed head.

The crowd, meanwhile, started to jeer. Not the students of Mr. V., not his colleagues, but the transient people, the gawkers and the passersby, the street vendors, the tourist-rickshaw drivers with calluses draped over their shoulders like a strange brown lichen. They booed at Mrs. V. and began yelling at her, "*Sa-ti, sa-ti, sa-ti,*" a common heckler refrain in our town at Hindu funerals, because the ancient Hindu wife-burning traditions were considered part joke, part dare, by the Muslims.

The religious man, realizing that Mrs. V. was incapable of setting the fire herself, decided, in view of the impending scheduling conflict, to take the inflammatory matter into his own hands. He extracted a red plastic lighter from his robe pocket; the lighter made fleshy snipping noises, but produced no flame. Beside us, our mother sighed. Hers was a sigh of impatience, of resignation, of the bone-weariness bred from always being the one in charge—a default position that she, a patently irresponsible person, resented being forced to occupy. She walked toward the pyre and pressed her lit cigarette stub against a wood protrusion, which smoked briefly, hissed, caught fire. Perhaps she was just being her usual martyred self, but it was also likely that her motives were tinged with malice. Perhaps she suspected—as everyone at the university did—that her husband had been going to bed with Mrs. V. for months, scrambling under her hemp jumpers on his mahogany desk during office hours, the desk's unforgiving surface softened by a sedimentary mattress of ungraded student papers two semesters old.

The fire pitched quickly to a roar, the flames eating their way through the wood, up toward Mr. V.'s platform. Mrs. V. moaned and stretched toward the flames. My father restrained her by wrapping his arms around her waist, his front against her back, his face pressed into her hair, and whispering urgently to her as she frenzied her hands at the blackened airborne remnants of her husband's books.

The crowd renewed their chant. *"Sa-ti, sa-ti, sa-ti."*

My father continued to talk to Mrs. V. He nodded in a detached, incantatory manner, suggesting that he was repeating the same phrase, over and over. Whatever he was saying to her, it hardened the woman. Her face, invisible to him but painfully visible to us, shrank up and made her look a hundred years old.

Unexpectedly, Mrs. V. twisted her head around to look at our father, her lips open and wet, as though wanting a kiss from him. Our mother raised a shrewd eyebrow, as did the academic dean standing across from us. *She wouldn't,* those eyebrows said. And indeed, she did not. Everybody watched Mrs. V.'s tiny Adam's apple tighten, we watched her disgorge a pert mouthful of spit into our father's face and wrench herself free from his immobilizing arm lock.

She stood beside him, arms extended and quivering, toes clenching and unclenching inside her sandals to the rhythm of the crowd's heckling mantra, *"Sa-ti, sa-ti, sa-ti."* Without seeming to move her feet, she leaned her body toward the fire. Edith clutched my arm, panicked; for a second, we both thought Mrs. V. might throw herself into the flames.

The religious man, apparently, feared the same. He tried to grab Mrs. V., but her silk sari served her well on this day; it was slippery and ran right through his fist. She picked up her hem in one hand and carved crazed circles around the pyre as the man chased her, his white cross-trainers visible beneath his flying robe. People started to laugh. Our mother, for one. She laughed a little, and who could blame her? Everyone later agreed there was something tragic yet blackly comic about the scene, at least until, midway through her fifth lap, Mrs. V. veered to the left and lunged, headlong, into the fire. Edith believed that Mrs. V. threw herself in with full volition, while I maintained it was possible, more than possible, that Mrs. V. had tripped. Although I never told Edith this, I witnessed our mother's foot extended, presumably to ease a tightness in her calf. Moments after Mrs. V.'s unfortunate hurtle, I saw our mother stoop forward to wipe a sandal smudge from her slingback with a corner of her dress.

Whatever the impulse, Mrs. V. plunged into the fire and disappeared from view. We all blinked, disbelieving; we all thought we'd seen wrong. But no. Her tumble was followed by a hideous shriek, which forced me to shove my thumbs in my ears or I would have started to shriek myself. These were Mrs. V.'s shrieks, or perhaps they were my mother's, or perhaps it was simply the sound of fire when it gets hold of a real, live thing. I unclenched one eyelid long enough to see two university students drag Mrs. V. from the fire. She moaned as the flames were smothered out with suit coats. The dean hefted her smoking body into his arms while our harried mother flagged a rickshaw. Our father hustled Edith and me home through the rice paddies; he became angry with me when I stopped to vomit off the bank of an irrigation ditch. He took me by the arm when I'd finished heaving; he pushed me ahead on the path, stomping behind me wordlessly as though I'd unfairly accused him of something.

Our mother spent the afternoon and evening at the hospital; she returned home sometime after dinner. She reported, her hands shaking as she poured herself a third drink, that Mrs. V.'s arms and scalp had only first-degree burns, and that, aside from the shock, she was otherwise fine.

Our father didn't say anything.

"Harold," she said, eyes and mouth and voice exhausted. "Harold, did you hear me?"

"A true miracle," my father said, scarcely glancing up from the back issue of *The Subequatorial Entomologist* he was reading on our rattan couch. In less than three months, my mother would move out, and my sister and I would be sent to Maplehook, where the wind howled with such ferocity against my dormitory window that nobody could hear my midnight homesick weeping, certainly not my bulimic roommate, who was as concerned with appearing happy as I was.

More than twenty years later, wind, still, was this to me: it was the sound of the burning body my father had fondled on his university desk. It was the sound of the moaning woman my mother had toted off in a rickshaw to be pronounced "otherwise fine." It was the sound of two bad marriages going up in smoke. It was the sound of our family expiring. It was the sound of fake remorse and resignation that nobody benefits from, nobody.

Beyond the control tower, the sun sprang out from behind the beige clouds. It shone through a window and permitted me to catch a reflection of myself. There was no mistaking my father's nose, a narrow cylinder that flared at the end; there was no mistaking his pinched, insincere cupid mouth, that had maybe told Mrs. V. "I love you" as a way of saying he was sorry, even though neither claim had ever seemed credible coming from him, the use of one contaminating forever the meaning of the other. But he had said, "I love you," his lame form of apology, as Mrs. V. knelt before her husband's cuckolded body, and she had possibly thrown herself into the fire because of his failure to sound convincing.

I spun around in the chair. I watched Verne's swaggling blond behind. I looked at my watch. I looked out the window, at our silver plane.

I stood up. Pitcairn. He wasn't coming, the bastard. I acted tough with myself, but underneath I was thinking, *This land is dead.*

"We're going back to the plane," I announced. I hauled on Verne's collar. He whined, but relinquished the bowl.

I stared into the bowl, licked clean of dog food. A word was scratched into the stainless-steel bottom: "Look."

I kicked the bowl lightly; I heard a rattle.

I flipped the bowl over.

A tiny pair of wire cutters. No bigger than tweezers, really. They were accompanied by a piece of stationery from the two-star Hôtel Deluxe, Bruges, onto which somebody had drawn a ballpoint design of the plane cockpit. An arrow labeled "Acceleration Cable" pointed to a box beneath the steering column. This somebody had even sketched people into the design for realness' sake, two sleeping pilots, *Zzzzzz*'s trailing from their poorly approximated mouths. In the upper right-hand corner, in a doll-sized penmanship that made my heart wheeze, were the words:

i'm sorry

BRUNO WAS LIVID when I returned from my trip to the terminal.

"He what?"

"He didn't show."

"Don't lie to me, Alice."

"It's the truth."

He ordered Stephen to rough me up. Stephen twisted my wrist behind my back.

"Christ!" I yelped. "It's not my fault if your negotiator's highly unreliable!"

Bruno ordered Stephen to frisk me; he complied, but reluctantly. It was nothing like the thorough frisking Edith had received from Tom. After patting me down cursorily in a few locations, he proclaimed me harmless.

"Take her back to coach," Bruno instructed. "I'm done with her."

I panicked. "But what about Pitcairn?"

Bruno sneered. "You let me worry about Pitcairn. You just try to do your job, for once, and find me a bargaining tool."

"I'll find you no one."

"Don't worry," Bruno said, smiling. "He or she will find *you*."

Tom met me at the curtain and deposited me in an empty coach seat, before returning to his post in front of the movie screen.

I hadn't been in coach since yesterday's food service, but I surmised, with a rapid once-over, that the plane had divided itself during the interim into three distinct social groups. The eight Moroccans constituted one, notable for the fact that they remained behind their makeshift tents; the two Germans and the American ophthalmologist formed the second, the three of them banding together for the sole purpose of playing poker; the third was the odd triad of Winnie Sunderland, Ponyskin Vest, and Work-Casual Indian Man. All three factions had colonized their own regions of the plane; I even detected a faint tension among them.

I stared down at my lap and listened to the rub of fabric as the Moroccans pushed aside their tent coverings to get a look at me. The ophthalmologist—an odd, possibly autistic man, with a perpetual-nodding disease—gave me a deeper nod before returning his attention to the card game.

The Germans ignored me.

Work-Casual Indian Man, however, was distinctly interested in my presence. He spoke in low, urgent tones to Ponyskin Vest while throwing furtive looks in my direction, the whites of his eyes flashing beneath a roguish flop of hair. Within minutes, he had disengaged himself from his two female companions and slid down an empty row. He did this with exaggerated stealth, tossing cautious glances toward first class.

He took a seat across the aisle, offered a hand, and delivered the following succinct vita: His name was Sadath Namboodiri (but I could call him Sad); he ran an import-export business in London; he'd majored in philosophy at Cambridge; he was married to a woman named Reeta, whose name he pronounced with an unattractive flaring of the nostrils. He pointed out his coalition members, Winnie Sunderland and Brita O'Kerrigan.

Brita waved. I waved back.

We ran out of things to say in no time.

"So," he stated. "I know why you've been sent back here."

"You do?"

I stared at the ruby ring on his right index finger. He had girl hands and a harmless, possibly bland face, every feature round or rounded, the skin unpinched by bouts of smallness or despondency. Yet his nickname fit him. He seemed to have an intimate knowledge of soulful impotence, which lent his haughty features a sweet, despairing quality.

"That blind fellow sent you back here to pick my brain. To begin the negotiations, so to speak. I thought I'd save you the trouble of trying to make my acquaintance."

"That was nice of you," I said. I had no idea what he was talking about.

"I don't know about *nice*," he said. "I'm feeling more wearied than nice, at the moment. You can tell your friend up there . . ."

"He's not my friend."

Sad gave an exasperated sigh and changed the subject. "You're not married." He pointed at my left fingers.

"No," I said.

"No apt candidates?"

I made an ambiguous motion with my head.

"Oh, dear. You're a romantic. I should have known it from the looks of you. A girl like you can't bear to witness the passionate devolving into the banal, is that it? No, tell me. I'm interested."

I nodded, even though I disagreed with him. I have witnessed very little banality in the devolution of relationships; bitterness, yes; unchecked wrath, ire, and repudiation, naturally.

"This is one benefit of arranged marriages," Sad continued. "You do not love your wife at the outset, but by the by you become fond of her. Quite the opposite of American marriages. In my culture, we experience an inherent increase in affection, rather than an inherent decline."

"I've always seen the appeal in arranged marriages," I remarked. And I had. I admired the emotional economy of poor Harja Veerappan's arranged marriage to a Hindu dentist when she was an unstrung twenty-three-year-old. I crossed adult paths with Harja at a social-work conference in St. Paul, and she invited me to her ranch house for tea. I had rarely experienced such a comforting evenness, such a secure lack of spark or mutual disdain in their mauve-carpeted home with the orange curtains, the glass case full of knickknacks, the chrome-framed wedding portraits. There is a lovely feeling of stillness in a house where love does not live, and where it is not expected.

"We always want what we cannot have," Sad replied. "I loved a ruddy New England girl once. She snowshoed. She knew a lot about firewood. But I don't fool myself into thinking that our marriage would have been any better than the one I've got. There is a base level to which all cohabitational arrangements descend, no matter what they're based upon."

I noticed Brita waving at us again. I waved back at her, but she wanted Sad's attention, not mine. He held up a single finger, urging her to wait. She beamed from the middle of her wrinkled face. I sensed that Brita was the kind of woman who never got close to the Sads and Winnies of the world. Mostly she'd believed herself undeserving, but now she realized it was just a matter of fortuitous proximity. Given the opportunity provided by, say, a hijacking, Brita would be welcomed into any old fold. Instead of fearing for her life, she was thinking: What good friends I've made on this trip. She was envisioning reunions in the future, she was envisioning sharing a ski house with her new buddies. It made me want to goddamn cry.

Instead I said, "There must be an unstoppable urge to bond with people you'd never talk to under normal circumstances."

Sad caught my meaning. He considered Brita from beneath the increasing droop of his hair.

"She's somewhat palpably desperate, isn't she, the old girl? Of course, her husband of eighteen years divorced her because she's barren, but not before he'd impregnated some office tart. Which is probably why I should steer clear of her. Among the more superstitious quarry workers in my village, it is considered terribly bad luck to encounter a woman with an empty vessel."

He twisted his ruby ring. I'd never met a man who seemed less concerned with the possibility of bad luck.

"Anyhow," he said, "you can tell your friend that my father will pay him whatever he wants. Then he will track him down wherever he tries to hide, and hang him by his eyelids. That is the difference between a man of his meager caliber and a man of my father's integrity. He cares only about money. My father cares about justice."

I looked at Sad and realized, *He's a nutter.* Miles called all his clients nutters, even the mostly sane ones. When he grew bored of being responsible and helpful, he would spur on the most disturbed ones, work them into hallucinatory spasms, just for the hell of it. He'd show up at my apartment two hours late and collapse on the couch, saying he was damned wiped out from "egging on the nutters."

I decided to give this particular technique a spin. What the hell, I thought. I'd been demoted. I was feeling mean.

"I've heard your father was a man to be reckoned with," I said.

"He was the Indian ambassador to Switzerland for ten years. It was inevitable that he would develop a taste for their banking practices. The Swiss have little else to offer as a culture."

"Your father's a banker," I said.

Sad grew huffy. "That depends on whose side you're on."

"Oh, I . . ."

"The Indian government chose his side, naturally, but only because he was making them pots of money on the deal. Pots and gobs, my sisters used to say. But a lot of my father's Swiss associates lost everything. He's always said that they would come after him. The Swiss are an aggressive nation. Don't let them fool you with their billy goats and their butter churns. They are a nasty, vengeful people."

I asked him if he happened to know a man named Pitcairn.

"Does he carry a cane?"

I claimed I couldn't remember. The subject of Pitcairn was dropped, and we encountered an awkward pause in our conversation. A few seconds later, Edith appeared through the nylon curtain. Her color had returned, and she'd applied lipstick—a sign that she'd been up to something in my absence. She had spotted an opening, and she'd taken it.

Edith nodded at the nodding ophthalmologist on her way to my row.

"Bruno would like to see you," she said.

"Well," Sad said. "Nice chatting with you. You'll pass along my message, I trust."

"No," Edith said. "He wants to see *you*."

Sad put his ruby-ringed hand against his breast with dramatized surprise.

She led us both to the front of the plane. Stephen gestured toward a seat. Sad took it. Edith and I continued forward and huddled in the galley.

"How's coach treating you?" Edith whispered.

I didn't answer.

She shook her head in a tsk-tsk fashion. "Bruno's really, really angry."

I gave her a look that said, *So?*

"Act tough if you want, Alice."

"Maybe I have a good reason to act tough," I said.

"I doubt that," Edith said.

I reached into my brassiere when Stephen wasn't looking. I flashed my palm so that she could see the wire cutters, just for an instant, before I stashed them back inside my bra, beneath the underwire curve. (Why did I show her the wire cutters? Why? Because I wanted her to see that I was the one with the ability to control our fate, not she, no matter what she'd been up to in first class while I wasn't watching. I was still the one in charge. This is why I did it. This is why.)

Edith peered at me, trying to figure me out.

"And?" she said.

"Wait and see," I replied.

Bruno coughed. We stopped whispering.

"Who have you brought me, Alice?" Bruno hollered.

"I haven't *brought* you . . . His name is Sad Namboodiri." Giving up now. What was the point of arguing when I had a pair of wire cutters in my bra? There was no point. Let the man think what he wanted. The rules of this game had changed, unbeknownst to him.

Bruno straightened the collar of his polo shirt. He rubbed his front teeth with a sideways finger. He counted his way to Sad.

"Mr. Namboodiri," Bruno addressed him. "A pleasure to meet you."

Sad grinned wanly. "Likewise."

"You're holding up under the circumstances?"

"Adequately, thanks."

"And how is Miss Sunderland?" Bruno inquired. "Quite an unexpected windfall, ending up with a woman of her stature on our flight. We certainly picked the right plane. She seems a sweet enough creature. Much more appealing than the tabloids might lead you to believe."

Sad stared at his ring. "She's rather trying, to tell the truth."

"She's pretty, I hear."

"Pretty? I suppose. And too rich. Which is what makes her the worst sort of American."

Bruno grew interested. "How's that?"

Sad scraped at his mud-speckled sandal with a thumbnail. "I am so exhausted by this notion that you can find something essentially true about yourself in an unknown place that you cannot find in a known one. Americans are pointlessly unhappy. Then they go elsewhere and they believe themselves to be happy because their friends and family cannot see their pointless unhappiness anymore."

"You disdain people who rely on public perception," Bruno clarified.

Sad didn't reply.

"And your family and your birthplace are so *affirming* that you feel others should find that same affirmation."

"We are born as we are born. The mistake is to think we have a choice in the matter."

"Choices nearly always lead to mistakes," Bruno said. "But I suppose you believe there is always a *right* choice, which means that there isn't a choice at all."

Sad leaned forward, eyes alive, his ease vanished. "In this case, that is true."

Bruno rubbed his chin. "Which case, I'm sorry?"

"This case of my captivity."

"*Your* captivity?"

"My captivity."

"And this differs, say, from Alice's captivity?" Bruno stared in Edith's direction.

"Come, now," Sad said, "we all know there's a difference. Alice isn't the reason we're here."

"Ah! And why are we here? I forget."

Sad grew stony. "Listen, Mr. . . ."

"Bruno."

"Mr. Bruno. I'm tired. I'm hungry and unwashed. It seems you ought to name your price and be done with this."

Stephen cleared his throat.

"It's hardly worth mentioning that I am worth far more to you alive than dead," Sad added, looking at Stephen's gun.

Bruno paused. "You have a high opinion of yourself."

"More to the point, it is my father's opinion of me."

"Of course. Your father." Bruno said this fondly, as though recalling a drunken gentlemen's evening of backgammon.

"So you did know him." Sad twisted his ring. "I didn't know if you had a personal vendetta, or if you were just the hired gun."

"Maybe I'm the hired gun with the personal vendetta. Or maybe I'm just the very personal gun."

Bruno spun on his heel, counting his way along the aisle. Stephen followed.

Sad remained in his seat. He flipped through the duty-free catalogue.

Stephen broke from the huddle, beelined for me, grabbed me by the arm.

"Cockpit," he said, pushing me forward. "Tell your friend food and fuel, Alice, or Mr. Namboodiri will be guaranteed to have a life-altering experience."

"How euphemistic," I said.

He tossed me into the cockpit. Aboul and Mjidd were asleep. They slept all the time now.

I was alone.

In the cockpit.

Yes.

I felt beneath my bra to ensure the wire cutters were still there. They were. But I didn't remove them. Not yet. I got on the radio, as I'd been instructed to do. I flipped around, yes, speaking whatever language, yes. It was all for effect. I didn't press the Talk button, so nobody outside the cockpit could hear me. Call this some kind of peculiar fore-play, call it what you will. But I didn't want Pitcairn's voice in my head. I wanted his face as I'd imagined it, with mousy hair and a mousy three-day scruff of beard, with eyes and lips that refused to come into focus. He was all sweet nimbus to me. I clutched his scrap of paper (*i'm sorry*), my lame little love letter. I stared at the curved ceiling overhead, the concave windshield, the teal carpet, the motionless pilots, so dead asleep they were barely breathing.

Outside the cockpit door, I heard Edith laughing. It was a loud laugh, engineered for me to hear.

Fucking, fucking Edith. She must be nervous right about now, wondering what I was up to with my wire cutters. At least I hoped she was nervous.

The cockpit was warm, claustrophobic. I pulled the wire cutters out of my bra. In my hand, they had the weight of a very small bone. I pressed my index finger pad into the tip. I could graffiti the walls in blood, I could write a clue for the investigators who might find us dead, or never find us at all: *In her heart of hearts, Alice never actually wanted to cut the acceleration cable.* Third person more convincing, less personal, less assailable. Keeping it real in third person, Miles used to say.

I studied the diagram. Aboul slept at an awkward angle, but I manage to nozzle a hand down between his splayed knees and poke around. I reached deeper and grabbed the wire that ran alongside the steering column.

It was a wire and only a wire. The power of acceleration inside this one plastic-coated vein. I rested it between the metal jaws. I started a countdown from ten.

Would I have done it? Would I? No one will never know. The cockpit door opened on the count of three. I froze. Hand between Aboul's legs. Wire cutters poised.

It was Bruno.

"Alice!" Barking, as always.

"Yes?"

Aboul gave a snort and shifted, clamping my forearm between his shinbones. I winced. He snorted a second time and released me.

"Why are you whispering?" Bruno asked.

"They're sleeping."

He stared right at my arm. He stared, and I imagined that his face tensed; I imagined that a very faint grin flirted at the corners of his mouth.

My head went black. *He knew.* This is what I thought at the time. He knew, and he was happy about it. I had no reason to think this. I was being paranoid, but I couldn't shake this sensation that people can "know" things on a different level, a level that has nothing to do with proof or even eyesight.

"Any success?" Bruno asked.

He stared at me, lying on the floor with my arm between Aboul's legs. His grin intensified. Maybe it was a wince. A wince betraying some kind of perverse pleasure.

"I . . . no," I said.

Bruno put a pair of fingers to his lips. He pedaled them there, one-two-one-two-one-two, a purposeful fortissimo. The wince disappeared, and with it my paranoia. I was imagining things. I was attributing the power of sight to a blind man.

"Well. Keep trying."

He disappeared.

Alone again. Aboul and Mjidd slept on. I sat on the floor, heart clubbing away.

I threw the headphones on the carpet.

Quiet now. Absolute. Too much quiet to think with any sort of lucidity.

Mjidd started to snore.

I held the wire cutters in my left palm. I bounced them lightly. I was conscious of making my decision on the basis of one set of overt desires—of wanting to manipulate my sister, of wanting to be, secretly, covertly, in ultimate control of this hijacking, which would stop the minute I chose it to stop. I was conscious of the fact that I wasn't ready to go home yet. I wasn't ready to return to my Revere vinyl-sided triplex and my three lunches, four dinners at the Tip Top. I had opportunities, here. There was room for advancement.

Although I couldn't have admitted it at the time, it would also have been true to say that I didn't cut the acceleration cable because of Pitcairn. He needed to need me longer. He hadn't needed me long enough, yet. I decided—unconsciously, and with self-defeating logic—that not cutting the cable would disappoint him and make him need me, because letting a person down in a drastic manner was the only way, in my experience, to make that person maybe love you.

WHEN I RETURNED to the galley, a remarkable thing was happening. I mean remarkable not in the grand scheme of things as things had come to be redefined, not even remarkable in a historical sense. But it was remarkable to me, I suppose, the way that Edith was so unstoppably *Edith*.

Her hair was loosened over her shoulders and face; her eyes, previously so sleepy and detached, were pin-sharp. I blame myself for this. I blame myself for showing her the wire cutters. She saw them, rightly, as a challenge.

Edith stood beside Sad's seat. She wore one of the stewardess's aprons.

"Would you care for a beer?" she asked. Hand on hip. Breasts tilted forward.

Sad peered up at her, bemused. "That would be lovely, thank you."

She returned to the galley and retrieved a can of Stork from a cabinet.

"Do you want a glass?" she called out.

"Please."

Edith emerged with the can in one hand, a plastic wineglass in the other. She popped the can and poured the beer, stewardess style, two inches into the glass, then set the can and the glass down on Sad's tray table.

He took a sip. "Thank you," he said.

"If you're hungry, I can offer you a stale bag of peanuts. Unless you'd prefer to chew on a Handi Wipe."

"I'll wait for a proper meal, thanks."

Edith placed a hand on the seat back in front of Sad; she bent at the waist, offering him a tempting sightline straight down her cleavage.

"A proper meal. You're so optimistic," she said.

A predatory glint narrowed Sad's otherwise indolent features.

"Is that unwise?" he asked.

Edith shrugged. She noticed Stephen's curious if benign attentions, and played to them.

"Depends on what constitutes a proper meal," she said, leering at Sad's crotch.

"Good Christ," I said from the galley.

"Do you hunt?" Edith persisted, ignoring me.

Sad sniffed. "For sport."

She nodded toward the bleached outdoors. "You could borrow a gun. Shoot us a game bird."

"Would you like that?" he asked.

"Immensely."

"I placed first in my club's riflery competition three years running," Sad boasted.

"I don't doubt that you've got exquisite aim. Another beer?"

"Of course," he replied. His eyes followed Edith's behind as she sauntered toward the galley.

Stephen intercepted her halfway.

"You're a natural," he said.

Edith rolled her eyes. She was well aware of her abilities, and was beyond needing validation from the likes of Stephen.

"We clearly picked the wrong sister, didn't we, Bruno?"

Bruno lifted his head. He was sitting in a window seat near the curtain divider, holding his temples.

"Pardon me?"

"I said, we definitely picked the wrong sister. I mean, in terms of innate hospitality."

"Alice, for all her considerable talents, is a bit lacking in the social arts," Edith offered. She winked at me.

"This next job isn't one I'd imagine Alice will be terribly well suited for," Stephen continued. He turned to me. "Alice, in fact, has proven herself a real dud."

"Live and learn," Bruno said, dully. "Trial by fire."

"So what do you say?" Stephen asked.

"Just make it *work*." Bruno used his hands to raise himself out of his seat. He appeared very fatigued.

Edith allowed herself to be led back through the curtain by Stephen, but not before shooting me a victorious look.

Stephen returned from coach. He gestured to Sad and me. "You too," he said.

Sad stood and tried to adjust his trousers. He had sweated through the back of them, and the fabric stuck to his buttocks and thighs so that he was as good as naked.

Stephen led me to an empty seat in the first row of coach. Tom was trying to get everybody's attention.

"Let's go," Tom said. "Everyone come out." He referred to the Moroccans in their makeshift tents specifically, who either didn't understand him or chose to ignore him.

This pissed Tom off. His face reddened, exposing the spots on his chin and forehead where he'd applied concealer. Working methodically, he walked down the aisles and ripped the fabric from its anchors in the overhead compartments. His progress was accompanied by the sound of tearing—the stutter of hemp cloth and the high zip of silk—as well as the miserable groans of the newly exposed. Winnie Sunderland was

especially afflicted. Her swollen face—from crying, from water reten-
tion, from the pills she took in abundance—shied away from light and
commotion, tucking itself beneath a raised forearm.

Tom wiped his hands on his thighs and took Winnie by the arm.
She stared at his gun with a druggy nonchalance.

Edith, meanwhile, stood before the movie screen beside Sad, fiddling with her blouse buttons. She was thrilled to be at the center of
the action, but trying to appear blasé.

Bruno explained the situation to us. We were being refused food,
fuel, water. He apologized for the inhumanity of this sacrifice, but
wanted us to remember that he had been forced to plumb such moral
abysses by people supposedly working to ensure our safety.

"Of course," he said, gesturing toward Winnie, "this woman's life is
negotiable. I'm willing to accept volunteers to replace her. It would be
a shame, after all, to have to kill two people instead of one."

The passengers looked down at their rumpled laps, their sour toes.
Nobody moved. I heard a timid sniffle, a swallowed cough. Perhaps I
should have volunteered, knowing (a) that Bruno was incapable of killing anybody, and (b) that this, surely, was just another game-show opportunity to humiliate an unwilling participant. But I must admit that
the scenario intrigued me; I was as interested as he was to see how the
rest of the passengers would respond.

The whispering began in the rear of the plane, a condemning wind
swirling low among the rows. It was the Moroccans who started it, or
possibly the Germans. Soon the entire cabin was staring at Sad. I
learned later he had boastfully announced that he was the cause of the
hijacking, and that his father's wealth ensured he, at the very least,
would never be executed.

People were happy to take him at his word.

Sad was not a brave man, a fact that failed to bother him until his
pusillanimity was on the verge of exposure.

He raised a hand. "I'll do it."

Bruno smiled. "Mr. Namboodiri. How kind of you to offer your life up to save the quote-unquote worst sort of American."

"She is a human being, sir." Sad stared with unchecked disdain at Tom and his gun, unbuttoning his shirt theatrically so that Tom could get a clean shot at his heart. A long, dark scar extended from below his right nipple down toward the waistband of his pants.

Tom ignored Sad's bared chest and gestured to Brita O'Kerrigan. Her eyes skittered around, her skin blushing, as Tom motioned her to the front of the cabin and made her kneel on the floor. He positioned Sad behind Brita and nodded to Edith, who took her place in line behind Sad. The movie-screen graphic—a northeast-pointing plane frozen over Melilla, the dotted line of the flight path erasing and then redotting its way across the skull of Africa—assured us that despite what we might be experiencing, we had, in the computer-chip version of events, reached our destination without a hitch.

"Since we're all a bit bored, I thought it might be fun to play a game," Bruno said.

Edith fiddled with her engagement ring.

"In this game—a relay of sorts—there is one gun."

Stephen displayed the gun.

"There is also a single bullet."

Stephen held the bullet by his cheekbone.

"There's no question of where the bullet is, this isn't a variation on Russian roulette. If you pull the trigger, the gun will go off. The rules of the game are as follows: I will count to ten. If Mr. Namboodiri fails to shoot Brita by the time I finish, then we will give the gun to Edith. If Edith fails to shoot Mr. Namboodiri by the count of ten, then Tom shall be given ten counts to shoot her. If Tom fails to shoot Edith—and I leave the decision to him entirely—then the game is over. Nobody dies. But the odds of that happening are not terribly good, I'm afraid."

Bruno instructed Tom to load the gun with the one bullet and hand it to Sad. Edith bit her lip, trying to retain her cool. When Tom and Stephen were preoccupied, she threw me a beseeching look through her loose hair.

Alice, her look said.

What? I mouthed.

Do something. Alice.

I wanted to say, *But his criminal profile* . . . Yet his criminal profile didn't apply here. Bruno was a brilliant bastard, I had to give him that. He could get out of this without killing a single hostage. Who needed to, when you had Sads and Ediths at your disposal? Bruno knew that Sad could pull a trigger. Edith, too. You can smell it on people when they'll do anything to save themselves.

I raised my hand.

Stephen whispered to Bruno, alerting him.

"Alice?" Bruno said.

"I'd like to volunteer to take Edith's place," I said. This was not about bravery or self-sacrifice. I knew he needed me. This was how I'd come to understand myself, even if I had been demoted. I spoke Sasak. I had a pair of wire cutters in my bra. I was the necessary creature. I was still immune.

This is how I was thinking.

"That's impossible," he said.

"But it's my fault we're still here," I pointed out. "I failed to find Pit-cairn, remember?"

"Then it is a worse punishment to watch how your failure ad-versely affects innocent people," he responded.

Yes, right, I thought. Damned *terrorists,* always living up to their name.

"Then it bears mentioning," I began, having no idea how I was go-ing to finish the sentence.

"Yes?"

I surveyed the line of people before the movie screen. This was a grim, grim scenario, the sort our father had drawn up at bedtime to keep us alert, he'd say, to the moral implications of everyday life, and yet my mind refused to see it as such. We *imagine* we will react a certain way to imminent tragedy, and yet the reality is that the mind fails to respond as we expect it will respond. Fear can desert you when you are most petrified, leaving you calm, composed, capable of constructing sober strategies; it can make you wonder, in the absence of any conventional emotional response, what the hell kind of monster you are.

I proved myself, in this instance, to be a monster of impressive proportions.

"Then it bears mentioning, given your fascination with moral tests, that the potentially most moral decision, in this case, is also the most self-serving," I said.

Bruno rubbed his chin. "Go on."

"True, Sad could refuse to shoot Ms. O'Kerrigan. But if he doesn't shoot her, then it's possible Edith won't shoot him—I could almost promise you she would not—in which case she would be in danger of being shot. By not shooting Brita, Sad is, indirectly, shooting Edith."

Bruno smiled. "I hadn't thought of it that way, Alice."

"I figured you hadn't."

"And how is it that you see Ms. O'Kerrigan's life as being of less value than your sister's?"

I looked at Brita O'Kerrigan—with her parched face, her balding vest, onto which she'd pressed Winnie's glittering forehead dot, her turquoise earrings that caught the stale blue of her eyes and tried to inspire some effortless sparkle. She stared at me with a ruined, resigned gaze, this woman who was so short on happiness, at least until now, this pinnacle in her lonely life, this hijacking in which she became friends with Winnie Sunderland, with Sadath Namboodiri. She could stand being thrown to the wolves; indeed, she expected nothing less. I could see it in her eyes. I had counseled my fair share of Britas in Revere, women who respected you most when you treated them like crap. You couldn't pull these women away from their beating, drunken, jobless husbands with a backhoe, and thus I began to wonder why I was so hell-bent on trying. It was part of the reason I dropped out of grad school, part of the reason that waitressing appeared to be a far more noble way to serve humanity. People tend to know what they want, and it's nice to just give it to them sometimes, without telling them they're wrong for wanting it.

"Because she is barren," I said.

Brita bowed her head. She did not cry. I was glad she didn't. It would have done me in.

Sad pulled his shirt tight around his exposed torso. It was at or around this time, I believe, that he first sensed his assessment of the hijacking had been vastly incorrect.

"She's barren," Bruno repeated.

I did not reiterate the fact.

"Is this true?" he asked Brita.

Brita nodded.

"Speak up!" Bruno barked.

"Yes, it is," Brita said.

"Alice seems to think this makes you less valuable as a human being," Bruno said.

"I didn't say that."

Bruno held up a hand to quiet me. "You implied it. Do you agree with her, Ms. O'Kerrigan?"

Brita started to cry. "My husband left me for a younger woman."

"I'm very sorry," Bruno said. Oddly enough, I believed that he was.

"He refused to adopt. He wouldn't adopt. He said, What if it's stupid? What if it's dull? And then he met Sharon. They already have a little boy. His name is . . . His name is . . ."

Bruno raised his voice. "Unfortunately, your personal problems fail to change our variables here." And to me: "That was a very admirable try, though, Alice."

"Thanks," I said. I couldn't breathe, suddenly.

"Of course, it was a little transparent. You're the last person to believe that the procreation of the species has been elevated to a moral level."

The plane graphic had resumed its motion, our flight path continuing from Melilla to Meknes, dotting and undotting, suggesting, *Everything can be undone.* Everything, that is, except the thing you didn't do. You can't undo the thing you didn't do. I didn't cut the acceleration cable.

"So," Bruno resumed. "Back to our game. Mr. Namboodiri, if you would be so cooperative."

Sad, still somewhat disbelieving of the circumstances in which he found himself, pointed his gun at the back of Brita's head. He cleared his throat, his eyebrows pursing and unpursing.

Brita turned to stare at the gun. A different woman might have begged for mercy or thrashed on the carpet so as to appear too pitiful to kill. Instead she folded her hands into a loose prayer by her groins.

Bruno started to count.

One.

Two.

Sad's arm shook. I stared at the stupid dotting and undotting line. In my mind, I reached under my left breast and touched the tip of the wire cutters. *You stupid idiot Alice you stupid fucking idiot.* In my mind, I pressed my thumb into the sharp tip. I wouldn't even wince as the metal pushed through the pad into softer territory. I wouldn't feel a thing.

On the count of three, Sad let out a vexed sigh. On the count of four, he lowered his gun. He stared ahead, face twitching.

Five.

Brita beamed at Sad, her cheeks so wet they seemed plasticized.

Six, Bruno said.

Seven.

Bruno parted his lips and began to form the next number in the bowl of his tongue. And because my sister and I have always been lucky girls—depending on your monstrous interpretation of luck—Sad lifted his gun and pulled the trigger before Bruno had closed his teeth around the *t* of *Eight,* and let loose that little aspiration that comes at the end of everything.

Sad's Shame

I AM THE YOUNGEST and only son of seven children born to a banker, who owned the largest limestone quarry in Kerala. My mother favored me over my ugly sisters, fussing over my soft head and instilling in me a taste for delicacy. For my tenth birthday, I asked for a silk-covered pillow and a horsehair brush. My father woke me the morning of my birthday with two packages. I unwrapped the pillow and said, Thank you, Father. I unwrapped the brush and said, Thank you, Father. He said, You're very welcome, Sadath, and kissed me on the forehead. Then he pulled down my pajama bottoms, pushed me across my new pillow, and beat me with my new brush.

No son of mine will sit on a silk pillow after he is beaten, he said. No son of mine will brush his hair like a girl. He hit me so hard that I urinated on my new pillow. I ran downstairs with my pants around my ankles and pushed my face into my mother's lap. Her legs spread and my head dropped between them; then she pressed against my ears until all I could hear was the underwater sounds of her fat thighs.

This became my habit when my father beat me for wearing my hair too long, or washing my face with rosewater. Sometimes my mother squeezed so tight with her thighs that my brain compressed and I saw red stars, dazzling things. But then I got too big for her lap, or maybe she lost herself in the planning of my many sisters' weddings. She didn't even protest when my father sent me off to work in the quarry with his brother's son, my cousin, a boy named Dido.

Dido was a ruthless boy with the sort of pinched face and rodent eyes usually found on more cunning individuals. He had pummeled a gypsy boy who sold him a broken fishing rod, smashed his skull open with a rock. As punishment for his stupidity, if not his crime, Dido was sent to work that summer in the quarry. My father decided that I should keep him company. On the first day, a foreman brought us down into a hole in a wooden crate that was lowered and raised by two men standing at the edge of the hole. The foreman showed us the little indentation in the limestone where we could store our things to keep them from getting wet. Then he blew a whistle around his neck, and the men pulled him out of the hole.

The work was, predictably, unpleasant. We were given dull, short-handled pickaxes and asked to chip a tunnel in a wall. The water in the hole came up to our calves; we had to wear rubber boots, which gave us blisters and caused a white puckered fungus to grow between our toes. We chipped at the wall for nine hours each day, five days a week. After a month of work, we had managed to create an indentation in the stone two meters high, three meters wide, six centimeters deep.

This was the same summer my father began to talk about his death. He was neither sick nor feeble, but he dreamed of his funeral the way my sisters dreamed of their weddings. He was fond of imagining how, should I not prove an able heir, the beneficiaries of his will would live marvelously changed lives after the dispensation of his vast fortune. He imagined lame children with new wheelchairs, or cricket fields and libraries bearing his name. Then he would say to me: Of course nothing would make me happier than to give my fortune to you, Sadath, but I'm not certain you're worthy of the responsibility.

I am worthy, I told him.

Words alone do not buttress a son's character against the doubts of his father, he said. Then—How is the tunnel coming along? When I complained to him about the tools, he was unimpressed. He smiled and tapped his temple. A man should not use a pickaxe to build a tunnel, he said. A man should use his head.

The next day in the quarry—a cold day; the rains had raised the water so that it slopped over the tops of our boots, making our feet as heavy as stone blocks and forcing us to shuffle over the sharp bottom and stub our numb toes—I appealed to Dido's wronged sense of violent ingenuity, because he was more of an evil dreamer than I.

We are being made fools of, I told him.

Huh? Dido said.

My father is making fools of us. He's testing us to see if we're worthy of his fortune. He's pitting us against each other, I said. He thinks that we'll destroy each other down here, like rats in a cage. Whoever emerges the victor will inherit his money.

Dido cursed and punched the rock, leaving the bloodied traces of his knuckles in the middle of our negligible depression. He was too enraged to speak the rest of the day, and when the men delivered us to the top of the hole, he shucked off his wet boots and ran home through the rubble in his bare feet.

He arrived at the quarry the next day with his feet and hands bandaged in stinking black cloth. He'd had an idea. We can steal explosives, he said, after we had been dropped at the bottom of the hole. Workmen were building a tunnel through the Western Ghats for a new road. Dido knew where the men locked up their dynamite during the nights and weekends when they were off duty.

We'll blow the whole place up, he said, splashing around in his boots. That will teach your father to play games with us.

I pictured with pleasure my father's ruined face when he learned that his quarry walls had caved in, that his equipment was crushed beneath tons of powdery scree. We decided we would ride our bicycles to the construction site the next weekend.

Dido and I met at the news kiosk. It was early, and the roads were empty. We rode side by side, and fantasized about the specific men who would perish in our blast, the two or three quarriers who laughed at us each afternoon when we emerged from the hole. We'd made it as far as the road that led to the mountains when we saw a girl walking ahead of us. Her too small sari was pulled over her wide back, her shoulders were black from the sun and from the dirt that her sandals scuffed into the air, her lusterless, messy braid had been slept on for who knew how many weeks. She balanced a water urn on her head with one hand. I could tell from how it tipped and wiggled that it was empty.

I should mention that superstition in our town had the power of a legal decree. I should mention that Dido and I understood ourselves to be witnessing nothing short of a bleak oracle proclaiming our imminent failure, for it was considered bad luck to encounter a woman with an empty vessel at the onset of a journey.

I stopped pedaling. We should turn back, I called to Dido. We can go to the mountains tomorrow.

Dido dropped his bicycle in the middle of the road. The girl turned. Her face was as wide and dirty as her back. She watched as Dido walked toward her, with the bland, unsuspecting acceptance of powerless people. She didn't even have the good sense to raise a hand to protect herself when Dido shoved her, hard, at the shoulders, knocking her to the ground. Her neck whiplashed, her head smacked the road. The urn split into pieces beside her, exposing its dry insides to the sun.

I dropped my bicycle and ran toward the girl. I straddled her waist. I poured water on her forehead from my canteen. She choked and moaned, and then, after vomiting a scant amount of clear fluid onto the dirt, she opened her eyes. One pupil swelled to the borders of the iris, while the other contracted to the diameter of a pinhead. She rocked her head from side to side. She reached out an arm and closed her fist around a shard of her broken urn. With a feeble grunt, she raised her hand and sliced diagonally across my chest with her makeshift knife.

I howled but did not budge. I tightened my legs around the girl's waist until her rib bones creaked. I could have snapped them. I could have crushed her heart. Instead I loosened my thighs, feeling sick. The girl dropped her shard and turned her head to the side and closed her eyes.

Dido touched my wound with a forefinger and started to laugh. He laughed and laughed, until the girl began to laugh, too. Dido shoved me off the girl. Get up now, he said to the girl, pulling her to her feet. Her head hung crooked, her hand on Dido's skinny forearm for balance. He held her around the waist and her forehead dropped onto his shoulder. The scene was very sweet, and no one seemed to have any bad feelings toward anyone else, despite all the bangs and cuts.

The two of them remained like this for a few minutes, before Dido—because he is the sort who thinks in cycles or seasons, because he is the sort to forget something so completely that he is shocked by the act of recollection—remembered the dynamite. He remembered the way it felt to stand in wet rubber boots in a stone hole, and the way you could scrape away at the white fungus between your toes with the sick, resentful suspicion that you would hit a bone before you found some uninfected skin, and the way he'd been made a fool of by a bunch of quarry idiots because—and this was how his mind worked—a dirty gypsy just like this girl had sold him a broken fishing rod.

Without any warning, he threw the girl hard against the ground, so hard, I swear, she bounced a little.

Ugly fucking whore, he said, and pounded her chest and face with his fist, in which he held a small rock.

When the girl stopped moaning, Dido stood and spit into his hands, then rubbed them clean on his pants leg. I watched the brittle hair of the girl blow in the wind as he tied my shirt tightly around my wound.

Of course, the day was a failure. Of course, the shed where the dynamite was kept was empty because the crew had long before finished with explosives and was now in the process of grading the rock with big machines whose tires Dido tried to slash with a small knife. We bicycled home on a different road. When we arrived at my house, my father was waiting for us. He stared at my bloodied shirt, tied like a corset around my ribs. He ushered us into his study, past the bored gazes of my ugly sisters.

He shut the door and made us sit on the floor.

The police have been here, he said.

I said nothing.

She got in our way at the beginning of our journey, Dido explained. Her water urn was empty.

I only want to know who is responsible, my father said.

I stayed quiet. I could not finger Dido, of course; I did not want to appear disloyal or a smarmy whistle-blower. I bowed my head, presuming that logic would lead my father to the correct conclusion.

Sad did it, Dido said. The girl sliced his chest trying to defend herself.

I called Dido a liar, but my father slapped me across the face and said, Nothing is more despicable than a boy who cannot stand by his own lowness.

The girl, my father explained, was in the hospital. The police wanted us to go there so that she could identify me as the one who had attacked her. He would escort us in the morning, he said, and sent Dido home.

I spent the night in my room drafting a letter to my father, detailing what had happened. I finally destroyed the letter and fell asleep, confident that the girl would clear my name in the morning.

At dawn, I heard a knock on my door. My father held a leather strap and told me to follow him to the field behind the house. As the sun rose through the dull grass—which looked not unlike the girl's hair, singed and dead and haplessly blown about—my father whipped my back until blisters sprang out on his palm, until the blisters broke open and bled. We stood together, sweating and bleeding in the big red sun. Come here, he said, dropping the strap. He hugged me with so much force that my new cuts pinched between his big hands and bled faster.

I didn't think you had it in you, he said, giving me an extra-tight squeeze.

Excuse me? I said.

Even bad luck will think twice before conspiring against any son of mine. Now I know that you're worthy.

I smiled and said, Oh. His eyes strained, and so I added, Um, thank you. He put his hand around my shoulder as we walked back to the house.

On the way to the hospital with Dido and my father, I had to hang my head out the car window to keep from vomiting. The girl would now confirm my innocence, and no one is as wrathful as a father who's been deceived into believing he has the son he always wished he had.

The girl's bed was surrounded by a curtain. A police officer pulled the curtain back, exposing her misshapen face, one eye swollen shut.

The policeman asked me to approach the bedside. He lifted the girl's limp hand and lay his index finger across her upturned palm.

Is this the boy who attacked you? he asked. You need only squeeze my finger if this is the boy.

The girl's lone eye wandered over me. Her hand remained still.

My father grew impatient. Come on now, he said. Tell the truth, you stupid ruffian. Nobody's going to hurt you.

The girl's eye rolled to the back of her head; her fingers splayed farther apart. My father pestered the nurse to give her some smelling salts. He suggested throwing a pan of cold water on her face. The nurse refused. My father's face reddened. He stared out the window and, I imagined, saw boys in polished wheelchairs, spinning across the athletic field that bore his name.

Now you, the policeman said to Dido. Again the eye wandered, again the hand hung motionless. Then it twitched, slightly, trying to clench shut, but failing.

The policeman grew irritated. Perhaps you didn't understand me, he told the girl. You must squeeze my finger when your attacker approaches the bedside. Do you understand? Squeeze my finger if you understand.

The girl's hand remained inert; the eye grew still. A nurse pressed a stethoscope against the girl's chest and pronounced her dead. My father gave the policeman a roll of notes and promised him a free tour of the quarry to forget the entire incident. He didn't speak to me on the ride home about the dead girl, or anytime afterward. The next day he rode the crate down to the bottom of the hole where Dido and I were chipping at the wall. He told us to throw away our blunt instruments, our sodden boots. He dropped Dido off at his house—we never did see much of Dido again—and took me out to an opulent lunch at his exclusive men's club, where I was soon made a junior member.

Six

EIGHT, BRUNO SAID. Edith's face constricted at the sound of *eight,* every feature recoiled in nauseated anticipation. It wasn't for a full two seconds after Sad pulled the trigger that her mouth untensed, fashioning itself into a semi-reverent smile.

"You sick, sick bastard," she said.

Brita giggled and said, "Good Christ, good bloody Christ." She whitened to the shade of an aspirin and lost consciousness, striking her head against an armrest as she collapsed.

Only Sad failed to react. He didn't even lower the empty gun. Tom stepped forward to pry the useless weapon from Sad's hands.

Bruno was in a perverse and giddy mood, bouncing on his rubber soles.

"Release them all," he told Stephen. "Everyone except the trumps and the shills."

Stephen ordered Edith and me to slide Brita's unconscious body onto the remaining first-aid stretcher, a request to which Edith responded with contemptible ease and compliance. Her brain had erased the fear she'd just experienced; she refused to look at me, so there was no reminding her of *Alice. Do something, Alice.*

"Let's play a little joke on Pitcairn, what do you say?" Bruno suggested to Stephen as the two of them towered above Brita's stretcher.

Stephen guffawed. He balled up a blazer left by one of the stewardesses and shoved it under Brita's shirt. He surveyed the oblong bulge, then removed it.

Edith spirited back to coach class and returned with our father's football helmet beneath her arm. Before covering Brita's body with a blanket, she placed the helmet, the one with the begging-prairie-dog decal, the one intended for the fabulously coordinated Antidote, atop Brita's hammocked pubic bone.

"Brilliant," Stephen said approvingly. Edith stationed herself beside Bruno and played with her hair.

I knew then that we were doomed.

Outside, I heard engines. A baby-blue bus, a baggage trolley, a fuel truck parked five hundred meters from the plane. The baggage trolley approached with provisions in clear garbage bags.

Stephen popped the plane door open and hurried the other passengers down the gangway. The five Moroccan men. The three Moroccan women. The pair of Germans, the American ophthalmologist. Tom guided Brita's stretcher down the stairs; the Germans caught it at the bottom and helped slide it into the back of the baggage trolley. The trolley driver drove a quick semicircle and sped off toward the bus, the wind whisking the blanket off Brita's lower body and revealing her tanned, overexercised legs.

I had one last chance. One more opportunity to cut the cable, before we were airborne again and any cutting of cables would be purely suicidal.

So I tried. I did try to sneak past Bruno while the seeing population on board was otherwise preoccupied. I swear I was soundless. Nevertheless, he swung his head around, he stared me down with his
opaque lenses before I'd even reached his row.

"Where are you going?" He lobbed a hand into the aisle, blocking
my way.

"The radio . . . I thought . . . Pitcairn," I said.

"Too little, too late, I'm afraid. You had your chance to be useful.
I warned you, didn't I?"

"It would be more accurate to say that you threatened me, using
the basest and most predictable form of sibling manipulation."

Bruno wedged a finger up beneath his left lens and scrubbed at his
eyelid. "Just return to your seat, please, Alice."

I returned to my seat and listened as our engines whined. I waited
for the moment when Pitcairn would discover Bruno's little gag, his
Counterfeit Winnie offering. But nobody attempted to stop us as our
plane sped across the rocky airfield and shuddered into the sky.

Then I saw him. I've been told by negotiators that Pitcairn would
never have been at the airbase, that a Brain Worm never stalks his prey
so closely. But I know it was he, standing at the edge of the tarmac with
a pair of binoculars. He was wearing the purple football helmet with
the black silhouetted prairie-dog decal. I swear that he picked my face
out, focusing on my particular window; I swear that he raised his hand
and, just before I became too small to curse to highest heaven, pushed
his shirtsleeve to the elbow and waved me away, with violent, impatient
flicks, as though I had disgusted him beyond the words of any language.

EDITH PROVED to be popular after the football helmet suggestion.
Nobody seemed to care what I did, so I walked back to coach under
the faint cover of bringing Sad and Winnie some food and water.

The reverberation of the engines was jarringly loud with so few

bodies to intercept and absorb it. I found Sad asleep in the seat abut-
ting the rear lavatories, the fingers of his right hand hooked into his
prominent collarbones, his palm resting over his heart. He had lost one
of the rubies from his gold ring. I did a U-turn through the rear galley
and started up the other aisle. A creature of habit, Winnie remained
in her assigned seat, a beach towel shielding her against the sun that
streamed through the windows.

I handed her an oily helping of chickpeas on a paper plate and one
plastic knife.

"We're above the Mediterranean," I said, having no idea where we
were. There was water beneath us. It might have been the Mediterranean.

Winnie delivered a few feckless stabs to the chickpeas with the
knife. We had run out of the more useful utensils. The chickpeas rolled
over her pregnant bulge and into her lap, leaving tiny trails of oil. An
empty pill canister lay overturned at her puffy feet. Her eyes were red
and smaller than usual, almost ugly. Her foul mood wizened her features into a forbidding scowl.

"I know I said you reminded me of my cousin Pammy," she said,
"but I've changed my mind. You're more like my sister."

"You hate your sister," I told her. I didn't care if she was in a bad
mood, I wasn't going to let her take unchallenged digs at me.

She rescued a chickpea between her thumb and forefinger and
mashed it flat.

"I don't hate my sister. My sister hates me."

"Hate's a two-way street," I said. "In my experience, at least."

"So you're saying you hate me?" Winnie asked.

"I . . . No."

"You're saying you find me pretty but irritating? You find me
needy and whiny, you find me to be painfully self-aware yet somehow
lacking in self-awareness?"

"I scarcely know you," I said.

"Don't mock me, Alice." Winnie threw her knife to the carpet. "You think if you mock me that I'll think you're marvelously bright and empathetic and tell you everything. You pretend to be such a compassionate listener, but you're not empathizing, you're *observing*."

"One must observe to empathize," I offered coldly.

"But you don't observe to empathize," she said. "You observe to keep score."

I leaned away from Winnie, stung. Our mother used to blame our father's failings as an entomologist on the fact that he didn't posess any innate curiosity about insects; he merely enjoyed keeping careful accountings of the ways lesser species mutate and destroy themselves.

I stood up. "Well," I said. "Don't hesitate to press the call button if you need anything."

I started toward first class. I paused.

"It seems odd," I began.

Winnie kicked her empty pill canister.

"It seems odd, given your rather low opinion, that you would, albeit under the influence of some impressively strong opiates, press me into hypothetical parental duties."

Winnie stared at me dispassionately. "It is odd. The world is odd."

"The world isn't that odd," I said. "The world tends to make a lot of sad sense." I didn't actually believe this.

Winnie looked out her window. "My astrologer said I would die far from earth, and that I would have to rely on the kindness of an accountant." She glanced around the empty plane. "As far as I can tell, you're the only one who meets that description."

She returned to her plate of squashed chickpeas while I stood stupidly in the aisle. I thought I heard Sad laugh, but when I turned around, I saw that he'd fallen back asleep.

In first class, I found Edith giving Bruno a hand massage, because, as she informed me loudly, he suffered from early-onset arthritis.

"So Alice," she said.

"What?"

"I've been telling Bruno about those stupid Shame Stories." Edith flashed a gaudy smile, all teeth.

"If they're so stupid, why bother?"

"He wants to hear a story, Alice. Just to get an idea of them."

"So tell him a story," I said.

"No, no, *you* tell it. Tell him the story of how Mom and Dad met."

"You know that story as well as I do," I said.

"Oh, but you tell it so much better."

I looked at Bruno. He was probing the cracks in his lips with his tongue. We were still terribly dehydrated, even after the water rations had been doled out and consumed.

"I don't feel like it," I said.

"Alice!" Edith whined.

"May I be excused to the cockpit?"

"You can forget about Pitcairn," Bruno said. "We don't need him anymore. We never needed him, if you must know, Alice. We were only running him around. The man's probably already out of a job."

I stared at him, dumbfaced.

"This surprises you?" Bruno asked. "There're many more surprises where that came from, if you're interested. And I imagine you must be. According to Edith, you're somewhat of a collector of humiliations."

"Preferably not my own," I replied.

"Ah," Bruno said, "but isn't that part of the deliciousness? How *shamefully* good it makes you feel to hear about other people feeling bad?"

"Something like that," I said.

"We have more in common than you might think. Why do you think I hijacked this plane?"

"The zillion-dollar question," I said.

"It's worth much more than that. How priceless is a scenario when you can humiliate a sibling *and* contribute to your own professional advancement at the same time?"

"You want me to believe you hijacked a plane in order to humiliate me? I hate to tell you, but my former boyfriend accomplished that with far less effort."

"He wasn't really a *boyfriend*," Edith pointed out.

"He's a boy and a friend and I gave him a handjob," I said.

"Ach," Bruno interrupted. "The blindness of the self-absorbed. No, Alice. To humiliate your friend Pitcairn. He's my brother, you know."

I blinked—dazed, slow-motion blinks. Then I realized: He was fucking with me again.

"You're a goddamned liar," I said, and the world resumed its normal speed. Bruno trilled his fingers in his lap. "And you're an anthropologist, and you were blinded by a girl with a poor throw. You have a real knack for storytelling. You'll not be without employment options when this gig is up. Nursery school teacher. President."

Bruno returned to ignoring me while Edith kneaded his fingers. Her phony servility repulsed me. I escaped into the galley and leaned my head against the stainless-steel cupboards. I felt the wire cutters in my bra and thought: I could do us all in. I could cut the cable and we'd all of us, the humiliated and the humiliators, be swimming in whatever the hell ocean we were over.

Stephen poked his head into the galley.

"Where are you going?" he asked. "You won't find Pitcairn."

"Who says I'm looking?"

He squinted at my hands. I hid them behind my back.

"I know you won't do anything stupid, Alice. You're a good girl, and good girls don't do stupid things."

"Except when people goad them by calling them 'good girls.'"

He smirked. I half entertained him. I could tell.

Aboul kept the lights low in the cockpit, so all I could see was sky and stars. I had never been in a sensory deprivation tank, but imagined it must feel like this: disconnection, darkness, exhilaration to be at the point where your feelings are stolen away by that lowest-common-denominator force of pure and absolute nothingness.

Through the open cockpit door, I could hear Edith trying to tell Bruno our mother's Shame Story. She'd stop and start over, say, "Wait, let me back up," and "I can't remember, was it a bone or a feather?"

I wiggled into the headphones and tried to reach Pitcairn. Nothing. The night was empty.

I wanted to talk to him, though, so I talked. It took my mind off cutting things I'd never have the nerve to cut. I turned on the radio and told the story about Machu Picchu and the fossil bog, even though nobody had asked to hear it, even though Pitcairn had probably burned my file and already forgotten my name. I told the story first in Thai, then I told it in Sasak, and when I didn't know a word, like "Incan," I talked it out, I said, *The men who built stone triangles and were poisoned by the water men from the sun-coming-up place.* Aboul could understand neither Thai nor Sasak, but I could see the lights from the instrument panel glinting off his gold teeth; merely the rhythm of a tragic love story, even if the language is impenetrable and the teller despondent, is often enough to draw a smile.

IT WAS STILL DARK when the seat-belt signs dinged. I'd been dozing on the cockpit floor. There was no land that I could see through the windshield, no solid threshold in the black, just a string of seven lights below us.

"Hold on," Aboul admonished. I grabbed the handle on a storage closet.

The wheels struck "ground," some shifty, midway substance between air and tarmac. Sand, again. The plane groaned to a stop, and the cabin filled with yellow smoke and the stink of rubber.

Stephen opened the side door and released the gangway. I heard a few jovial *Alhamdullilah*s and the thumping noises of men greeting one another.

Bruno sent me back to coach to gather Winnie and Sad. Winnie was still asleep. Sad had switched seats during the night. I couldn't find him at first, then saw his sandals upended in the aisle, a pair of sock-covered feet protruding from a distant row.

"We're here," I announced.

Tom marched back to inform us that we were each allowed to take a single bag. I helped Winnie stuff her towel into a quilted tapestry carry-on. Sad abandoned his briefcase, his fancy overcoat, his leather satchel.

"You're leaving this?" Tom asked, fingering the overcoat.

Sad didn't reply.

"Mind if I have it?"

Sad blinked, meaning, Yes, no, I haven't an opinion on the matter, go ahead, you bastard, take my bloody slicker.

One by one we descended into the desert. The air was cold but the sand was still hot. A pair of Berber men in white djellabahs squatted before a dead fire. They stared at us, but did not greet us. They jabbed at the fire with sticks and then, having determined it was lifeless, tossed the sticks onto the cold coals and groaned to a standing position.

Sad and Winnie huddled together while the Berbers spoke broken English with Stephen and Tom. They pointed toward a dune, and Stephen gave them a canvas pouch, which the skinnier one tucked inside his hood.

I reached into my brassiere to scratch a pretend itch. I withdrew the wire cutters, lowered my hand, and dropped the damning evidence into the sand, where I buried it with my foot.

Edith shook her head, trying to wipe her hair off her face. The cold, dry desert air made it staticky. It clung to her cheeks, a persistent blond growth.

"Don't look at me like that," she said crossly.

"How am I looking at you?"

"It's the cutthroat who survive, Alice, not the most virtuous." She pulled a wad of cocktail napkins from her pocket and blew her nose.

"We have to walk," Tom informed us.

"Walk?" I said.

"Not far." He gestured toward the same sand dune.

We gathered our bags, those of us who had bags, and hefted them onto our shoulders. Edith had begged Bruno to allow her to take more than one, and so she struggled to load herself up with her garment bag and her Samsonite. Stephen led the way; Bruno and Tom stayed by the plane. I took one of Winnie's arms while Sad took the other. She wore his leather sandals, because her own shoes no longer fit. She made whimpering noises as Sad and I hauled her up the dune. Edith toiled behind us, limping beneath the weight of her bags.

We reached the top of the dune and paused, all of us struggling to catch our breath. Down on the other side of the dune, I could see Verne sitting in the center of a two-rut road that came and went through the sand drifts, more a dotted line than a mindful vector, depressingly reminiscent of the meaningless airplane graphics. Beyond Verne was an old ambulance, the red cross painted on the roof missing its left-side protuberance, leaving a mathematical *therefore* sign.

Looking back toward the plane, I could still see the silhouetted figures of Aboul and Mjidd, staring out the lighted cockpit window. I raised a hand, but we were too dark to be distinguished, and they were too bright to see any further than their own reflections.

"Won't they call for help?" I asked Tom.

He reached into his bag and pulled out a handful of severed wires.

A dullness came over me as I stood on that fulcrum of sand, the silence from all directions pressing against my head. Tom dangled the wires in front of me; he might have been exhibiting my cut-out tongue.

Edith was still less than a third of the way up the dune. She had to stop every few steps and rearrange her luggage, switching the garment bag from left to right, the Samsonite from right to left. Frustrated, she sank onto her knees and unzipped the garment bag. She pawed through it, pulling items off their hangers and stuffing them into the Samsonite. The white glow of her wedding dress grew smaller and smaller as she rezipped it into the garment bag, to which she then gave a little push. The bag undulated over the peaked sand with a hiss, its metal zipper mercury-colored in the moonlight. It came to rest near the bottom of the dune in a tarry clump.

Edith wiped her hands on her thighs. Sprightly now, she mounted the dune with giant strides. I fixated on the crumpled bag as she flung her way upward. I wondered what the goatherd who discovered her wedding dress would make of it, what string of logical happenings he would try to attach to a wedding dress, unworn, zippered into its plastic garment bag in the middle of the desert. He would think, *A wedding dress in the desert, therefore . . .*

But there was no suitable answer; I feared our *therefore* would be equally haphazard, a mere attempt to elicit some meaning from a situation that was, at its heart, illogical, solipsistic, and absurd.

TOM AND STEPHEN took turns driving beside Bruno while the rest of us, including Verne, huddled in the back of the ambulance. I could hear the desert swishing against the undercarriage, the occasional moan from Winnie. Sad got sick in a coffee can. Edith looked green, even in the dark. The road was not a road in some places. The ambulance ran down the back faces of the dunes like a boat surfing waves, and we could hear sand surge through the grille and tick off the underside of the hood. We stopped every few hours to pee, or to refill the gas tank from the plastic containers that functioned as our seats.

By the time the tires forsook the sand, finally, for a tooth-jarring surface of cobblestones, it was nearly six o'clock the following evening. We turned left, then right, then right again, before braking to a stop.

"Move it," Stephen ordered.

Sad, Edith, Winnie, and I crawled out of the back of the ambulance, dumb and disoriented and very, very smelly. I peered around for some sign of police, but of course there was no sign of anyone, not even a mordantly surprised pedestrian. We were hastened inside a building made of pale pink mud, the name "Hotel Itzal" stenciled over the crude lintel. Once my eyes adjusted to the dark interior, I could make out a giant blonde surveying us from behind a reception desk. We never officially met our "hostess," Gesina Guistot; she walked around the reception desk to shake Stephen's hand wordlessly, her hair clamped beneath a red scarf, her body hidden beneath a white djellabah. She was too tall, too full of Bavarian brusqueness and utility, to require an introduction.

Gesina took us on a tour of the hotel, speaking English with alternately German and French accents. She showed us the dank center courtyard, so choked with sturdy fan palms that you could not see through their jagged layerings to the second story, much less to the sky. Our room—located on the gallery floor, above the courtyard—featured a drain in the center of the floor and an attached lavatory without a door or curtain. Sad, Winnie, Edith, and I were each assigned an iron cot, over which a clingy, musty mosquito netting dangled. We were too nauseated and otherwise destroyed from our trip to care much about eating or showering; we tumbled onto our cots. Gesina locked the door behind herself as she left.

Sad and Winnie fell asleep within minutes (Sad did not snore so much as flubber his lips), but Edith and I lay awake in the oven-intensity heat. Edith, I could tell, was fairly miffed at having been assigned to sleep with the coach-class losers. She flounced about on her cot and sighed indignantly. "Christ," I heard her say to herself as she rolled her legs over the edge of her cot and stomped toward the bathroom. The sound of her urinating echoed around the tiled room.

"Such luxury!" she hollered from the toilet. "I give this place four stars for ambience."

"Shhh," I whispered. "People are sleeping."

"I could give a damn," Edith said sourly.

"Is there toilet paper?" I whispered.

"It shares more in common, molecularly speaking, with asphalt, but call it what you want."

I stood on the end of my cot to get a better view out of our high-up windows. I could see the pointy tops of date palms, and farther off, wavering in the heat of the lowering sun, a blood-colored mountain range.

Edith emerged from the bathroom and dried her face on the corner of her bedsheet. "Where are we?" she asked.

"A place with some mountains."

"A place exactly like every other place we've been in the past five days," she grumbled.

"Your 'boyfriend' is consistent," I said.

She reveled in my jab; my referring to Bruno as her boyfriend gave her a proud little thrill.

"Maybe Bruno's making a point, Alice," she said.

"About?"

"About the pointlessness of the human condition."

"Right."

"About how, in modern times, we've lost touch with that crucial, alienating sense of human futility. He is an anthropologist, after all."

"So he says."

"But wouldn't this make Dad drool?"

"Talk about controlled experiment."

"Or maybe we're just the controlled test audience," Edith said. "In the not too distant future—depending on our valuable feedback—people will be signing up for this sort of experience willingly. People will pay to be hijacked, so that they can attain some transcendent, triumphant sense of resignation about their slogging, awful lives. The motto could be: No matter how far you go, there you are again. You know. Familiarity. Remember what Dad said about familiarity."

"It breeds intent."

"He said people don't want new things. People don't want to be surprised."

Winnie struggled to turn over in her narrow cot. Her sheets untucked, exposing a rust-stained stretch of mattress ticking.

"Are you saying you're no longer surprised by this?" I asked.

"I'm just saying there's something *comfortable* about it. It's not a bad way to live, having no responsibilities, even if you do have to deal with a fair share of futility."

"Too much freedom is no freedom at all, is that what you're saying?"

"I don't know what I'm saying. I'm just trying to be optimistic."

"You should stop that instantly," I said. "I'm terrified of your optimism."

"On the other hand," Edith offered, "maybe this was simply meant to be."

"What was?"

"If we hadn't been hijacked, I might have married the wrong man." She corrected herself. "I *would* have."

"What are you talking about?"

Edith paused. She watched a spider on the ceiling. She turned to me with a look of martyred resignation.

"I'm not going to marry X, Alice. I never wanted to marry him."

I didn't respond.

"You look upset," she said.

"I'm not upset," I lied. Why was I upset? I had tried to tell Edith at the airport in Casablanca, hadn't I, that she shouldn't marry X. My heart felt small and mean as a chicken gizzard. My reaction gave me a hideous start; it made me consider the fact (as Edith often forced me to consider) that I was not so much interested in helping people as I was addicted to their failures and unhappinesses. The fact that she was marrying the wrong man pleased me, on some level.

Edith put a hand on my shoulder. This was not a comforting hand, despite her sincere expression. She squeezed so forcefully that my neck muscles cramped.

"Ow," I said.

"You said it yourself, Alice," she reminded me as she kneaded my shoulder.

"What did I say?"

"There's nothing like a hijacking to make you put a finger on the things that really matter."

I pushed her hand away.

Edith attempted to pry her engagement ring from her index finger, where she'd wedged it for safe travel; her skin accordioned above the knuckle as she jammed the ring as far over the bone as it would go. She put her finger in her mouth and disappeared again into the bathroom. The pipes rumbled. Water sloshed into the basin.

"Voilà," she said, thrusting the ring into a patch of sun. The room exploded in frenzied light spots. One skittered across Sad's REMing eyelids; he flinched in his sleep.

Edith crouched by the drain grating in the center of the tile floor. It took some artful turning and twisting before she was able to drop the ring into the pipe below.

She wiped her hands on her thighs. "It's so much nicer, isn't it, Alice, when the world makes sense."

She replaced the grating, but her ring was still visible through the openings. I felt an extreme and yawning wretchedness for that ring. Those stones had been crushed by a million tons of subterranean pressure, they had survived unimaginable tortures to become so bright, and this was where such stoicism led: to a grotty drain in the middle of the desert, to be shoved out of existence in the name of someone's idiotic notion of sense.

WE WERE NOT ALLOWED out of our room the next morning. Tom brought us bread, olives, and books to read from the hotel's common area. These included a fifty-year-old Fodor's travel guide and a set of children's encyclopedias called *Pictured Knowledge*. For old times' sake, I looked up "Roe" (*See* CAVIAR; SPAWN). I looked up "Spawn" but was sidetracked by "Sentence": *Paul, a good captain, sailed to Easter Island. As Paul was a good captain, he sailed to Easter Island. As Easter Island was,*

Paul, a good captain, sailed to it. A good captain was Paul, and to Easter Is-
land he sailed. Good for Paul the captain! He sailed to Easter Island!

At about five, we were ordered to dress for dinner. I tried, and
failed, to get Winnie out of bed. She coughed and flopped about on her
mattress. I gave up.

Our first dinner at the hotel proved an oddly formal occasion. We
had all showered, and we smelled of the pink soap Gesina had given us
to scrub off the days of filtered, recirculated airplane air. My hair,
when I washed it, yielded a pale-green silt.

Everyone except Sad wore new clothes, and this was perhaps the
real cause for celebration, as neither the food nor the company was
worthy of commemoration. New clothes, even if they are old clothes
one hasn't worn for a while, have a way of bestowing the most tired
event with much-needed pomp. I wore a sarong, a clean T-shirt. I'd forgotten my shoes in the desert during one of our fuel stops, so Gesina
loaned me a pair of her double-wide Moroccan babouches. Edith was
by far the most conspicuously turned out of us all. She wore her wedding "escape suit," a skirt and jacket of Chinese-red poplin meant to
replace her wedding dress as she and X fled the ceremony on his
motorcycle. I found it hard to look at her; in Chinese red, she bore an
unsettling resemblance to our mother.

We might have been guests at a normal dinner party, had it not
been for the guns.

"Shall we have wine?" Bruno asked, waving the list about.

None of us replied.

"Mr. Namboodiri?" Bruno said. "You're a well-bred individual. Why
don't you choose us something venal and preposterous." He thrust the
list in Sad's approximate direction, whacking over the pepper mill.

Sad had not shaved; there was dirt under his fingernails. His shirt
smelled. He accepted the list and scrutinized it.

Gesina towered over Sad, waiting for him to choose. I figured her
to be in her fifties, but then, it is difficult to be precise with dispro-
portionately large people. Their measurements are all off. Her eyes ex-

hibited a fright distance of nearly three inches; her features ran scared from one another.

"We'll have the, um," Sad said.

"Pardon?" Gesina leaned closer.

"We'll have the . . ."

I worried that Sad might faint or say something upsetting. We watched him nervously, as one does a too drunk uncle.

Sad swallowed. "We'll have the red wine." He glanced at Bruno for approval, seeing everything as a test now, poor fellow, which he feared failing; even selecting his cot had been a fraught process.

"Excellent," said Gesina. She opened a dirt-encrusted bottle and set the decomposing cork on Sad's plate. He pressed his fingers to the crumby bits. He held them to his nose, his lips, his tongue. He chewed pensively. He giggled that giggle which is usually a reliable segue to complete dissolution.

Gesina poured the wine around the table. Stephen declined, and requested a glass of tonic.

I picked up my wineglass and sniffed. The wine was the color of iodine. It smelled of pickle water.

Bruno held up his glass. "Cheers," he said, and took a large swig.

"Cheers," Edith responded with a bright socialite grin.

"Sorry for the rough trip," Bruno said, lighting a cigarette. "Hopefully you'll find the present accommodations more amenable than the last."

We picked up our menus. The meal was prix fixe, three courses. Penned-in asterisks denoted the specials of the house: *"soupe de thon,"* tuna soup, and *"coux de poulets à la sauce Itzal,"* chicken necks, as well as I could translate, with a local sauce.

The kitchen door opened. Gesina emerged with a big metal tray.

"But we didn't order yet," Edith protested as Gesina dropped a sloshing bowl of *soupe de thon* in front of her.

"Choice is overrated," Bruno said. "Isn't that right, Mr. Namboodiri?"

Sad stared at his reflection in the back side of his spoon.

"It's *monstrously* overrated," Edith said, placing a hasty and placating hand on Bruno's forearm.

Ethically vacuous suckass, I glowered to myself. I tried the soup. It was salty and fishy and cold. I reached for my glass and drank all my wine, even the sharp silt that had collected in the bottom.

I felt myself growing peevish.

"So"—I pushed my soup away—"how long do you foresee us staying here?"

Bruno tweedled his cigarette. "Poor Alice. Are you already bored?"

"I'm just curious what the point is."

Stephen smirked. He bent his face low over his tuna soup.

"The point, Alice. You sound like a debate coach. Why must everyone have a point?"

"Okay. Forget point. Let's talk about desire, then. What do you *desire* from our continued captivity?"

Bruno smiled. The wine had dyed his teeth a dark gray. I glanced around the table. Everybody's teeth and lips, save Stephen's, were a blackish gray.

"Okay, Alice," he said. "Let's talk about desire."

He reached into his jacket pocket, jabbing around in there for a few seconds, before swearing to himself, "Dammit," and hurrying a bleeding index finger into his mouth. He switched something into his other hand and opened his palm, to reveal a pair of wire cutters.

My first thought was: The nice thing with blind men is that you can be incontinent with your physical self, as long as your voice remains modulated.

"Let's talk about your relationship to desire and these wire cutters," Bruno said.

"It is so tiresome," I began, "the way you reverse every mode of inquiry to attack the source."

"Maybe the source should learn to cease inquiring," Bruno suggested.

"Fine. Forget I ever wondered a thing." I retrieved my bowl and shoveled soup into my mouth.

"No, no, it's an interesting and valid question," Bruno said. "And I might answer it, if you agree to answer mine. Surely your friend Pitcairn taught you that much—never give unless you get. He was always adamant about fairness, wasn't he, Gesina? Adamant to the point of being unfair. You know how virtues can flip-flop when you take them too far."

"It seems you're similarly obsessed." I examined Gesina with more interest. So she knew Pitcairn, too.

Bruno thrust his empty wineglass in the air. Gesina refilled it.

"I'm obsessed, but with other things," Bruno said. "I'm obsessed, for lack of a better word, with *artistry*."

"Artistry."

"Try this on for size, Alice: If terrorism is a craft, then antiterrorism is an art."

"Then it seems you've found yourself on the layman's side of the skirmish."

"That may be so," Bruno said, "but there's always room for advancement. The board planer can become a wood sculptor; the house-painting slog might someday learn to rival Ingres."

"If odalisques are your bag."

"Odalisques are everybody's bag," Edith chirped.

"I'd imagine you've blown your chances to be an antiterrorist with this stunt of yours," I said. "Sorry to inform you."

Bruno leaned forward over his soup. The tip of his tie (he was wearing a tie, a god-awful mauve and gold jacquard tie) lily-padded in his soup. "But have I, Alice?"

"I believe so," I said.

"But don't you think that one should be the actual thing before he or she becomes the anti-thing? In the same way that abstract painters frequently studied figural painting before they rejected it, before they became *antifigural,* so to speak?" He reclined in his chair, dragging his tie and his soup with him.

"Then why don't figural painters train first as abstract ones?" I asked.

Edith daubed at Bruno's shirt with her napkin.

"Fine, I give you that, but it doesn't disprove my argument."

"But that doesn't ever happen."

"You miss my point."

"So you have a point now."

"My point is that *maybe it should* happen that way. Perhaps the best way to train to be a figural painter is to be an abstract painter. Perhaps the best way to train to be a terrorist is to be an antiterrorist. Don't you see?"

I didn't see.

Edith piped in. "You used to be an antiterrorist!" She blew a strand of hair out of her mouth.

Our conversation paused as the soup bowls were cleared and the main course, the *coux de poulets* with Itzal sauce, was delivered. Gesina opened a second and a third bottle of wine and poured them around the table. Each time she passed behind Bruno's chair, she put a motherly palm on his shoulder.

"Bon appétit," she said.

Bruno nodded toward the swinging doors, even though Gesina was standing by the wine cabinet.

"You were an antiterrorist," I said.

"A graduate of the International Institute for Terrorist Studies in Lucerne, just like your friend Pitcairn."

"Your brother," I said sardonically.

"Half brother. He studied with a man named Seymour Packs, I studied with Guiomar Atxaga. We were students during some virulent times." He was clearly wistful about virulence.

"What was so virulent about them?" Edith asked.

"It hardly matters. But statistics show that virulence breeds excellence. Since the Packs crowd has come to run the Institute, that is, since the dissension died away, the Institute has fallen on minor times."

"So what you're saying," I said, "is that you went to school to become an antiterrorist so that you could train to be a terrorist."

Bruno's face darkened. "No."

"No?"

He picked up the wire cutters. He felt around for his bread, then thrust their tip into the soft middle. They failed to stand, toppling over onto a pat of butter.

"Answer me this, Alice: How do you think I knew about the wire cutters?"

"Tom saw me drop them in the desert."

"Tom didn't see any such thing. Tom is chronically unobservant, as are you. These aren't even the same wire cutters."

I reached across the table. I held them in my hand, approximating their heft. I had no idea whether they were the same ones or not.

"I knew about the wire cutters, not because Tom found them, but because Pitcairn told me."

I scoffed. "Bullshit." I drained my wine and held up my glass as Bruno had his for a refill. "He lost his job because of you."

"He lost his job because he deserved to lose it. Pitcairn used to be an innovator in his field. Now he's just an Institute wonk. It's because of him that enrollment has dropped to a historic low, that we've had to stoop to accepting people like our Tom here, men who are barely cunning enough to sell a bum wristwatch to a five-year-old. And why is this, Alice? Why do you think?"

"Because the world is a safer place?"

"The world is never more dangerous than when it is a safer place," Bruno replied. "It never pays to be optimistic. You can tell that to Pitcairn when he next foams you up a cappuccino at a Heathrow coffee bar. That's as close to any international work as he'll find."

"You're gloating," I said.

"I am gloating, Alice, and you know why? Because Pitcairn, with his fancy set designers and his multimillion-dollar Role Play Complex, has turned out a bunch of virtual thespian sissies who have made our Institute a laughingstock. The key to international protection is four-fifths menace, as Guiomar Atxaga used to say. It wouldn't be so appalling if Pitcairn hadn't once been a fit opponent."

"So why did he change?"

"Because they made him the director. He likes to challenge authority, but he hates to have his authority challenged. A frustrating double standard embodied by all administrators. It practically defines the job." Bruno put an entire bird neck into his mouth, switched it from one jaw to the other. He produced the bones, clean, from his lips, and dropped it on a side plate.

"If people change," I said, "it is not always in reaction to something. Sometimes a person is inclined to be different, all of a sudden."

"Bah!" Bruno tossed a piece of bread in my direction. "Whether you revolt or continue to mindlessly inhabit your station, you are always reacting in harmony or reacting out of harmony. You are reacting *to*."

"Me? I am reacting *to*?"

"You. Pitcairn. Your types suffer from the classic good-girl syndrome, as we call it at the Institute. 'Good girls' are people, men as often as women, who do what they think they should, rather than what they want. They are pleasers, not survivors. They cannot make decisions without a biased context."

"Not making a decision is a decision," I said. I threw the bread back at him and missed by a wider margin than that by which he had missed me.

"Spare me the college freshman clichés, Alice. Not making a decision is a lazy, fatalistic way to view the world."

"What about those of us who are willfully lazy?" I volleyed.

Bruno ignored me and lit another cigarette. Our plates were cleared and *"les fruits"* were served—four canned-peach segments on a saucer. The peach segments were so lacking in moisture that they might have been wiped dry with a cloth.

I watched as Edith speared a puckered segment. Again, her resemblance to our mother was uncanny and upsetting. She had gone far, far away, as our mother would do at dinner parties where our father took full advantage of his trapped audience, airing his unintelligible and deeply unpopular views about the increased rate of mite mutation versus the decreased use of pesticide.

"So," Bruno said. "Where are we?"

I shrugged. I noticed Sad white-knuckling the table edge while fixated on the saltshaker.

"Ah," Bruno said. "We were talking about how the good girl didn't cut the acceleration cable. We were talking about how she had the opportunity to reverse her situation. She could have saved herself, and arguably all of us, from this continued state of captivity. But she was unable to do so. She choked. Didn't she, Alice?"

You misunderstand, I thought. But what did he misunderstand, exactly? Well, this: If I had suffered from the so-called good-girl syndrome, it was because "good girl" was my assigned role, as far as my family was concerned, and I had traveled with it into adulthood. I learned Sasak; I stayed away from exploitative sex; I agreed to fill the underdog position and generally became whomever people needed me to be, regardless of what I needed. And look at who I was, because of my consummate cooperation. I was a lonely dropout grad student in Revere. And yet this good girl didn't cut the acceleration cable. She didn't cut it—not because she was lazy or scared—but because a person can grow tired of loneliness and self-defeating obedience. *Sometimes a person is inclined to be different, all of a sudden.* If this isn't indicative of free will, what is? I opened my mouth to say so, but was interrupted.

"Shut up!" Sad yelled. His eyes popped out of his head, still fixed desperately on the saltshaker. "Shut up! Shut the fuck up!"

"Why, Mr. Namboodiri," Bruno said. "Have we been monopolizing the conversation?"

Sad started to cry. He bunched the tablecloth in both fists, toppling a bottle of wine. The ominous brown stain extended toward him. He lurched from the table. Stephen grabbed his gun and followed him. Soon we heard the echoing, exaggerated sounds of Sad retching on the tiled floor of the nearby communal showers.

"Fabulous," Edith said. She wiped her stiff mouth and tossed her napkin onto the table.

Bruno patted her hand. He seemed pleased with the evening's conclusion, as though he had masterminded this quick disintegration all along.

"Well," I said. "It's been a scintillating evening. If nobody minds, I might go check on Winnie." I grabbed a saucer of peaches and a glass of water for her. Tom gripped me by the elbow and steered me past the showers, where I could see Sad kneeling in a pool of his own bad sentiments.

The air was cold and the night sharply refreshing. Tom and I mounted the stairs to the second floor.

"Stars," he said, pointing.

I looked. There were zillions of stars, so many that the night was powerless against them. Edith was right. There was something comforting about our captivity, something deeply safe about being told when to go to bed and what to eat and how to spend your days. It was a relief to be denied any responsibility. It made it easier to forgive myself for the dumb things I'd done in the interests of being different, all of a sudden.

I was still perplexed as to how Bruno had known about the wire cutters—had Pitcairn really told him? Impossible. He couldn't have told him. It didn't make any sense to me, nor did I need to make it make sense. Sense can be overrated sometimes; sense can be terribly misguiding.

Tom opened the door to our room. It smelled of sleep, of several people's sleeping. Winnie remained curled against the wall, her bare feet protruding off the end of the mattress. She had not, to my eye, shifted her position since I'd left her more than an hour before.

"What a drama queen," Tom said. "This isn't a movie, princess. No one's going to give you an award for bonelessness."

"Winnie," I said. "I brought you some food."

She didn't answer.

"Winnie."

She rolled herself over, left arm flapping.

"The critics would say, 'Over the top,'" Tom deadpanned. "The critics would say, 'Boneless women do not make me, de facto, care.'"

"I brought you some food," I repeated.

She blinked at me. Mute.

I sat on the side of the cot. I didn't know much about pregnant women, but I had read somewhere that they enjoyed having their feet rubbed. I took a sandy mutt in one hand and jabbed at it with my thumbs while Tom urinated in the lavatory.

Winnie stared at my hand on her foot.

"Your accountant doesn't usually touch you this way, does he?" I said.

She refused to talk to me, so I tried to make her eat a peach. She clamped her lips shut. Water she conceded to. She managed a meager sip and turned back toward the wall. I patted her on the hip and re-arranged her sheet.

I stepped outside the room, where Tom was sitting on a stool, smoking, his gun leaning against his thigh, the barrel pointing directly at his jawbone.

"Got a spare?" I asked.

He looked around. He handed me a cigarette from his shirt pocket and produced a plastic lighter from his shorts pocket. He flicked the lighter for me. I leaned into the flame.

"Chivalry?" I inquired. "Or an act of precaution?"

Tom ignored me. "Didn't know you smoked."

"Only when I eat chicken necks."

He didn't smile. He stared up at the sky, and I suspected that despite his bad skin and poor powers of observation, our Tom might be some measure of a dreamer.

"So," I said to him. "What's in this for you?"

"What do you think?"

"A good pension. Padding for the résumé."

"Seriously," Tom responded, "didn't you learn anything at dinner?"

"You don't have to tell me specifics. I'm just curious about your macro intent."

"My macro intent."

"You know. Experience? Notoriety? Peer pressure? To make a point?"

He frowned. "You know what happens to people who ask questions."

"After a while," I said, "they get answers."

"Or they get shot."

I grinned at him. "But at least they die trying."

Silence now. A not uncomfortable one. Then voices.

Tom and I watched across the seething palms as Edith helped a slumping Bruno up the tiled staircase. I was surprised to see that he was so drunk. He was one of those practiced drinkers, I guessed, who are good at one thing but never two—they can walk straight but slur, they remain articulate but stumble, they can take a steady swing at their wife but miss by a mile.

"This is all going to hell," I whispered under my breath.

Stephen appeared on the stairway with Sad's body slung over his back. "Mind giving me a hand?" he called out, breathless and irritated.

Tom tossed his cigarette over the balcony. "Stay put," he told me.

The desert made everything loud. I could hear Sad muttering to himself, "Fucking whore, ugly fucking whore." The three of them struggled up the stairs, Tom and Stephen holding their noses against Sad's renewed stink. They stumbled and Sad whacked his head on the tile. He stopped mumbling after that.

❧

EDITH NEVER CAME to bed that night. In the morning, her bed was empty, the sheets patterned in the exact same gullies of disarray in which she'd left them the day before.

I might have been more bothered by this if it hadn't been for Winnie. She'd bulleted me awake at dawn with a croupy coughing fit. Another dramatic show, I'd figured, and allowed myself to be hugely, gratifyingly annoyed with her, at least until the sun came up and I tried to give her water. I propped her up against the wall. Her skin was hot and sticky. I yanked out her lower lip and poured water from a cup into the crevice, then tilted her head back so that the water might chance down her throat. Instead it sluiced out the sides of her mouth and ran along her neck and collarbone.

I received permission from Tom to walk across the landing to talk to Bruno.

The desert in the morning was colder than a northern place. My teeth knocked together as I slippered across the grit to knock on Bruno's door.

Nothing. Then a tired, throat-sick "Come in."

The room was a mess. Two double beds, one covered with Edith's getaway suit, bra, stockings, and underwear, the other a sparse tangle of flattened pillows and untucked sheets. There were crates everywhere, stacked against the walls and on either side of the French doors.

Edith was seated on an overturned crate on the balcony, in a robe I'd never seen, drinking coffee from a soup bowl.

"Pull up a crate," she said. She appeared to be alone.

"Is Bruno here?"

"He's with Gesina."

I picked up a crate. It was light. Inside was a polystyrene insert, hollowed out in the shape of a wine bottle.

I stepped onto the tiled balcony. Edith's hair was newly washed. The ends hung by her hips, wetting the thin fabric of the robe.

Three waterbugs the size of dates lazed on the edge of a drain.

"Nice room you have here," I said. Without a hint of sarcasm. Which meant to convey, through its conspicuous absence, sarcasm of the highest order.

Edith ignored my nonsarcastic sarcasm.

"I suppose a congratulation is in order," I said.

Edith shivered theatrically. She was the master of the bogus reflexive response.

"And what about X, Edith? Doesn't he deserve a candid brush-off before you start sleeping with criminals?"

She took protracted sips from her coffee bowl. "You're so worried about X all of a sudden? How touching."

"Even a formerly provincial Spaniard deserves better than this."

"Better than me, you mean."

"Perhaps."

"Then I'm performing him a generous service. His mother never liked me, anyway. I don't even know how much *he* liked me."

"Spare me the convenient revisions."

"He tried to break it off with me once, did you know that?"

I did not know that.

"Remember when he flew to Boston on such short notice? He'd decided to break off the engagement. He said his mother found me—I believe the exact wording was 'whimsically immoral.'"

I did remember that trip. Edith brought X into the Tip Top and I refused to pull any strings, making them wait forty-five minutes in the corral-fenced customer line that zigzagged up from the parking lot. I seated them next to the kitchen, where they could best overhear the chef-gripe-narrative loop, hear the sound of badly aimed partially frozen white rolls thunk against the walls and roll on the linoleum, hear the howl as a sixty-plus waitress twisted her ossified ankle on one of said rolls and hurled expletives that would curdle the stomach of a teenager. X had been stiff, I did recall this, so I'd brought him a Cowpoke Cooler on the house, a caustic mixture of rum, lime, and Tabasco.

"But then he saw you being so nice to all these overweight Americans," Edith said. "He figured if you were such a bleeding heart, then I couldn't be as bad as his mother made me out to be. He's Spanish, you know. They still put a lot of faith in bloodlines."

Tip Top epiphanies, I wanted to say, should never be trusted. They were as cheap as the tea bags.

I noticed then how awful Edith looked, how her eyes were no one color, not blue not gray not green not brown, but some unappealing muddle of the four. Her neck was covered in a rash.

She picked at a toenail while I told her about Winnie.

"Can't you talk to her, Alice? You're four-fifths a social worker."

"I've tried," I said. "She's on a hunger strike or something."

Edith wrinkled her nose. "I told Bruno she'd be trouble."

She finished her coffee and dropped the bowl onto the tiles. It rolled onto its side but did not break. She stood and her robe fell open.

"I have a terrible rash," she announced. She pulled her left breast aside to show me the raw skin.

I stared at her naked breast.

"The heat," I offered, with very little sincerity. It was not unusual for Edith to get a rash when she started sleeping with a new man on the heels of an old man. Her body was her only loyal aspect, her skin protesting the hastiness of her physical transitions by becoming raw and untouchable. Possibly she was allergic to each new man, until her body grew accustomed to his; possibly she was allergic to herself and her own crude ways.

"Probably just the heat," she agreed. She noticed the trio of waterbugs sunning themselves near the drain. She lifted her bare heel and crushed them. Their bodies made an audible crunch.

She scraped her heel against the balcony railing. "This place is a freaking dump."

"So Winnie," I said.

My sister sighed. "Let's go talk to Gesina."

Edith slipped into a pair of sandals and knotted her bathrobe. She kicked some underwear beneath one bed. She gave Tom a cursory wave as I trailed her down the stairs.

"So Gesina and Bruno know each other from way back, huh?"

Edith shrugged. "Somebody's mother was somebody's French teacher. I think."

"Didn't he tell you?"

"He's vague about his personal background. It's very goddamned sexy," she said, tonelessly.

She walked me through the empty dining room, where our dinner dishes still sat, now dotted with flies. She pushed through the kitchen door.

"Watch your head," she advised. I ducked to avoid a broken cuckoo clock, hanging low over the doorway.

Gesina was cleaning her knives and copper bowls with a blue-white paste. "He's out," she said.

"No kidding," Edith said.

Where could he go? I was thinking.

Edith fingered a leftover peach slice from a saucer. She slurped it down.

Gesina eyed Edith as she ate a second slice, then a third. There was something confrontational in the way she ate those peach slices, glugging them down without even chewing.

"Tell her," she instructed me, her mouth full of orange.

I explained the problem with Winnie to Gesina.

"In addition," Edith said, wiping her sticky fingers on her robe, "I've developed a medical issue of my own." She opened her robe and presented Gesina with a welty breast.

Gesina was unimpressed. "We do not have bugs in this hotel," she said.

"I wasn't saying that you did," Edith said. "Although you goddamned do."

Gesina removed her apron and pulled a cloth bag from beneath the butcher block. "I was about to go to the market."

The cuckoo clock emitted a jangled yelp. We turned. Bruno stood in the doorway, in his usual pastel polo shirt and khaki pants. Verne panted at his side. His fur was mottled with something brown and deep-sea-smelling.

"Winnie's sick," I announced.

Bruno rubbed his head.

"I mean, she's really sick. We need to get her to a hospital."

Bruno nodded. "That's impossible."

"It is, Alice." Edith shook her head. "It's impossible."

"Edith, just shut the fuck up, okay?"

She poked at her rash through the thin robe.

"You have to do something," I appealed to Bruno.

"I don't *have* to do anything, Alice."

"Free will and all, is that it?"

Bruno mashed his lips together. He was visibly irritated, not necessarily with me.

"We need a doctor," I repeated.

"Fine. Gesina will bring you to a doctor."

"*I* don't need the doctor. . . ."

"There are no house calls here. Just tell him what the problem is. He'll give you something for Miss Sunderland."

Gesina tied a hair scarf tight around her forehead. "I don't want to be responsible for her," she said. "I have errands."

"She'll be responsible for herself," Bruno replied. "She knows what will happen if she runs away. Or perhaps I should say, it is precisely what she doesn't know that will guarantee her return."

"I find your threats less and less convincing," I informed him, but he was already out the door. He deftly dodged the cuckoo clock before disappearing into the dining room.

MUCH TO GESINA'S obvious irritation, I remained glued to her side as we walked through the confounding Itzal medina. She had given me one of her djellabahs, whose hem I had to bunch in my hand to keep from tripping over the excess fabric. Gesina led me to a corner stall where the air was pixelated with flies. She bought six rounds of bread, smelling them for freshness and shaking the flies off before sliding them into her bag. We returned to the central walkway and followed a bony horse with a microwave oven strapped to its back.

I'm not sure at what point I started thinking we were being followed. Soon after we visited the bread stall, I turned to find a man staring at me. He appeared again when Gesina paused to purchase salt and cumin and a handful of cilantro.

She looked at her watch and said, "Let's stop for tea." We sat at the counter of a stall, the sun beaming down on us through the stick roof. Gesina spoke French to the spindly tea man, who had black calluses on his elbows and a thumb bundled in masking tape. He pulled two cups from a tub of brown water and shook them with a loud *splat splat*. He sloshed them full of green water and placed them in front of us.

I peered around. The follower had apparently lost interest in us, or we had managed to shake him.

Gesina proved a reluctant conversationalist. She pretended to be preoccupied by the bare propane flame that burned in the center of the stall, then pushed back her coarse sleeve to check her watch again. She slapped at the back of her neck, which was covered with bites.

"So," I said. "You've lived here your whole life?"

"More or less." She delivered a panicked swat at a spider the size of a crab apple that dangled under the countertop.

"Where else have you lived?"

Gesina eyed the spider. "France. Switzerland."

"Switzerland?"

"Switzerland. Who says you get to ask so many questions?"

"I'm making polite small talk."

"Oh."

"It's one of the greatest social misunderstandings of our era, mistaking small talk for actual concern." What the hell was I talking about? I was just babbling.

"Right," Gesina said.

"So, Switzerland," I said.

"Yes, Switzerland, what about Switzerland?"

There once was a blind man from Switzerland.

"Is that how you know Bruno?"

Gesina blew on her tea. "Maybe."

"You were an exchange student," I guessed. "He introduced you to your first fondue experience."

She laughed. "Hardly. That would require skewers. There were no skewers in his family's house. No skewers, no sharp objects. No balls. No bats."

"Did you meet at reform school or something?"

Gesina flashed her teeth at me. She had nice teeth, very white. An aunt in America, I conjectured. Camp. College. Who knew, but those perfect teeth spoke geography to me.

"My mother tutored the boys in exchange for room and board. It was an estate. On a lake. Their father had spent his teenage years in a juvenile prison, or so that was the rumor, for killing his own brother on a hunting trip. Both his wives had left him by then. You think those boys turned out oddly, you have no idea how much closer to normal they are than to its opposite."

Those boys. My stomach flurried. What boys?

"Not that I really know how they turned out. Don't get the wrong idea. We are not close. Bruno's the only one who stays in touch. I get letters from him and a box of chocolates for Christmas. The chocolates are always runny and full of ants. Now when he needs something from me, I see him. This is the way with them. You are necessary only when you are necessary. Otherwise, you're just a far-off person who requires the occasional placating box of infested sweets. I've learned not to take it personally."

"That's more understanding than I might be in your shoes," I said. I didn't say, *But I am in your shoes! I am in your djellabah!* I had caught sight again of the man whom I was sure was following us. I could not see his face inside his hood. He passed the tea stall and involved himself with the neighboring olive vendor. He tried each kind of olive twice before purchasing a small plastic bag of green ones.

"Well," Gesina said. "It's an unspoken understanding between us that they owe me."

"Who owes you?"

"Bruno and Pitcairn."

Okay, stunned now. But trying not to be. Trying to keep up the small talk. Trying to be an unstunned small-talker.

"Of course," I said, dazed. No, I thought. Not possible. Bruno had been lying. Gesina was lying. Everyone was lying, they all had to be. *Brothers?* Truly? The djellabah scratched my neck. The darkness of the medina was stifling. I felt stupid, as stupid as I had when I found out Miles had been sleeping with a girl in our graduate class named Kim. He'd told me so, but I didn't believe him. Then Kim confirmed that he'd slept with her without his stupid nightgown, he had fucked her, even, and I had never before felt so goddamned suffocated.

"Their father claimed they were cognitively challenged," Gesina continued. "My mother told him that was just a clever way to call a child stupid. They were stupid, too. Some children don't know how to be curious. They believe every little thing they're told, and never question the fact that their lives are miserable. You can make a child stupider than he might naturally be."

"Indeed," I said. I saw the follower wander into an alley.

Gesina drained her tea and checked her watch again. "This is unfortunate," she said. "My peach supplier is late."

"Are we in a hurry?" I asked.

"The clinic closes for noon prayers in ten minutes," she said.

"I could wait here while you go."

Gesina frowned. "It's better for you to go to the clinic."

She procured a pen and a scrap of brown paper from the tea man, and sketched a map. In the center she drew a star and a line, and wrote a name: Alani Younossi Driss.

"Head that way," she said, handing me the paper and pointing down the alley the follower had taken. People had started to leave the medina, hurrying in silent droves.

I scrutinized her map.

"Go on," Gesina said. "And no funny games, Alice."

I gave her a trust-inspiring pat on her broad shoulder and struck off. Bodies pressed by me on both sides. It grew darker as I walked, a close and fecund darkness, slit open here and there by bright slashes of sunlight through chinks in the roof. I was good and lost in no time.

Behind me, I heard a faint shuffling. The follower. He stood before a closed stall, pretending enthrallment in a sack of grain. He tapped a wooden cane on the muddied cobblestones and raised his eyes, dark and inscrutable inside his hood.

We faced off, twenty paces, neither of us moving, frozen by the unnatural quiet. I heard a distant dripping of condensed water.

It was Pitcairn. How did I know? I knew. I knew. I thought I knew, at least.

He caned toward me, his hood still obscuring his face. I did not move, not even when he brought his head alongside mine. I could feel his breathing against the fabric of my hood. His hand picked at my sleeve, discovered my elbow, turned me to the left.

I did not resist.

We walked by the inactive businesses of the deeper medina and made our way past the potters' quarter—the wheels still, the raw clay vessels fetal and unpolished, the air redolent of low-tide bogginess—and the herbalists' square, where the stall fronts were hidden behind thatches of desiccated mint. The alley leveled out, and the trickles of condensed water formed stagnant puddles rather than meandering downhill streams. We were at the dead center of the medina, the alleys sparking off in all directions. Pitcairn steered me toward a doorway, which was studded around the perimeter with metal spikes. With his free hand (the other still confidently clamped to my elbow) he palmed his pointy hood and mushed the fabric back to expose a leathered, gray-fringed pate, bony Berber eye sockets so deep in his head that no eyes were readily apparent.

This was not Pitcairn.

Not-Pitcairn smiled at me, revealing a mouthful of silver and a blue tongue. My first thought: Does silver tarnish in the mouth? And does it render the tongue blue? Then I thought: Let me go. Let me go let me go.

Not-Pitcairn opened the door and pushed me into a large court-yard. It was blindingly bright after the dim medina, the noonday sun beating down through the open roof onto the tiles. I heard a delicate patter near my feet. Orange peels. The peels formed a perfect line, leading toward the back of the courtyard. Not-Pitcairn grasped my elbow again. We followed the trail.

THE ROOM—on the third floor, lined with bookshelves—had possibly been a library at one time. The shelves were vacant, the books stacked on the floor in waist-high piles. A man was seated on one of the stacks, peeling an orange. He was not remarkable-looking, and in this, he exuded some quality of remarkableness. His was a face that would grow on you, as you got to know him; you could love him like a mother, however, and you'd be unable to conjure that face once it was no longer in front of you, because his physical presence was inexact and best perceived with eyes closed. He was all sweet nimbus to me. But in fact: He had small eyes, close together, and a narrow, pointed nose. White skin, too white, with an irregular, patchy beard and green-gray eyes, did I mention the color? He wore a T-shirt, a wool V-neck sweater, brown trousers, bright new American running shoes that reflected the light from the window behind him. His chest was narrow, hips narrow. He might have been a droll schoolboy who knew too much at too young an age, the way he was sitting cross-legged on the pile of books, the way he was tossing orange peels onto the stone floor with an expressionless face.

He didn't look up from his task. He didn't say a word. Not-Pitcairn released my elbow and pulled his hood over his skull. I listened to him descend the staircase *slap-thunk, slap-thunk*. I heard him strike tentative bottom and cane away. His hard leather babouches echoed in the courtyard. The front door opened and shut.

Quiet now.

"Hello, Alice," Pitcairn said. He had the vaguest laze of a southern drawl this time, his demeanor as dry as toast. His insouciance made me feel overexcited by comparison.

"Hello," I said. "Nice office you've got."

"It's a defunct medieval college—the Medersa El Attarin. Completed in 1325 by a Merenid sultan."

"Ah," I said. I gazed around the room, trying to achieve my very own brand of nonchalance. I recorded a massive wooden desk, a chair with an embossed leather seat, more of those vicious metal spikes, protruding from the window frame. There was an out-of-date calendar on the wall, behind Pitcairn's head. It appeared, from a distance, to be a nudie calendar.

"Pretty racy scholarship for medieval times," I said.

"Go take a look, if you're interested."

"I'm not."

"Even if you're not, then."

He cracked the small orange in two; it released a sharp, misty tang into the air. I waited for him to offer me half. He didn't. He separated the segments and lined them up along his thigh before eating them.

I walked behind him, maintaining a prudent distance. The pages of the calendar had thickened and warped in the years of heat. The models were depressingly interchangeable—with their deeply unhappy happy faces, their fat cheeks and small eyes, their agile breasts extending below their collarbones, and (this was the perverse kicker) their long, unruly patches of pubic hair hanging between their legs.

"There's quite a market, or there used to be, for merkin pornography in Morocco," Pitcairn explained. "People used to be treated for syphilis with mercury, which, as a side effect, caused baldness. Also, prostitutes wore pubic wigs to cover up sores. Do you know of the one-act by Lord Beecham? *The Bearded Wife?*"

I shook my head.

"One of the most poignant moments in post-plague theater. A woman, humiliated by her husband's sexual exploits, decides to dress as a man and seduce his mistress for revenge. As she prepares herself, donning her husband's knickers and inserting the codpiece, she speaks to her reflection in the mirror, 'Pity me, for here am I, an embattled lady, forced to wear some stinking merkin for a beard.'"

Next to me, a pile of books collapsed. I hastened to straighten them, but Pitcairn waved me off.

"You must read a lot," I said.

He pulled a second small orange from his pocket. He began to peel it with his fingers.

"As a terrorist negotiator, I spend a lot of time on planes. I watch movies. I read."

"This experience has given me a whole new perspective about the possibilities of air travel." I picked up a book from the nearest pile. It weighed ten pounds. I opened it. It was full of Arabic and termites. I dropped it on the floor. The spine shattered.

"Whoops," I said.

Pitcairn discharged four staccato sneezes into a pocket handkerchief. His face turned an alarming magenta. I saw a movement in the rafters. A pigeon locked its black eyes on mine and ruffled its neck feathers.

Pitcairn blew his nose endlessly.

I don't want to say the man was a disappointment to me, but I was still trying to get my head around the fact that he looked *vaguer* than

I expected, as though he had begun to recoil from his own face. I searched his countenance for any resemblance to Bruno, his presumed half brother, and had to admit that I found very little. Where Bruno's face was round and cabbagey, with far-flung eyes, Pitcairn's face suffered a certain cautious efficiency, his intense, all-pupil orbs hugging the bridge of his nose, seeking cover from the rapid fire of other people's looking. It was hard to locate the shared person, the father, from what I knew of the two of them; it was hard to assemble a single composite man from their widely varying features.

"You've got a cold," I said.

"I contracted dust pneumonia in the Middle East three years ago, and now, as the doctors say, I am predisposed. But an oxygen tank becomes a little unwieldy when you travel as much as I do. As I did."

His face turned bleak.

"You've been sacked," I guessed.

"No, Alice, I haven't been sacked. Is that what Bruno told you?"

"He . . . he said you probably would get sacked. He said you would deserve it."

Pitcairn shivered from his loins upward. He was clearly quite ill, with a flu or a respiratory infection. He reached behind the desk—it was made of a dark wood and was as big as a bed, legs chunky and carved with vines and cows, very ugly, really—and grabbed a djellabah. He slid it over his head and pushed his hands through the openings. He hunched inside the shapeless fabric and resumed his peeling.

He did not speak for nearly a minute. Then he said, "If I get sacked, Alice, it will be in no small part due to you."

This was not an accusation. This was just a very tired thing to say.

"Well. You didn't really treat me as a proper conduit."

He raised his bloodhound eyes to mine. I was zooming in the veins. Whatever feeble exhaustion his body conveyed, I was pulled toward him by a deeper vital force.

"I did not treat you as a proper conduit," he conceded. "Then again, this is not a proper hijacking. Regardless, I thought you were on my side."

"I was. I am."

"But you worked against me, Alice. You didn't cut the acceleration cable. Why?"

I swallowed. Shrugged. Stalled for time. "Dunno," was the best I could do.

"You don't know."

"At least I didn't *tell* Bruno about the wire cutters."

He stared at me, inscrutably. He stared at me and I couldn't take it for more than a thousandth of a second, because I am a coward when it comes to staring and sincerity is involved. This is why I will never be able to get married unless in a dark room. This is why I will never be able to make love unless giggling is tolerated from start to finish.

"This operation has spun out of control," he said. "My Institute is in an uproar. There is no man, so to speak, at the helm."

"I thought you were at the helm."

"I am," he said. "But I am hardly a man. Not these days."

"How self-pitying," I said. I remembered this much from social work—tell themselves back to themselves. Nothing hurts more than an apt description.

"You understand the uncomfortable position you've put me in. Instead of a conduit, you're an accomplice. You could be prosecuted."

"Excuse me?" He'd skipped right past the *listen-reject-reject-hear* response pattern experienced by most healthy, ego-invested individuals, forging onward to the more hostile *ignore-deny-accuse.*

"That old Stockholm-syndrome defense doesn't hold up in court any longer."

"But I . . ."

"Love, even love as a means of self-defense, is no excuse to abet a criminal."

I was stunned. "Is that what you think? Honestly? You think I did it—or didn't do it—for him?"

He held up a hand that said, *What should I think, Alice?*

"You blocked my attempts to infiltrate the operation."

"Using me," I said.

"Of course using you. You were my conduit."

I shot him a skeptical look. We both knew I wasn't just a conduit. Was I?

"This is all Brain Worm protocol, Alice. I'm not specializing in any new form of exploitation. I can show you the book if you want. But instead of helping me out—and everyone on the plane, I might add—you purposefully made me and everyone working for me look foolish."

I reddened. A combination of shame and anger. He was right, but he was also so, so wrong.

"Clearly you *should* lose your job," I retorted. "I'd have to say you know less about human beings than I do, and I'm a relative novice at the human. I dropped out of Human school, remember? I flunked Human. But I'm leagues beyond you."

He chewed. Stared at his knees.

"I'm sorry for speaking with such candor," I said. "But you misunderstand."

He nodded. Not agreeing with me. Then: "Have you ever surprised yourself, Alice?"

I frowned. "Never. And I don't say that boastfully."

"Neither have I. Or I hadn't, until a few years ago. Now I surprise myself regularly. As it turns out—and this was my first surprise—power doesn't corrupt. Corruption implies high levels of cunning and clever manipulations. No, power, contrary to what people say about it, enforces mediocrity. Maybe it's self-congratulatory to think that I've 'sunk' to mediocrity from a previously more elite position. But sunk I have, Alice. I have sunk. I am sunk."

More coughing. The remaining orange segments toppled from his knees; he squished them flat as he stumbled behind the desk. He emerged with an inhaler and stuck it in his mouth.

After a few frantic tokes, Pitcairn placed the inhaler on the desk and explained to me, in layman's terms, the schism that had divided the Institute for decades, until he was awarded the directorship and banished his opponents from the classroom. He told me about Brain Worms and Incursionists, about Seymour Packs and Guiomar Atxaga.

"Anyhow"—Pitcairn glanced with regret at the flattened orange segments—"Bruno was right. He told me he could *hijack a plane blindfolded*—hah!—he told me he could manipulate the people on board to do his bidding more readily than I could—Mr. Namboodiri, you, your sister—he told me I'd never catch him unless I employed his tactics, his brutal Incursionist tactics, which I had long banned from the Institute curriculum. I do not believe in violence as a way to combat violence, Alice. Even if I have been forced, due to this unpleasant incident, to consider violence as an occasional necessity. It does not mean I have to endorse it as a world vision."

"Maybe it's a good thing you're getting sacked, then."

He grimaced. "Men in my position don't get sacked. One day your ID card isn't returned to you when you insert it at the security gate. It's all very tasteful, really. Embarrassment is kept to a minimum. There are no scenes. There is no humiliating walk down a hallway with your desk contents in a cardboard box."

He picked up an orange peel and tore it in two. "Which is fine with me. The king has been inviting me for months to play golf at his new course in Casablanca. And there's always the commencement-lecture circuit."

I kicked at the shattered book with my babouche. "Sounds dreary," I said.

The pigeon overhead cooed.

"Maybe to a good girl like you."

I examined his bent head, thinking he must be mocking me. He had my file, after all. He'd read testimonies from Miles Keebler describing my feeble stabs at a sex life, he'd perused photos of my apartment in Revere, the Indian-print cotton throws covering the kitchen table, the bed, the couch, the gaping, doorless closet. He'd scanned lists detailing the objects inside my medicine cabinet (a book of Tip Top matches, a bottle of Robitussin, a rusted disposable razor, a crudified packet of lavender bath salts), my refrigerator (four different brands of Pommery mustard; hot sauce, fish sauce, duck sauce, oyster sauce; mint jelly, mango chutney: I was the condiment queen of Revere), my desk drawers (many, many boxes of discontinued square paper clips). He knew that I was never above dreary, that I was beneath it, even, that I had made an art form out of drear. On me, it was almost fashionable.

But he didn't appear to be mocking me.

"Seymour Packs used to say, 'The way to a man's heart is through his heart.' Do you know what that means?" he asked.

"No."

"I never did, either. Until now, that is. If you can't talk a man into acting like a human being, then you have to kill him. I believe that's what he meant. It makes me think that maybe Packs wasn't so opposite to Atxaga. They were both aiming for the same organ. They just attempted to pierce it with different objects."

"Then maybe you and Bruno aren't so different."

"And maybe you and Edith aren't so different, either."

"We are," I insisted. "We are very different."

"I think you're more like her than you're comfortable admitting. The thing about Bruno is . . ." He paused.

"The thing about Bruno is that he's your brother," I said.

He stared at me with an unreadable face. Which is to say he strove to be unreadable but I could read him anyway, because you are always legible to the person who thinks she might adore you.

"Half brother," he corrected. Then he doubled over, hacking. What a seducer he was. In retrospect, he made the best of those reed-quick, swashbuckling Institute men I'd come to know too well look full of a laughable braggadocio, with their confident gum soles and their corduroy suit coats and their digital thermoses. He knew the way to a woman's heart was not through suavely geekish gadgetry, but through gestures of abject infirmity.

"He's not blind," Pitcairn added.

"Metaphorically speaking," I said.

"Blindness is a tempting metaphor. It's almost more metaphor than anything else."

"Not for those people who actually can't see, I'd imagine."

Pitcairn grew quite pale.

"And what does this have to do with the Institute?" I asked.

He cradled his chin, lost for a moment. "I was teaching at the Complex three years ago when Bruno stopped by after a disastrous stint in West . . . Well, I shouldn't say. But the Complex was my baby. Packs and I, we created it, after a complicated diversion of funds from an Atxaga project. . . . Sorry. More information than you need. My point is, Bruno stormed into my classroom, he dragged me into the hallway, he related, at a decibel level audible inside the lecture hall, his disastrous experience with a few of my trainees. They'd all received glowing recommendations from the Complex training evaluators, but he claimed they were dangerously unprepared for real terrorist situations. I can't get into the specifics, but it was bad, it really was a doozy of an operation. Bruno issued a formal complaint about the lack of real-life training at the Role Play Complex, and began a campaign to change the Institute training policy. Then I became director, and, well, I buried his campaign. Bruno's a lateral thinker, and somewhat conspiracy-minded. His ideal Institute is one in which many 'apparent' hijackings are staged as a form of real-life combat training. It's an apprentice program."

"Except there are civilians involved."

"The presence of unknowing participants is the only real difference between a game and life."

"But he killed somebody," I said.

Pitcairn got a queer look on his face. "He didn't kill anybody."

"Not directly, but indirectly he killed Cyrus Bing."

"Survival is a game, Alice. People who play it well persist unscathed. People who play it poorly fall prey to actions they think they're being forced into, but to which they succumb of their own volition."

"Like dying, you mean?"

Pitcairn cleared his throat. "Sometimes it takes that 'form.'"

"Interesting. And I suppose this is your more humane, less invasive Brain Worm approach to problem solving?"

His skin darkened from regular gray to an alarming gray.

"Is it?"

"I'm not sure anymore," he said. He put a trembling hand atop my knee, squeezing it carelessly and hard. I put a hand on top of his. The act was pure instinct. His knuckles were quite warm, with an unexpectedly soft nap.

"Are you okay?"

"Sure I am. Sure I am, Alice. You know, I've never lived very well in the moment."

"So you've told me."

"Yes, but . . ." His closed his eyes. He was casting around for a way to tell me something.

"That's why I've never understood that Greek myth," he said.

I regarded him curiously. "Excuse me?" What was he smoking in that inhaler?

"That one where Orpheus is allowed to lead his kidnapped wife out of Hades, on condition that he not turn around to make sure she's following him. The condition is trust. The human flaw is suspicion. Orpheus believes he's being tricked. He falls prey to his suspicions and sends his wife back to the underworld forever."

"That's the standard interpretation."

"But it never made any practical sense to me. I mean, it's supposed to indicate something essential about human beings, is it not?"

"I believe so."

"And yet, I would never have turned around. The scenario doesn't even tempt me."

"Because you're too trusting," I said.

"No." He squeezed my hand, hard. "Because I despise certainty."

I squeezed his hand back, as hard as he was squeezing mine, harder. We were practically arm wrestling now.

"Do you see what I'm saying?" Pitcairn asked.

I nodded. I had a muddied idea of what he was saying.

He smiled. "You're a strange one, Alice. Don't take this the wrong way, but you're a highly artificial creature."

"Who isn't?"

"True, who isn't, but most people pretend to be more impressive than they truly are, while you strive to be more mediocre than you could ever be."

"I'm ambitious," I kidded.

"You don't fool me."

"I'm not trying to fool you."

"The real question here is how committed you are to maintaining this façade of mediocrity."

"Meaning?"

"Hypothetically. Would you, if the situation required it, be willing to save yourself if it meant sacrificing your sister—whom, I should point out, you seem very invested in projecting as being a more successful, more valuable creature?"

"To a pack of wolves? Angry Berbers with stones? Give me some specifics, please."

"Real-life specifics, you prefer? How about on the plane, when Cyrus Bing was deciding between Winnie and your sister. You can tell me how you responded to that very real situation."

Huh. Well. I had balked back on the plane, hadn't I, until it was too late to say what I'd been willing to do. Maybe I'd seen Cyrus start to falter before I offered myself in Edith's stead. Maybe I'd waited until my gesture was superfluous, a dramatic and convincing show of sibling self-sacrifice and nothing else.

"Hypothetically, yes. In practice, I couldn't say."

Pitcairn tugged on my hand. He bounced it against his kneecap as he talked. It hurt a little. He had a bony knee.

"Let's say, then, *hypothetically*, that something is going to happen tonight at nine forty-five. Everybody will run out of the hotel, but I want you to remain inside, because it will be the only safe place. I'll meet you there. But you cannot tell your sister. You cannot urge her to stay with you. You cannot give her the slightest hint, because anything you tell her will be transmitted to Bruno posthaste. What will you do, Alice?"

"Hypothetically, as I've said . . ."

"This is not hypothetical, Alice. You must meet me in the hotel at nine forty-five."

"Is this a test? Or real life?"

He seemed terribly confused all of a sudden. "If you can tell me the difference, you're a smarter man than I."

Pitcairn's face grew dangerously white, his breathing irregular. His head fell onto his chest as he balanced atop his book pile, suspended for a brief moment between states of consciousness. Then his body doubled up on itself and the whole dusty bundle tumbled to the floor.

Of course, I knew it was a ploy, a tactic, a strategy, this fainting spell. This was all a test of hypotheticals, wasn't it? He'd admitted that he had a hard time living in the moment, he'd admitted that he'd buried his brother's attempts to infuse the Role Play Complex with real-life scenarios. So this was his seduction, maybe. This was the only way we'd ever be able to interact romantically, he and I, through make-believe scenarios in which one of us had supposedly lost consciousness.

I won't deny it: I was intrigued.

I made a gesture toward helping him, but then forced myself away, deciding to wait him out. I didn't understand the parameters of this game yet, and wanted to be strategic in my approach. The library was a quiet place, quiet except for the pigeon. It paced back and forth on the beam above, its peaked feathers forming a wrathful collar around its neck.

I located a bar of sunlight moving across the scholar's desk. When the light covers the rightmost crack in the wood, I said to myself. Then I will help him. I waited and watched the sun travel. Tiny bugs emerged from the desktop's many potholes as the heat made their homes unbearable. They scurried to new ones, just beyond the reaches of the sun. Then it would catch up to them, and they would scurry again, not learning, not expanding their fright distances, willing to settle again and again for the first available shelter.

The sun covered the rightmost crack in the wood and an exodus of bugs struggled over the edge. Pitcairn had not moved. As an experiment, I picked up a chunk of plaster and tossed it at him. It struck his shoulder and bounced out of sight. Pitcairn did not react.

Old, old dog or not, the man was a role-playing pro.

I picked my way through the bookslide and slipped an arm beneath his shoulder blades, to lift him to a seated position. I listened to his breathing; I put a hand over his ribs and felt the distant intentions of his heart.

He was not in need of CPR, of course he wasn't, but then again, that is only if you subscribe to the medical uses of such acts and forget that you are *giving the breath of life,* that you are *giving,* and it is the thought that counts. I pulled down on his bristled chin and his mouth fell open. His teeth were smooth. He had not a single cavity, not one, and a comforting smell, of tea or pipe tobacco, desiccated and sweet.

It required very little effort for me to lift him onto the desk. I cannot say why this small human touch felt necessary, but it did. I was going to perform an operation on this man, and I required elevation. This was not the sort of activity meant for dusty floors, this activity was not debased or hasty. This was methodical, this was in the interests of that peculiar medieval form of scholarship.

I smoothed out his djellabah and unlaced his shoes. They fell *plunk, plunk* onto the floor. I did not remove his socks, because I was not interested in skin. I explored his entire body. His arms were well muscled beneath the wool. His calves were firm, his ankles delicate but not dangerously so. He was, as they say, small-boned. This is why I could touch him the way I did. Because he was a man. The sleeping princess is always awakened by her seducer, every tale will tell you so, while the sleeping prince revels in his somnambulist emissions. Women must be cognizant, while men can enjoy intimate encounters from an unconscious place, because to have physical experiences as a man, one does not need to be present. I challenge any man to think about his own mental absence from a place, and how it counts as having been there. This is why I have modeled myself after men, or at least that's how I present myself to people—as a person with a strategic emotional plan, one with absence as its cornerstone.

Anyway, this was all hypothetical.

As my hands moved over Pitcairn's body, its shape began to change. I felt a reluctant tightening under the tented fabric between his hipbones. I could say I was committing an act no less offensive than his brother's, testing the outer limits of his role-playing abilities. Could he refrain from engorgement while pretending to be unconscious? Could he maintain a gray pallor, without succumbing to the blotchiness of the sexually inspired?

He could not.

But perhaps I was not testing. Perhaps I was seducing the only man I was capable of seducing—an unconscious man, a man who could not look me in the eye or see my shameful hesitation, who could not hear my nervous tittering, who would accept me as a ready apparition of his illness, a laughing girl in a muddy wool djellabah, clumsily shaping him toward ecstasy. The "Sentence" entry in *Pictured Knowledge* flashed through my mind in all its twisted syntax. *Alice, a good girl, shaped the unconscious man toward ecstasy. The unconscious man was shaped toward ecstasy by Alice the good girl. A good girl was Alice! She shaped the unconscious man toward ecstasy!*

I lifted our respective wools. I unbuckled and unzipped. I was silent, so silent, so weightless; there would be no trace of our shushing fabrics, no blackened spot of fluid on the wood desk, no single hint of "me." Pitcairn was so thin, so chalk-pallored and hot to the touch, so defeated. I experienced a surge of pity for him; it fanned my lust until I was breathing harder than he was. I straddled him, leaned over his flushed head and put my lips against one fevered cheekbone. I worked my way down that slope, angling inward toward his mouth. I could feel his breath on my temple, ratcheted and strained. I kissed him on the lips. They were hot, they were springy. I kissed his top lip, then his bottom lip. I positioned my mouth directly over his and felt his breathing. We were no longer two bodies. We were one body, living on the same air. Our lines were erased and we intermingled, two kinds of compatible water. My head was quiet, it was so damned quiet that I could hear the nonexistent Itzal wind blow between my ears.

But then, gripped by an abrupt Styx-like chill, I stopped. I zipped, buckled, I listened as Pitcairn's breathing wound down, his body withered.

Why did I do this? Why? Because I didn't want to ruin myself for love, by actually experiencing it? I don't know. I doubt it's that clear-cut. I would have happily been ruined at that moment, but then I would have failed my first test. I understood, in an instant, that this was a test not dissimilar to Orpheus's, and by falling for him in a very real, very *certain* way, I was failing it miserably.

I stole Pitcairn's watch, a cheap Swiss Army knock-off that could serve as a second-place souvenir, and searched for a pencil. What sort of bloody medieval scholars, I thought, haven't got a stupid pencil. But it was all hollow indignation. It was all for some kind of lousy tough-guy show, put on for my own benefit, because I wished I were the sort of girl who was too unpredictable to be melancholy about the souvenir she failed to bring home with her—her loss of innocence.

In my haste to find a pencil, I leaned against one of the metal spikes protruding from the windowsill. The pinprick pain was disproportionate to the amount of blood that fanned across the sleeve of my djellabah. I touched the wetness on my sleeve. I wrote on the calendar beneath Miss April with my bloody index finger:

9:45 p.m.?

I should have left off the question mark. It would have been more honest to leave off the question mark. But I wanted him to believe in me, hypothetically. I wanted to be the sort of elusive person he evidently hoped I might turn out to be.

Gesina's
Shame

When I was ten years old, my mother left my father in Morocco and took me to Switzerland to stay with her sister. It was summer, and my mother answered an advertisement for a French literature tutor. She was very optimistic about the job, despite what her sister told her about the man who had placed the ad. My mother didn't seem to care that this man was rumored to have killed his own brother, when they were boys.

A taxi dropped us at a granite house surrounded by an iron fence; a manicured lawn dwindled down to a colorless lake the size, to my small eyes, of an ocean. I sat on a bench in the man's office while he interviewed my mother. He didn't ask her about her education or experience. He challenged her to three hands of rummy with a deck of cards he kept locked in a drawer.

My two sons must be protected from their own destructive im-
pulses, the man said, as he shuffled with a lightning quickness, or I fear
they will not both see the youthful age of eighteen. Boys are dangerous
creatures, as you may not know, being blessed, as you are, with a single
daughter. When I was a boy, as you've no doubt heard, because the
tongues in this town wave more freely than the flags in a brisk wind . . .

The man trailed off as he dealt my mother her first losing hand.

My older brother tried to kill me from the time I was an infant in
the crib, the man said. He tried to drown me in that very lake. He took
my clothing, my books, my food. He was a rabidly competitive fellow.

What happened to him? my mother asked.

An archery debacle, the man said absently. He lay down four jacks
and a trio of kings.

My mother lost three consecutive hands of rummy. He hired her.

We were given an apartment over the carriage house, furnished
with wicker porch furniture. The furniture had wheels, and my mother
rearranged our apartment three times a week. I was forbidden to play
with the boys, and my yoyos, my blocks, my marbles were confiscated
by the man, who locked them in his desk drawer with the promise that
they would be returned to me once we were packed to leave.

I was very bored in Switzerland. I chased squirrels with a toilet
plunger. I spied on the boys, who spent most of their time in the library
and wore identical loden-green trousers and overcoats. I preferred the
older son, who was my age and wanted to be an anthropologist. He was
quiet and had a knack for listening to the things I didn't say. I would
tell him a story about the Hotel Itzal and he would say, You hold your
arms so tightly over your chest, are you ashamed or merely cold? Do
girls in Morocco always travel with their toilet plungers? And would
you care to borrow a green sweater?

I wore the older son's green sweater until his father saw me and ordered me to take it off. I removed the sweater and hurried upstairs, and
rode a chair around the apartment until one of the wheels fell off. The

older son explained to me that in his father's culture, a scrap of green tapestry worn about the torso by a woman symbolized to the world that she had sexual intentions toward the owner of the tapestry, and he toward her. In his father's culture, the older son explained, tapestry was exchanged between the sexes not just to suggest intent, but also to symbolize a state of clotheslessness. It was only proper in Switzerland, for example, that symbolically naked people blend in seamlessly with the landscape, thus the importance of green. Tourism, he said, depended on it.

One afternoon, I was standing at the library window talking to the two boys. I remember the blandness of that day. The sky was dun-colored, the water, too. I saw a red ball floating in the lake, the only real spot of color.

Come on, I said to them. I have something to show you. The boys put on their overcoats and followed me. I pulled off my leather shoes, my socks, my dress. I dove into the lake and took a few confident strokes from shore before floating on my back and waving to the boys, who stood above me on the lawn, their hands gripping the bars of the iron fence, which narrowed, at the tops, to arrowlike points. The boys did not wave back. I pretended to throw the ball at them. They ducked. I took a deep breath and sank below the surface. I exhaled and spiraled downward, pretending to drown. I waited to be rescued, but no such rescue occurred. When I popped to the surface, the lawn was empty. I could barely make out their green shapes against the lawn as the boys retreated to the library.

I found them later, reading. I informed them that I had nearly drowned.

We don't know how to swim, the younger brother said, but what he really meant was, Who cares?

You should have drowned, the older brother said. People are not meant to go into water, unless to get clean, and even then a green tapestry must be employed. Do you know how many people drowned in the lake last year?

I shook my head. He flipped through his book, pretending to search for the figure.

Many, he said, finally, closing his book.

I rescued the ball, I said. From the lake.

The boys didn't answer me. They paged through their books, backward. They were terrified.

I have the ball, and it's in the carriage house, I said. If you're interested I'll teach you how to use it.

Still the boys did not respond. I saw the younger one draw in his book with a finger. He passed the book to his brother, who made a dotted addition with his thumb.

I went back to our apartment. For days I waited for the boys to come around, but neither of them came. I decided there was something desperately wrong with boys who preferred to draw in books with their fingers, who did not care about swimming or balls, who did not care about saving pretend drowning girls in slips. They did not resemble the boys or even the girls I knew in Itzal, who competed over the height of a urinary arc or the distance they could hurl a mouthful of spit. They took time out from quantifying their effluence only to kill things—waterbugs and rats, a vulture once—with whatever pipes or brooms or bare hands were available. It came to them naturally, this need to torture, to pummel, to win.

These brothers, I decided, required fixing.

I cornered the older brother after breakfast one day. He had toast crumbs and honey stuck to his lips.

Your brother's been to visit me, I said. I had tucked a green tea towel into my skirt waist. I reached up and wiped his mouth for him with the tip of the towel.

Has not, he said.

I shrugged. He'll lie if you ask, so don't bother.

I don't need to bother. I know him too well. He is more frightened of our father than I am.

That may be, but haven't you read Shakespeare?

He stared at his green brogues. Which version?

The King James Version.

He shook his head.

It is the province of the younger brother to stab out the eyes of the older brother so that he can sleep with the mother and play cards with the father.

He looked alarmed. We have different mothers, he said.

Metaphorically, I'm saying. See Oedipus 3:14.

He returned to the library and paged through his books. Meanwhile, I found the younger brother in the old dairy barn and told him the same story, more or less. He began to cry.

But I don't want to, he said, weeping.

Which part?

All of it, he said. And besides, my mother is dead.

It's metaphorical, I said.

He appeared bewildered.

A metaphor is something that stands for something else, and it's up to you to guess, I explained. Come and let me show you my ball.

The younger brother followed me, his overcoat collar turned up around his face. I shut the carriage house door behind him. He blotted his runny nose with his knuckles. A clear mist rose off his woolly green body.

He took off his overcoat. Where is it? he asked. He was scared, but pretended to be impatient. I saw a touch of the father in him.

I pointed at the wooden ladder.

You go first, he said.

Up the ladder was a crawl space, located beneath our apartment's floorboards. I climbed across the beams on all fours. The younger brother appeared through the bright hole. He swatted at the cobwebs that stuck to his face.

Where is it? he whined.

Here, I said, reaching behind me.

He stared at the ball. He did not desire it, I could tell. He had no idea what to do with a ball.

Let me show you how to use it, I said.

I lay down over the rafters and balanced the ball on my stomach.

Here, I said. Now you lie on top.

It was difficult to accomplish because the ceiling of the crawl space was so low. He pried himself on top of the ball. It squashed into an oval under his slight, seven-year-old's body.

Now what? he asked.

Lift up your arms and legs, I said.

I can't, he said. He looked ready to cry again.

Do it, I said.

This isn't fun. I thought this was supposed to be fun.

It's never fun the first time, I said. Nor the second nor the third. But it is intriguing how it makes you feel dirty, and that's why you will do it.

He held his breath and lifted his hands to the sides. He raised his feet, his green brogues knocking against the low ceiling. The breath was forced out of me as his entire weight rested on the red ball, which squeaked and rolled between us.

See? I said. See?

I hate you, he grunted. He raised his sweaty head and looked out over the rafters. Then he said, remorsefully: I'm flying.

OF COURSE WE MADE a pact not to tell his older brother, which I instantly broke.

Your brother's been to see me, I informed the older brother.

Again? he asked, expressionless.

I nodded.

You are a lying African, he said.

How would you know a liar from an unliar? How would you know an African from an un-African? You don't even know how to play with a ball.

I've read about it, he replied.

Okay, I said. So where does it go?

He pointed into the air.

And then what?

It disappears, he said. You can only play with it once. Which is how I know you're lying.

You should come and see if I'm lying, I said, but he ignored me.

I badgered him for three days. I had to be careful, so that the younger brother didn't see me and grow suspicious. Finally I persuaded the older brother to come to the carriage house, because the dentist, who drove through the neighborhoods in a truck, ringing a bell, was busy polishing his younger brother's teeth in the kitchen.

The older brother did not take off his overcoat. Where is it? he asked.

I pointed upward. If you toss a ball inside, I said, it cannot disappear.

The older brother followed me into the crawl space. This time I made him lie with the ball on his stomach while I flew above him. He said, You weigh too much for a girl. Afterward I picked the splinters of wood out of the back of his wool overcoat.

The man should have been suspicious, but that is the problem with parents who purport to have an overall child-rearing design—they are usually trying to mask their complete lack of interest in their actual children. Despite his interdict against toys, guns, even verbal bets about what the cook would singe for dinner, the boys had begun to bite their toast into gun shapes, the honey dripping off the bread handles as the guns unloaded imaginary charges across the tablecloth. They pelted each other with grapes and kept score by scratching white-red marks on their forearms with fork tines. The man failed to pay any attention, even after my mother reported to him that his sons, usually very dutiful students, had stopped listening to her. They stared out the windows and flicked paper pellets at the glass. They slouched in their chairs. They had grown contemptuous, mispronouncing words on purpose. Instead of *"je suis"* they said "Jew Swiss." Instead of *"hors d'oeuvres"* they said "whores and ovaries."

The boys had, meanwhile, also grown desperately fond of the red ball. They'd each developed a different playing style. The older brother would insist on putting the ball between my thighs and sitting astride it while I held his outstretched arms by the wrists, while the younger brother preferred to dispose of me entirely, cornering the ball and bouncing against it with his back, alone. Neither of them knew of the other's intimacy with the ball. Each believed he'd achieved something unique.

On my last night in Switzerland—a gruesome and humid evening— my mother and I sat on the couch, rolling around the living room and holding ice cubes to our wrists. I looked at my watch. I had arranged to meet both brothers in the crawl space in ten minutes; my mother and I were leaving in the morning and I wanted them to understand what was really important about the ball. That there was only one of it. That they couldn't both possess it and remain unique. That jealousy and ire formed the basis of any successful sibling relationship.

My mother and I jumped as thunder exploded over the south end of the lake.

Grâce à Dieu, my mother said. I heard what she didn't say, as well. She said, I hate this goddamned stone house, may this thunder cleave it in two. I hate these peculiar boys and their peculiar father. It's time to go home, my darling.

The thunder boomed again. Beneath my feet I felt a *bang* against the underside of the floorboards.

My mother looked at me.

It's nothing, I told her. Rats.

I put on my raincoat and hurried down the exterior stairs to the carriage house door. One of the boys had come early. One of them was taking liberties in the crawl space without my knowing it. Who knew how long it had been happening? I suspected the younger brother, with his playing style of rubbing against the ball in such a guilty, self-assisted fashion.

I dropped my raincoat on the floor. I climbed the ladder to the crawl space. It was completely dark, I couldn't see anything. I listened for the telltale squeak and groan of the red ball.

As I picked my careful way across the rafters, my hand fell on a hot piece of rubber. I found another piece, then another. I collected them and climbed down the ladder. I spread the pieces of the former ball on the floor, triangles and continents of red. I laid them out like the sky undone.

I had invited the younger brother to come first, because he was always late to everything. The older brother arrived before him anyhow, because he was always early.

I gestured to the former ball on the floor, but the older brother was distracted. Thunder jammed its mouth against the roof, and we grabbed each other—he my dress, me his green wool coat.

Marry me, he said.

I leaned down and picked up a piece of red rubber. I stretched it over his mouth.

In my culture, I said, women cover the faces of the men in red rubber, and you know what that says about intention.

The older boy breathed in and out, in and out, behind the tight rubber.

Bahwah mah, he said.

I pressed my mouth against his rubber mouth. He did not kiss me. He made a chewing motion.

Another explosion of thunder and the rattle of rain. I turned to see the carriage house door open, the black clouds moving above the lake at a laughable speed, the younger brother staring at us from beneath the brim of his dripping green hat.

We could not have spoken if we'd wanted to. The storm was too loud. I released the piece of red rubber from the older brother's face. I bent down and selected a second perfect piece. I moved toward the younger brother, offering it to him.

In my culture, I said.

The younger brother did not care for my offering. He slapped my hand and the red went flying. He bent down and collected the pieces of red together into a limp pile. He pulled a matchbook from his green wool coat and tried to set the mound on fire.

The rubber refused to catch. The edges smoked and shrank, pulling into themselves like a hurt, live thing.

The younger boy gestured toward us with his lit match, which was promptly extinguished.

Come outside, he said to his brother.

The boys dropped their coats *whomp!* to the carriage house floor. They chased each other into the rain. Once they were a safe distance from the carriage house, they hugged each other. They hugged and hugged, then fell onto the lawn in a single mass, kicking and scratching. They rolled under trees and around shrubs. Lightning fired up the sky and the lake, and the boys were the only solid things I could see. They slammed into trees; they slammed against the flagstones. Eventually they rolled into the fence with a loud clank. Somebody's father-issue buttons or somebody's father-issue zipper against the iron bars. Lightning struck at the far end of the lake, a brilliant crack. Through the rain I could see the father standing on the back porch of the granite house. He held a rifle in his hand, as I had seen him do before, using the sight to get a closer look at boats on the lake. He observed the boys grappling at the fence like prisoners trying to escape. He raised the rifle and peered through the sight—to shoot them, I thought. But maybe just to get a better look.

There was another mean lightning crack, followed by an animal yowl. When the lightning struck next, the fence was empty. The arrow bars stood blackly against the sky, but all traces of the boys had disappeared. They had been zapped out of existence, or turned into light.

The wind slammed the carriage house door shut, and I ran up the ladder to the crawl space, where I hid throughout the duration of the storm, and the lighted whooping of the ambulance, and the chirping calm of the subsequently clear night.

We left the next afternoon, my mother and I. The man arrived at the carriage house door with our tickets and a bag with my marbles, my blocks, my yoyo. He did not mention what had happened to his sons. He did not seem to be someone who had witnessed a tragedy or narrowly escaped one; he seemed to be the same strange man. As we drove off, I saw a ghost in the window of an upstairs bedroom. A ghost or a bandaged person, with a white-wrapped head.

It was ten years before I heard from the older brother. The younger one I never saw again. I was living in Morocco, had lived there since we left Switzerland. A young man with a cane and a pair of dark glasses pressed against me as I was buying salt in the Itzal medina one day; he slipped a note into my djellabah pocket that read, "Oedipus 3:14." We had tea at a tea stand, and I asked him about his accident.

Was it an accident? he said.

Lightning is always an accident, unless you believe in things I doubt you believe in, I replied.

But was it lightning? he asked.

Don't you know? I said.

He shrugged. Could have been lightning. But I have this dream a lot, he said. My brother and I are watching my father burn things. He has built a bonfire on the lawn and he is tossing in tennis racquets, playing cards, writing tablets, pencils. He is tossing brooms and forks, he is tossing coat hangers, he is tossing anything that could double as a mallet or a spike or a bat or a club. He is hurrying, and I am worried that his green coat will catch fire. My brother is standing next to me. He starts to laugh.

Why are you laughing? I ask him.

He holds up a single stiff finger and pushes it into his own eye until his eye disappears into the back of his head. My brother holds his finger out to me. He waggles it in a taunting fashion.

Your turn, he says. Want to play?

Seven

GESINA WAS SEETHING by the time I surfaced at the tea stall, almost two hours later. Her net bag banged off her left thigh as we hurried to the clinic, the peach cans swinging with a pendular intention to bash me in the ribs. Dr. Driss—an animated badger of a man who wore a beard shorn tight against his face and a lemony cologne—insisted on looking down my throat and taking my blood pressure before sewing up the cut on my arm (three stitches). He gave me a poultice for Edith's rash, and some antacid tablets for Winnie, who, he would not be convinced otherwise, suffered from a mere case of tourist tummy.

Gesina and I arrived back at the hotel, according to Pitcairn's watch a few minutes past three p.m.

I put Edith's poultice in a cast-iron pot and read *Pictured Knowledge* in the dining room while waiting for the water to boil. I looked up "Poultice." The accompanying illustration showed a woman in medieval garb pressing a kidney-shaped object over the rib cage of an unconscious monk. A spider crawled up the monk's wrist, while a second woman cried next to an empty birdcage. It was a morbid tableau, especially for *Pictured Knowledge*, which seemed determined to take the pain and pathos out of its every subject, including "Accounting" (*If your son selects accounting as his profession, you can be sure of one very important thing: He will be welcomed with open arms!*).

Edith wandered into the dining room, scratching.

I regarded her from behind volume eight of *Pictured Knowledge*. "Can you name the Seven Wonders of the Ancient World?"

Her eyes strayed toward the ceiling fan, which had been coaxed to turn in a listless counterclockwise fashion by an otherwise imperceptible cross-breeze.

"Cleopatra's Pessary, I know that's one," she said. "It was made of gold, and it was stolen twenty-five times."

"By her lovers?"

"By road bandits."

"On the way to the forum, then."

"She wore it incessantly. Word got around."

"A woman after our mother's cautious heart."

"She'd get mugged and they'd pry it out of her."

"Dear me," I said. "Although it clearly deserves to be, Cleopatra's Golden Pessary is *not*, as a result of some grave oversight by the editors of *Pictured Knowledge*, one of the Seven Wonders of the Ancient World. Do you want to take another stab at it?"

"Is that poultice boiled yet?"

"Just make a guess," I said.

"I did make a guess."

"You didn't guess seriously."

"I hate games," she said.

"You love games."

"Not when I have a rash. How's my poultice doing?"

I pulled the poultice from the water. Edith reclined in a wicker chair with the poultice resting on her chest. She demanded that I read to her about whales from volume ten, and we learned about a whale that feeds off the tongues of other whales, flippering between its victim's strainer teeth and making off with its tongue like a big carpet.

Edith's rash turned a brighter shade of red, but failed to abate.

That evening, the mood presiding over our dinner of chicken necks and canned peaches was audibly grim. Edith shuffled into the dining room in her robe, her face pruned into an expression of such dourness that I didn't even attempt to joke her into a more resilient humor. She rolled her bread into pea-sized pellets and pushed them, one at a time, into her disapproving mouth.

Gesina was unusually attentive with the wine, never allowing the levels to fall more than a few sips below perilously full. We slopped and spilled as we grew drunker and more intolerant of one another's company; the tablecloth was stained with wine, with sodden crumbs, with dead conversation. Tom drank bitterly and fast. He'd chug his wine and clang his spoon against the glass to demand a refill.

Bruno sat motionless with his nose pointed across the table wreckage at me. As if this were a board game. As if it was my turn. His nose was the only true indicator of where his attention was directed.

"So Alice had a little adventure today," he said, after a lengthy and sordid silence. "Didn't you, Alice?"

I said nothing.

"Alice?"

"If you say so."

"Why don't you tell us about it," he insisted.

"I prefer not to."

"Humor us, why don't you. The dinner conversation's been lagging all evening."

I replaced my soup spoon onto the greasy underplate.

"I got lost. I got unlost. I met Dr. Driss. Gesina's still mad at me." I smiled at Gesina, leering by the highboy.

"How about the long version? Surely you don't tolerate this sort of sardonic abridgment with your clients."

"I dream of sardonic abridgment. Sardonic abridgment is the goal. It's not what you say that's revealing, but what you leave out."

"Exactly," Bruno said. "So, then."

"It's up to you to interpret. The 'client' cannot supply the missing pieces. That's cheating."

"Fine, then. I'm all for playing it tight to the rulebook." Bruno patted Edith on the wrist. "Maybe your sister can help supply the missing pieces."

Edith didn't respond. She resembled a mental patient, in her dingy bathrobe and the misery-mottled interior that had imprinted itself on her body.

"Edith?"

"Yes, let's hear it, Edith," I goaded.

She scowled at the pellet of bread pinched between her thumb and forefinger. "Who cares," she said.

"Who cares?" Bruno asked. "Who cares? This is an insightful question. No, really. Tom, do you *care*?"

Tom looked at his watch. "I plan to stop caring in about fifteen minutes."

"Is that right," Bruno stated.

"My contract expires at seven o'clock, at which point you will no longer be paying me to 'care.'"

"Interesting." Bruno wiped his lips with his napkin in a rough, rubbing manner. He would rub them right off, I thought. "And what is the price of your empathy? If I were to pay for a contract extension."

Tom worried a blemish on his neck. "You mean, what price do I demand to suspend my disbelief indefinitely? Sorry. There's no amount of money you can offer me to *pretend* we're about to succeed with this stupid little insurrection. We gambled, and we lost. I need to go home and update my résumé."

Edith and I exchanged perplexed looks.

"We haven't lost yet," Stephen said under his breath.

Tom slammed his fork on the table. "Give me a goddamn break, Stephen. We'll never manipulate Pitcairn into doing something he doesn't want to do. The guy's unmanipulable. Like all those Brain Worms, he's hardly even human. You're going to the glue factory with the rest of us." He swung his arm around to include everyone at the table, even Gesina, who was attempting to clear the dirty plates. She ignored him, but I could see the blush creeping up the back of her neck, seeping into her thicket of yellow hair.

"Shut up, Tom," she said.

"You're a fine one to be tossing orders around. You're a hotelier by trade, but have any of us ever had a more repulsive meal? Anybody with half a brain for details could pick this operation apart in five seconds."

"Tom," Bruno said.

"I'm just a little cranky that I didn't get what I signed up for."

"I apologize for not fully anticipating your needs," Bruno said icily.

"I only anticipated what was promised to me. I was promised French cuisine in a desert oasis. I was promised a goddamn occasional phone call."

"What's going on here?" Edith asked.

"Ask your 'boyfriend,'" Tom sneered. "I doubt you'll get a straight story, but I guarantee you'll get a story out of him."

Tom pushed his chair away from the table. The tablecloth caught on his belt buckle, and he dragged what was left of the meal—dirtied plates, wineglasses, trivets, pats of butter, bits of bread, saltcellars— onto the floor as he charged from the dining room.

Gesina humped into the kitchen for a broom and a dustpan. Sad picked peach slices out of his lap. Stephen stared at the food-covered floor, despondent. He lifted his feet as Gesina worked the broom, pushing wet and dry and hard and broken, mixing everything together to form a dusty-wet gruel.

"I told you," she muttered as she swept beneath Bruno's chair, pricking his ankles with short, mean jabs of the broom.

Edith trembled in her seat; she made a few pitiful attempts to scrape the wet salt off her robe. "I'd love to know what the hell is going on," she said to Bruno.

He removed his eyeglasses and pressed his fingers into his crimped sockets. Stephen leaned forward in his chair. He opened his mouth but then thought better of it.

Bruno waved his hand in the direction of the hotel's front door, the medina, the desert beyond. "You're free to go now."

Uniform silence, reflecting various levels of confusion.

"You're free to go," Bruno reiterated.

Stephen stared at the bare table. "You're sure about this?"

"Your contracts are up, are they not? As promised, I've arranged for your transport back to Lucerne. It's waiting for you at the preappointed location."

Edith stammered. "What contracts?"

"Get out of here. All of you. This is done." As he pronounced the word "done," the cuckoo clock in the kitchen sounded the first of four guttural chirps. It had not chimed once in our two-day tenure at the Hotel Itzal.

Creeeep-croop! Creeeep-croop! Creeeep-croop! The bird had sand in its works.

Gesina ceased her vigorous sweeping. Her eyes drifted down toward her hands; she seemed surprised to find them clutching a broom, and cast the mawkish domestic tool away. She pulled out a chair. From a pocket of her djellabah, she extracted a tin of expensive-looking cigarettes.

"Must you?" Stephen inquired.

Gesina lit a cigarette and exhaled in his face.

Stephen scowled. "Do you mind?"

"This is *my* hotel," Gesina said. "I can do what I damned well please."

"I don't understand," Edith whined. "Alice?"

I didn't have the faintest idea what was happening. Bruno *had* won, hadn't he? Then again, there was no way to assess anything truthfully, which I was beginning to suspect was the point of all this.

"Alice?" Edith repeated, pleading.

"I don't know, Edith."

Bruno wiggled a hand at Gesina. "Could I have a cigarette?"

Gesina lit a cigarette for him, then paused, unsure which end to present first—the lit end? The filter? She handed it to him filter first.

Bruno accepted. Inhaled. Exhaled. "Looked" at me. I got the impression that he hated me, really hated me.

"Since no one else seems interested, Alice, maybe I'll try to supply the missing pieces to your sardonically abridged day," he offered.

"Be my guest."

"You pretend to be such an unflappable creature. To be honest, I find it a tad creepy."

"Yeah, well."

"Unflappable and secretive. Your sister has no idea how secretive you are, does she? You've behaved rather falsely toward her, I'd imagine."

"It's become boring and predictable, this little sibling refrain of yours. Really. You need to find another angle to worry."

"Then you've told Edith what you did this afternoon."

"I went to Dr. Driss."

"And . . ."

"And I cut myself on a piece of metal when I got lost in the medina."

"So you also told her you met Pitcairn this afternoon."

Wait a minute.

"You've also, no doubt, mentioned to her that he's asked you to remain safely in the hotel while you allow the rest of us—including Edith—to run outside and risk our lives due to some unexplained 'danger.'"

Aghast. I was purely aghast. I said as much.

"Aghastness aside, I imagine your sister deserves an explanation," Bruno said.

"How about me? Don't I deserve an explanation?" I stalled for time, but inside I was frantic: Did Pitcairn sell me out? God damn him. God damn him and his hypothetical convalescing act.

Bruno intuited my distress.

"Relax, Alice. Pitcairn's a good girl, remember? You can trust him to play by the rules. That's how I knew about the wire cutters. That's how I know he's met you, and offered you a deal. He follows the Brain Worm playbook to the letter, which is unfortunate when your opponent's read the same playbook."

"You've lost me," I said, although I wasn't so lost. Bruno was saying that if anyone was ready for the glue factory, it was Pitcairn. Every old dog has his old, old day. The thought of Pitcairn trying to be secretive with his oranges and his playbook was too much to bear. My heart cleaved open with affection for the guy.

Edith enacted her own version of aghast across the table. "Alice. Is this true?"

"No. Yes."

"You were going to abandon me in the hotel?"

"It was all hypothetical," I offered lamely.

Edith rescued a bread pellet from her lap, set it on the table and flicked it across the room. It ricocheted off the highboy at a forty-five degree angle, striking Gesina in the bosom.

"That is so incredibly fucked up of you," Edith said. She flicked another pellet of bread, with less spectacular results. Edith wasn't yet hurt, or even acting hurt. She was being objective. *Nothing hurts more than an apt description.*

"I could have told you, I know. . . ."

"But you had a good reason, I'm sure. One of those stupid social-worker reasons you and Miles enjoyed cooking up on your sexless nights in Revere."

Please don't, I thought. Even if I have a file that everyone in this room has read. I don't need my sex life critiqued in front of these people.

Mercifully, she dropped it.

"Did you ever think that you're too much of a misanthrope to be a social worker?" she asked. "That you fucking *enjoy* other people's failures too much to be of any help to anyone? Did you ever think of that, Alice?"

"It has occurred to me."

"I've always said that you were too smart to have a profession. Smart people are hopeless in the face of anything *actual*. They are terrible cooks. They cannot dress themselves. They are children who need guidance and protecting."

She smiled and dabbed again, somewhat neurotically, at the salt stain on her robe.

"In fact, I don't believe that Alice has even begun to appreciate all I've done for her. Oh yes, she'll tell you how she's the one who's made sacrifices, she's the one who's allowed me to live a life in full bloom while she withered away beneath my officious tutelage."

"I've never said anything of the kind," I said.

"You've thought it," she shot back.

I did not disagree with her.

"And yet," she continued, "have I mentioned how shameful it is to have a sister in her thirties who is plump and plain and has still failed to get screwed by the spleeny likes of Miles Fucking Keebler?"

"I am plump. I am plain."

Edith shook her head. "Excuses, Alice. Pitiful excuses. Plain girls get fucked. They get fucked *especially*, because men are fond of convincing themselves that they can philanthropize with their dicks."

Sad laughed; an unchewed peach slice rolled in his mouth. Gesina stubbed out her cigarette on the bare tabletop. She turned to Stephen and whispered, "Who knew she was such a cynic?" She had a strong Cockney accent, suddenly.

Edith turned to Gesina. "When you're not born smart, cynicism is the only form of shrewdness available to you. I prefer to think of it as bludgeoned acumen." She tapped her blond head with the back of a spoon. "Had the smarts beat into me."

Bruno interrupted. "Enough yammering," he said.

Edith's face fell. "Christ," she said. "Pardon me for 'yammering.'"

Bruno ignored her, delivering clipped orders to Gesina and Stephen.

"Alice," he said. "Go wake Winnie up."

I scoffed. Not a real scoff, a sort of half-scoff. "Aye, aye," I said.

"Please. Alice. I need to talk to your sister alone."

Edith refused to acknowledge me as I exited the dining room.

It was cold in the hallway. Nobody watched me walk through the courtyard. Nobody seemed to care what I did anymore.

I could just leave. There was the door. Beyond that the cobble-stoned street, the medina. I could just start walking. Instead, I ambled up the hotel stairs. The sun was just setting, the stars were firing up in the darker parts of the sky. The constellations were different in Africa, because we were closer to the equator. I no longer saw *Varicoscadera*, the embittered waitress at the Tip Top; I no longer saw *Haggiopeia*, a hunched shrew blathering out her dying days in a vinyl-sided triplex in Revere, relishing the hate she has for the cat she found and thought she might grow to enjoy because cats are the ultimate symbol that a per-son has embraced the inevitable fact that *she will die alone*, her body undiscovered for weeks in her Revere triplex, until the UPS man, who delivers the cat food, gags at the odor seeping beneath her uninsulated door frame and hears the mewing of her hungry, stupid cat.

Down here, nearer to the equator, the stars told a different story. My Revere triplex burned to the ground, the stupid cat and the grease-stained Tip Top pinafores were incinerated as I replaced this constel-latory life of underpaid servility with a more blazingly exotic one. *Amourion*'s glowing passport in the sky spoke of a life in hotels as my husband—I thought, truly, *husband*—played golf with Arab leaders and delivered commencement speeches at undistinguished, overendowed embassy schools. I would spend my days beneath the mosquito netting, sipping tea and nursing our single child—really, to have more than one child when you moved around as much as we did would be impractical—until it became old enough to learn, at which point I would school it in the few subjects for which I exhibited any affinity, namely non-Romance languages and layman's sociology and informal table service. We would vacation at an empty beach, and we would play breezy card games together, without a hint of competitive tension. Also backgammon. Never chess. I would wear more feminine attire, adopting head scarves to keep back my newly long hair, so long that it fell to my bottom when my husband picked the pins out with his teeth. This was only the beginning. I can say, more generally, that convertibles were also involved, and wooden sailboats equipped with Asian-style rigging. There was always wind. There was always wind, and thus I could never hear what we were saying to each other; but I could see our faces, and we were smiling.

These were the fantasies that "lust" unleashed. I was a fool for comfort. I was lusting for a home.

I continued to walk, unhurried, toward our room. Winnie was on her cot, motionless, her body covered with a sheet. My head still blinded by starry futures, I stumbled over to my cot to retrieve my passport from beneath the mattress. I would need this, I thought, for my new life. I was assaulted again with images of this hypothetical life when the floor drain caught in my peripheral vision.

Edith's ring.

I dropped onto all fours and picked at the drain with my fingers. I levered the corner of my passport beneath the lip and thrust a hand down into the pipe. My hand emerged, the ring caught in the talon crook of my index finger, covered in esophageal plumbing slime. I wiped my hand on my thigh, I cleaned off the dirty diamonds, I slipped the ring on my finger. Edith's ring looked far better on me than it did on her; my hands were more delicate, and took to this kind of filigreed nonsense better than her muscular fingers ever could. I held the ring against my forearm. I steered an imaginary convertible. I trimmed an imaginary sail.

It's kind of pretty, isn't it?

It is. It's absolutely pretty.

I put my ringed finger on Winnie's sheet-covered leg. The stones glimmered against the dingy white.

"Come on," I urged, shaking her calf. "Time to wake up."

I pinched her toes. I tickled her instep. I pulled the pillow out from beneath her head. No response. I pulled off her sheet and screamed.

There was blood. Rivers of it.

Gesina charged through the doorway within seconds, pulling off her djellabah. Underneath, she was wearing a navy skirt suit, sheer white stockings, loafers.

"Get Dr. Driss," she commanded Stephen, who stood, horrified, in the doorway.

She removed her jacket and rolled up the sleeves of her blouse. "Alice," she ordered. "Go to the kitchen and get me some water."

I hustled down the stairs, through the disaster in the dining room. The kitchen was a disaster of empty cans and dirty pots. Evidently Gesina had known it was her last day as hotel proprietress, and thus failed to take her usual pains with the kitchen. The roaches had been quick to capitalize on her neglect; they slalomed in and out of dishes, they twinkled their feelers at me, they gave up no ground.

I filled a giant tureen and slopped through the dining room, reaching the courtyard in time to catch Dr. Driss scurrying up the stairs, followed by a pair of men—white men, with white uniforms and white shoes. The white men returned moments later with a silent and uncharacteristically stoic Winnie bouncing on a stretcher. Stephen and Sad followed, then Gesina and a sulking Tom.

"Let's go," she said. I dropped my water tureen and followed her.

Outside, the Therefore Ambulance idled.

"Oh, no." Sad balked. "No. No."

"Don't be a buffoon." Gesina tried to force him into the back of the ambulance. "We're taking you to a helicopter."

Sad eyed her disbelievingly.

"Cross my heart," Gesina said, jabbing an X over her abdomen with a double-jointed thumb. "We're going home."

"Where's Edith?" I asked.

"She and Bruno have gone ahead to meet the transport," Stephen said. "Get in."

I glanced at my wrist. Pitcairn's watch read seven thirty-five.

This wasn't the plan. We were supposed to be in the hotel at nine forty-five.

I set one foot on the back bumper.

"Move it, Alice," Stephen said.

"I, uh, forgot something in the hotel," I said. I'd write Pitcairn a note. I'd tell him about the transport point. He could meet me there.

"Too late." Stephen gave me a gentle push.

Gesina, Stephen, Tom, Dr. Driss, and I followed Sad into the back of the ambulance, where Winnie's contractions cruised along quietly, gaining in strength and shortening in frequency.

Dr. Driss poised himself over the patient.

"Will she make it to Melilla?" Stephen asked.

Dr. Driss pressed the stethoscope over Winnie's throat, her wrists, her hair.

"Doubtful," he said. "Claims will have a field day with this one."

Gesina harrumphed. "Claims? We don't have to answer to Claims anymore, remember?"

"That's the problem, isn't it?" Dr. Driss said. "There's no one to answer to now."

"I thought that was the point," Gesina replied acidly. "You always lose your courage in the face of deregulation."

Dr. Driss smoldered in his corner of the ambulance. We bounced all over the place, hitting our heads on the ceiling, then crashing down with a collective *uuufff* onto our coccyx bones. Gesina pulled a cigarette from her pocket and tried to light it, but succeeded only in singeing her bangs. The smell of cooked hair filled the back of the ambulance, and mingled with the odor of overworked brakes and Dr. Driss's lemony cologne.

"You know," Dr. Driss said, "this is precisely the sort of outcome that made me hesitant to be involved with this operation."

Gesina groaned. "You and your regrets! Maybe if you hadn't flunked out of the Institute . . ."

"I failed my physical," Dr. Driss interjected. "That can hardly be perceived as 'flunking out.' "

"Maybe not by you," Gesina said under her breath.

"You should watch who you throw stones at, *you* who were suspended for unapproved steroid use!"

"That was a role-play!" Gesina yelled back. "I was a Ukrainian gold medalist in the two-hundred-meter butterfly!"

Dr. Driss observed Gesina's broad shoulders. "That was a role-play?"

I feared Gesina was about to strike the citrus-smelling man.

"Enough!" I said. "Please! Have some pity on the innocent civilians!"

Gesina sneered at me. "I'm sorry, Alice—do you find us unprofessional?"

"Just tiresome."

Gesina laughed. "Tiresome! Well. There will be comment cards available in the helicopter. We'd love to know how we can improve your experience."

I put my head between my knees. I was nauseated again—from the lurching Therefore Ambulance, from the utter absurdity of it all.

"Don't throw up," Stephen said. "We're almost there." It was the first considerate thing he'd said to me.

I looked up at him. His eyes had lost their cold shrewdness and appeared almost kind.

"You know him?" I asked.

"Who?"

"Pitcairn," I said.

"Sure I do," he said. "Or did. You know, you should watch out for him."

"Thanks for the warning, but I doubt I'll ever see him again," I said, hoping I sounded convincing. Or hoping that I didn't. Would I ever see him again?

"Make sure you don't," Stephen said. "Pitcairn hates anyone who tries to get close to him. The more you actively admire him, the more he'll come to despise you. He used to be my mentor. I admired the hell out of the guy. And look where it got me."

"It got you in an ambulance with me," I said, my nausea redoubling as I ingested this new information.

"Exactly," Stephen said. "Not that I mind your company. The rest could stand to be improved upon."

Moments later, the ambulance came to a sliding halt. Gesina flung the doors open and hopped out, her ankles buckling as she landed in sand.

"Where's the helicopter?" she yelled.

Stephen climbed out, followed by Dr. Driss. I remained in the ambulance. I put a hand on Winnie's foot, palpating it. The poor narcissistic girl, I thought. Lucky for her she's not here for this.

"It should be here," Dr. Driss said.

"Should be!" Gesina howled.

"Don't get mad at me! It's not as though I lost it!"

Gesina scraped a hand through her hair. "It's simply, *Doctor,* that you said it was here."

"It *was* here."

The two of them stood an angry distance apart, squinting up at the sky, as if you could discern a helicopter in the dark before you could hear it.

I continued to massage Winnie's swollen foot. Her body relaxed and her breathing evened out. She was sleeping, or so I believed, but then she bucked upright in the stretcher, her mouth contorted in a silent, agonized yowl. I dropped Winnie's foot and scrambled backward on all fours, tumbling out of the ambulance. Dr. Driss shouted instructions to Stephen, words I could not hear because the air was being chopped into noisy black bits by an approaching helicopter.

During all of this, I lay in the sand. I lay in the sand and watched the stars, as I listened to the helicopter's approach. Sand blew over my face and suddenly there were more stars—stars stuck to my eyelashes, stars in my mouth, tiny, cold, tasteless grains of star. I felt a gentle *bump* reverberate through the earth. I raised myself up on an elbow. There was a helicopter in the desert, and people running toward it. The pilots did not cut the engine, and so it resembled my fantasy of life with Pitcairn, lots of wind and nobody talking, or people talking but nobody listening, because there is very little to say when the wind is so loud that whatever seems to be happening to you probably isn't happening, it is just the deafening weather inside your head.

I replayed my Pitcairn fantasy, but it didn't seem so convincing anymore. There was a possibility other than happiness to consider, if I somehow managed to escape and meet Pitcairn at the hotel. I would forge through the courtyard, I would find him speaking into a cell phone, we would make stunted conversation, we would return to our respective homes, he would never call me, in fourteen years' time he'd appear at the Tip Top and I would hide in the kitchen, spying on him through the greasy porthole before sneaking out the side entrance and returning home to feed my cat. Or: The hotel would be abuzz with Brain Worms, looking at criminal profile spreadsheets while Pitcairn patently ignored me, we would return to our respective homes, et cetera, et cetera. Or: I would sit in the empty hotel and wait for him, but he would never arrive. Or. Or. Or. Regardless of the scenario, the fallout was always the same. The Chinese junk faded from view, the hotels we stayed in grew increasingly mold-ridden and serviced by a dyspeptic staff, our life on the road exuded an aura of gruel and desperation, our child screamed in the backseat of our flea-infested Hyundai rental, our mouths were tight, there was no wind, no sound, nothing but a terrible sun overhead and the unspoken agreement that we'd made a horrible, horrible mistake.

I lifted my hand to look at Edith's ring. When I squinted, it appeared to be just another misleading arrangement of stars.

"Alice!"

Stephen signaled to me. The two white men led Sad to the helicopter and pushed him aboard. A hand reached out to help. A woman's hand. Edith's, I assumed. She and Bruno were already aboard. I watched as the white men returned to the ambulance and yanked the bloodied stretcher from the rear. The blanket over Winnie's body blew away, and I saw her huddled in fetal position, clutching her knees.

Dr. Driss climbed out of the ambulance, one arm bent to his chest. He knelt beside me in the sand and moved his lips at me. *Gum wun*, his lips said.

Under the furred canopy of the propellers, everything was quiet. Dr. Driss smiled and revealed the blanketed infant he had hidden in the crook of his elbow. I took it in my arms. It smelled terrible, worse than rotten. I passed the baby into the resistant arms of Gesina, intending with every fiber of my body to follow it, intending to get into the helicopter to be spirited away from this desert where the stars filled my mouth with their stale taste of old sky.

I glanced in the direction of the hotel, which I would no longer have the opportunity to be tempted to enter at nine forty-five p.m. *In part, I feel relieved,* I thought. *I am tired of playing games.* This is what I said to myself, at least.

I stepped onto the helicopter ski and braced my hands on the door. I scanned the interior. "Where's Edith?" I yelled.

Stephen shook his head and pointed at his ear.

"Edith!" There was no meaningful sound above the *chop-chop-chop*. Gesina shrugged. Tom yelled, "I think she went back to find Bruno!"

Stephen grabbed my forearms and hauled me into the helicopter, which had already started to buck and jump. We rose a few feet and bobbed above the ground. I could see the lights of Itzal, murking up the night above.

"Hold on," Stephen hollered. Gesina clutched the baby to her suit jacket; the baby oozed from her tight grasp, fists winging incensed and hopeless punches at the air.

That's not right, I thought. Why I was so compelled by this squalling creature I cannot exactly explain. This baby appeared to represent the single bit of sincerity in a scenario that otherwise lacked the usual sincere footholds. For this reason, its presence was a cool guarantee of humanity. For this reason, our captivity seemed done with; for this reason, we were really going home.

We were going home. I was going home.

Without Edith.

I must have had time to think about this queer, disquieting fact. I had minutes, or seconds, before the helicopter dropped with a gut-twirling directness straight toward the desert, knocked out of the sky by wind shear. I looked up and saw stars, or maybe it was the glint of Edith's engagement ring, still wedged on my finger as my hands flailed madly. I do not remember thinking anything; I do not remember being scared, even when it became clear that I was falling. Falling, yes, although it is possible, too, that I simply let go. On purpose? By accident? Because I exerted my free will? Because I was a "good girl"? God knows. All I can say for certain is this: I dropped fifteen feet and landed in a heap on the sand.

I lay on my back and watched the helicopter's unimpeded ascent into the night sky, its blinking taillights becoming another pair of anxious stars. The silence that closed in after the chopping died away was enough to crush the life out of me. I sobbed for reasons that were not wholly apparent. Soon the night grew too cold for crying. I walked toward the silhouetted shape of town.

❧

I t z a l   w a s   e m p t y, so there was no one to avoid as I hobbled through the unfamiliar streets, my hair and clothes clotted with bits of desert that rained off me and made a ringing noise on the cobblestones. I wandered aimlessly before stumbling on the recognizable hotel façade of closed shutters, through whose numerous cracks no light was visible.

I hurried through the reception area and into the courtyard. According to Pitcairn's watch, still buckled to my wrist, it was five minutes after nine. Even if he meant to meet me—which I was beginning to doubt—he wouldn't be here yet. His promise that "Something is going to happen tonight" was a big ruse; he was as much of a manipulator as his brother, putting human beings in stressful conditions to see how they would react. Which was why I didn't want him to catch me here. I didn't want him to think I'd misunderstood the implicit rules of our hypothetical courtship.

The wicker chairs lining the courtyard had been overturned, some even appeared to have been tossed, a bored afterthought, as during a successful party. Edith and Bruno's room was empty and in its natural state of disarray. I heard noises coming from our room. Terrible, thunking noises, punctuated by a woman's "Ugh! Ugh! Ugh!" I recognized that voice. Or perhaps I should say: The voice was unrecognizable, but the constricted despair it conveyed was all too recognizable. It was the sound of Edith losing her shit, really losing it, not for any effect, not to exploit or manipulate anyone.

Through the door, I could see my sister standing amid the broken tiles, the pulverized grout, clutching a tool that resembled a big, skinny hammer. She'd changed into her wedding escape suit. Her hair was so tightly braided that her face looked slicked back by a destructive wind.

She lifted the hammer and brought it down on the tile floor, what was left of it. She'd hacked up the area where the drain once was.

I pulled her ring off my finger and hid it in my bra. I could have said "Edith," but I did not. I watched her. She was nearing the end of her tantrum, her arms too tired to lift the hammer above her knees. Lift, drop. Lift, drop.

The hammer wedged itself between two wooden joists. She grunted as she attempted to lever it free.

"Fuck it," she said, kicking at the handle. She dropped onto a mattress. She looked at me.

And looked at me.

Was I invisible? Her eyes didn't focus. She hawked up a dramatic wad of spit, fired it at the floor. Wiped her mouth. Did it again.

"Fucking dust," she said. "What the hell are you doing here?"

I leaned against the door frame. "I came back to get you."

Bitter laugh. "Well, aren't you the martyr. Or did you come to sell me out a few more times?"

"I didn't sell you out."

"No? What do you call it, then? Protection?"

"It was all hypothetical," I said.

"I'm not feeling terribly hypothetical at the moment."

"Well, but . . ."

"We've always looked out for each other, or at least that's how I understood the arrangement."

"Which is why I came back to make sure you were all right."

"I'm fucking fab." Her lips warbled. She swiped her nose with her forearm.

I grabbed the roll of gray toilet tissue from the lavatory and tossed it at her. She failed to catch it. Unlike the Antidotes, Edith and I had terrible hand-eye coordination. We had never deserved a sporty relic from the fatherland. We would have dropped it, broken it, rested it on the hipbones of an unconscious woman, lost it to a sacked hostage negotiator in Kashmir.

Edith unrolled the tissue. Blew her nose and tossed the tissue on the floor.

"Where's Bruno?" I asked.

"Lost in the desert, for all I care."

"But he was here, wasn't he? Isn't that why you came back?"

Shrug. "I don't know why I came back. Because he told me not to."

That's right. *I need to talk to your sister alone.* "What else did he have to say for himself?"

Shrug. Weeping. The real stuff. Now that she had her grief partner, her misery spectator. Now that this wasn't a wasted display of wretchedness.

"Said I should go and get married, even if I didn't love the guy. Said it was 'high time' for a girl such as myself to accept my moral limitations."

"What moral limitations?"

"Some anthropologist hooey. He said he'd been using me to prove a point about the 'moral no-man's-land of sibling relationships.'"

"And did you prove his hypothesis?"

"I'm not a sibling on my own, you know. A person needs a sibling to be a sibling."

"Okay. Did *we* prove it?"

She made vague flapping gestures with her hands. My insistence on precise recall was annoying her. Or there was something she didn't want to tell me.

"Who cares? Bruno was using me. He bragged about it. So I told him that I'd been used plenty before he'd used me, and there was no being first in this world anymore. Chances are someone's always been there before you, and he might as well rub that smug smile off his face." She folded her arms, squishing her breasts together. She peered into the dark crease morbidly.

"I'm sorry," I said.

"Yeah, well, you should be sorry."

"I'm shamefully, mortally, world-record-breakingly sorry. Now stop crying."

"I'm not crying about you. I could give two hoots about you and your fair-weather loyalties."

I was confused. "But you came back here."

"Yes."

"Why?"

She paused, allowing the forces of sadness to rejoin, the lips to strike a pout, the shoulders to tremble.

"I don't want to marry X, Alice." This confession produced a dissolution nearing total. I sat next to her on the hunched mattress, I put a hand around her sweaty shoulders.

"So don't," I said.

"But I have to!"

I frowned. "That's really what this is all about?"

"*All?* I'm talking about the rest of my life!"

"Not necessarily."

"I do not share your cynicism about matrimony, as you well know. When I marry, it will be for a longish time."

"But nobody's making you marry X."

"That's not true."

"Name one person."

"*No,* Alice."

"Edith."

"*No.* Somebody is making me marry him. I'm making me marry him. *Me.*"

Hysterics, of the soundless variety. She collapsed into my lap, the whole mewling, unchecked mess of her. I rubbed her arm. I patted her head. I curled her braid around and around and around, forming a pastry shape. Dear Lord, I thought. What happened to us?

"So you came back to get your ring?"

"I don't know why I came back here. Because I'm just so goddamned tired."

She yawned and shut her eyes, resting her chin in her hand. I thought she might take a nap.

Finally she said, "Do you remember the day of Mr. V.'s funeral?"

"Of course."

"Do you remember when Mom took Mrs. V. away in the rickshaw, and we never saw Mrs. V. again?"

I nodded.

"Well, I saw her again."

"You never told me that."

"I'm telling you now. I went to her hospital room. I returned the next day, and the next. She ordered me to stop visiting her. She called in a nurse to remove me, but the nurse gave Mrs. V. a tranquilizer instead. Mrs. V. started to cry and begged me to leave her alone. I said I would leave her alone if she'd answer one question."

"Which was?"

"I'm *getting* to it. She said, 'What is it? What is your one question?' I told her I wanted to know if she'd thrown herself onto the fire on purpose, or if she'd tripped."

"Good question."

"She was very rude, naturally. You remember what a bitch she was. She thought I was too idiotic to hang around with her brilliant fucking daughter. She was always speaking Hindi to Harja when I was around, and because I couldn't understand Hindi, I was, according to her, stupid. The question made her nervous. She upended the pudding on her lunch tray. And then she lied to me, Alice."

"How do you know?"

"I was wearing a red sweater. I looked just like Mom. I remember thinking when I left the house that day: This will freak the hell out of her, I look just like Mom. And it did. Even after the tranquilizer, she was shaking. I'd be lying if I didn't say that I enjoyed it. It was her fault that Mom and Dad divorced, after all."

"That's not true."

"Of course it is."

"She was, as Miles would say, the marital succubus."

"Screw Miles," Edith said.

"A marital succubus is the event or person upon which a marriage's failure is wrongly blamed, because everyone needs a scapegoat. Miles wrote his thesis paper comparing divorce proceedings to the Salem witch trials."

"In my opinion, it was Mrs. V.'s fault, and Miles, King of the Succubae, will never convince me otherwise. Anyhow. Mrs. V. told me that she and Mom had planned the whole thing together, as a way to punish Dad for his philandering."

"What whole thing?"

"I mean, from the very beginning. She claimed that Mom had come to her crying one day. She was being cheated on by Dad, and needed Mrs. V.'s help. Mrs. V. said that mom *asked* her to seduce Dad, which she did, and that they planned to scare the pants off of him by making it appear as though he'd driven Mrs. V. to kill herself. She said that a few superficial burns were worth making a fool of the man. It was her feminist duty. She said that she and Mom laughed all the way to the hospital."

"Bullshit."

"Of course it's bullshit. But it's cool to think of Mom having the forethought and organization to play a trick like that on her own husband. All married couples should work out their problems that way. Deceive and conquer, as Bruno said."

"But that's, so . . . so . . . *peculiar.*"

"Is it peculiar? I thought it was the most marvelous thing I'd ever heard. And I decided, from that day forward, to make everything that happened to me appear as if I'd engineered it. Every heartbreak, every failure. I dated wounded people, and when they wounded me back, it was all because I'd orchestrated it to happen that way. There was no longer any need to be ashamed about anything. I had eradicated shame."

"That's so peculiar," I said again.

"It's not peculiar, Alice. It's *brilliant.*"

"I don't know if I'd go that far."

"Well, that's because you're such a fucking moderate."

"I just think that, in the long term, it's bound to make you a touch unstable."

"Oooooh, what, are you going to invoke the denial clause, Miss Almost Social Worker? Are you going to invoke subsection B, Revisionist History, under Roman numeral two, Delusions of Invulnerability?"

"Did I say anything about . . ."

"Because of course you'd have no idea what it was like to be the black sheep of the family . . ."

"Hold on now. . . ."

"To have to throw myself off the back of a goddamned *camel* to get anyone to pay me any attention, I mean, really, Alice, you've been Alice your whole life, and I've just been a number of different people, none of whom have managed to stick very well."

"That's not true," I said.

She started to cry again. "It *is* true, Alice. I know you like to think of yourself as the loser, the ugly duckling, the late bloomer, but maybe you should face up to the fact that that's as much of a goddamned fiction as anything I've come up with."

Was it true?

"Deny it if you want. As I know you'll probably deny the fact that you've proved yourself to be as much of an opportunist as me these past few days."

I didn't say anything. I was trying to work through the *listen-reject-reject-hear* response pattern. I was stuck in the *reject-reject* part.

Edith burrowed her head in my lap, as she did when she wanted her head rubbed. Reluctantly, I dug through her hair, hair that was so familiar to me in texture and smell that it might have been my own. I leaned back against the lumped-up mattress and closed my eyes, feeling as though I was in a museum-restored site where people had been snuffed out or experimented on. It made me uncomfortable to think that I had been as inconsiderate and selfish as Edith when it came to the suffering of the other passengers. She had treated it as a game. I had treated it as an opportunity to be different, all of a sudden. Now I found my hunger for "opportunity" had abated; now I wanted to go home.

Home, yes. And where was home, exactly? Home was a vinyl-sided triplex in Revere without so much as a cat to resent. Home was a wait-ressing job at a Route 1 western-themed steakhouse. Home was the scene of BB gun blow-outs with the neighbors and regular garbage re-moval. Home was proofed with a figurative vinyl siding against exhila-ration and glee, similarly against failure, disappointment, humiliation. What did that crotchety old humbug of a poet say? *Home is the place where, when you have to go there, they have to take you in.* In other words: Home has exceedingly low standards.

This is what I'd said to Clifford after we'd finished our sandwiches on that fateful day of role-playing in Øn. We were exhausted, both of us, in a deep-body, Scandinavian way. I let Clifford do the dishes while I collapsed in a wingback before the fire.

"What do you say, Alice?" Clifford said, emerging from the kitchen, her gaunt face inflamed. "Now that we're completely warmed up, perhaps we should return to the 'home.'"

Home has exceedingly low standards, I told her. Meaning: One did not have to be at the top of one's game to revisit it. Meaning: I was tired. I wanted to go to bed.

Clifford persisted. "This is an opportunity," she said. "I'll play you, while you play Edith."

"Don't be predictable," I said. Clifford was desperately attracted to my relationship with Edith and was convinced I was hiding something from her.

"Are you uncomfortable?" she asked.

"Of course I'm uncomfortable," I replied.

She said, "Discomfort is your weakness, Edith."

"Don't call me Edith," I said.

"Are you so uneasy being yourself?" she asked. "Or are you uncertain who 'yourself' is?"

Clifford/Alice sat there fingering her whistle. Fuck it, I thought. If she wants to go down this road, we can go down this road. It wasn't a very interesting road. I'd told her everything. She'd learn nothing new from me.

We time-traveled without much respect for chronology, moving from Mr. V.'s funeral, to our discovery of the Shame Books, to our last real conversation, at the Hotel Itzal. Clifford circled me around and around before arriving, in a sneaky, back-door fashion, at "Camel Ride."

"We are at a hypothetical country house," she said.

"In Sweden?" I asked.

"Why not Sweden," Clifford said. "We are at a rented vacation house, Edith. The weather is poor. You're bored, and true to your usual disdain for personal boundaries, you decide to poke through the family's conceits in the attic. In doing so, you find a home movie camera and a cardboard box full of old movies. You want to set the projector up and have a matinee. We do so, and the movies are tedious. Lots of babies wobbling around in diapers."

"What did you expect?" I asked. "Scenes from an adulterous relationship? Father frontal nudity?"

"No," Clifford corrected. "What did *you* expect?"

"I really don't want to play this game," I said.

Clifford put her whistle to her lips, but did not blow.

"Wait," she said. "It's getting better. I propose the following idea: to reenact all the home movies Dad shot of us when we were kids, and record it with the camera."

"What a dumb idea, *Alice*," I said sarcastically.

"Why is it such a dumb idea?"

"Because you know we don't agree what happened in those films."

"That's why we should reenact them," she insisted. "If we're both present during the filming, how can we disagree?"

I was tired of fighting her. I conceded to the reenactment.

There were no camels in our pretend Swedish rental house, so we pulled an old couch out from the wall, stacked pillows on the backrest, and straddled it, with Clifford in front, me behind.

"Here come the women with the yarn," Clifford said. She waved. She accepted a pretend twist of yarn, she licked it with her salmon-colored tongue.

I couldn't have cared less. Honestly. I did not care about the yarn, about Clifford's pretend popularity. I could not inhabit my sister's head; it was impossible for me to be Edith given the oppositional way we defined ourselves. I was everything she was not. To cross that line, to become "Edith," was too great an insult to my person.

"Can't we go back to the plane?" I said.

"Here come the women with the grain baskets," Clifford said, ignoring me.

"So?"

"So you want to impress them. You're terribly envious of me, and you want to impress them."

"No I don't," I said.

"You do," she said. "Don't be such a chicken."

Clifford started to pinch my hands, little tiny ant pinches.

"Stop it," I said.

"I won't stop. You're jealous of me because I'm more powerful than you and always will be. The only power you have over me is to resist my taunts, but you can't resist, Edith. Do you know why?"

"Because discomfort is my weakness?"

"Exactly. Discomfort is your weakness. You'll do anything to be left alone, even if it means calling attention to yourself."

"That's so complicated," I said.

"I know," Clifford said. "I don't expect you to grasp the subtleties, because I'm far more intelligent and devious than you. Just imagine yourself as my dancing puppet."

"Your dancing puppet," I said.

"You can have all the attention, while I'm invisible. You will make me invisible. I've realized, you see, that invisibility is the way to go. I've been the popular one up to this point, as we both know, but I've realized, after some lengthy analysis, that this is not the way to go."

"What lengthy analysis?" I said. "What are you talking about? You're five years old."

"I haven't articulated this to myself, of course. But"—Clifford stepped out of character for a moment—"children as young as eighteen months have proven, in tests, to possess the manipulative sophistication of an adult."

"Clifford," I said.

Clifford glared at me.

"Alice," I said. "I believe you've read too much into 'Camel Ride.'"

"Have I, Edith?"

"It's just a dumb home movie."

"But it represents a defining moment in our relationship, does it not? It communicates something unarguably true about us. Isn't that what you believe?"

"That's how I've represented it, yes."

"You're saying you've lied?"

"No."

"You're saying you've invested a random event in our life with more meaning than it deserves?"

I looked at Clifford. "What do you want from me?" I asked.

"I want to know: Did you invest a random event with meaning it never possessed?"

"I—I don't know," I said.

"What is the meaning of this event, then? Is it meaningless?"

"Of course not. It happened."

"How did it happen, Edith? After I said, 'You can have all the attention, while I'm invisible. You will make me invisible.'"

I didn't say to Clifford, "But I never said that." It was clear she wasn't going to let me off the hook, so I tried to get into the spirit of the thing, whatever the thing was, and whichever spirit it demanded.

"After I said, 'You will make me invisible,'" Clifford repeated.

"I don't want to be watched," I said. "Someone's always watching, in this family."

Clifford picked at her lips. I thought: I don't do that. Edith does that.

"You're older," Clifford said. "And prettier."

"Not yet," I said.

"But you will be prettier, because being watched is addictive. You might even develop a taste for being observed. I promise."

"Being watched means you're abnormal."

Clifford's lips started to bleed. "How do you figure?" she asked.

"Dad's always looking at things. He watches things mutate. Being watched means you're abnormal," I repeated.

"Not necessarily," Clifford said. "Being watched means you're notable."

I raised an eyebrow.

"I am, as I have always been, too scared to be notable," I said.

"That's my line," Clifford said.

"No it's not."

"It is." Clifford pinched my hands again.

"Stop it," I said.

"But that's my line," Clifford said. "Give it back."

"What are you talking about?" I asked. The room was starting to morph. The gingham curtains oozed into the wainscoting, the lamps into the floor.

"You've been playing me all these years," Clifford said. "I'm goddamned sick of it."

"What years? We're only five and six years old."

Clifford scoffed. "This isn't about 'Camel Ride.'"

"It's not?"

"'Camel Ride' was just the beginning. It was simply the first time."

"The first time for what?"

Clifford grew impatient.

"We switch roles, Edith. Don't you get it? We've been switching roles our entire lives. You're no such thing as a fixed person."

"I never claimed to be a fixed person," I said.

"You did," Clifford countered. "You thought you were a fixed person. That's why you believed you were better than me."

"Wait," I said, "who are you talking to? Edith or me?"

"Does it matter?" Clifford said. "It's all the same, isn't it?" She pinched my hands, harder and harder.

"Leave me the fuck alone," I said.

"What are you going to do about it?" Clifford taunted. "What are you going to do?"

It was stupid of me to stand on that couch. It was a hundred years old, a cranky, arthritic heirloom, lacking the appropriate ballast. But I stood on the back of the couch because I wanted to escape this woman, whoever she was. The sleet spattered the windows as I tried to balance, the sleet sounding like grain. I was not waving enthusiastically to get anyone's attention. I was not looking to steal anything from anyone. I was simply trying to escape. But escape what, exactly? I couldn't put it into words—not then, not now. Whatever it was, it felt more oppressive than a preexisting home movie. It ran deeper, like a blood obligation. It was, as they say, *in my contract*.

The couch overturned and I hit my head against the curtain rod. When I woke up, Clifford was crouching beside the fire, blowing on her whistle so lightly that the sound she made was barely distinguishable from the Swedish wind, whistling through the eaves.

"What did you learn?" she asked, fidgeting with her skirt hem.

"Hell is other people," I said. I touched the bleating lump beneath my left eyebrow.

"And?"

"I am other people," I said.

Clifford beamed at me. "And we all know what that means, don't we, Edith?"

I nodded, sick. I knew myself better than I had ever had known myself, the paradox being that the better I got to know myself, the freer I was to be anybody but me.

"It means," Clifford said, pulling an unopened bottle of scotch from beneath the coffee table, "Welcome to our sorry, hellish club."

T HERE WAS A SPIDER on the ceiling, the same damned spider that had been on our ceiling for days. Edith had fallen asleep.

I looked at my watch. Panicked. Nine twenty-five p.m. Pitcairn could be here any minute.

I poked Edith.

"Wake up," I said.

She grunted.

"Come on. We have to get out of here."

I pulled her to her feet and we stumbled over the mattresses, the chunks of tile and old grout.

Edith scuffed along the walkway with a vacant expression on her face.

"Come on." I pulled at her sleeve. She was dawdling.

She refused to be hurried. She leaned against the railing and looked up at the sky.

"It's so beautiful here," she said.

"Right."

"I mean, North Africa is really beautiful. I've always wanted to live here, ever since I was a girl."

This wasn't true or untrue. She'd also wanted to live in Finland, in Saskatchewan, in Potsdam (she liked the sound of "Potsdam").

"But what a dream to be able to spend the rest of my life here. Well, not *here*, but Melilla."

I shot her a quizzical, sideways look. "Huh?"

Edith delivered a joshing punch to my forearm. "You didn't really believe all that nonsense, did you?"

"What nonsense?"

"About not wanting to marry X, about me being the black sheep, and well, whatever else I spewed out. I'm just a little upset."

I blinked. The spots were branded on my eyelids. Star burn. This was all too psychotic.

"Once a girl's bought a dress," I said dully.

Edith brushed the plaster off her skirt. She spread her arms to the sky and took deep breaths, before lowering her arms with an overanimated exhalation.

"I need to get a few things from my room," she said. "Meet you outside?"

I nodded and started down the staircase, one numb step at a time. I felt light-bodied, unfamiliar to myself, as though someone had just suctioned out all my gray matter and bone and muscle, leaving a rubbery human suit in which no sentient creature lived.

I was at the bottom of the staircase when I heard Edith call my name.

I turned. She'd hoisted one hip onto the railing; she played with the frayed end of her braid.

"So," she said. "I have a question."

"Yes?"

"Just a little question, Alice."

Did you do it on purpose? Or did you trip?

"Do you still think I've lost my spark?"

She twirled her braid. Twirled it and twirled it with a nervousness that verged on mad. She couldn't keep that smile on her face much longer. It would be the death of her. I wanted to say *No.* So I did. I said *No,* I said it a few times. *No no no no,* emphasis on the *No.* But what I meant by it was different from how it seemed. I didn't mean she still had her spark. What I meant by it was, *No,* you haven't lost anything that you didn't ever have in the first place.

❧

I STOOD OUTSIDE the Hotel Itzal and waited for Edith. I didn't know where Bruno was, and can't say that I cared. I assumed that the helicopter, once I had fallen out of it, had flown back to town and picked him up. They were all on their way back to Lucerne to update their résumés, while Pitcairn coughed up a lung at the Medersa El Attarin and drafted his letter of resignation. I still hadn't decoded in what way Bruno had "lost," and assumed he was just like a lot of people, always wanting more than he'd initially thought he'd wanted, so that every victory could conveniently appear a failure.

This is called, in some circles, ambition.

As for my own ambition, what remained of it, I had the following goals in mind: Edith and I would hitch a ride out of town on the next supply truck. She would get married; the Antidotes would batter each other over the head with letter openers; the weight of happiness would descend upon the head, et cetera, et cetera; X and Edith would go to Greenland; I would return to Revere. It would be as if none of this had ever happened.

Except.

Except that each night before falling asleep, I would have a new imaginary future to entertain. I would make my love interest slowly less pitiable, I would reshape him and reshape him until he was a raucous, glowing Institute man, playing golf with the king of Morocco, pontificating in an open-collar shirt and a new corduroy jacket to an auditorium full of eager prep school graduates. Soon he'd be in my head even when I was wide awake, striding about in jodhpurs or adjusting the mainsail on our Asian-rigged boat. Soon I would elevate my moment with him at the Medersa El Attarin, and the liberties I did not take with him, as the greatest symbol of my lack of will and the single most fulfilling regret of my life.

I had it all planned out. I was, as I said, ambitious.

It was dangerously late now, and cold. Overhead, I heard a noise. When I looked up I thought: A falling star. How perfect. How apt. Heading straight toward me (or so it seemed). Except. This falling star, well, it wasn't exactly *falling*. It originated at the horizon and arched overhead. Just a trick of light or latitude, I thought. I watched the falling star rise above me, and then behave more predictably, curving down toward the earth.

It was quite beautiful. Blue in color, with sparking instances of green and orange as the gaseous core was exposed. I heard sighing as the star descended and hit with a tremendous blast, maybe a hundred meters west of the Hotel Itzal. The palm trees on the far side of the western wall exploded upward, thin chimneypipes of pure flame. Heat, instantly. A wind of heat. It propelled me toward a small alley in the lee of the fire. I landed on the cobblestones. They rolled beneath me. My knee throbbed. My lungs, too.

What the hell?

A second star fell, also beyond the hotel walls. Then a third. And a fourth.

Because I was not thinking clearly, the giggling did not take me by surprise. The high-pitched, thrilled eruptions of delight did not strike me as out of place in the back alley of a Moroccan desert oasis town, in the midst of what appeared to be a violent meteor shower.

It was hard to see in the dark, even with the light from the fire. *Because* of the light from the fire. It obliterated everything, as an eclipse can obliterate everything, singe the world right out of existence. So I didn't see him at first, dressed in his dark burnoose. He was sitting mere feet from me. The fire reflected maniacally in his lenses, and if the eyes were the windows to the soul, then I was gazing into the house of some kind of madman.

He must have heard me. I was singing to myself, a nervous rhyme, *Once there was a falling star made of dynamite, it landed on my sister and it turned her into light*. He lunged at me, taking me by surprise and trapping my head in an unshakable bear hug.

"I knew it, Alice!"

I tried to wrangle free.

"Alice!" Bruno screamed. "Alice! We've won!"

"*We* won?"

But he wasn't listening to me. "*We won we won we won!*" He ran into the street, rammed his shin against a ceramic planter. He didn't even notice. He yelled up to the sky. He limped over to a junky bronze-colored sedan—idling, its headlights shining on the hotel and illuminating the smoke that drifted through the street—and turned on the radio. Loud. Distorted zither music twanged into the stone alleyways, amplifying the hysteria.

"*Pitcairn!*" he yelled. "*You bastard! Pitcairn! You may have surprised yourself, but you sure as hell didn't surprise me!*"

I walked into the street. The bombs (bombs, right, *not* meteors) seemed to have stopped. The trees just beyond the hotel were dangerously afire. The wind shifted to the east. I noticed this because the air became hot, hard to breathe. The wind blew predictably west in Itzal, meaning the flames from the bombs should have blown away from the hotel. Instead, they arched up and over the roof.

Edith. She was nowhere.

"Alice," Bruno said. Grabbing my arm.

"Let—me—go." Calm now.

"Alice," he said. He had to scream to be heard above the burning and the zithers. "Can you believe it? He's an Incursionist! A goddamned Incursionist of the worst kind! Willing to kill innocent civilians! Willing to raze villages!"

"I need to find Edith."

Bruno grinned, and I wanted to be sick, right there, on the goddamned cobblestones. I wanted to be sick.

"Is that really why you want to go back in there?" he asked.

"What are you implying?"

"He told you he had a hard time living in the moment. He told you he despised certainty."

"This has nothing to do with Pitcairn," I said. "I'm going in to get Edith."

"That's an even worse reason. Forget her, Alice," Bruno said. "She's no sister to you."

"Says you."

"I hate to be the one to tell you this."

He grabbed my arm harder. He shook it. I would have a bruise on that arm for six weeks; the skin where his fingers were would never fade to normal. He had tarnished me for good.

"She's the one who sold you out. She told me about the wire cutters. I asked her to follow you through the medina. It had nothing to do with Pitcairn or his rulebook. She will never have your best interests at heart, do you understand that? She will forever try to sabotage your life. You should let her fend for herself for a change. Do you both a favor."

He threw me away from himself. Toward the hotel. Daring me to ignore him.

"Fuck you, Bruno."

I started toward the hotel.

"You're willing to risk your life for her?" Bruno called after me. "You're willing to die for someone who will always screw you over, always? Where's your sense of self-preservation? Where's your indignation? Where's your goddamned pride?"

"Maybe I'm doing this for selfish reasons," I yelled over my shoulder. "Did you ever think of that? Did you ever think I might be doing this for self-serving reasons?"

Bruno didn't respond. Then I heard him say, "Never, Alice. I never once thought that."

You misunderstand, I wanted to say. *Alice is a good girl, you think. But you have no idea, no idea at all.* Instead, I left him there. He kept yelling at me. I could hear him all the way from the reception area. He didn't even know that I was gone.

❧

I PEEKED INTO the dining room, hoping to find Edith in her red escape suit, deranged as a desert Miss Haversham.

The dining room was empty. Edith's Samsonite, however, was on a table.

I stood by the wine cabinet, listening for human sounds. Edith's human sounds. Pitcairn's human sounds.

What the hell was I doing in here? It was nine thirty-nine, by Pitcairn's watch.

I needed to leave. I understood the parameters now, and (since Bruno had asked), this was where my goddamned pride was located— in beating Pitcairn at his own game. In passing his stupid test. I would be damned if I was going to be branded as yet another adoring person, willing to be despised. I got halfway through the courtyard on my way to the front door before pausing by an unfurling wicker chair.

Was it true, what Bruno had claimed? Had Edith sold me out? God damn her. God damn her and her pretend insecurities, her need to one-up me even when I was trying to be modest and invisible. If I was a loser, she had to be a worse loser; if I was a person on the rise, she had to stick a pin in my balloon. There was no winning with her, there was simply no winning.

It occurred to me, though, that Bruno might be lying. He was lying to see what I'd do, because people were just one big experiment in humility, as far as he was concerned. If I thought my sister had screwed me over, would I let her burn? Or was I such a deplorable whipping post that I wouldn't even be able to exact revenge on my worst enemy? I would risk my life to save hers, even though she'd never do the same for me.

Or would she?

I was feeling dizzy, short of breath. It was hot in the courtyard, and my brain was beginning to liquefy, the fatty excess of my larded thought processes rendered by the heat to reveal a dilemma that was obscenely clear. This was the choice, if there could be said to be one: Pitcairn or Edith. It was easier than contemplating whether or not I'd let my sister burn to death; that felt melodramatic and beside the point. The real choice was what sort of person I wanted to become; the real choice was what kind of future I would have, one in which I was involved in strange, faraway seductions with a man who couldn't live in the moment, or one in which I'd continue my life as an intimate partner with my worst enemy.

This was my choice. It wasn't about them. It was about me.

Instead of making a choice, I looked at my watch. Nine forty-one. I had four minutes to find Edith and ask her whether she'd sold me out. If she had, if Bruno was telling the truth, I'd leave her here, I'd leave her and get out of the hotel before nine forty-five.

It wasn't that I wanted to save her. I just wanted to know whether she'd sold me out. I needed to know.

I returned to the dining room and touched the metal plate of the kitchen door with my palm, intending to push it open and search for Edith inside.

The door was hot. Very hot.

I had not grown up in the States, at least not during those formative kindergarten years when caution is the main course of study, when children are cajoled by knowledgeable bears and singing fish to fear cavities and sudden quiet and other harbingers of doom. Edith and I were not taught to crouch under desks, take refuge in doorways, swish with fluoride, wield a key through dark alleys, avoid baths during electrical storms, suspect old men of bad habits. The rest of the world is not so taken with self-preservation because there are humans to excess, and so I had not learned from any singing bear or knowledgeable fish that a hot door is a bad door.

I opened it.

That I was not instantly incinerated was the true miracle of the day. I was knocked to the side as the flames pushed across the dining room floor. I heard the pop and crack of wood-boring insects as their bodies kindled and combusted. The fire stole all that was breathable from the room. I felt my way along one wall and opened the first door I could find. I did not feel it to test if it was hot. It would not have mattered if it was. I had no choice, so I opened it.

The back hallway felt arctic in comparison with the dining room. I dare to claim I remember shivering, even though I could hear the sound of burning wood—erratic explosions and loud cackles. It came from everywhere.

There were two doors in this small hallway. I opened one. A closet. The second, I knew, led up a back staircase to Gesina's room. The metal railing was more than warm, it was downright hot. At the top of the stairs, another door. Closed. Extremely hot to the touch. Is this sounding too ludicrously like a dream? I won't deny that I believed I was in the midst of a scalding dream, a dream with the ability to leave welts on my body.

I opened the door. There was too much smoke to discern anything, but I could hear coughing. If I squinted, I could make out two fetal forms in a corner. I dropped to my hands and knees and shuttled toward the coughing noises. My eyes stung, watered. I couldn't see. I felt around and encountered a hot, breathing mass of fur.

Verne.

He licked my hand. He whined.

Next to Verne I found Edith. I mistook her for part of Verne at first, because his fur and her hair had identical handfeel—slippery, coarse, and very warm.

I poked her in the ribs. I pinched her nose, hard. Nothing. She was out cold.

I pulled her floppy head into my lap. Verne rested his snout on my leg and licked my hand with a dry tongue.

I tried again, and again failed, to revive Edith. She wouldn't wake up. *"Did you sell me out?"* I yelled at her. *"Did you?"*

The fire was making me tired, but my curiosity continued to flare.

Lord knows what Edith was doing in Gesina's room while the hotel smoldered. Playing out, in real time, one of the childhood dilemmas my father only dreamed of us facing. I couldn't breathe, I couldn't even open my mouth, but in my head I let fly a cretinous laugh that fanned the fire. *Let us burn!* I thought. Daddy, you poor bastard, you sham of a scientist, you adulterer of colonial feminist scholars with a taste for theatrics, you dispirited, weak-willed failure of a man. Your children are your crowning experiment! Your children will get you tenure!

Edith roiled in my lap. If we get out of here, I thought to myself.

If. If. The terrible if.

If a jeep on a cliff, she thinks (keeping it real in third person). No. If a bear in a cave, if a hungry blizzard, if a blind half brother and a bullet-free gun. Wait a minute! I'm thinking! If a stupid, pretty sister, if an asthmatic Institute man, if a Hun-sized hotel proprietress, then we have a party! Bring out the dancing tunes, Miles. Bruno, strike up the zither! Tip Top steaks for all you Spaniards with cold feet, and drinks on the lousy cunt with the stale white roll in her eye. Hello, Gesina, straight from a Ukraine locker-room pep talk: Go, go, you effeminate men, swim for the gold or be uselessly androgynous, be pelted with old potatoes and hung from your mannish teats. And Sad, how sweet of you, of course you can bring your father, the old sick goat, of course we won't mind if you suckle his pinkie finger while he applies a slow but increasing pressure with his slippered foot to your groin area. And look who's back! It's Cyrus! Lovely to meet you, Mrs. Cyrus, your husband's such a rogue, just kidding, dear, the rogue's been cooked out of him, all those years in Bristol without a dab of sun cream, and these must be your daughters! What fabulous football uni-forms, did you sew them from old tea cozies and dye them in milk? Did you! Well, well, and a balm for your sadness, too, my dear, and you're a regular regional sales star, from Winchester Falls to Lady-on-Croton, you've sold the most creams, and there's not a liar in the south of En-gland who smells of lavender and old ladies! A new bum-pink Mini for you! Bravo! And Tom, dear fellow, perhaps a little Lying Cream for your eruptions, may your pustules recur until your teeth drop out. An eye for observation! And an eye for boils, dear man, how can you *stomach* that soup? Stephen ate his, darling, no peaches for you until every chicken neck is gone. I mean it now! You signed a contract, darlings, and the fine print says, *No dessert until the fat one loses her shit.* Haven't you read the fine print? Don't use that old blindness excuse, don't tell me you coughed so hard your eyes flew out. I'm not such an idiot. I'm not about to lift my djellabah for the pathetic likes of you, no matter if we live in hotels together and play backgammon, never pinochle—or was it poker, never bridge? Lord, I can't remember what we promised *to have and to hold and to never indulge in cribbage, so help me*—and what about the baby? Shall she learn table service? Shall she grow up to live in a vinyl-sided triplex in Revere? Shall she ever find love, shall she ever be worthy of it? Shall she ever be able to lift respective wools and keep a straight face? Hers is the sort of pestilence you want to quarantine, no lovers for her, no threat of passing the weakness along. We've enough pathetic sopbottoms clogging the social services. Give her love, and let her shut up for once! I'm telling you, it's the same old thing, over and over, if you cannot count on the same old thing, what have you got to look forward to? What have you, I ask? Exhilaration is overrated. Home is the place where, when you have to go there, they strike you across the bottom and feed you a soupy pot pie. Home is the place where you are alone if you are lucky. Home is the place where the cat will gnaw your bones clean after you strike your head on the toilet, trying to catch a glimpse of your fat, unlovable self in the shaving mirror, preening about and thinking, *This land is dead.* Keeping it melodramatic in the third person, Miles says. Home is her own fucking ridiculous fiction.

So maybe I was crying. So maybe I was. Laughing, crying, what's the bloody difference? It's all a sign of emptiness. And so I laughed, I cried, I drooled and spurted from the face, but nothing would put out this fire, nothing could spring me from this joyless snare that I had goddamn bred myself for.

I held Pitcairn's watch an inch from my face. The time. It was late. Too late. Nine forty-four. As I looked, the last digit dotted, undotted, redotted.

Nine forty-five.

And here I was. I was here. I'd lost.

Verne tried to hide his nose under my shirt, his heavy head resting on a sharp object that ground into my ribs. Edith's ring. I pushed his nose aside and dug the ring out. It didn't glimmer any longer; the smoke made the stones quiet and dull, no more valuable than a silly little trinket you'd get at the dentist's.

I held the ring in my palm, thinking I would throw it. Throw it like an offering toward the encroaching fire. The smoke pinched my eyes shut and I was giving in to it, I was, when I had one final, brilliant impulse. I held the ring between my thumb and forefinger, and said, "Do you take me as your awfully wedded humbug?" I picked up Edith's hand and jammed the ring over her knuckle.

Edith stirred.

I slapped her face. I slapped her and slapped her. I said, "Did you do it? Did you sell me out? Did you?"

Her mouth trembled open. She started to laugh.

"Answer me!" I yelled at her. "Squeeze my finger, if you must! Squeeze to indicate in the affirmative! Just tell me if you sold me out!"

Edith's eyes were bloodshot from the smoke, and she peered up at me with a red-devil gaze, pure teary adoration or pure Satanism. She hugged me around the waist, refusing to answer my question. Because she didn't need to answer my question. I knew she'd sold me out. I knew it as clearly as I knew that I was a lonely person to the bone, a person whose choices reflected her inability to ever love anyone as much as she loved this woman whom she goddamn, goddamn hated.

I cannot remember how Edith and I got outside, arms around necks, stumbling down the narrow staircase, Verne at our heels. We might have been chanting a limerick we'd concocted as a family fight song, as we tramped through the rice paddies, strangling each other with our desperate, vengeful girlishness. *There once was a man from My-landrum, Whose life was unbearably humdrum. He lay on his desk with a mad feminist, now his wife causes headaches and bedlam.* I cannot remember the feel of the cobblestones rounding up between my shoulder blades as I lay on my back and tried to ignore the face that loomed over me. I watched, semi-unconscious, as he pulled off his glasses and, to the tune of a zither, reached into his head and yanked off a bit of dried glue. A single, angry eye rolled into place. It wobbled. It stared in shock at the world. It wept for me. It said: *Alice is a good girl. Alice, a girl, was good. A good girl was Alice! Good for Alice, the girl. Good girl, Alice. Good girl.*

Epilogue

TRUE, THERE'S NOT MUCH in the way of tourist opportunities in these parts, but that's why we prefer it. We like to watch the clouds roll in. We like to watch the fishermen moving about in the dawn hours, revving up the engines in their brightly painted snub-nosed punts, making certain to hit the more strident diesel notes when they pass beneath our window, which hangs, not unprecipitously, as this hotel is four hundred years old, over the West Ghost Cliffs. The cliffs are named not for any supernatural sightings, not for any unwilling maidens tossed into the sea during fishless times, but because the rocks have been enameled (I have tried to chip it with a walking stick, there is no other word for it) with birdshit. There's an endangered-tern rookery in these cliffs, the hotel brochures claim; the birds are permitted to defecate all over everything, and do, with a vitality that affirms their resurgence as a species.

At night, without a moon, the cliffs glow. They are not poorly named.

Fanny is at the pool. She is just pretty enough that her pre-adult life will not be conscripted to either proving herself more attractive than she is or proving herself more intelligent than she appears. She has her mother's wild hair; she keeps it long, but prefers to wear it speared up with whatever stick or pencil she can lay her hands on. She has a practiced speediness to her coiffing that does not linger and invite spectators, that does not imbue the moment with anything more seductive than utter pragmatism. She is not without her unconscious charms. She is reedy and quick enough to seem athletic when necessary, able to catch keys tossed from windows and perform respectably at tennis. I have been told, by her blood relatives, that she most resembles her maternal grandmother and namesake, the perfume innovator who was murdered on her Connecticut estate by a group of drugged-out prep school girls. The girls claimed in court that Fanny's grandmother had killed herself; nonetheless, they were sentenced to three years in a girls' penitentiary, and all seven of them have published memoirs, none of which sold especially well despite the preponderance of field hockey photos and nubile dormitory snaps.

Fanny and I have read them all.

To this day, I have not determined for certain whether Fanny's biological mother, Winnie Sunderland, was involved with the Institute or not. I have broken into file rooms to try to satisfy my suspicions, I have hired amateur hackers and smuggled microfiche from the library in a hollow tampon applicator. I have made every attempt since receiving the certified letter from Plumb, Plumb and Chesterton informing me that Winifred Sunderland had provided in her last will and testament that, in the event of her death, I should be the guardian of her then nine-year-old daughter. I have failed to uncover anything of note or suspicion in Winnie's death. The Goan police, an intractable bunch, leafed through their unalphabetized manila folders, stacked on a broken television set and fingerprinted with curry sauce and coffee, and confirmed that Winifred Sunderland was the only person to die in the Keppalle Pass bus misfortune, in which fourteen others were injured. The bus was headed for a spiritual retreat in the mountains, run by Guru Han of the New Delhi Hans. Winnie was impaled through the epiglottis with a bamboo tent spike, which had shaken loose from somebody's batiked rucksack and shot backward like an arrow as the bus struck Elephant Rock, elevation 1,498 meters, at a speed of forty-six kilometers per hour. The bus driver's epilepsy was confirmed by numerous Goan doctors, all of whom had at one time or another agreed to vouch for the man's perfect health on the physical examination sheet for his driver's permit. None of the other bus passengers remembered anything out of the ordinary before the crash, save one woman, Berenice Mandelbaum, a Canadian, who believed the accident was prophesied by the black stork she saw fly past her window at breakfast that morning, a noosed rope dangling from its beak. I even tracked down Winnie's astrologer, Sue Aspic, now of New Rochelle, New York, who told me that she had never told Winnie she would die "many miles from earth." I inquired as to how she could remember so distinctly after all these years. She stared me down with her third eye until I bundled myself into my white rental car and drove away.

None of this, however, has served to dull my suspicions. Okay. My paranoia. Edith and I were told (Bruno debriefed us while he drove the bronze sedan, fifty kilometers outside Itzal) that all the passengers had signed a contract upon their release and had been paid a considerable sum to ensure their silence. Our "hijacking" was never reported in any papers. Rather, the Moroccan Air officials explained our delayed arrival in Melilla to family members and reporters by releasing a quarantine statement. One of the pilots had tested positive for smallpox, the statement claimed, necessitating that we be quarantined in a military hospital in Rabat. Bruno handed Edith and me a typed narrative of our "experience"; we were told to memorize it so that our stories would be consistent, should we ever be questioned by reporters.

For this, we were each paid $10,000.

I can't help wondering the extent to which the other passengers might have been involved, no matter what Bruno told me. To which *everyone* was involved. The only one I can be certain about, after all, is me. Some days I even convince myself that Edith was working for Bruno, which seems ridiculous, and never more so than when I receive her annual family photo Christmas cards. These inevitably show a tensely thin woman lording over her unfocused husband and two red-haired daughters, their spiteful arms clamped around the torsos of two obese Pekingese. Edith speaks barely three words of Spanish, even though she's lived in Melilla for almost two decades. She is quite attractive—her hair is still long, and she wears it in a graying bun—if a bit too fond of Sauvignon Blanc. Sometimes she calls me when she's drunk, alone, and it's night; she'll slur into the phone, "Stupid slut, you're a stupid, stupid slut," she'll leave the receiver off the hook and I can hear her in the background, crying. It takes all my willpower (ah, yes, *that*) not to jump on a plane, kidnap her, and whisk her away with me to Potsdam or wherever she wants to go.

But I have never once done this. I am an ersatz mother now, and must cultivate my weak survival instinct for my daughter Fanny's sake.

Still, I must admit to experiencing moments of paranoia—no, long, endless tracts of it. Maybe Edith *was* involved, I think. Maybe Sad. Maybe Winnie. There's not a spent tissue I have not noticed, not a water stain, not a dust bunny, not a crumpled lobster bib. I have been taught to see everything, and I have seen so much that I am always, always tired; I sometimes wear an airplane sleep-mask in the middle of the day. I sit in an easy chair with a mask and earplugs and face out to sea. But I have not been given answers, because answers are not Institute protocol. The Institute favors obfuscation over clarity in every regard. Bruno sank millions into transforming the Role Play Complex, with the idea that students could slip, without awareness, from a dramatized scenario to a real one and back, until the dividing line between authentic and virtual grew so frail as to seem foolishly archaic. Thus I was never allowed to know what happened to Pitcairn. I submitted my questions in writing to Director Smythes, and he replied, in writing, "To know is to never be certain."

I responded in my finest penmanship: "Go to hell."

And as for the Hotel Itzal: I have been to "Itzal" (International Institute for Terrorist Studies in Lucerne, *IITSL*—so clever, you people). Fanny and I took three buses, two cabs, and a camel from Ouarzazate to the exact longitude and latitude of Itzal. I recognized the date palms, those not incinerated in the fire. I commanded her to dig, and we came up with very little—an American penny, a rusted lug nut, a tan button. Those people were thorough. I imagine they must have vacuumed the desert after they'd blown up the buildings and yanked the cobblestones. There is no Itzal, God damn it, and if there is no Itzal, why have I never seen Pitcairn strolling down the fluorescent hallways of the Institute, why have I never seen him at the annual Ottawa Summit dressed in his finest corduroy suit, why have I never heard a single word from him? He didn't blow up innocent civilians; he blew up a stage set. A bungle for a Brain Worm, yes, but a bungle in which the damage was only "hypothetical."

I'll admit that it was in some sense—okay, many senses—because of Pitcairn that I was even moderately interested in Director Smythes's letter inviting me to matriculate at the Institute. The letter—on a sturdy cream bond, his director's "signature" applied at the bottom with a rubber stamp—found me in Revere after a particularly grueling Tip Top Mother's Day brunch, vulnerable to opportunity. I thought it was a rejection letter for a grant I'd forgotten I'd applied for. The envelope was fancy and thin.

> Dear Alice,
>
> It has come to my attention that you may be looking for a change. Many people your age believe that change is over-rated. They have gone to medical school, then law school, then abandoned all ties to professionalism in order to bake bread or build salvaged-wood furniture, with no greater degree of satis-

faction than if they'd finished their ob-gyn residency and spent their adult lives peering between women's legs. They believe that change, after many strenuous adjustments, merely leads a person back to the same dead end.

The people your age are not wrong.

Their cynicism is apt, hard-earned, applauded even, at least by me. The problem is that people your age believe change to be the act of trading one static arrangement for another. That is not change. That is merely trading one static arrangement for another.

Ask yourself the following questions: Are you living a static life? A predictable life? Do you really want to initiate a "change"? Do you want to trade one personality for another with the same unconscious ease with which you hate yourself?

These are rhetorical questions. They are rhetorical, because I know your answers. Yes. Yes. Yes. Yes.

A few months later, I stood in front of the discreet gates of the Institute with my duffel bag full of clothes and my introductory letter in my coat pocket. I strained to catch a glimpse of the building beyond the sharp curve in the pebbled drive, a gardener I could signal (there was no bell). Instead I saw a helicopter, I saw the glass-bubbled cockpit. And I nearly pissed myself. I recognized those two pilots. Aboul and Mjidd, their heads framed by fancy earphones. They took off into the sky, dragging a dank, noisy wind over me.

It is possible, of course, that it was not Aboul and Mjidd. I was jet-lagged, I was disoriented. I never saw them again. But what I am saying is that I was starting to think as an Institute man should, before I'd even had my first baffling encounter with Professor Barbara Clifford. I soon learned that a little bit of doubt goes a long way; a little bit of doubt can cast everything you thought you knew into question, until everything is related, until every unknown is known to you, because the world is a terrible net of certainty. All it takes is one minute of paying attention, and suddenly you realize—at first with a sense of comfort, then with a sense of claustrophobia—that everything is connected. The people you see in Peru are the people you see in Kashmir. The Peugeot your father drove to work each day in Mylandrum is the Peugeot your hirsute Institute roommate drives to her weekly electrolysis appointments. Despite your fear that the world is a lonely place, it is precisely the opposite that should unnerve you.

And yet, despite the fact that the world is a terrible net of certainty, I never saw Pitcairn again. I know why, of course. Because he thought I went back into the hotel for him. He thought that I was willing to grab the moment, that I was willing to sacrifice a perfectly untainted fantasy for the real, inferior goddamned thing. Nevertheless, I didn't stop hoping. I hoped he might hunt me down at graduation, I hoped he might swing me up in my black commencement robes and take me to the airplane in the Role Play Complex. We would wear headphones and talk to each other on the radio; we would eat oranges until he asked me, talking into his hand and pretending there was static and he was far away, to marry him. I can't even tell you what else I imagined. I can only humiliate myself to such a degree; at a certain point it becomes humorous, and this story is not meant to be humorous. This story is meant to winch your ribs open and tamper with your heart. This story is meant to make you realize that your chances of happiness in this world are terribly slim if you lack a fine imagination.

Next week, Fanny departs for university. En route, she will stop in Melilla to visit Edith and X and their two children. She will write a letter informing me that Edith is drinking more or less, that when she is drinking more she accuses X of being homosexual, that their daughters are more or less bound for early deaths in windsurfing accidents or suicide pacts. Edith and I have drifted apart since her marriage, my career, my accidental motherhood. I do not regret our distance, although it frequently makes me feel both sad and lucky. I am lucky to have broken away from her so naturally, without a lot of pain or hostility. Yet I could get sucked back into that old family contract with her at a moment's notice, I know this about myself, and so I keep our personal interchanges to a minimum—a New Year's card, a birthday card, and one long weekend's visit per annum, during which very little permanent regression can occur. Fanny has helped with this immensely. Fanny has helped me define myself anew.

But now Fanny is leaving me. It is this looming solitude that gives me frightful pause; it is her imminent abandonment that prompts me to complete what I believe amounts to my letter of resignation. Take me off the Institute mailing list. I no longer wish to receive veiled requests for money. I am no longer interested in subscribing, for a *criminally low price*, to Terrorist Trade publications.

Moreover, I suspect I enrolled at the Institute under false pretenses. I know I claimed that I had no attachment to the undivided self, I know I promised that I wanted to be an Institute man for the purposes of making the world a safer place, but in fact, I joined the Institute only because I thought I might find Pitcairn there, and I wanted to increase my terrible net of certainty.

Here is what I think I'm trying to say:

I did not go back into the hotel for Pitcairn, no matter what he thought, and possibly still thinks. I knew the arrangement, that old Orpheus-and-his-wife arrangement. No looking back. Forge forward blindly, and you'll always have your hopeful fantasies to entertain you. But I went back into the burning hotel. I went back, thereby proving I didn't trust the terrible net of certainty. I sent him flying back to Hades. He was hiding in the bathroom or spying from a nearby parapet. He thought I was looking for him, the idiot, the man who flunked Human. He never imagined that I'd trade a life with him to save that sister of mine—oh yes, I know I said I was simply *curious*, but we all know the truth—he never imagined that I'd ruin my chances with him forever, that I would sacrifice not her, but him.

Now that Fanny is leaving me, I will choose to live a fuller life in pretend places for my own benefit. This is my personal shame. That I am not a stronger person. That I cannot outgrow the hypothetical. This is what a gift for playing roles boils down to: A penchant for loneliness. A life in hotels. This is why winning isn't everything, because you are never yourself to enjoy it. You've been keeping it real in third person for so long that your I has atrophied out of existence.

Isn't this true? Isn't it? I am the same old mediocre failure of my own design, am I not? Ostensible motherhood didn't change me. Work didn't change me. People don't like new things, my father said. People don't want to be surprised, especially by themselves. They want to hear the same story. Tell them the same story and they'll listen. So here's my story. I am Alice, I am Alice, I am Alice.

And so (keeping it real), Alice plans ahead. She imagines those evenings she will be alone, when the phone hasn't rung, and the Fannys of the world—those creatures who feed off moments, who chew big granite blocks of time to pea gravel, because they are damned if they're going to take after her—are off in the night with their mouths full of immediacy, while Alice resuscitates her old regrets, because they are most comforting to her. They are her masterpieces. They are the hidden canvases of her secret oeuvre. She flips through them with a careless hand, a cloth over her mouth to protect her from the dust. She settles on the one she's cultivated for this very purpose. And she composes in her head a letter on hotel stationery that she will never send, because it would indicate that she is not the same old person, oh no, because it would indicate, despite her attempts to present herself as tough-skinned and pragmatic, that she is just a silly romantic ready to stuff her mouth full of immediacy.

It says:

Dear Sirs,

Pitcairn has made a grave mistake. His error was understandable, of course. But if you could tell him, please, tell him when you see him next, that I am alone again and just my plain old self, not Cyrus, not Sad or Winnie or Bruno or my mother. I am simply looking for a companion with whom to spend my days, a companion who will cherish as much as I the stupidity of living in the moment, and spend every dull, amazing second with me. Tell him, please, that he can find me at this hotel if he likes, wearing a sleep mask and staring out to sea.